Vespers

Vespers

Jeff Rovin

ST. MARTIN'S PRESS ⚌ NEW YORK

Design by Nancy Resnick

Library of Congress Cataloging-in-Publication Data

Rovin, Jeff.
    Vespers / Jeff Rovin.
      p.   cm.
    ISBN 0-312-19351-3
    I. Title.
PS3568.08894V47   1998
813'.54—dc21   98-19398
                                                          CIP

First Edition: October 1998

10 9 8 7 6 5 4 3 2 1

Acknowledgments

Dozens of people contributed information to this novel. However, there were several whose assistance was indispensable:

The bat scholar who wished to remain anonymous but provided patient explanations of echolocation, bat reproduction, and bat flight.

Betsy Herzog, spokesperson for the New York Police Department. If she didn't know something—which was rare—she knew who did or knew what manual to find it in. She was, in a word, terrific.

Jerome Hauer, director of the Office of Emergency Management in New York. Even when buildings were collapsing and avenues were disgorging water and flame, he found time to answer questions about crisis management.

Larry Steeler, deputy superintendent of the Statue of Liberty. While he was forced to keep some of the Lady's secrets to himself he revealed—he insists—some of the best ones.

And Frank Pascual, director of public affairs for the MTA. He loves those tunnels and bridges, and his enthusiasm is contagious.

Vespers

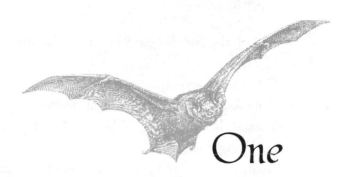

One

The bat sliced through the warm night air. Wood met hardball with a sweet, loud crack that sent it arcing through the twilight.

Thirteen-year-old Tommy Fitzpatrick dropped the bat and ran. The gangly boy couldn't watch. He lowered his head, exploded toward first base, and prayed. He saw his white Nikes flash against the baseline. He felt the cotton uniform rub his thighs and forearms. Through his batting helmet he heard muffled cheers from the Thurston Thrashers grandstand. There was a runner at second. If the hit was a double, it could tie the semifinal game. A home run and they'd win. An out—

As he neared the bag he heard the drowning-out cheer from the Fortelni Fighters grandstand. He looked up just as big first baseman Rick Boots raised his arms in triumph and ran toward home with the rest of the infield. Boots didn't even look at him.

Tommy slowed and stopped at the bag. He stood there breathing hard, his shoulders rounded, his back to home. He looked out at the picnic area and the street beyond. His dad was probably dying behind the cage.

So much for staying alive. So much for playing in the championship, for taking home a trophy, for being the talk of the lunchroom tomorrow.

One of the Fortelni coaches patted Tommy on the shoulder as he ran past.

"That was a good shot, son."

"Thanks," Tommy muttered. But the man probably didn't hear. Tommy barely heard it himself. His mouth didn't want to move. It just wanted to hang there.

Tommy pulled off his batting helmet and shook out his long, black hair. He wanted to cry but didn't. It would be bad enough facing the school tomorrow as a loser. He didn't want to face it as a water baby.

The boy took a short, deep breath. Somewhere inside he found the energy to crank up his arms, turn toward home, and join the rest of the Thrashers as they congratulated the winners.

The bat swept through the deepening twilight. Small, hairless wings carried it on a zigzag course through the woods. Crossing in the open field beyond, the vespertilionid quick-coughed an ultrasonic trilling from deep in its throat. The sound saturated the air for several yards, ten pulses a second alternating with the beats of its wings. The bat's large ears were turned forward, listening for any change in the returning signal. Whenever the echoing pings came back as a low drumbeat, it meant another bat. When they returned as a long, high rasp, it meant that the fluttering wings of an insect were somewhere ahead. Finding a bug, the bat would pinpoint it more precisely by increasing its bleating twentyfold, processing up to two hundred beats per second. The amplitude, direction, and sharpness of the returning signal indicated exactly where the prey was as well as its size and texture. The bat would then change course, fix on the insect visually in a sharp, bright, black-and-white image, and snap it cleanly in its small jaws. During the moment it took to swallow, the vespertilionid rerouted the pulses through his nose. On an ordinary night the bat repeated this process an average of six hundred times an hour for five hours.

But tonight was not ordinary. The colony would begin to migrate at dawn, and the bat was a field picket, one of nearly three hundred rear-guard bats spread across the woods and flying up to two miles high. In addition to feeding, its job was to watch for any movement toward the forest. If it detected any, or if the echo of any bat within its range began to fade, it was to follow, reconnect, and defend the perimeter.

After gulping down two mosquitoes in swift, left-right bites, the bat detected something moving below. It was large and headed toward the woods. He nosed down, snaring a moth as he did. Speeding up to compensate for the loss of tailwind, the bat dove straight toward the object.

Tommy crossed the parking area adjacent to the woods. He stopped in front of his father's forest green Blazer and thumped backside-first against the hood. He looked back at the diamond. Scott Fitzpatrick was talking with coach Don Breen and assistant coach Bob Kidd and several other fathers behind the cage. Some of the mothers were sitting and talking in the grandstand while little brothers and sisters ran around the picnic area near the pond. The rest of the Thrashers were sitting on the bench, eating chips and drinking soda and grumbling. The Fighters were in the field, exuberantly throwing the ball around.

The boy didn't feel like talking to anyone. Why should he? He blew it. Even if no one said so, they'd be thinking it.

Tommy looked down at the glove on his left hand. At least he still had next year. And he had his glove. He loved the way it felt, the way it smelled, the heft when there was a hardball in the pocket. Win or lose, it always sucked putting this part of him up in the closet. But the Little League season was over and fall was starting to show in the trees. Soon it would be too cold to play catch. There was football, but it wasn't the same as being out in the warm sunshine with school far off and—

The boy heard the fluttering. He raised his head an instant before it struck. The bat dug its ten strong claws deep into Tommy's forehead. It held on, its wings beating against the boy's temples while its wide mouth pushed through his hair. The pin-narrow teeth found the boy's scalp and bit through the flesh.

Tommy screamed. He pushed at the bat with his right hand and screamed again when he felt the creature's furry body. He screamed even louder when a piece of skin came away with the bat's mouth. Panicking, Tommy hammered it with his glove.

"Dad! *Dad!*"

The men looked over.

The bat held on as two more bats arrived from the left and right. The first bat snagged another piece of scalp just above the hairline while the other bats landed on the tops of Tommy's ears. Their claws easily pierced his skin. The boy fell to his knees. He shook his head violently, but the feathery slap of their wings stayed with him.

Scott Fitzpatrick started running toward the parking area. "Tommy?"

Portly coach Breen slowly jogged after him. "Scott, what is it?"

"I don't know, Don. I can't see."

Behind them, members of the Thrasher bench stood. Several of the Fighters stopped playing and watched.

"Tommy!" Scott shouted as he craned to look around the cars.

A fourth bat charged across the field and latched onto Tommy's upper lip. The boy wailed as it bit the underside of his nose. He tasted blood. A fifth bat snagged the flesh between the thumb and index finger of his right hand. The bat bit the back of Tommy's wrist.

"Dad, help me!"

Scott scrambled around the haphazardly parked cars. "Hold on, I'm coming!"

Tommy tried to shake the creature off his hand as a sixth bat grabbed the inside of his elbow. It chewed through his jersey in three quick bites and scissored through the flesh. Its upper and lower fangs perforated the pulmonary artery. Blood pumped through the tear in the uniform.

The boy's screams became yelps. He tried to raise his glove as two bats dive-bombed his left arm. He flopped to his side by the front fender and kicked along the ground, frantically trying to wipe the bats off. The flailing wasn't his own; pain told him where to swipe and push and swat. Blood from his ears, hand, and arm dribbled onto the dying grass.

The boy's wild motions attracted a second wave of bats. They descended steep and sharp like a monstrous arrowhead, breaking up as they came out of their dive. Most of them slipped around the buttons of the boy's jersey. They crept up his chest and along his arms, gnawing relentlessly. Tommy shuddered; his movements suddenly slowed and then stopped. He felt nothing more, as pain, exhaustion, and the loss of blood triggered neurogenic shock.

A new swarm of bats sailed low over the boy. They didn't stop but headed toward their next target. Scott Fitzpatrick swore as they knifed toward him. He wrapped his arms around his head, dipped it like a charging bull, and kept weaving through the parked cars. The bats slowed and covered him like a giant hand. They picked at his windbreaker, tore away pieces of nylon, burrowed into the rips. The man uncrossed his arms and slapped at the lumps beneath his jacket.

"Tommy!"

Another swarm arrived, attacking his now-exposed face.

"Shit! *Shit!*"

They raked his eyelids, his forehead, the back of his neck. Blinded by wings and blood, Scott slammed into the back of a car. He shouted with pain and rage and dropped backward onto the trunk, trying to crush the bats that were under his clothing. He reached up to his face, squeezed two mouse-sized bodies with each hand, and threw them aside. They darted back.

"Fuckers!"

More bats swooped down and piled onto Scott's face and hands. He slid from the trunk, wriggling and yelling as the tiny, slashing teeth and long hooked claws opened dozens of wounds.

Don Breen was a car length away when he saw Scott Fitzpatrick writhing on the ground. Breen stopped.

Scott was bucking violently beneath a layer of small bats. They crawled over him like an oil slick until he was covered from foot to forehead.

"Jesus!" Breen said.

One of the parents shouted, "Don, what's wrong?"

"Stay away!" Breen yelled.

"Why?"

"Just do it!" he screamed.

None of the men moved. Slowly, Breen removed his team jacket. He held it like a matador and leaned forward. He crept ahead, measuring the distance with his eyes, intending to throw the jacket on top of the bats.

Suddenly, Scott stopped moving. A moment later, so did the bats.

Breen stood watching as a gentle wind slipped through the cars. It blew across the fist-sized animals, stirring their fur and lifting the thin skin of their wings, but their spindly feet and five-wing digits held them fast. Then, using those claws, the animals turned themselves around. They moved like little dials, rotating clockwise, nearly in unison, and looked at Breen. Small, dark eyes gleamed from blood-smeared faces, and their wide, dangerous jaws hung open.

One of the kids yelled from the field. "Yo! Coach! You sure you don't need help?"

Breen didn't tell whoever it was to shut the hell up. A parent did that. Breen waited for the bats to attack. When they didn't, he wondered if it had anything to do with not moving. Or maybe not moving forward. Tommy and Scott had both gone toward the woods.

There was only one way to find out. Slowly, very slowly, he lowered his jacket away from the bats. When the animals didn't react, he took a cautious step back with his right foot.

Almost as one the tiny heads clicked to the right. He moved toward the woods.

Breen wanted to swear and run. He did neither. If the bats had wanted to attack, they would have. He waited several seconds. When nothing happened, he took a second step back, this time to the left. The twenty-odd small heads didn't move.

"Okay," he said softly. "Okay. If you'll let me go that way, I'm leaving."

Breen stepped again. Then again. The bats still didn't move. When he reached the edge of the parking lot, Breen finally turned toward the diamond. The players and all of the parents were standing and watching. He walked swiftly toward the cage.

"What happened out there?" Bob Kidd asked. "Is Tommy—"

"I don't *know*," Breen snapped. Cold perspiration dripped from the band of his cap. He picked up the pace as he approached the grandstand. He looked up at the parents and children. "All right," he said. "I need everybody to go that way *slowly*." He pointed toward the picnic area. "If you've got jackets, use them to cover your heads. Does anybody have a phone?"

"I do," one of the mothers said.

"Call nine-one-one."

She punched in the number.

"Tell them we've got bats—maybe thirty of them. Two people are seriously injured. Tell them *not* to come along Forest Road. Tell them they should pull in by the pond."

The woman said all right. Coach Breen walked with her as she placed the call.

In less than a minute, the diamond and grandstands were empty.

When there was no longer a threat, the bats returned to the skies. They continued scooping down insects, watching one another, and making certain that nothing but wind and moonlight approached the forest.

Two

One of the things Detective First Grade Robert Gentry liked about running the Accident Investigations Squad at Midtown South was that when he left the station house he left the work there as well.

Fender benders and buckets kicked over by window washers and pedestrians tripping over gas or water hoses didn't depress him the way being a narc had for more than ten years, five of those spent deep undercover. Minor accidents didn't have the same kind of despair and deterioration and rippling consequences as drug addiction. And major automobile or structural accidents were handled jointly by the NYPD and the Fire Department, with the ranking Fire Department official in command. All Gentry had to do was show up. When he came home at night he also didn't have to wonder whose footsteps or shadows were behind him. And thanks to those long years he'd spent pretending to be Nick Argento, buyer and seller of hard drugs, he no longer had a wife to worry about. For Gentry, worrying that he'd been found out by a pusher or smuggler and that he'd gotten to the house and to Priscilla had always been his greatest fear.

Police Commissioner Joe Veltre had personally selected Gentry to run the small, relatively cushy AIS nearly six months before. It was the equivalent of a papal dispensation, since Veltre's appointment as top cop had been given a big boost by Gentry's successful antidrug efforts.

Gentry usually quit the station house around six P.M., leaving the report writing to Detectives Second Grade Jason Anthony and Jen Malcolm. Anthony in particular enjoyed the detail work. He'd come over from the Multi-Agency Salvage Yard Task Force and said it was gratifying to make order out of chaos.

Maybe. All it did for Gentry was make him want to look out the dirty office window and think. Think about the past. About that one here-then-gone instant that had taken him from narcotics to where he was. Think about Bernie Michaelson and what it had been like to have a partner, to be closer to someone than he'd ever managed to be with his wife. Think about how he missed that—and Bernie. They had been so attuned to each other that even when they hadn't been able to speak, the movement of an eyebrow, the slope of a shoulder, the shape of a smile told the other one everything he needed to know.

As he usually did, even in the most inclement weather, the thirty-three-year-old NYPD veteran walked downtown from the station house on West Thirty-fifth Street. It was nearly two miles to the West Village, and he enjoyed every block of it. He loved the half sentences of lives he heard as people passed. He loved the smells of restaurants and delis and roasted peanuts hawked by street-corner vendors. He loved the loud tabloid headlines and magazine covers he caught as he passed racks or shop windows. There was always something small to enjoy, and when small got boring there was always something big to savor: the Empire State Building over his left shoulder, the World Trade Center straight ahead. They were different every day, sunshine glinting off both like sequins or clouds hanging low over the tops. There were also old facades, a low-flying dirigible now and then, and the parade of automobiles and trucks and buses. Gentry especially enjoyed the Fashion Institute of Technology on Twenty-seventh Street, and he always slowed on the wide sidewalk to watch the young people coming and going with portfolios. There was life and energy among the young, not just the emaciation and death that he'd become accustomed to during those ten long years.

He walked, too, because he had nowhere to rush to.

There had been women for the first three or four months after he'd quit narcking. Women he met on the job, in coffee shops, on blind dates, at dances. Women who helped him forget, for a few hours, the loss of his wife and then the loss of his undercover partner. But sometimes, in the small hours of the night, he'd look at the woman sleeping next to him. He knew how to turn her on but not *what* turned her on. He'd try to remember her name. And he'd feel dirty inside. They were using each other the way they'd use a back scratcher. He'd spent enough time as a narc watching people destroy their spirits while they thought they were doing happy things to their bodies. So he put a stop to that. He hated being alone, but being with those ladies was worse. They were like mirrors that showed you your own scars. They were alone too.

Walking also gave him time to finish the serial thinking he'd started in his small office. To come to terms with the event that had ended his career as Nick Argento. It was tough, still.

Gentry was married to the Seventh Avenue route. It took him a little out of his way to the east, but Ninth Avenue was too sedate and Eighth Avenue was too damn crowded with people waiting to get into the trendy bar, jazz club, or café of the week. However, he did vary a key part of his routine each night. Sometimes he stopped for Thai takeout, sometimes he grabbed a salad, and sometimes he ate in at a sushi place on Hudson Street because he loved the monster-sized dragon rolls and there was a waitress who was simply the most elegant woman he had ever seen. Old Mrs. Bundonis who lived next door to Gentry warned him that he was going to die of malnutrition or worms. Also of not dressing warmly enough. He was actually glad she did that; he'd always wondered what it would be like to have a mother.

Tonight was Thai night, and Gentry stopped at his favorite hole-in-the-wall on Seventh Avenue. He got caught up on the saga of the counter guy and his four old aunts who had come to visit from

Bangkok and showed very little interest in leaving. When Gentry got to his one-bedroom apartment on Washington Street—with a double-order of mei grob, since the portions were appetizer-small—he slipped off his navy blue blazer, white shirt, and cobalt blue tie, pulled on his gray NYPD sweats, and crashed in front of the tube.

Three

For years, the Bronx meant only one thing to Nancy Joyce. It was the ultimate killer place to use in the game Geography, until her older brother Peter discovered there was a place called Xochihue-huetian, Mexico.

Her view of the borough changed when she moved there. What she discovered was that the past, the present, and the future all coexisted in the Bronx.

The past were the remnants of the thousands of families that had settled here in the first two decades of the twentieth century. That was when New York City's northernmost borough offered spacious apartments with central heating, refrigerators, and private bathrooms—amenities that were undreamed of in the older, more crowded Manhattan.

The present were the families that had moved here in the years following World War II, when affordable public housing went up and the exclusive nature of the borough ended.

The future were the families that had come to the Bronx, lured by fire-sale prices and a near-evangelistic desire to rejuvenate neighborhoods that had surrendered to drugs and crime and the homeless.

Twenty-nine-year-old zoologist Dr. Nancy Joyce was part of the past. The things that were real but foggy, just out of reach. Two years before, when she had been hired by the Bronx Zoo and became what her coworkers and school groups affectionately called "the bat lady," she had moved into the three-bedroom Bronx apartment that belonged to her eighty-seven-year-old widowed grandmother. Nancy Joyce and her brother had spent very little time here as kids. They grew up in rural Connecticut, and more often than not Dad drove down to get Grandma Joycewicz and bring her up to the country.

When Joyce came to the Bronx after obtaining her Ph.D., the apartment was a revelation. The walls of the living room and dining room were almost entirely covered with browning, frame-to-frame photographs. They were a shrine to a lost world. Her grandmother's family, the Cherkassovs, had been Russian aristocrats—starched men and formal women who stood or sat in studios, in salons, and on porticos of beach homes or country cottages. Her grandfather's family had been Polish laborers, and the pictures of them showed rumpled, tousle-haired men and women holding scythes or working oxen in the fields. The Cherkassovs fled after the Russian Revolution, and they ended up sleeping in woods and fields where they were found one sunrise by Joseph Joycewicz. He took one of the refugees as his wife, and they sailed for America.

Even if she hadn't heard that story when she was growing up, Nancy Joyce would have been able to read it in this picture diary, its fragile pages lovingly preserved behind glass.

There were also some newer pictures. Her father and his older sister as children. Joseph up in Westchester hunting with his son. The family at Coney Island and Atlantic City and on Forty-second Street taking in a double feature. Probably a western, which her grandfather was said to have loved. He believed that westerns were accurate depictions of history. Just like the black-and-white photographs on the wall.

It wasn't just the photographs that had a story to tell. There was the porcelain statue of the Greek hunter Orion holding a dead stag. The arrow had been broken off by her father, who had tried to pull it out and fire it from a homemade bow when he was three years old. There was the sofa that her grandfather had gone to lie on at night when the pain of the cancer that consumed him kept him awake. He went there to read the Polish novels he loved or to cry because he would be leaving his Anya far, far earlier than either was prepared for. He was forty-nine when he finally succumbed. There was the worn and faded rug that Joseph had bought Anya for their tenth wedding anniversary. The tattered seat cushion on the rocking chair, from the first cab that Joseph had driven. The radio that her father and his older sister had grown up listening to. Their schoolbooks on the shelf. The rifle with which Joseph had taught his son how to hunt. The old Victrola and the elderly woman's large collection of 78s.

When Grandma Joycewicz died, her granddaughter kept the apartment but refused to change very much in it. She put cable TV and a VCR in the living room and added a CD player and small speakers. She also replaced the old black rotary phone on the nightstand with a cordless. And she put in an extra phone jack so she could go on-line with her laptop. Joyce had never found it strange to be on-line in "this old place," as her grandmother used to call it. An on/off switch let the present in and then sent it back out again. The apartment remained a comforting retreat.

Her handful of semiclose friends thought Joyce was being trendily retro. It didn't matter. The place had an air of the melancholy that suited her fascination with things dark and haunting. "This old place" was a reminder of a time when lives that had been upheaved by chaos were set right by love. A time where the pace was slower but hopes were much, much higher. A time when each day was precious because twentieth-century medicine was still in its adolescence.

On her days off, like today, the young woman thoroughly enjoyed staying at home and catching up on current research and reports about bats, answering E-mail from former classmates and other scientists, and then relaxing by reading trashy novels, planning hunting trips, or talking on the phone with her mother or her sister-in-law, Janet.

For reasons she couldn't quite pinpoint, those calls always left her feeling as if she'd done something wrong.

Both her mom and Janet worried about her living alone and also—more so, she suspected—about her *being* alone. No husband. No boyfriend. No prospects of one. As Joyce had told them both many times, it wasn't that she was uninterested in meeting men. It was that she was uninterested in seeing most of the men she did meet. Except for a couple of five- and six-year-old gentlemen she'd caught smiling at her from school groups, most of them were aggressive and charmless.

Joyce had been in an unusual relationship during school, followed by years of fieldwork abroad, so she'd missed the "window" of the early twenties that both her mother and sister-in-law had caught. And then she'd been with Christopher, who had heard her give a talk at the zoo. That relationship went from chummy to kinky—it was the only way he could stay interested—and made her question the entire concept of trust. Today, the men who asked her out were either single men in their late twenties or early thirties who were interested in relationships that lasted until the next prospect came along; divorced men who were like concrete, poured and set in bizarre ways; or married men who were interested only in sucking up some passion before going home to familiarity and comfort. None of which was for her. She'd rather stay home or go to a movie or work late. Occasionally she'd have dinner with her mentor, Professor Kane Lowery. She had always been alone, and she functioned just fine that way. Not that she felt her mother or Janet believed her. Joyce could imagine the conversations the two women had with each other.

The telephone rang while Joyce was heating some lentil soup and reading about computer simulations that proved that bats, like dogs, see in very sharp black and white. The caller was Kathy Leung, a TV reporter who covered the Westchester County beat. There had been a large-scale bat attack at a small-town park an hour north of the city. It had sent two people to the hospital in very serious condition. Kathy had gotten Dr. Joyce's number from the zoo and was calling from the broadcast truck. If they swung by, would she be interested in coming up to provide some professional commentary from the site?

Not really, Joyce admitted, but that's what she'd do if it were her ticket to the scene of the attack. Kathy said they'd be there in ten minutes. Turning off the burner and covering the soup pot, Dr. Joyce was out the door and on the curb as the van pulled up.

Four

Following this evening's *unprecedented* bat attack, which left two people in critical condition, authorities in the small Westchester town are looking for *answers*."

"They oughta be looking for exterminators, Kath," Robert Gentry said to the TV.

Gentry was leaning back on the sofa. The nineteen-inch TV rested on a typing table on the other side of the snug living room; there was a small desk with a computer next to it. The half-eaten container of mei grob sat on the folding chair to his left. He held a large black decaf, no sugar, in his right hand. The blinds of the one window were pulled up, and he had a partial view of the Hudson and the sparkling lights of coastal New Jersey.

Gentry's dark eyes lingered on the young Hong Kong–born reporter. Her silky brown hair was bobbed to just above the collar of her maroon blazer, and she had beautiful, dark eyes. He liked Kathy Leung. They had dated several times after meeting at a Police Athletic League function when she came to New York from a Connecticut TV station. It didn't work out. She went for taciturn lugs like her six-foot-six, red-meat-eating camera operator, Tex "T-Bone" Harrold. But Gentry still liked her.

Kathy was standing in front of a cordoned-off, very flat field. A trio of hefty state troopers stood stiffly behind her. Occasionally they motioned for people off-camera to stay away. Behind the state troopers were rows of parked cars and a dark forest.

"One person who may be able to *provide* those answers," said Kathy, "is Dr. Nancy Joyce. She's the Bronx Zoo's expert on chiroptera—*bats.* We're with her, live."

The newswoman turned to a head-taller young woman with short, raven black hair. Nancy Joyce had a long, very pretty face with full lips and large hazel eyes. She looked a little pale, but Gentry didn't imagine that bat scientists got out much during the day.

"Doctor, I understand you'll be going into the field when your assistant arrives with protective gear."

"Correct."

"At this point, is there anything at all you can tell us about what happened here?"

Gentry nodded. "Yeah. The final score was bats two, people zero."

The slender scientist squinted as she looked into the TV spotlight. "Only that this attack is not indicative of ordinary bat behavior. Bats are normally quite docile creatures. They live in colonies, but they don't hunt in packs. And they don't hunt people."

Gentry sipped his decaf. "Didn't, Doctor."

"Typically," Dr. Joyce went on, "the worst kind of human-bat encounter is when a bat gets into the house. That usually occurs when the bat pursues an insect through an open window."

"High-speed chase," Gentry said. He liked this woman, too. He liked her husky voice and the fact that she seemed a little ill at ease on camera.

"What about *vampire* bats?" Kathy asked. "There's been some talk of that because of the amount of blood spilled here—"

"No," Joyce said emphatically. "Sanguivorous bats are found in South America and usually attack sleeping prey. And they don't inflict the kinds of lacerations that were found here. The incision is so fine, in fact, that most victims seldom even wake."

"There's also been talk about microwaves," Kathy said. "Is there any way that radiation from the town's cellular phone tower can affect bat behavior?"

"Only if they kept getting disconnected," Gentry said. This lady, Dr. Joyce, was a professional. He liked people who knew what they were talking about.

"Again, no," Joyce said. "Those towers put out signals in the one-thousand- to three-hundred-thousand-megahertz range. That's a lot higher than the thousand-kilohertz upper range of bat echolocation."

"So, no effect."

"None," Joyce assured her.

"Are rabies a concern?"

"We won't know until we've had some medical reports," Joyce said. "But again, that's unlikely. Bats are highly symptomatic carriers of the virus. Unlike dogs which can turn violent, a bat that develops hydrophobia usually becomes very sick and dies. Bats can also carry other diseases, from a protozoal sleeping sickness called Chagas disease to histoplasmosis, an airborne fungus that comes from inhaling dusty bat guano. But those are extremely rare."

"I see. Finally, Doctor, what exactly are you going to look for here?"

"What I hope to find are one or more of the bats that were involved in this assault," the scientist said. "With any luck they'll attack me so I can observe their behavior—"

"*Ohmigod! Ohmigod!*"

Mrs. Bundonis's voice soaked through the thick wall behind Gentry. The detective muted the TV and listened.

"Mrs. B?" he shouted.

"Get *away!* Oh God!"

Gentry dropped the remote, swung from the sofa, and hurried to the door. He slipped his revolver from the holster hanging on a flea-market coatrack, listened, then walked into the hallway.

It was after eleven. The seventy-nine-year-old widow usually went to bed by ten. Maybe she was having a nightmare. She did sometimes, though usually it was just a moan or two. This was something he hadn't heard before. She was still screaming as he crossed the old linoleum tiles on tiptoe.

There were three apartments on the first floor of the four-story building. A composer rented the big one across the hall; he tended to work at night, in earphones. Mrs. Bundonis's apartment was on the west side of the Washington Street building, near the front. It was possible, Gentry thought, that someone could have gotten in through a window, which was unbarred; there were no signs of forced entry at the front door. He held the gun in his right hand, barrel down, and knocked with his left.

"Mrs. B?"

She was shouting in Lithuanian now. Her voice came from high in the room, as though she were standing on a chair.

"Mrs. B!" he yelled. "It's Bob Gentry."

"Oh—*oh!* Detective!"

He heard a stomp as the woman got off the chair. Then she tromped across the floor. She undid the chain, turned the latch, and opened the door.

"Detective, it's *terrible!*" she said as she moved aside. Her fine gray hair was in a long braid, and she was wearing red silk pajamas. He never would have imagined the pajamas. Mrs. Bundonis pulled on Gentry's sleeve. "They're all over! Come. Come!"

"Who is?"

He saw them before she answered.

Cockroaches large and larger were pouring from behind a light switch on the riverside wall of the apartment. Hundreds of them fanning across the living room floor. Some were rushing into the bathroom, others into the recessed kitchen area next to the door, still others into the radiator. Some were congregating on the bed, scurrying under the blankets, the pillows, the mattress.

"I didn't do this," Mrs. Bundonis said. "I keep the bread closed tight, all the time. I keep a clean house."

"I can see that," Gentry said quietly. "It's all right, Mrs. B. This isn't your fault."

The detective had never seen anything like this anywhere. Even in apartments where bodies had been sitting for a day or two, cockroaches didn't swarm. And they couldn't have come from just one nest. There were too many. But what was most amazing was that the cockroaches weren't just moving. They seemed to be in flight, running away from the wall.

Gentry told Mrs. Bundonis to wait in the hall.

"What are you going to do?" she asked. She was still holding tight to his sleeve.

"First, I'm going back to my apartment to put some shoes on," he said calmly. "I'll call the super and then I'll have a look around. Maybe something died somewhere. Or maybe there's a cockroach war going on."

"A war?" she said.

"That's a joke, Mrs. B. You stay here. I'll be right back."

Mrs. Bundonis released Gentry's sleeve but only to swat at her leg. There was nothing there. She followed Gentry to his door.

The detective phoned Barret Neville, the super. Neville lived several blocks away on Perry Street, but he wasn't in. Gentry left a message telling him what was happening. Then he put his gun back in the holster, pulled on the Frye boots he'd had for fifteen years, grabbed a flashlight and small screwdriver from the cupboard and stuck them in his deep pockets, and went back to Mrs. Bundonis's apartment. The woman watched from the doorway as he went in.

The stream of cockroaches had abated somewhat, though the bugs were still moving east. Gentry knew they'd find their way into his apartment before long; all these bastards did was eat, drink, reproduce, and infiltrate. Not that he was knocking it. That was all he did for ten years as an undercover cop.

Gentry walked toward the light switch. It wasn't possible to avoid stepping on bugs, and he didn't try. The crunching was ugly, slippery; he made a face. It surprised him that after sixteen years on the force, half of them spent undercover in the drug world, something like this could disgust him. But it did.

He stopped at the light switch. There was an opening of roughly a quarter inch along the bottom. Gentry wondered if the bugs had created that in their crush to get out. But get out *why?*

He started unscrewing the faceplate. There was a strange smell coming from behind it, like cleaning fluid or ammonia. A fire would certainly drive cockroaches from their homes, but there was no smoke. And the tiny basement had a fire alarm. So did the apartments.

He removed the two screws and carefully slipped the plastic plate from the wall. He shook a few cockroaches from the inside and set it on the windowsill. The smell was stronger now.

There was a two-inch space between the age-hardened plasterboard and the old brick wall behind it. He shined his flashlight into the area behind the light switch. He pressed his face to the wall, closed one eye, and looked down.

Cockroaches were everywhere except on what looked like small, dark anthills. The mounds were tucked against the plasterboard about an inch apart. The cockroaches were circling wide around them. He angled the flashlight to either side. To the right was a pipe—probably from the kitchen sink—and went down into the basement. Where it went from there he had no idea.

Gentry shook off a bug that had crawled from the flashlight onto his hand. He turned to Mrs. Bundonis, who was still in the hall.

"Have you heard any kinds of noises in the wall?" he asked.

"Just the pipes."

"No scratching or tiny little feet?"

She shook her head.

He looked back down inside the wall. Mice didn't leave waste like that, but something did.

"You have a wire coat hanger?"

"Over there." She pointed to the closet beside the kitchen recess.

Gentry strode over to the closet like a titan, crushing bugs as they continued their flight. "What about a Baggie?" he asked after he'd retrieved the hanger. He began untwisting it.

Mrs. Bundonis pointed to a cabinet over the sink. Her bare feet remained planted in the hallway, as though the cockroaches could never find their way past the threshold.

When Gentry had the plastic bag and had straightened the coat hanger, he went back to the wall. He began feeding the wire past the light switch and down the plasterboard.

"If I electrocute myself, call nine-one-one," he said.

"All right," she said helpfully.

Gentry's mouth twisted unpleasantly. The only person who ever got his dry sense of humor was that shit-wad Akira Mizuno, head of the drug-running operation he helped to bust last year. That was one of the reasons Gentry had been able to get as close to the crime boss as he did. Between wiping out his Armenian, Colombian, and Vietnamese rivals and getting kids addicted to crack—he had a wall chart with target "enrollment" on it—the murderous fuck liked a good joke, liked to chill. Gentry wondered if laughing boy was enjoying life-without-parole at the Attica Correctional Facility.

Gentry managed to poke the tip of the wire hanger into one of the mounds. He carefully withdrew the sample and shook it into the baggie. The substance came off easily, like powder. Gentry repeated the procedure four more times to make sure he had enough. Then he zip-locked the plastic bag, threw the hanger into a wastebasket, and went back to the hallway.

"I'm going to knock on doors and tell the other tenants what's happening," he said. "Then I'll pack some of your things and get you up to your daughter's place. You can call her from my apartment."

"Thank you." She patted his arm. "It's nice having you next door. You're a good man."

Gentry smiled as Mrs. Bundonis walked past. The septuagenarian ladies loved him. They really did. Then he glanced down at the Baggie. He had no idea where he was going to sleep tonight.

But he knew where he'd be early in the morning. Giving his old friend Dr. Chris Henry a little shit.

Five

Dressed in a white blouse, black slacks, and a blue sweater she'd borrowed from one of the mothers, Dr. Nancy Joyce stood alone at the edge of the parking lot. She was waiting for her assistant, Marc Ramirez, and the bat-resistant Nomex safety suits he was bringing up from the zoo. Designed to protect the wearer from bat droppings as well as from claws and fangs, the suit was typically used to explore caves where there could be as many as a million bats.

When she first spoke to Westchester wildlife commissioner Cliff LoDolce—he reached her in the van as the TV crew was driving down—Joyce hadn't expected to need the outfit. From LoDolce's description of the attack, she assumed that Tom Fitzpatrick had disturbed a small bat maternity roost or harem, prompting the assault. Female bats could be extremely protective and a little cross, especially early in the evening when they hadn't yet fed. Until she saw some home video footage shot by one of the parents, Joyce hadn't realized that the bats actually had charged the boy and his father. Unfortunately, she couldn't speak to either of the victims about what had happened. Both were still in intensive care and heavily sedated.

The scientist looked up. Against the near-black sky she could see bats zipping here and there in perfectly normal fashion. A pass over the woods in a police helicopter had failed to tell her anything because of the darkness and heavy leaf cover. She would have to go in on the ground.

She glanced out at the grandstand, which was partly lit by two large spotlights well behind first and third base. A large pack of reporters and TV crews was huddled there, along with resident state trooper Bill Anderson and six other troopers. Initially, the Little League parents and children had been there as well. Most of them lived in wooded areas and were afraid to go home. But when the crowd began to grow, Bill Anderson had had enough. He consulted with LoDolce and Joyce, who agreed that people stood a greater chance of being attacked here in the open than in their homes. The trooper then imposed a curfew and told everyone to leave. He made sure that people who didn't have a ride got one.

The scientist was glad when everyone left. Not only was it quieter, but she'd felt pressure while they were there. She'd caught the glances, the nervous smiles, the pointing fingers. She'd volunteered to go in because *she* needed to know what was going on. Now everyone was waiting for her to give them answers. One of the reasons she'd stayed apart from them was that she didn't want to speculate. Privately, she didn't believe a disease was behind this. Once in a while nature whipped up a mutated virus or bacterium. One of her two colleagues, Dr. Carla Kelly—a specialist in veterinary diseases—had gone back to Columbia University with blood, fur, and guano samples. The blood came from the boy's wounds; if they could find traces of bat saliva, that might tell them if there were a new kind of illness. But Nancy didn't think that was the case here. From all accounts the open-field attack had been coordinated and demarcated. Healthy or sick, bats were smart. But not *that* smart.

The other colleague who had come up here was Dr. Herman Berkowitz, who added nothing to their limited body of knowledge. Dubbed "überputz" by the people who worked with him, the self-promoting, German-born zoologist from the Central Park Zoo had come up with one of the other camera crews. After doing his TV bit, talking about how gentle bats normally were, he headed back to his third wife's Central Park West penthouse. He was not a man who liked to dirty his hands with science.

The other reason Joyce stayed by herself was that as long as she had to think, this was how she enjoyed doing it. Alone, outside, in the dark.

Joyce grew up on eight isolated acres in the hills of Cornwall, Connecticut. Whatever the season she'd walk the wooded grounds after twilight. She would watch bats in their crooked flight and listen as foxes moved through the crickety silence. She marveled at the great horned owls—big birds with deep, throaty hoots—and at the smaller, faster screech owls. She had never seen a field mouse get away from one of those birds. Never.

The kids at school thought Joyce was spooky and avoided her. Her teachers and guidance counselor and Father Joseph thought she was troubled. Her mother worried because her fascination with nocturnal predators wasn't ladylike. Her father, a local GP, was concerned because she was always using vines to rappel into deep gullies to catch frogs, wading through lagoons because the swirling silt felt cool around her toes, or climbing high ledges to see how trees grew out of them. He absolutely forbade her from doing any of that; she did it anyway and got punished.

Only her grandmother understood. The older woman once confided that she never felt as free or as important as when she and her parents were fleeing from the Bolsheviks. She said that sleeping beneath the stars or clouds in woods and on hillsides made her feel like she was part of all nature. Compared to that, being a member of the aristocracy faded to insignificance.

Grandma Joycewicz also taught her that it didn't matter what other people thought. Joyce liked what she liked. And what she liked was dangerous, compelling nighttime. Old books, just like her grandfather had. Solitude. Candy corn, which she wished she had a bag of right now.

Joyce looked back across the picnic area just as Marc Ramirez arrived on his motorcycle. The wiry graduate student stopped on the other side of the baseball diamond, killed the engine, dropped the kickstand, and slid off. Even before he removed his helmet—which was black, save for a large gold bat silhouette just above the visor—he began unstrapping the silver case from the large luggage rack behind the seat.

Joyce walked over.

"Hey," Marc said.

"Hi."

The young man hefted an armful of aluminum case to the ground. Camera crews and reporters, followed by the police chief, the wildlife commissioner, and the health inspector, hustled toward them.

Marc pulled off his helmet. He used his fingers to comb his short black hair as he looked at the cameras. "How are the victims?"

"Critical." Joyce bent and unlatched the top of the case.

"What happened?"

Joyce removed the folded headgear. She nodded toward the parking lot. "They walked in over there and didn't walk out again. Four volunteer firefighters in helmets and full-face masks had to go in and pull them out."

"Were the firefighters attacked?"

Joyce nodded. "And they were there for only a few seconds."

"Amazing," Marc said. "A bat line in the sand. Any idea why the bats pack-attacked?"

Joyce lay the floppy headpiece and gloves on the ground. "My guess is there's something in the woods. A bear or a big cat might cause a bat frenzy. Or a chemical contaminant like amyl nitrite or some kind of amphetamines might have made them disoriented, aggressive."

"You mean the bats could've gotten into someone's stash?"

"Don't laugh. The police chief said that people go into the woods to do drugs."

"I'm not laughing. I'm actually wondering how many of those people were in the grandstands tonight giving statements to the police."

Dr. Joyce frowned. The twenty-four-year-old Queens native was an enthusiastic zoologist-in-the-making. Though he hadn't quite outgrown his MTV sense of priorities, at least he'd limited his visible body piercing to one ear and one nostril.

Marc picked up the rubbery suit and shook it out. "Anyway, drugs wouldn't explain the boundaries those bats set. Or the timing. Why now?"

"I'm hoping the bats will give us some of those answers when I go in."

With the bright TV lights on and the news cameras turning, Joyce took off her shoes. Then she slipped into the leggings and built-in boots. Though her mind was on the bats, there was no ignoring the invasive cameras and the hot white lamps. They answered a question her unlamented, was-I-really-that-lonely boyfriend Christopher had asked over and over and over. Getting dressed and—especially—undressed on camera was not something she could ever get into.

The one-piece antibat outfit was heavy and loose-fitting, like a radiation suit. It was colored Day-Glo orange with reflectors on the front and back to prevent her from being shot by hunters. There was a zipper in the rear, another around the neck, and one more around each sleeve to attach to the gloves. When the headpiece and gloves were attached, the suit was completely sealed, except for the faceplate, which was made of rigid plastic mesh. That allowed her to communicate and to breathe.

Marc helped Joyce finish dressing. Before donning the headpiece, she slid on a lightweight radio headset. Marc donned his, and they checked the reception. Then the young man took a large flashlight and Nomex sample bag from the compartment under the motorcycle seat.

"Doctor," Kathy Leung asked. "Will it be all right if we light you up out there?"

"Sure." Joyce pointed up with a gloved hand. "See the way those bats are zigzagging?"

Kathy said she did.

"They're echolocators." Joyce slipped on the hood. "Roughly

half of all bats are. Vision is a secondary sense to them. Bats that rely on smell or eyesight to hunt tend to be frugivorous or nectarivorous."

"Meaning you're safe in the light unless you're a banana," Marc said.

"Fruit, nectar, pollen, leaves," Joyce added. "They'll eat any food that doesn't move."

One of the newsmen shouted, "Are you nervous, Dr. Joyce?"

Joyce paused and peered into the lights. "I don't think so," she replied. "Just awfully curious."

"We all are," said the health inspector, a chunky, balding man whose name Joyce couldn't remember. "So if you'll all just stay back and let Dr. Joyce do her work—"

After zipping up the "bat hat" as Marc was fond of calling it, Joyce turned toward the parking area. Marc handed her the flashlight and slid the sample bag over her arm. He gave her shoulder a little pat. "Good luck," he said.

"Thanks."

Trooper Anderson stepped closer. "Anything we can do?"

"Just keep everyone away," Joyce said.

The cameras followed Dr. Joyce as she ducked under the yellow tape that had been stretched along the backs of the parked cars. Though the spotlights from the baseball diamond didn't reach this far, the camera lights illuminated most of the parking area and about twenty feet of airspace. Joyce stood for a moment looking out at the forest some five hundred yards distant. There was something mysterious and seductive about it, like nights in Cornwall. For a moment Nancy Joyce felt like a little girl again.

She took a deep breath and slowly walked forward. Her footsteps and breathing sounded very loud inside the suit. When she neared the spot where Scott Fitzpatrick had been attacked, she stopped and tilted her head back. Her vision was limited by the sides of the visor, but it seemed as though the bats were still going about their business, just above the treeline.

"Marc?"

"Here."

"What're you seeing?"

"Bats bug-eating."

"Nothing else?"

"Nope."

She started walking again. "Odd," she said. "They don't seem to be exhibiting any of the behavior the townspeople—"

Joyce gasped as a bat slammed against her face. Its claws and teeth locked onto the mesh and its wings batted fiercely.

"Shit!"

"Nancy?"

"I'm okay," she said. "Just a little heads-up."

"It must've come in pretty low," Marc said. "Damn. Sorry. I didn't even see it."

The bat twisted and tried to nibble at her nose, but it couldn't get through the mesh. Joyce grasped the creature's fat, round body between her thumb and index finger and pulled it away from the visor; the bat felt soft, like an overripe peach. The animal flapped and screeched, but she held firmly. She examined the wriggling creature under the flashlight.

"It's a vespertilionid," she said. "Genus *Myotis,* a little brown bat with—man, he's jumpy—with what appears to be a normal physiognomy." She angled the head back. It continued to squirm. "Enough, you." She shoved a thumb under its jaw, steadying the head and forcing the mouth open. "No rabid salivary accumulation or discoloration. Also no discharge from the nose leaf or eyes to suggest a viral infection. Weight seems normal, about ten grams." She pushed aside the fur of the lower belly. "And it's a young male, so scratch my theory that they could be females protecting a nurs—"

Joyce's head snapped back as three more animals flew at her face. They attacked the mesh, and she lost the first bat. The new sets of teeth twisted left and right, trying to bite her nose, eyebrow, chin, and cheeks. Joyce angrily pushed them away. They came back.

"Nancy, you *sure* you're all right?"

"I'm fine," she replied. From the corner of her visor Joyce saw the first bat circle up, stop, then shoot down to the back of her glove. It clutched her knuckles and tried to bite her wrist. "They're just getting a little pushy. Hold on a second. I want to check something."

Joyce leaned her head forward slightly. She breathed deeply through her nose. Then again. She smelled the distinctive dampness of the bats' breath. A meal of a few thousand bugs a night produced a "swampy" odor that the bat shared with no other animal.

"The nose lab gives me a normal on bat halitosis," Joyce said. She felt a flurry of tiny punches along her arms, legs, and torso as other bats struck. She continued walking. "That would rule out a toxin or bacteriological or parasitic infestation that might affect the stomach acid, give them bad breath." She inhaled lower. "The fur smells musky, as it should. Except for the violent behavior, I'm not seeing or smelling anything unusual."

"I am," Marc said. "You're wearing four bats."

"Don't worry about it."

"I *am* worried. That suit was tested for guano and a bat or two, not catastrophic exposure. Listen, why don't we just take one of the cars. We can drive in closer."

"No. The gas fumes and noise might change the bats' behavior. Besides, there are still far fewer bats than attacked the field before. Can you see if they're flapping?"

"They are. Why?"

"Because if they were only trying to bite me they wouldn't be moving their wings."

"Right. Well, they're not feeding. This is definitely an attack."

"Bats as territorial carnivores," Joyce said. "There's your doctoral thesis, Marc—"

The scientist started as another bat slapped against the mesh. It cried in a high, ululating chirp as it joined the other bats, snapping and pushing its flat muzzle at the plastic.

"This is unbelievable!" she said.

"What?"

"The way they keep throwing themselves at me."

Joyce stopped and shoved the flashlight in her sample bag. Then she dug her fingertips under the bellies of the squealing bats and roughly pushed them off. Retrieving the flashlight with her left hand she began rapidly waving her right hand back and forth. Though the bats continued to fly at her, Joyce was able to swat them aside.

"That's better," she said. She picked up the pace slightly and looked skyward. "It's odd, though. Only a few are attacking. The rest are still going about their business."

"Someone forgot to tell them the war's over," Marc joked.

Joyce was about twenty-five yards from the forest now. It loomed large and dark, like the woods in Cornwall. But there was something unnaturally still about this place. Uninviting. When Joyce reached the edge of the woods, the bats suddenly flew off. The silence was complete. The scientist stopped and swept the flashlight beam slowly across the trees. Nothing seemed to be moving. She stooped, picked up a large rock, and heaved it ahead. Except for the *thunk* of the rock there was no sound.

"What's happening?" Marc asked.

"Apart from my escorts leaving, nothing," Joyce said.

"The bats just took off?"

"All at once, like they had somewhere else to go."

"More pack behavior. Nancy, I don't like this. Are you sure you want to go in there?"

"Answers don't just walk up to scientists, Marc."

"I heard a scientist say something like that in a movie once. Right before he was eaten by the 'Beast from 2,000 Fathoms.' At least talk to me."

Joyce said she would. She moved cautiously into the woods, shining the flashlight left and right as she proceeded.

"It's strange. I'm about ten feet in and it's dead quiet. I also haven't seen any flying insects." She stopped at a rotted log and poked it with her toe. There were beetles in the soft wood; after a moment they rushed into the cracks and under moss-covered bark. Grubs glistened under her light. "There are some shelter bugs, but that's it."

"Maybe the bats got the others."

"An entire airborne population? Very unlikely." Joyce continued walking. "Besides, I don't see or hear anything else here. Nothing in the grass, in the leaves, anywhere."

At about twenty-five feet in, the ground sloped downward slightly. The soft earth was knit with large, looping roots and creeping vines. Bare patches of dirt were interspersed with tall grass and occasional thorn bushes. The incline ended in a small marsh that was about fifty yards across. Joyce crouched at the edge and shined her light across the murky water. The grasses, cattails, and motherwort were bowed, and the water was still. There were no minnows, no frogs, no waterbugs. No animal life of any kind.

She stood slowly. "This isn't natural, Marc. There aren't even any sounds coming from—"

There was a loud crack, and then something crashed into the water in front of her. Joyce stumbled back, swearing.

"What's wrong?" Marc demanded.

"Something fell." Joyce turned the light on the marsh as she got back on her feet. "A large branch." She watched as the four-foot limb settled into the mud beneath the shallow water. Then she pointed the light up. "And I see where it came from. Very interesting. We've got what look like otherwise healthy limbs of all sizes. They're broken and hanging from a row of red oaks along the right rim of the marsh." She started walking along the water's edge, looking up at the shattered limbs. "Strange."

"What?"

"The trees are severely damaged from top to bottom but only on the marsh side."

"That could mean there was a weather event. A small tornado could've touched down and scared the bats. They get those little twisters here."

Joyce stood directly under one of the trees. "True. But some of these branches are pushed down and others are leaning *up* against the trees. They're broken in the middle and folded back."

"A funnel could have snapped them going in, then sucked them up again going out."

"Possibly," she said. "Do me a favor. Ask one of the TV reporters to call their meteorological people. Find out if there were reports of any ministorms in the region."

"You got it," Marc said.

Joyce continued to circle the marsh. A small twister *would* explain many things. The condition of the trees. The absence of anything living aboveground. The agitated bats.

She stopped as something shimmered on an old tree to the right. She turned her light toward the trunk. It took a long moment before she realized what she was looking at. The bark was covered with blood. It was running down in a thick coat, like paint. She stepped closer and angled her head so she could see up through the leaves.

She froze. A twister wouldn't explain the deer carcass flopped across a massive branch roughly fifteen feet up. The buck was lying on its side, its head and hindquarters hanging down, its eyes staring lifelessly. From where Joyce stood it looked as though the midsection of the animal had been torn open and gutted.

"Marc?"

"Wait a sec. I've got Kathy Leung checking—"

"Forget that."

"What?"

"Forget the weather report," Joyce said. "I'm coming out. Tell Trooper Anderson we're going to need the chopper again. And tell Commissioner LoDolce something for me."

"What?"

"Tell him I don't think his problem is little brown bats."

Six

The Hudson River is one of the most heavily traveled waterways in the world.

The river begins in upstate New York at Lake Tear of the Clouds in the Adirondack Mountains and flows 315 miles in a mostly southward direction. It divides New York State from New Jersey for seventeen miles before spilling into the Atlantic Ocean.

Grant's Tomb, the final resting place of President Ulysses S. Grant and his wife, Julia, is among the most famous landmarks along the river. This is primarily due to the old joke about "Who's buried in Grant's Tomb?" and not because the mausoleum is a popular tourist stop. Located in an isolated area off residential Riverside Drive and West 122nd Street, inconvenient to pedestrians because of heavy vehicular traffic to the east, the monument has become a hangout for drug dealers and graffiti artists.

At 150 feet tall, the top of the domed rotunda is one of the highest points on the upper New York City side of the river. Whether travelers are coming south by water or by air, it is considered the beacon that welcomes them to Manhattan.

. . .

The bats glided gracefully to the top of the tomb.

Their powerful feet found clawholds in the wind-pitted stone, on the marble knob at the top, at the decorative ridges. Their wings settled gracefully on the sloping sides of the dome, and their bodies slumped forward. Many hung upside down from the eaves. They preferred letting gravity work for them to help them take flight or keep their ears erect.

A strong, persistent river wind washed over and around the monument. A tiny claw at the apex of each wing helped the bats hold on wherever they were. The wind carried with it the strong scents of the city and of the streets directly below.

They listened. First, they listened for the high, drumming cries of their kind. Some of the voices were faint, bouncing here and there before reaching them. The bats focused on the location of the nearest members of the colony. They were coming from a cave in the direction of the lightening sky. They marked the mouth of the cave not just by sight and sound but also where it was relative to the direction of the wind and the first glow of the new day.

The bats would go there—but not yet.

They also listened for the sounds of insects flying toward them. Nourishment for themselves. They listened for the sound of the bat that had summoned them. The bat that had not yet arrived.

A short time later a sound reached them from the north. It grew louder, until finally a large shadow passed over them. A shadow accompanied by a high, whistling cry. A sound that stirred them to activity by its strength and the ringing pain it caused inside the head.

Relaxing their claws, the bats released their grip on the tomb. Some walked awkwardly down the sides as they raised their wings and flew into the dawn. Others just dropped off the sides, snapped out their wings, and took off like flying devils in the wind.

. . .

It was days like these that made Barbara Mathis glad she hadn't gone into another profession.

Look at her husband. Hal had once said that there was nothing worse than being a stockbroker who was heavy into the European markets. He was right. He left their home on the Upper West Side at three A.M. each morning and headed down to Wall Street. He came home dead tired at six P.M. They had dinner together, and he was asleep by eight.

Barbara's brother was a journalist. He was never home. Her sister-in-law wrote computer software. Things changed so fast that no sooner was something written than it had to be rewritten. She was never home.

But Barbara was smart. She'd turned her teenage fancy into a profession and became a makeup artist. She freelanced for several modeling agencies in town. Most of the time her hours were ten A.M. to two or three P.M. Models didn't like to work early in the morning or late in the afternoon. They didn't look their best then. That worked for Barbara. It left her time to work out in the afternoon, play around with her oil paints, and read.

But once in a rare while one of her clients had a great idea to shoot on top of a building and catch the sunrise. Like today. So Barbara had gotten up with Hal, who seemed way too happy to have her with him. She'd loaded her makeup kits into the baskets on the back of her ten-speed, armed herself with helmet, cellular phone, mace, and a loud battery-powered siren bracketed to the handlebars—to use against reckless drivers or would-be attackers—and headed into the morning.

She was happy that days like this happened only once every few months.

Barbara left the old building she and her husband had bought, gutted, and renovated and pedaled quickly down Riverside Drive. The morning air was smooth and the streets cooperatively deserted. She hunkered down over the bars and turned up the speed. She smiled, savoring the healthy slap of her heart and the just-short-of-painful burning in her thighs.

Suddenly there was a burning in her neck, then along her scalp, up the backs of her arms, and across her shoulders and down her spine. She saw something flash past her on the left, then come back at her. Something small and black that her mind registered as a pigeon. When it doubled back and flapped at her face and closed her left eye with its claws, she saw that it wasn't a bird.

She tried to hold the handlebar with her left hand while she reached for the bat with her right. She screamed with shock and then pain. She had trouble seeing. The bike wobbled.

A moment later Barbara thought she'd hit a pothole. The nose of the bicycle dipped. She felt herself being thrown forward, but she didn't fall. She continued forward. The muscles of her shoulder cramped for an instant, and then knife-sharp pain ripped across her back from the tops of her arms to the middle of her neck. Her back stiffened and her mouth fell open and she wanted to scream. But she couldn't. The pain had slapped the air from her lungs, and all she could do was squeal.

She felt her throat tighten with sound, but she didn't hear it. All she heard was the rush of the wind and something beating all around her. It sounded like when she was a little girl and hid in the sheets on her mother's clothesline and wondered if that's what it felt like to be an angel in the clouds.

Barbara was dimly aware of the bicycle falling to the ground in front of her. Or the street growing dark and her back trembling and weak, hot and then cool. She tried to reach up, but there was no strength in her arms. Then her lungs stopped. Her eyelids sagged.

For a moment before they shut, she thought she saw the comforting clouds of her youth. . . .

Seven

Robert Gentry spent the night at the Hotel Windermere on West End Avenue and Ninety-second Street. The manager, Dale Rupert, was one of his oldest and closest friends.

Rupe used to run the Hotel Dixie on West Forty-fourth Street. When Gentry was still a beat cop, the Dixie Hotel was the "Midtown Eden" for junkies and pushers. Rupe hated the drug traffic and had Gentry boot the pushers out. The one-armed Vietnam veteran hated it even more when swaggering drug boss Stevie "Cool" Kuhl came to see him one day. Cool threatened to break Rupe's remaining arm with a mallet if he stopped his people from dealing in the lobby.

That was all Rupe had to hear.

With the veteran's full cooperation, Gentry brought in the Special Narcotics Enforcement Unit. The SNEU fitted Rupe with a wire, and thanks to his efforts they sent Stevie Cool to prison for fifteen years.

But the Dixie operation uncovered a larger New York–southern Connecticut drug chain that SNEU agents in both states wanted to break. Having completed his requisite two-year tour as a patrolman, Gentry asked then–Precinct Commander Veltre to be transferred to SNEU. He spent several weeks undergoing intense tactical training at

Camp Smith in upstate New York, then came back to Midtown South and worked as a plainclothes narc running buy-and-bust operations. Later, in order to break the Mizuno ring, he went undercover. Tearing down that smuggling-and-dealing chain consumed the next five years of his life. It sent fourteen major dealers to prison and earned Gentry a Medal of Valor for bravery. He gave the medal to Rupe. He wasn't sure why, but his partner Bernie was gone, and it seemed like the right thing to do. Gentry and Rupe remained friends. Rupe stayed at the Dixie until it was torn down in 1990.

There were no rooms available at the Windermere, but Rupe let Gentry have the couch in a psychiatrist's office on the first floor. The leather couch was comfortable, though Gentry had trouble sleeping for more than an hour at a time. Some paranoid kept calling the answering machine and waking him. The man was complaining that his apartment building was too quiet. He was sure the neighbors were listening to him. He said he could hear them putting drinking glasses against the wall and moving them around. By four A.M. Gentry seriously considered calling the man back, informing him he was listening from the room next door, and telling him to go the hell to sleep.

Early the next morning Gentry pulled on the beige slacks and white shirt he'd brought with him. He had coffee with Rupe at the front desk and looked at the *New York Post.* A front-page article said that the "bat boy and bat man" up in Westchester were recovering, though wildlife officials still had no idea why they were attacked. Thanking Rupe and throwing his overnight bag over his shoulder, Gentry took the Number 2 subway down to Twenty-third Street. The shrink's paranoid caller would not have liked the ride. The passengers seemed unusually quiet. As if they were waiting for something to happen.

Or maybe it was him waiting for something . . . or imagining that people were quiet. Either way, it was weird.

Gentry felt better as he walked crosstown through the warm, bright morning to the police academy building on Twentieth Street between Second and Third Avenues. He always felt good visiting the thirty-four-year-old academy. Whether it was to talk to plebes about the Accident Investigations Squad or his days with the SNEU, recruit new talent for the precinct or to see Chris Henry, it was exciting to watch enthusiastic young cadets move in and around the eight-story building. Just like the kids at the Fashion Institute, it renewed his spirit to see the up-and-coming generation. To see that they cared, that they weren't afraid to put everything on the line for others.

The forty-nine-year-old Henry was the head of the crime lab—more formally known as the Scientific Research Division—specializing in ballistics, bombs, and what they called "unidentifiables" found at crime scenes. Though the FBI lab at Federal Plaza had the whiz-bang public reputation, and the NYPD Crime Scene Unit on Tenth Street got the press and big bucks, Henry ran the smartest little group of scientific sleuths in town.

The short, chunky physician was sitting at the chrome table that filled his laboratory. He was reading the *Daily News* and drinking coffee when Gentry stepped into the open doorway.

"Get your big goddamn nose out of the personals," Gentry said. "You're married."

Henry looked up and smiled. He slid off his stool and extended his hand. "Well, look who's here! You know, Bobby, I was just telling my new lab assistant about you yesterday."

"Male or female?"

"The latter. Bright, and gorgeous, and engaged, so forget it. How the hell've you been?"

"Not bad."

"You look tired."

"I am."

"Been working late on a case?"

Gentry shook his head. "It was something else."

"Well, pull up a stool and tell me all about it. I *am* married. I need to live vicariously through my single male friends."

"Sorry, Chris," Gentry said. "It wasn't that either."

"Too bad." Henry sat down heavily. "What I was telling my assistant, Laurette, was that I miss the days when you were with the SNEU. While everyone else was giving us bullets and bomb parts, you gave us real nutbusters to unravel. ID-ing dried blood on a safety razor, looking for traces of gunpowder in water from a fish tank, trying to find heroin in saliva somebody spit onto the street." Henry frowned. "Lot of liquids, now that I think of it. But challenging."

"Right. The good old days."

"Hey, they were rewarding days for everyone. You don't give the crime lab that kind of stuff anymore. A hit-and-run once every three or four months. Mortar analysis of falling cornices. From everyone else it's still bullets and bomb shards. You ever think of going back to the SNEU?"

"No. You ever think of going back to the army?"

Henry winced. "Touché. On the other hand, you did do it over ten years. Most men would've burned out."

"Flattery won't work either."

Henry shrugged. "Anyway, here you are. What can I do for you?"

Gentry unzipped his overnight bag, withdrew the Baggie, and handed it to Henry. "I fished this from the wall of my apartment building last night. I was hoping you could tell me what kind of animal it belongs to."

Dr. Henry held the bag up to the fluorescent light. He shook it lightly, opened it, sniffed it, then pressed it shut. he handed it back to Gentry.

"Well?"

"Like I told you," Henry said, "there was a time when you made my life interesting."

"What do you mean?"

"This was way too easy."

"You know what it is?"

Henry nodded slowly. "It's a waste medium consisting primarily of nitrogen, phosphorous, and potassium. Also millions of microscopic, undigested insect parts."

Gentry looked at him blankly.

"It's bat guano," Henry said. "Not only that, but it was collected almost straight from the bat."

"How do you know that?"

"Because very early this morning we were given a sample almost exactly like yours."

Gentry had been slumping. He straightened. "Explain."

"Laurette was here and ran the analysis," Henry went on. "She identified it and also noticed the lack of any bioremediation microbes—meaning no decomposition. Hence the freshness."

"Who brought the sample to you?"

"A Metro North cop sent it over. He had a strange name—what was it? Arville something? Arvids?"

"Arvids Stiebris. Works under Ari Moreaux. I know him. What happened?"

"One of the MTA maintenance workers went out on his weekly inspection early this morning and didn't report back or answer his pager. The shift supervisor called for a police escort. Arvids and he went out looking for the guy. They found the man and the guano."

"What was wrong with him?"

"Physically, not much. He apparently passed out from the smell. There were scratches on his face and neck, but the EMT personnel who were called in said he got them when he fell."

"Where did all this happen?"

"I'm really not sure. Somewhere along the subway tunnels, Lexington Avenue side of the station, I think. Arvids said the dung heap was a big one, about two feet high."

"Jesus."

"Yeah. That's a lot of shit."

"Anything else?" Gentry asked.

"About the sample, no. But totally by coincidence, when I saw the bat attack on the news last night, I called Al Doyle at home. He's the Health Department's Dr. Pest Control. You know him? Looks like a field mouse."

Gentry said he didn't know him or know of him.

"He's not one of us I Love New York guys. Sees the burg as a pit stop to the federal level. Anyhow, he didn't think the Westchester bats were anything to worry about. He said the attack up north probably happened because too many migrating bats tried to feed on too few bugs and ended up colliding with one another and with people who got in the way."

"The news reports said the two people up there were practically gnawed to death."

"I mentioned that to Doyle," Henry replied. "He said bat attacks make good copy."

"Horseshit. I saw the home video footage on the news report."

"Me too. What can I tell you?"

"That you'll call Doyle later and ask him what he thinks about the guano in Grand Central."

"Actually, we had that discussion last night. He told me that we've had bats in the subways before. He said they usually migrate late in the summer or early fall. They look for a warm place to hibernate and give birth, and the subways fill the bill. He said there are thirty to forty thousand bats in the city parks, and it's not uncommon for many of them to head underground."

"I've lived in the city for eighteen years, Chris. I've never had bat guano in my wall. And that maintenance guy was obviously a little surprised by what he found on the train tracks."

Henry shrugged. "There are renovations going on at Grand Central. There's been a lot of new construction where you live in the West Village. Maybe that's opened new niches for the bats or closed some old ones."

"Oh, come on. How many displaced bats would it take to create a pile of shit two feet deep?"

"Listen," Henry said, "I'm no bat expert. Maybe *you* should talk to Doyle. He gets in around ten o'clock. I'll give you his direct line at the Health Department."

"No, thanks." Gentry zipped his overnight bag and slung it over his shoulder. "I saw a bat lady on TV last night. I'm going to see if I can get in touch with her."

Henry smirked. "I'd take a lady over Doyle too."

"She seemed to know her stuff, Chris. That's all."

"Sure. Well, let me know what you find out."

"I will."

"And it was good to see you," Henry said. "Come back with a real problem next time."

"I'll try."

Henry waved the Baggie. "You want this?"

Robert shook his head. He had a feeling he'd be able to get more where that came from.

Eight

Midtown South is known as the busiest police precinct in the world. It's responsible for Times Square and its millions of tourists, for Hell's Kitchen and its mix of aspiring actors, old-timers, and human predators, for busy Grand Central Station, the residential elite of Park Avenue, and the heart of the popular Fifth Avenue shopping district.

Gentry took a cab to the station house. He wrote "in" beside his name on the duty blackboard, then made his way through the crowd of officers and people with problems. He said good morning to Detectives Jason Anthony and Jen Malcolm who sat at desks in "the squad pit," as they called it, then tucked himself into his small, bright office in the back. He shut the door and fell into his swivel chair. There was a pile of folders on his desk about a foot deep. Bike messengers who ran people down. Cars that hit poles. A model plane that flew off a roof and struck a pedestrian in the eye. Gentry decided that most of these cases would keep. He ran his finger down the sun-faded auto-dial list taped to the desk beside the phone. He punched in 34# and looked for a pen.

Gentry couldn't remember the name or title of the bat expert who had been on the evening news with Kathy Leung. He also couldn't remember whether she worked at the Bronx Zoo or the Central Park Zoo. He assumed he'd get Kathy's assistant, get the number, and get off the phone. He was surprised when the lady herself answered.

"Kathy?" he said.

"Who's this?"

"Robert Gentry. Midtown South."

"Detective," she said flatly. "Hello. This is a surprise."

"A pleasant one, I hope."

She said nothing. This wasn't going to be easy.

"I saw your report last night," Gentry said. "I didn't think you'd be in this early."

"I slept here. Look, I'm really kind of busy right now. Things got weird last night."

"In what way?"

"You ought to watch more morning TV. We get late-breaking news the papers miss."

"Sorry. My dad set type for the *Trib.*"

"The what?"

"The *Herald Tribune.* Never mind. What happened last night?"

"They found a dead deer way up a tree. Its side was torn open and it was partly eaten."

Gentry stopped looking for the pen. "Eaten as in decomposed?"

"No, eaten as in 'for dinner.' The body was very fresh, dead only a few hours. The police thought at first that it might be some kind of prank. That whoever put the deer up there also scared the bats into doing what they did. But there were no footprints anywhere near the tree, either human or deer. The police used a chopper to pull the deer out of the tree and had it brought to the zoo for an autopsy. I'm waiting to hear about the results."

"What the hell could have carried a deer up a tree?" Gentry said. "Even if this were a joke, a deer weighs—what?"

"This one was full-grown, about three hundred kilograms."

"Which is how much in English?"

"A little over six hundred pounds," Kathy said. "That's a lot more than your average puma or college jocks can haul twenty feet up a tree. You know my camera operator T-Bone?"

"I do."

"Used to be a Con Ed lineman. Big guy. He said that four of him couldn't have carried it up there. Everyone's hoping the autopsy will give us some answers. Police are also asking parents who video-taped the game to turn over the cassettes. Some of them might have picked up something going on in the woods."

Gentry was silent for a moment.

"So why were you calling?" Kathy asked.

"Oh. I wanted the number of that bat lady you had on the air last night."

"Why?"

"I'd like to talk to her."

"I got that part. Is it personal or professional?"

"It's business."

"Did something happen I should know about?"

"No," Gentry said. "I just wanted to ask her if there's anything we should be worried about regarding bats."

"Detective?"

"Yes?"

"Don't bullshit me. You're with the accident squad. Since when are bats your beat?"

"Since trains come into Grand Central from Westchester nine-teen hours out of every day," he said. "I'm worried about tiny little fare-beaters flying at people in the station." Now that he thought of it, he wondered if they should be worried about that.

"That's a Metro North concern, not yours. Come on. I shared with you. What's going on?"

"Nothing, Kathy. Really."

"I don't believe you."

"Kath, if I can help you, I will. I promise. That's the best I can do."

Kathy exhaled loudly. "Her name is Nancy Joyce, Bronx Zoo. And don't call again unless you want to play ball."

The next thing Gentry heard was a dial tone. He still liked Kathy. But he didn't want to tell her what they'd found. Just in case Doyle was right. He didn't want to see the media turn this into something it wasn't.

Gentry got the zoo number and called. He got the switchboard recording, entered the first three letters of Joyce's name, and was put through to her office. A young man answered.

"Marc Ramirez."

"Hi. This is Detective Robert Gentry, New York Police Department. Is Dr. Joyce in?"

"She had a long night. She's trying to get some sleep. Is there something I can help you with?"

"Are you a bat expert?"

"I'm working on it, Detective."

"All right," Gentry said. "What do you make of about two feet of bat guano piled next to subway tracks under Grand Central Station? Enough of it to make a man pass out. Also a massive cockroach exodus, apparently from a pile of guano inside an apartment wall?"

"I'll get Dr. Joyce," Ramirez said.

Gentry smiled. He liked that about today's young people, too—the smart ones knew when to duck.

He was on hold for less than a minute.

"This is Nancy Joyce."

Gentry recognized the husky voice from the newscast. It sounded thicker now, probably from lack of sleep. But it still sounded nice.

The detective introduced himself and told her about the guano in Grand Central and also in Mrs. Bundonis's apartment. When he was finished, Joyce was silent.

"Doctor?" he said, after a long moment.

"I'm here." Her voice no longer sounded groggy. "I was just thinking."

"While you're doing that," he said, "I was wondering. Have you found out anything about the deer?"

"We don't know much about that yet," she admitted. "There are large marks in the hide, backbone, and organs. They look like teeth, though they could have been made by an unserrated knife. The animal appears to have been killed by a large predator, but there were no bark splinters in its hide."

"Bark splinters? From the tree?"

"Correct. Meaning it wasn't dragged up. And there are fractures along the right-side ribs. Those could have been caused in an attack—you see it in bear assaults all the time—though the breaks appear to conform with the shape and size of the limb I found it on."

"Wait a second, Doctor. Are you saying the deer *fell* onto the branch from above?"

"Fell or was dropped," Joyce said. "Maybe from a plane or a helicopter—we just don't know. The carcass is with Dr. Nadler. Even-toed ungulates are Caryn's bailiwick."

"I see." Gentry couldn't decide whether this was comical or sick.

"Detective, can you find out anything more about the guano in Grand Central?"

"Like what?"

"I need to know more about the dimensions and consistency. It's not uncommon for bats to nest in subways, tunnels, and basements. But a two-foot-high mound of guano, even if it's only a foot in diameter, would take a hundred bats about a week to produce. And that's if they were all living on one vertical post."

"Is that unlikely?"

"With all the subway traffic in those tunnels? Yes."

"Al Doyle at the Health Department says we get plenty of bats in the tunnels," Gentry said.

"He's correct," she said, "only they don't stay there long. Bats don't like loud noise, wind, bright light, or moving objects."

"I see. Then how do you explain the guano?"

"If I had to guess, I think someone's playing a trick on you."

"Subway workers aren't noted for their sense of humor," Gentry said. "And even if that were true, it wouldn't explain the guano I found in my building."

"True," Joyce admitted. She was silent again. Then she asked, "Can someone take me to where the guano was found?"

"Absolutely," Gentry said. "I'll arrange it. When can you—"

"An hour," she said. "Meet me at the upstairs information booth in Grand Central. What are you wearing?"

"I'll find you," Gentry said. "I saw you on TV last night."

"Fine," she said and hung up.

Gentry placed the receiver back in the cradle. Women didn't seem to want to stay on the phone with him today.

After calling over to Captain Moreaux at Metro North to make certain that Arvids was still on post this late in the morning, Gentry left his office. As he stopped to write his destination on the blackboard, Captain Chris Sheehy entered the station house.

"Good morning, sir," Gentry said as the short, round captain walked past.

"Good morning," Sheehy replied. He stopped. He seemed uncharacteristically chipper. "Detective Gentry, do you know what the sweetest thing in the world is?"

"I think so."

"No, Detective," Sheehy said. "It's not. It's payback. Three times in the last month I was supposed to have breakfast with Captain Di-Fate of Central Park. I got paged away each time. So we made a deal. The next one who canceled had to pick up dinner—not breakfast—at the Old Homestead. Well, guess who got nailed this morning?"

Gentry smiled. "Not you."

"Not me."

"I'm happy for you, Captain," Gentry said.

"Bless the beasts and children," Sheehy laughed as he walked toward his office. "Especially the beasts at the zoo."

Gentry's smile evaporated. He put down the chalk and called after the captain. "What happened at the zoo?"

Captain Sheehy stopped. "An attempted jail break," he said. "Seems a couple hundred bats in the bat house decided they didn't want to live there anymore."

Nine

Gentry walked up to Forty-second Street and headed east to Grand Central. This time his mind was not on the sunshine.

According to Captain Sheehy, Captain DiFate said that the bats at the Central Park Zoo had gone wild shortly after sunrise. They were trying to escape through the two grated air ducts in the bat house. So far they hadn't succeeded, though DiFate said that many of the bats were bloody from the effort and still wouldn't give up. He added that the police deployment had nothing to do with the bats per se. It had to do with zoo and park authorities being concerned that nearly one hundred squealing bats might upset the other animals. They didn't want people trying to get in to see the "wild" lions and trumpeting elephants.

Captain Sheehy added that he wasn't worried about the bats in Central Park or Westchester or anywhere else. If they got loose in the city and the Health Department couldn't handle them, NYPD sharp-shooters would. "Skeet," he called them with a chuckle.

Gentry wasn't so sure about that. Any animal that could terrify a cockroach had his cautious respect. He hoped that Nancy Joyce had an explanation for what was going on.

Gentry entered the busy terminal and headed toward the grand staircase on the western side of the concourse. Just like when he walked home at night, he loved the crowds. The life. The energy. He needed to get that back. As he walked, he looked up at the newly restored constellations on the hundred-foot-high ceiling. It was green and bright, and it helped take his mind off bats. He thought back to how his father used to tell him about the constellations. Only in New York would builders have been audacious enough to block out God's heaven and put up one of their own. He admired that.

Metro North ran most of the trains coming in and out of the city from upstate New York and New England. They had their own police force, which was chartered by the city and worked closely with the NYPD. They were based in the most elegant headquarters in New York: the former Vanderbilt apartments. The rooms, made of marble and stone, had been erected in 1912 for the convenience of the family that ran what was then the New York Central Railroad.

Gentry paid a call on Captain Ari Alberto Moreaux. When Moreaux was the operations coordinator for Midtown South, he worked closely with Gentry at SNEU. Moreaux got burned out just nine months before Gentry had his own problem up in Connecticut. The long hours and slime stains they all had to deal with were bad enough. But for Moreaux, the capper came when a major heroin dealer got stopped on lower Broadway for a routine traffic violation. The officer found a joint in the car ashtray. One of Moreaux's undercover boys was in the car with the dealer and saw two years of work going down the toilet for a simple pot bust. Instead of letting the cop arrest the dealer, the undercover guy flashed his badge to the traffic cop, blew the scumbag dealer away, and put a "throwaway" in the hand of the corpse—a gun he kept for just that purpose. The traffic cop covered for him and said the dealer reached for the gun to discourage the arrest. Moreaux couldn't take it anymore. Now, as the captain freely admitted, he was happy to be dealing with the menace of drunken commuters, panhandlers, and cigarette smokers who lit up while they were still inside the station.

It was good to see Moreaux. He still had his son Jonathan's

framed second-grade history report on the wall, a one-pager on the origin of the word *cop.* Gentry hadn't known until he read that when the New York state legislature gave the city its first police force in 1845, the officers had refused to wear uniforms. As a compromise, they agreed to wear copper badges to identify themselves as peace officers—hence the name.

Jonathan Moreaux was now a "copper" cadet himself.

Gentry explained to the captain that he wanted to take Dr. Joyce out to the tracks where the guano had been found. Moreaux had no objection and asked the desk sergeant to radio Officer Stiebris. The rookie was told to meet Detective Gentry and Dr. Joyce at the main information booth in half an hour.

Gentry thanked Moreaux and they agreed to have dinner the following week. Moreaux said he'd picked the spot, someplace he could get a burger instead of the stomach-burning shit Gentry ate. Then the detective went downstairs to wait beside the small kiosk.

As Gentry stood there, he watched the midmorning crowd. The people were mostly commuters hurrying from the tracks on the north side of the station to subways and exits on the south, west, and east. Very few of them bothered to look up at the constellations.

That's what the world is all about, Gentry thought. Rushing. Rushing to work, rushing from work, rushing to entertainment and shopping and eating. It was ironic. Gentry had the siren at his disposal, but he rarely rushed anywhere. His life on the force had been about patience and waiting. Cooling off arguments when he was on the beat. Nurturing the trust of gang members when he was undercover. Taking part in stakeouts. When he was off duty all he wanted to do was relax. With a lady if possible, but alone was fine too.

Gentry saw Nancy Joyce coming toward him from the east side of the terminal. That was where the Number 5 subway train would have dropped her. She was moving briskly against the human wave, ducking and weaving gracefully. The scientist was slightly shorter than he'd expected, about five-foot-five. She was carrying a bright orange shoulder bag and was still dressed in the clothes she'd been wearing on television the night before.

Gentry stepped away from the kiosk to greet her. She had a firm handshake. She made and held eye contact. She really did have beautiful eyes.

"Thanks for coming," Gentry said.

"Thanks for calling."

"I don't know if you heard, but there's been some kind of bat uprising at the Central Park Zoo," Gentry said.

"I know. That moron Berkowitz called as I was leaving. I sent my assistant Marc to have a look."

"How bad is it over there?"

"It must be pretty bad if Berkowitz called," Joyce said. "He's not really a bat guy, he's a rodent guy. Handles everything from chipmunks to chinchillas. He waited five hours before calling—doesn't like anyone messing with his fiefdom, especially if it's a woman." Joyce shook her head. "The joke is, if Berkowitz's rich wife hadn't given so much money to that place through all her not-for-profit charities, he'd probably be writing flash cards instead of helping to run a zoo."

"You know, I never realized that about—"

"Berkowitz?" Joyce said. "Oh, yeah. The man's great at self-promotion. He brings his cuddly little animals to schools and goes on TV, but he doesn't know half as much as he should for that job."

"No," Gentry said. "I never realized that chinchillas are rodents."

Joyce looked at him. Then she looked down, embarrassed. "Yeah. They are." She suddenly seemed to have the weight of all those constellations on her back.

"Y'know, when I was a kid I used to love learning things like that," Gentry said.

"Me too. Look, I'm sorry."

"About?"

"I shouldn't have gone off like that. Patronage in science is a major sore spot with me."

"Patronage bothers me, too," he said. "The worst thing about it is when we have to do their jobs plus ours because they're incompetent."

She looked back at him. There was a hint of a smile in her eyes. "Right. I'm also very tired, which isn't helping my mood any."

"Understood."

Joyce seemed a little peppier now. "You want to get going?"

"We're waiting for Officer Stiebris. He knows the way. He'll be here in a couple of minutes."

Joyce nodded. She leaned heavily against the information booth.

"You want some coffee?" Gentry asked. "Maybe a bottle of water? We've got a long hot walk ahead."

She shook her head. "Thanks, though."

"So, the last day's been pretty tough?" Gentry asked.

"Yeah."

"What *do* you think is going on?"

"I wish I knew. The only universal explanation I can think of is that we're seeing some kind of bat dementia, though there's no precedent for it and I have absolutely no idea what could be causing it. The initial lab results from the two patients and the deer carcass came in just as I was leaving. Unfortunately, they don't tell us very much."

"What do they tell you?"

"In terms of the two people, nothing more than we already knew. In terms of the deer, only that there's definitely bat saliva in the blood. But it's possible the vespers simply lit there—"

"I'm sorry. The who?"

"The vespers. Vespertilionids," Joyce said. "That's the breed of bat we're dealing with."

"Oh."

"It's possible they landed on the deer after it was already dead," Joyce continued. "But vespers very rarely eat meat, and they definitely aren't scavengers."

"Unless they were suffering from dementia, as you said."

"Yes. Unfortunately, though we haven't exhausted all the tests, we didn't find any kind of microbe in the saliva that might cause the bats to act this way. In fact, except for rabies there really *isn't* a condition we know of that would do this. And rabies wouldn't cause the kind of—I'll call it cooperation, for lack of a better word, that the witnesses reported."

"So you really haven't got much to go on, have you?"

"No. Though there was something else—what look like several large teeth marks in the deer carcass. They're about two to three inches long. They look like a mountain lion could have made them, but there were no footprints anywhere. Dr. Nadler made a mold from a gnaw mark in one of the shoulder bones. When Marc is finished at the Central Park Zoo, he's going to run the mold over to Dr. Lowery at the Museum of Natural History. Maybe he can identify it."

"I didn't realize big cats live in the region."

"They do. The problem is they wouldn't be strong enough to haul a deer up a tree."

"Well, I don't know anything about bats or cats, but I can't help thinking this deer thing is a prank. Some kind of antienvironmentalist statement."

Joyce shook her head. "The wildlife commissioner up there said he knows those groups. They print leaflets and bitch on-line. Besides, nobody's taken credit for killing the deer. But if and when they do, I want to know how they got the damn thing up there." She looked at Gentry again. "Do you mind if I ask why you're so concerned about this?"

"Like I told you on the phone, I had a late-night run-in with bats myself. They chased a couple hundred cockroaches from my neighbor's wall."

"But you didn't actually see any bats."

"That's right. When I took a look behind the switchplate they were coming from, I found bat guano."

"How much?"

"I probably could've filled seven or eight sandwich bags."

"Actually, Detective, that's pretty consistent—"

"Robert," he interrupted.

"Excuse me?"

"You call me Robert and I'll call you Nancy."

"All right," she said. "Anyway, that much guano is consistent with transient bat habitats in the city's tunnels and subways. Manhattan has always been a stopping-off point for bats migrating from Canada and New England to the warmer states in the South."

"It's funny," Gentry said. "I never thought of any animals migrating except for birds."

"Bats do, and for exactly the same reason as birds. Insects are extremely scarce during the winter. Bats usually start the trip in late summer and get where they're going by midfall. Whenever bats are en route, they'll usually duck into a shelter to stay cool, eat or drink, stay out of the wind, and hide from predators like cats, hawks, snakes, and owls. That could be the case here."

"As far as I know, we've never had a bat problem or even a bat sighting in my building before."

"Did you ever have a cockroach problem?"

"Not much of one. And I'm right on the Hudson."

"I'm not a bug expert, but they could have been chased into your building from somewhere else. A small colony of bats in a subway tunnel might have found a pocket of them. Or they could have been chased in by an upswing in predation near the river."

Arvids Stiebris arrived as Joyce was speaking. The tall, powerfully built railroad officer clasped Gentry's hand tightly. Arvids had been a rookie pitcher on the Metro North softball team during the season that just ended. Gentry had played left field from Midtown South and whiffed during three at bats in the last, crucial playoff game. The kid had an unhittable sinker. Robert Gentry was an okay loser and he admired talent, but the "Heroes from Westchester" profile Kathy Leung had done on Arvids really rankled him—"Hartsdale's gift to Grand Central . . . and the pitcher's mound."

Gentry introduced the officer to Dr. Joyce. Arvids fixed his dark eyes on her.

"I saw you on TV last night with Kathy. That was great spin you put on the bats. Makes you almost want one as a pet."

"That wasn't spin, it was the truth," Joyce said. "If bat diets were compatible with captivity, they'd make wonderful pets."

"Maybe," Arvids said. He started toward the ramp that led downstairs. "But I wouldn't want one unless it was housebroken. That is one potent stench they produce."

"It's no worse than that of any other animal," she replied, "including humans. You're just not used to it."

"I'll take your word for that," Arvids said.

Gentry thought Joyce was being a touch defensive. But then, he didn't like it when anyone outside of the department criticized cops. Stereotypes could be frustrating to people who knew better.

"Anyhow," Arvids went on, "I checked with station maintenance. No one's been back in the tunnel to clean up the mound. Because this whole thing involved a medical situation, the health inspector has to do an on-site report. You know, tell everyone there's no danger before they can clean up the guano. That's supposed to happen later this afternoon."

"Not that I'm complaining but why are they waiting so long?" Gentry asked.

"They just did a major rat sweep in the north end of Central Park," Arvids said. "Quiet operation, ethyl chloride—every effective. But a lot of people are still in the field cleaning up the bodies."

Arvids led Gentry and Joyce to the lowest platform on the east side of the subway terminal. The clerk buzzed them through the service entrance. As they entered and made their way across the crowded ramp, Gentry got the same feeling he'd had earlier—that there was something "off" down here. Subdued. He couldn't explain why he felt that way.

They walked to the end of the platform. When they reached the far side, Arvids hopped down. Joyce jumped down after him. Gentry sat on the concrete and slid off.

A moment later they were in another world.

Ten

Grand Central Station is the largest train terminal in the world. It covers nearly fifty acres in the heart of Manhattan and is laced with tunnels stacked seven levels deep in places. The lowest of these tunnels lies more than two hundred and fifty feet underground.

Dozens of the tunnels are used for either commuter or subway trains. Most of those are on the top two levels. On the other five levels are dozens more tunnels, many of which were begun but never finished. They were abandoned, sealed off, and forgotten when funds ran out, when walls or ceilings or floors leaked, or when needs or technologies changed. At least half of these dark, damp labyrinths are unmapped. Over the years, homeless people opened many of the tunnels and began living there.

Joyce knew a little of this history from her studies of urban bats and their habitats. But she had never imagined she'd be down here. Like the night, it was fascinating.

Arvids slid a flashlight from a loop in his belt and shined it ahead. They could see about ten feet down the tracks.

"Stay behind me, single file," he said.

They walked nearly toe-to-heel, with Joyce in the middle. She looked back. Leaving the station was like pushing off in a rowboat. The land sunk away quickly, and the sense of being in a new and dangerous element, on an adventure, quickly took hold. Apart from Arvids's flashlight and the dull, yellowish bulbs stuck in the ceiling every ten feet or so, there was no illumination down here. No hint of daylight. No fresh air.

"What do we do if a train comes along?" Joyce asked.

Before Arvids could answer, Joyce felt the ground begin to quake. It wasn't like the gentle rumble a rider felt on the platform. It rattled up her ankles, rolled to her waist, and crawled down her arms. She felt it in her fingertips. A moment later the iron columns and tracks began to brighten and glow to the left. Then everything was washed out in a blast of white light from the headlight of the train. The sound was painfully loud.

Arvids had motioned for them to stand to the right, closer to the wall. They stopped walking and covered their ears as the train lumbered past. It squealed loudly as it stopped at the station. Joyce's body was still trembling, fine and fuzzy like a tuning fork.

Arvids shouted back through the cottony silence, "What we do is just step aside!"

"I see," she said.

When the train left the station, the platform was empty and the sense of isolation was even more pronounced. The white-tile wall continued for another few yards. When it ended there was only darkness to the right, to the left, and beyond the glare of the flashlight. Walking here was a little like descending a staircase without looking down.

Gentry leaned close to her ear. "In case you were wondering, you're nowhere near the third rail."

"That did cross my mind," Joyce admitted. "Where is it?"

"Over to the left, underneath the current bar. See it?"

She looked. She craned. She squinted.

"That raised, L-shaped piece outside the running rail," Gentry said, leaning close and pointing.

"Got it," she said. "Have you spent a lot of time down here?"

"As a matter of fact, I have," Gentry said. "When I was on the narcotics squad."

"You were a narc?" Arvids said. "I didn't know that."

"Why did that bring you down into the tunnels?" Joyce asked.

"Dealers from Connecticut used to toss stuff from the trains, just in case cops were waiting for them in the station," Gentry said. "They had goons down here to pick the stuff up."

"Man," Arvids said. "I'm impressed. You were a narc. I don't see much action here and I've been thinking about a change. Narcking, Violent Predator Task Force, Worst-of-the-Worst Task Force—those are the kinds of thing you do to *really* test yourself. To do some good, too, but also to see if you've got the stuff. You know what I mean."

"I do. That's one of the reasons I did it."

"It's like when my dad was in the army and he said he wanted to get some combat in," Arvids went on, "even though he didn't really. He just wanted to see how he'd do. He ended up in Vietnam, and it turned out he had more steel in him than he thought."

A second train charged by, its light harsh in the deepening darkness. The train was farther from the station and was moving faster than the first train. This time Joyce didn't hum when it passed. She rattled.

When the train had receded, Joyce tapped Arvids on the shoulder and stopped. "Would you shine your light up for a second?"

"Sure thing." Arvids turned his flashlight toward the top of the tunnel.

The ceiling was about twelve feet above them. There were concrete ledges, iron girders, and discoloration from water seepage. There was a lightly metallic odor coming from the damp metal. Beneath it, in the distance, Joyce could already smell the distinctive odor of the guano.

"What are you looking for?" Gentry asked.

"Cockroaches," she said. "If bats moved in somewhere ahead, the roaches would have moved out. Like at your apartment."

Arvids shined the flashlight slowly along the ceiling. "I don't see any, but they travel pretty fast. And they could have gone in about a million different directions. This is a very long tunnel."

"How long?"

"This particular trunk heads up to the middle of Central Park, which is about two and a half miles north. Then it doubles back and heads southwest to Penn Station."

"I didn't realize the two stations were connected," Joyce said.

"*Everything* is connected through these tunnels," Arvids said. "All the train lines—commuter, subway, everything."

Joyce felt a cool draft from the left and asked Arvids to shine the light over. About six feet away was a concrete wall with a hole cut in the center. The opening was about two yards up from the ground, a yard across, and nearly a yard tall at its highest point. The edges of the hole were jagged, as though it had been punched out with a hammer.

"What's that?" Joyce asked.

"It's probably the work of the tunnel people," he said.

"The who?"

"The homeless people who live underneath the train tunnels. We had most of them cleared out, but they keep coming back. The tunnel people live on this level, and the mole people are on the lower levels. We think there are about five hundred homeless living down here altogether, but we're not sure."

"You're kidding," Joyce said. "There are that many homeless people here?"

Arvids nodded. "They've got communities with a mayor, teachers—it's really very organized."

"Does anyone ever go to them?" Joyce asked. "Help them?"

"We have an outreach program here at the station," Arvids replied. "But they don't like intruders. Some of them come up for food and supplies, but most of them never leave the tunnels."

"And why would they make a hole like this?"

"Could be a short cut. Or sometimes they do it for ventilation, especially during the summer."

"Amazing." Joyce asked Arvids to keep the flashlight on the jagged hole. Stepping high and long over the third rail, she went over and examined it. There was no guano and no smell of guano coming from inside. She returned to the group. Gentry didn't look happy.

"I was careful," she said.

Gentry made a face. "Nothing there?"

"Nothing. Let's go."

They continued walking between the tracks. A third train passed. This time Joyce felt as if it was the intruder, not her.

It was not at all surprising to the scientist that the deeper they went into the tunnel, the more excited and contented she became. The act of creeping around had always made Nancy Joyce feel free. It probably came from growing up with a father and an older brother who liked war movies and Westerns. Some of Joyce's earliest memories were of sitting on the floor to the side of a big TV. She would play with Colorforms or her Etch-a-Sketch and look up whenever the TV grew quiet. She didn't like the shooting or talking parts, but she always watched when cowboys or soldiers crawled through the mud, crept under barbed wire, or moved stealthily around corners or mountainsides. Soon Joyce began creeping around by herself, daring her brother, Peter, to catch her, and then squeezing behind the sofa or under the piano bench where he couldn't fit. But Peter's arms *could* fit, and he usually dragged his sister out and punished her with a tickle attack to the sides and underarms. When Joyce was seven she began poking through the thick, nighttime woods on her own. There was something bold about taking each new step. Something a little claustrophobic about the dark. She realized much later that that was one of the reasons night appealed to her. Everything seemed so close, so intimate. Even the danger.

But . . .

There was always a but. While Joyce felt at home with the unknown, she hated not knowing things. And the past fifteen or so hours had severely tested her patience. When she was a graduate student at New York University, doing fieldwork with Professor Lowery—who also became her first lover, deep in a bat cave in the Pyrenees—the older man worried about her low threshold for frustration. He advised his pupil to look at puzzles with a relaxed mind, to view them as an opportunity to add something to the annals of science. Unfortunately, Joyce just couldn't think like that.

"You doing okay?" Gentry asked.

His voice startled her. For a moment, Joyce felt as if she'd been alone. "I'm fine. Why?"

"Just making sure. A lot of things can get to you down here. Sore feet. Thirst. Nerves."

"No, I'm good."

Gentry put his hands on her shoulders and moved around her. He sidled up to Arvids. "How well does your radio work down here?"

"Depends on how far down you go or how many walls get between you and the operator. So far I've never had a problem. Why?"

"Just curious. We've had trouble with our radios with all the new construction in midtown. The layers of electronics going into offices and residential buildings are acting like walls. Say," Gentry turned to Joyce, "you said on TV that bats aren't bothered by microwaves."

"That's right."

"What about electronic noise? Could a city full of it draw them to a place or disorient them?"

"Draw them, no. Most bats ignore any sound beyond an average radius of fifty yards. And within that radius they pay attention only to sounds made by fellow bats or potential prey or predators."

"Do they listen the same way humans do," Gentry asked, "or do they use those echos?"

"Mechanically, bat hearing is the same as human hearing, albeit much more sensitive. When they echolocate, they ignore other sounds, pretty much the way people do when they're talking in a subway or at a bar. The rest of the time bats listen the way other animals do."

Arvids asked, "If there are still any bats down here, will they hear us coming?"

"They can hear an insect walking on sand six feet away."

"I guess that would make us sound like a brass band."

"Fife and drum corps would be more accurate," Joyce said. "If there are bats within a mile of here, they heard our breathing and heartbeats about the time we entered the tunnel. To answer your other question, Detec—Robert," Joyce went on, "electronics can disorient bats. Certain kinds of tiger moth emit high-frequency clicks that turn the normal flow of echo information into gibberish. We've been able to duplicate those signals in a lab."

"Stealth moths," Arvids said. "Nature is amazing."

"Totally," Joyce agreed. "Electronics can also confuse bats, but only if they happen to replicate a known sound—for example, a baby bat calling to its mother or a female to a male. And once the bat got a look or whiff of the computer or fax machine or whatever it happened to be, and saw that it wasn't a fellow bat or prey, it would break off at once."

"Pretty clever creatures."

"They're one of a kind," she said proudly. "Did you ever hear of Operation X-Ray?"

Gentry said he hadn't.

"During the Second World War, the Allies came up with a plan to drop thousands of bats from high-altitude bombers over Japanese cities. Each bat was going to be equipped with a large wax capsule strapped to its back. As the bats flew down, their body temperature would slowly melt the wax. Inside the capsule was a highly flammable liquid that would ignite when exposed to air. The bats were trained to fly toward certain sounds—air raid sirens, railroad whistles, maritime bells. They were also conditioned to fly toward searchlights. The idea was that they'd roost in strategic buildings in Japanese cities, self-immolate, and burn the buildings to the ground."

"You're kidding."

"No. And there was no way to stop the bats. At night, even the best sharpshooters would have had an impossible time trying to gun them down. And even then there was always the risk that a bullet would penetrate the wax, set the bat on fire, and accomplish the mission."

Gentry said, "I can just imagine what you think of the plan."

"Why? Because bats were dying?"

"Well, yes."

Joyce shook her head. "I'm not an animal rights activist. I hate cats, I enjoy hunting and eating deer and boar, and I'm all for using mice as medical test subjects. I lost a father to brain cancer and a grandfather to pancreatic cancer. I'd rather lose mice."

"Hear, hear," Arvids said.

"Besides, the bats were bred especially for Operation X-Ray. I think the plan was inspired. By targeting specific buildings the military could save human lives on the ground and in the air."

"So what happened?" Gentry asked.

"During test runs in the desert, several dozen bats proved to be smarter than the scientists who'd conditioned them. They flew off and returned to where they were trained—bats have an incredible homing sense—and burned down the barracks."

"Stealth moths and commando bats," Arvids said. "Man, even zoologists see more action than I do."

It took nearly half an hour of moving slowly through the darkness before they came to where the maintenance worker had fainted. The mound of guano was lying beneath a girder, between two sets of tracks. Joyce took the flashlight from Arvids. She circled the mound slowly. Arvids put his hand in front of his mouth. Gentry winced.

"I've never seen anything like this," Joyce said.

"Jesus," Gentry said. "The size alone probably put the maintenance man out, once he realized what it was."

"The size is incredible, but so is the singular consistency," Joyce said. "This is not a typical bat mound. This is like something you'd find in the elephant cage at the zoo."

"That'd be a new one for the Transit Authority," Arvids said from behind his splayed fingers. "An elephant infestation."

"No, this was definitely left here by bats." Joyce moved in closer. "The smell alone tells you that. The point is, when bats cluster in a small area like this, the guano falls in different ways, at different times. You can usually see the separate segments, different color and texture."

"Like horse apples," Gentry said.

"Exactly."

"Excuse me, but this is more than I wanted to know," Arvids said. He turned away.

Joyce shined the flashlight almost directly overhead. There were two horizontal concrete columns built perpendicular to the track. A naked metal girder, rusted from seeping water, was stuck between them. There were traces of guano from one side of the girder to the other. "What I don't understand is why the bats would have come here, done this, and then left."

"Like you said before," Gentry pointed out, "this could be a migration rest area."

"No. In that case the guano would have been spread across the tunnel, not centralized here."

"Then how many bats do you think did this?" Gentry asked.

"I don't know that either." The scientist turned the flashlight back on the mound and walked around the base. "There's a lot of spread at the bottom of the pile. See that?" She shined the flashlight on a wide, murky pool of liquid surrounding the mound.

"New York's an extremely leaky island. River water and rain are constantly seeping in and dissolving soft biodegradable matter. Groundwater like that along with vibration from passing trains caused the waste to settle. And the weight of the mound caused the fluid content to sink and separate, compacting the mass above. So it's impossible to say how many animals contributed to this or when it was started. It could have been a hundred bats over a few days or several thousand bats over a few hours."

"Several *thousand* bats?" Gentry asked. "There could really be that many bats down here?"

"If this tunnel goes on for as long as Arvids says it does, a thousand bats could easily have gotten in. Even though cockroaches scatter when attacked, there would be enough insect life down here to sustain them. Silverfish, bugs of that type. Possibly bats from the park moved in here, not migratory ones."

"Why?" Gentry asked. "It's still warm."

"All of the human activity during that rat sweep might have scared them away," Joyce suggested. "The question is, why would bats have come to this one spot?"

"Would it help if you had samples of guano to study?" Gentry asked.

"No," Joyce said. "But I do want some pictures. I can scan them into a computer and run some simulations."

She tucked the flashlight under her arm and pulled a digital camera from her shoulder bag. She snapped photographs from several different heights and angles. Then she put the camera away and shined the light around. Across the tracks to the left was a tunnel.

"What's that?" she asked.

"It's a service tunnel," Arvids said.

"Meaning?"

"The train crews do repairs there, store equipment."

"Does it lead anywhere?"

"I don't think so," Arvids said. "Service tunnels are usually closed. They're like caves."

Joyce and Gentry both looked at Arvids.

Arvids grinned boyishly. "I knew it even as I said it. You want to go in there."

"Bats are at home in tunnels," Joyce explained, "but they really like caves."

Eleven

They swung around a rusty iron column, then ducked low under a concrete overhang. They approached the service tunnel in the pale glow of a single, dusty, sixty-watt lightbulb hanging over the track. They moved ahead slowly. Joyce had informed them that if the bats were there, each next step could bring them into what the animals considered "their territory." The instant a bat moved toward them, they would retreat.

No bats appeared.

Arvids found the light switch and turned it on.

Joyce stopped nearly halfway into the tunnel and looked around. The far end of the long room was dark. There was a crane to the right, ladders, lockers, and toolboxes to the left. There were also what looked like pneumatic platforms in the ground just outside the tracks. From the oil stains, it looked like railroad cars were probably put on these and raised. She didn't see guano anywhere. She looked up. The ceiling was about twenty feet high and made of smooth concrete. She was surprised and disappointed.

"Heavy-duty tools, grease stains, and dusty coffee cups," Arvids said. "No bats."

Joyce walked ahead while Gentry looked inside the lockers and

Arvids checked behind them. Water was dripping down the walls in thin streams. Bats would probably try to follow that to a source; she wondered if there might be another way to get to it.

"Maybe the bats stayed the night in the tunnel outside and then left," Gentry suggested.

"Like I said before," Joyce replied. "Not with all that train traffic moving through. No, this is their kind of resting place. Arvids?"

"Ma'am?"

"Are you absolutely sure this is a dead end? No vents, no stairs leading to other levels?"

"I'm positive. There probably are other levels, but they aren't accessible from this tunnel."

"When was the last time anyone was in here?"

"I don't know," Arvids said. "I could call the stationmaster—"

"Approximately. Hours? Days?"

He looked down at the concrete floor. "The oil stains look pretty dry. I'd say it's probably been about two or three weeks."

"No human habitation," she said. "That would be a definite plus as far as the bats were concerned. So where are they?"

While Arvids and Gentry made their way toward the back of the tunnel, Joyce went to the wall on the left. She walked along, peeking behind the toolboxes and ladders. Then she went to the wall on the right. The crane sat on a platform that resembled the undercarriage of a train car. It rested on a short spur of track connected to the rails in the center of the room.

She squeezed behind the crane. She couldn't squat there, but she sniffed. There was a smell like ammonia. She smiled. "Bingo!"

"What've you got?" Gentry asked as he and Arvids hurried over.

"A bat cave," she replied.

The men squeezed in behind the crane, and Arvids pointed the flashlight down. There was an oval hole just above the base of the concrete wall. It resembled the hole in the main tunnel except that it was close to the ground and was only about two feet tall by two feet wide.

"It's another entrance for the tunnel people," Arvids said.

"Yes," Joyce said, "but smell."

"More guano," Gentry said.

Joyce reached up. "Arvids, can I have the flashlight?"

Arvids went to hand it to her. Gentry stopped him.

"What are you planning to do?" Gentry asked.

"Go inside."

"That's what I thought. I can't let you do that."

"What are you talking about? I have to see if the bats are still here. If they are, we'll have to come back with bat suits, get specimens. See if there's something wrong with them."

"I'll go in," Gentry said. "You're going back to the station."

"No way!"

"Did you take a close look at the wall?" He pointed to the corner.

She looked back down. "I don't see anything."

"The lower left corner. See that jagged piece like an *M?*"

Arvids turned his flashlight in that direction. Joyce looked closer. There was blood on the sharp edges.

"That could be from anything," Joyce said. "A homeless person could have cut himself when he went in. Or it could be blood from a wounded rat or bat. Anything."

"You're right. But until we know for sure, I want you out of here."

"Robert, that's crazy! This is a scientific puzzle. Let me do my job!"

"You did the job you came out here for," Gentry replied. "You saw the guano on the tracks. You took pictures. That's enough."

"No! My job isn't finished until we've *found* the bats. Can you feel the air coming from behind the wall?"

"Yes."

"It's warm and damp. This is where the bats have gone. I *have* to go in and look around."

"Maybe later," Gentry said. "After I've checked it out."

"This is insane! I've picked my way through quicksand fields, I've explored caves with just matches—"

"That was the wild. This is New York."

"Oh, please!"

"Listen to me," Gentry said. "Those tunnel people Arvids was talking about can be extremely territorial. I used to bump into them when I was down here. There might also be structural deficiencies behind the wall that we don't know about."

"The detective is right about those things," Arvids said.

"I'll take my chances," Joyce replied.

"I'm sorry," Gentry said, "but that's not an option."

"I don't believe this—"

"It's nothing personal," Gentry said.

"No, it's insulting!"

Gentry excused himself. He went over to one of the lockers and got a flashlight. He tested it, then walked back to Arvids. "Let me have the radio."

Arvids handed it to Gentry.

Joyce's lips were pressed tightly together. "And what exactly are you going to do inside?"

"Look for bats."

"Look for bats. And how are you going to read what you see? Genera, guano color, maternity roosts—"

"I'll make very careful observations and report back. That's *my* job."

"It won't be enough," she said. "You won't be able to tell an invasive species from an indigenous one, a sick bat from a healthy one. You need someone who knows what to look for."

"You can come back later—"

"If you do find bats and they're anything like the Westchester bats, there may not be a later."

"In that case, your being there won't help."

"I disagree. I've had to improvise in the field."

"Me too. Look, I understand and I'm sorry." Gentry glanced at Arvids and cocked his head toward the main tunnel.

The young officer backed away from the crane. "Come on, Dr. Joyce."

Joyce balled her fists. "Gentry, don't!"

He said nothing.

"This is moronic!" Joyce turned away from Gentry. She faced the main tunnel then swung back around to Gentry. "Don't do this. I hate it. God, I hate it."

"I'm sorry," Gentry said, "but I've been down this road before—"

"So have I!"

"—and no one except me is taking a chance."

"This is my field!"

"I don't care. You're not going with me. You're not even staying here."

Arvids moved gingerly toward the scientist. "Come on, Doctor."

"You're all the fucking same," she said angrily. "Every damn one of you!"

Outside, another subway train passed. Then, as Arvids led a furious Dr. Joyce back down the tunnel, Gentry walked toward the crane.

Twelve

Gentry didn't like bullying good people, and pushing a young woman around left an iron-heavy weight on his conscience. He felt like he'd done that with Priscilla the entire time they were married—forced her to do what he wanted, which was not to have kids and not to have a life together because he couldn't think of anything except bringing Akira Mizuno down. He hadn't felt like this in a while, and he didn't like it.

Maybe you should have blamed it on the city, he thought. You can't let civilians into a suspected crime scene because of insurance regulations. If anything happened, she or her estate could have sued the city. It was true; it was on the books. And it would have made New York the villain, not him. Except that wasn't the reason he'd done it.

With effort he squeezed behind the crane, where the slender woman had fit so comfortably. At the opening, he shimmied down, sliding his backside along the train carriage and feeding his legs through. It was not a place for the claustrophobic. When his feet finally reached the ground he wriggled into the dark. If the bats or some territorial tunnel people were in there waiting for him, he was going to be in serious, serious trouble. He continued worming through, until he was inside and was able to shine the flashlight around.

The room he was in was slightly larger than a garage. The walls were made of brick and the floor was a heavy iron grille. A metal staircase, like a fire escape, disappeared into the floor on the opposite side. There were open ducts and bundles of wires overhead. He didn't see any bats, but the smell of guano was definitely stronger in there. Drops of blood led straight ahead. He followed them across the room.

He wondered what this place had been built for. Once a floor was put down, it could have been a storage room or an office for maintenance personnel. He looked up. Or it might have been designed as a power room. It was large enough to hold a large gas turbine, and the ducts could have vented fumes through the roof.

He headed slowly toward the steps, walking on the balls of his feet. What Joyce had said about the bats' hearing made him realize that walking softly was useless. But he did it anyway so that he could hear. He shined the light down through the grate. It looked as though the rooms went down several flights. That would make sense. Everything in the station was probably built in layers to maximize space. And if this was going to be a generator room, they might have wanted access from underneath.

The smell of guano was stronger the deeper he went into the room. The drops of blood were thicker as well. They reminded him of someone who got popped in the nose and was trying to hold it in. He was going to have to go down the stairs. Before he did, he tried to call Ari Moreaux, just to let him know where he was. All he got was static. Out of communication, without a roadmap, and with blood on the floor—he knew it didn't make sense to go ahead. But Gentry didn't intend to go back and tell Joyce he didn't check the place out.

He had no idea how far down the stairs went. He turned the light on the steps. He could see the bottom twenty steps below—and more small drops of blood leading down.

That could be from tunnel people fighting over food or clothes, he tried to persuade himself, without success. His sixth sense was telling him whatever left the mound in the tunnel left the blood here as well.

He held tight to the damp, rusty railing as he descended. He toe-touched each step tentatively before putting his full weight down. The stairs groaned and listed slightly to the left, toward the inside of the room, as though the entire structure were coming away from the wall. Maybe it was. It probably hadn't been safety-checked in half a century.

The blood continued in a thickening line down the steps. As he neared the second-level landing he stopped. There was a rank, metallic smell coming from the room—not guano, something else. He brought the flashlight around. His eyes, increasingly accustomed to the dark, saw the hint of shapes on the floor. They were too large to be bats, and they weren't moving. They were also just out of reach of his light. He continued down.

Upon reaching the landing, the toe of Gentry's shoe bumped against something on the grate. He shined the light down. And swore at what he saw.

Within days of joining the police force, Gentry had helped lift the bloated, partially decayed body of a young woman from the Hudson River. He had entered a former crack den where a kid had died and been left to rot for nearly a week. He'd seen pedestrians who had been run down by cars and one who had been crushed under a crane. There were mugging victims who had been stabbed in the chest or side or back, and he'd once come to the assistance of an officer who'd been shot through the throat. All of those events were memorable as tragedy, and none of them had prepared him for what was in the room.

The grate was carpeted with blood and bodies. There were fourteen corpses in all, two of them very young children. All of them were fully clothed, a few were in sleeping bags, and some were lying face-down. A couple of bodies were sprawled across other bodies, as though they'd tried to get out or to help someone before falling themselves. Countless small but deep gashes scored the throats and faces that were turned toward him. The bloodied hands of some of the victims were splayed across their eyes, as though they'd been trying to protect them. There was guano on the bodies, and the grate below some of them was clogged with gummy patches of blood.

He knelt beside the body closest to him, the one his shoe had touched. She looking nothing like the other victims, not her dress or her condition. It was a young woman—or what was left of one. She was wearing sweat clothes and a bloody bicycle helmet. She was lying on her back, her left foot near the bottom of the steps. Her shoulders had been flayed, her throat had been crushed flat, and her chest had been torn open. The woman's rib cage was pulled out, not pushed in, and the bones had been flung to the left and right. The heart and lungs and most of the face were eaten almost entirely away.

He looked closely at the blood on the grate. It was still relatively moist. It couldn't have been more than three or four hours old. This had to have happened shortly before or after the maintenance worker found the guano. He wondered if the bats had been coming or going when they did this, whether they'd wanted to take this spot over or were just using it as a pit stop.

He could almost feel Nancy wagging a finger at him and saying, *"I told you so."* But he wasn't going to risk another partner. Especially one who wasn't even a member of the force.

Gentry rose. He felt light-headed and slightly nauseated. Grabbing the rail behind him, he shut his eyes and breathed deeply. The worst part of feeling dizzy down here was that taking a deep breath only made it worse. It filled his nose with air, guano, and the smell of fresh death. He put his teeth together and slowly sucked air through them, the way he'd been taught at the academy. No smells, no hyperventilating.

When Gentry felt better, he opened his eyes, breathed one more time through his teeth, then walked slowly down the steps toward the third level. There were no more victims there and no bats. Only drops of blood that had seeped through the grate.

Returning to the second level, Gentry went to each of the bodies in turn. He wanted to make certain that everyone was dead. Not just so that he could help anyone who might still be alive but also to make sure that one of the bodies wasn't a psycho pretending to be dead.

There was no one left alive.

As he stood and backed away from the corpses, Gentry noticed that there was artwork spray-painted on the far wall. Not-bad portraits and a panorama of bright blue sky. Tucked into corners of the room were garbage bags stuffed with clothes; pieces of carpet were spread under some of the sleeping bags. These people obviously lived in this part of the underground. They weren't intruding in a bat area like the people in Westchester.

The bats had come here wanting something. And then there was the woman in the bicycle helmet. He turned and looked down at her. He didn't want to search for an ID until the forensics team had a chance to take photographs. But he wondered where she fit into all of this.

As he looked away, he suddenly noticed a thick trail of blood. It began about a foot from the dead woman's left ear and thinned the closer it got to the landing. It continued up the steps in closely spaced dollops.

That's where the blood on the steps came from, he realized. But there was something odd.

Gentry crouched and looked at the blood more closely. The trail thinned as it went up, as though it had been dripping *up* the steps. Which meant the killer did this and then left by the stairway. It was also a slow, thick, steady drip, which meant it probably wasn't made by a creature in fast flight. He wondered if that ruled out a bat as the killer.

He turned the flashlight up.

"Oh, shit," he said.

There was blood on the underside of the grate above him. It was left in hash marks all along the grate. They looked like large chicken scratches.

Or bat scratches? he wondered.

What seemed curious, though, was that the bloody marks above were thicker than the ones below. And they followed the trail on the stairs exactly—

Like they dripped down.

And then it hit him, though it didn't make sense. Someone, something, could have left this way without using the steps.

The killer could have been hanging from the grate.

Thirteen

Gentry went back to the main tunnel to call for assistance. Captain Moreaux told the detective that they'd get a team down as soon as possible.

Gentry asked if he knew where Nancy Joyce was. Ari told him that she'd gone up to the Museum of Natural History.

That made sense. It was where her assistant had taken the mold from the deer bone.

Feeling guilty again, the detective went back to the walled-off sublevel. He sat on the landing and looked into the room. The only sound was the occasional distant thunder of a subway train.

It was difficult for him to process the horror of what had happened down here. The pain. The speed—these people were slaughtered where they lay. But it also underscored what he had always believed, despite the years his father had made him go to church. That human beings are animals. Not just the perpetrators but the victims. The reverential funerals and talk about immortal souls notwithstanding, people inevitably bear an unnerving resemblance to beef.

Captain Moreaux arrived nearly half an hour later, with Arvids and four other officers from Metro North. Two of the men got sick. In the heat, the smell was becoming intolerable. The officers were joined by three transit police—under whose jurisdiction the subways typically fell—and five officers from the police Emergency Service Unit. This mobile force of 350 elite officers is not attached to any one precinct. They're divided into ten regional squads and are called in to assist precinct police in extreme situations ranging from hostage standoffs to river rescues. Lieutenant Gary Holmes of ESU, City South, was at the end of his two-to-ten shift when he arrived with his team.

Gentry stayed for a while in what was already being referred to as "the butcher shop." Police were always quick to assign lighthearted nicknames to places of violence or danger. This was done not out of disrespect but, Gentry believed, to give them a way of denying the extreme horror until the situation could be dealt with and processed.

A Metro North police officer photographed the scene before ESU officers began placing the bodies in bags. While Gentry watched from the landing, two officers gently searched the outside woman's body for identification. They found a blood-soaked pouch beneath the body, attached to her leather belt. Her wallet was inside, along with a can of mace, a Swiss army knife, and an I Love New York key ring. No money had been taken. Arvids looked at her driver's license. The woman's name was Barbara Mathis and she lived on Riverside Drive. She was smiling in the photograph and attractively made up. She was twenty-eight years old. About the same age as Dr. Joyce.

Most of the bodies would be taken to the city medical examiner. Before they were removed, Gentry went over to Captain Moreaux.

"Ari, I need you to do me a favor. I want you to take Ms. Mathis's remains to the Scientific Research Division."

"Chris Henry?"

Gentry nodded.

Moreaux winced. "Ouch. The medical examiner will not be pleased if I do that."

"I know. But the medical examiner is going to have his hands full with the tunnel people. This lady came from someplace else."

"Obviously—"

"I need to know where and I need to know it soon. Chris'll do this fast and right."

Moreaux thought for a moment. "Okay. I'll go set it up."

Gentry thanked him. Moreaux looked pale as he took the wallet and went back to his office. The captain was the one who was going to have to call the young woman's family.

Before leaving, Gentry went over to Arvids and thanked him for his help. Then he started up the stairs.

"Detective," Arvids said.

Gentry stopped and looked back.

"I just thought you should know that Dr. Joyce was still pretty steamed when she left."

"I'm not surprised. And I don't blame her."

"What I'm saying is, maybe you should talk to her. Keep her in the loop. She wants to help. And this"—he gestured behind him—"is gonna take some explaining."

"Don't worry, Arvids. I'm going to involve her."

Arvids thanked him. Gentry wondered what the hell that was really about.

It was much easier getting out of the tunnel than it had been getting in. In order to accommodate the evacuation team, subway traffic had been rerouted along the tracks leading to the underground rooms. The detective was surprised at how cool and clean the air tasted and how bright the daylight seemed when he reentered the terminal. The concourse was much less crowded than it had been before.

Gentry stopped at a pay phone and called Chris Henry. He told him to expect Barbara Mathis's body within the hour and to front-burner the autopsy. He wanted to know as soon as possible whether the woman had been sexually assaulted and if there was anything on her that would place her whereabouts at the time of her death—dust particles in the lungs or eyes, muffin crumbs in her mouth, anything. Henry thanked him and said he'd be back to him as soon as possible.

As he left Grand Central, Gentry's mind was on the bats. As he walked west toward the station house, he wondered whether the attack and possible infestation were going to be a small problem or a big one; or whether it was a small problem that would become a big one when the media got their teeth into it. Nancy had been right about one thing. He wished he knew more about bats. Unlike human perps, he had no way of knowing what, if anything, they were going to do next. That was frustrating.

People were ambling along Forty-second Street, self-absorbed or talking to whomever they were with. Some were looking at Bryant Park or toward Times Square or the Chrysler Building. They were oblivious to the hidden worlds of the city, to the hidden dangers behind walls or beneath their feet. Which was how it should be. The job of the city's forty thousand police officers was to give them that luxury. He was proud of the way they handled that responsibility even when, as now, the problem was moving faster than he was.

After the silence of the underground world, the Midtown South station house seemed unusually raucous. Gentry got himself coffee, shut the door to his office, opened the window, and stared at the street for several minutes before starting through the folders on his desk.

The phone beeped. He snapped it up.

"This is Detective—"

"What's going on in the subway, Robert?"

"Kathy. How are you?"

"Not good."

"Sorry to hear that. . . ."

"Come on, Robert, talk to me. What's going down?"

"Nothing."

"Bullshit," she snapped. "Subway service has been disrupted, and I got a solid tip that there was a dismembered bicyclist down there and that you found her among a bunch of dead homeless people. True?"

"If the tip's solid, why are you asking me?"

"Because I need two sources, and that's all my other source would tell me."

"Which source was that?"

"Don't do that," Kathy warned.

And then it hit him. "*I saw you on TV last night with Kathy.*" Not Kathy Leung, just Kathy. Officer Arvids Stiebris, you dumb, beauty-struck, horse's ass of a rookie. He'd been sticking up for Nancy, too, the Romeo.

"I'll tell you what, Kathy," Gentry said. "I'll tell you what we found if you promise to do me a favor."

"That depends. What kind of favor?"

"I want you to spin it as an aberration, a one-time event. You go tabloid on me, give me a subway system under siege, and I'll make sure Arvids Stiebris is transferred to a place where he'll do you absolutely no good in the future."

"You've got a deal," Kathy said quickly.

"We found the body of a young woman in a bicycle helmet down there. We also found several dead homeless persons. We have no idea who the woman was," he lied to protect the privacy of the family, "but it looked like all of them were killed by animals."

"What kind of animals?"

"We're not sure."

"Dogs? Rats?"

"We're not sure."

"How old was the woman?"

"Our guess is late twenties."

"How'd she get down in the subway?"

"We don't know. Maybe she was some kind of outreach worker—we just don't know."

"How long will subway service be disrupted?"

"Until the bodies have been removed."

"Good," she said. "Now that you've told me not very much, how about the truth?"

"Sorry?"

"You're playing me. I want to know about the bat guano that was found on the tracks."

What did that dopey bastard Arvids do? Tell her everything?

"Kathy, there's nothing unusual about bat guano on subway tracks," he said. "Ask Al Doyle over at health."

"I will. In the meantime, what really went on down there?"

"I told you, we don't know."

"What do you *think?* Is there any connection between the dead people in the subway and bats? Could this be related to what happened in Westchester?"

"We don't know that either."

"What *do* you know?"

"Nothing other than what I've told you," Gentry said. "Maybe your source can tell you more. Why don't you go back to him?"

"I will. But frankly I'd rather talk to you. I'd rather that you help me—that we help each other."

"I know. Wasn't that the real reason you agreed to date me after the Mizuno bust?"

"Not entirely—"

"That didn't do a lot for my ego."

"Look," she said, "I went from Connecticut to Westchester, which isn't exactly a step up. I want off the fucking beat. If these incidents are connected, the story's still mine. That puts me in the big city with a big breaking headline. Help me and I can help you in the future. Promote the work you're doing."

"I don't need help, thanks."

"Maybe not now. But one day you will."

Gentry said nothing. The idea of cooperating with Kathy was not an option. When he worked undercover his policy was to trust only those people who were with him in the trenches. He paid for help or information in cash, not trust.

"Kathy, I'm sorry. No."

"Detective, I'm *going* to get this story."

"I know."

"I can call Dr. Joyce. She went on the consultant payroll last night."

"Fine."

Kathy hung up.

Gentry placed the receiver in the cradle. He looked out at the street. He smelled hot tar from a roof across the street.

Part of him actually wished he could have helped Kathy. He admired independence and tenacity, and she had a lot of both. And he still liked her. But until he knew exactly what had happened in the subway, he wasn't going to say anything.

Gentry put in a call to Moreaux to find out whether he'd discovered anything about where Barbara Mathis had been before they found her. Captain Moreaux said that a patrol car had found her abandoned bicycle and makeup kits on Riverside Drive near 120th Street at 5:22 A.M. There were traces of blood on the seat. They found the address inside one of the kits, went to her apartment building, and contacted her husband at work. He gave them her destination and they confirmed that she never arrived.

"What was the condition of the bicycle?" Gentry asked.

"Absolutely intact," Moreaux told him. "Spokes, paint job, everything. It was just lying near the curb. A little later in the day, with more traffic, it probably would've been ripped off."

Gentry thanked him. He got on the computer and asked the interlinked citywide Stat Unit for a list of any reported carjackings or parked-auto thefts the night before, anywhere from the Bronx down to the Upper West Side. Nothing had been reported. Often, joyriders will stop and grab a "snack" for the road. A lone woman on a bicycle would have been a perfect target, bumped and abducted. Sometimes the kidnappers will kill them and dump them when they're finished; that was what had happened to the dead woman Gentry had pulled from the Hudson River. But joyriders don't typically stop, crawl into a subway tunnel, gut a body, then leave it underground. Besides, a good nudge from a car usually leaves a mark on a bicycle.

Gentry went down the hall and refilled his coffee cup. Then he turned to accident reports that had been filed last night and early this morning by personnel in his unit. A horse-drawn carriage colliding with a bicycle deliveryman. A window box falling onto a woman walking her daughter to school. Nineteen others. He signed all but one and left them to be filed. Then—leaving his door open in case the phone rang—Gentry went over to the squad pit with the unsigned report, an investigation into an early morning fire at a Times Square movie theater. Apparently, a broken wire had shorted inside the wall of the projection booth. There was a little bit of smoke and no one was injured.

"Do you have any idea what caused the wire to break?" Gentry asked.

"Looks like a nail might've gone through it during renovation," the officer said. "The Fire Department's bureau of investigation has that one."

"Did you make it to the booth?"

"Yes."

"Was there any kind of unusual smell up there?"

"Just the burning insulation."

"What'd it smell like?"

The officer shrugged. "It smelled like burning rubber, Detective."

"Not ammonia?"

"No."

"Any cockroaches running around?"

"Not that I noticed."

"Thanks," Gentry said.

"Can I ask what this is about?" the officer said.

"Yeah. I was thinking some bats might've gotten into the wall and chewed through the wire. Their guano smells like burning leaves and they scare the hell out of bugs."

Gentry went back to his office and signed the report. He turned to the computer and input the keyword *bats*. He restricted the search to the past two days but asked it to include all of New York State. The database would provide any instances where local or state police had been called regarding bats.

There were four. In addition to the incident at the Central Park Zoo and the assault in Westchester, a motorist fixing a tire on Interstate 87 in Kingston, New York, had been bitten by "a group" of bats. He managed to get back in his car and drive himself to a hospital. That happened two nights ago. One night ago a woman leaving work at the South Hills Mall in Poughkeepsie was attacked in the parking lot. A security guard who was on patrol heard her cries and pulled her into his car. In both cases the bats left when the people did.

The phone beeped and Gentry jumped. He picked it up just as he realized that Kingston to Poughkeepsie to Westchester to New York was a straight line down the Hudson.

"Detective Gentry here—"

"Robert, it's Chris Henry."

"Hi. You get everything okay?"

"I did," Henry said. "I appreciate it, I think. It's a nasty one. What about the missing organs?"

"The Metro North police are going to keep looking. If they find them, you'll get them."

"Good. I also wanted to make sure you don't need a full rundown right away. This one's gonna take time."

"I figured."

"I will tell you what you probably already know: Whoever did this is some fucked-up piece of work. I took a quick look for signs of sexual attack. There's nothing. But there is one thing I noticed. Some very strange marks on a couple of the rib fragments."

"Strange?"

"Yeah. Deep gouges, like knife wounds. Only they're fatter and rounder than a knife blade. I've never seen anything like it."

"Any guesses what made them?"

"A lion," he snickered. "If it wasn't that, you got me."

Gentry felt his stomach burn a little. Nancy had said something about big cat teeth too.

The detective asked Henry to make exact measurements of the gouges and to beep him when he had the figures. Then he hung up.

A mountain lion, he thought. What the hell did that have to do with bats? Nothing. It made no sense. Gentry was about to call Nancy at the museum when the phone rang.

It was Nancy.

"You're back," she said. "I'm glad you're all right."

Her enthusiasm sounded a little on the light side. Or maybe that was just his own guilty interpretation.

"Thanks," he said. "I got in a few minutes ago. I was just about to call you."

"Did you find anything in the room that I should know about?"

"As a matter of fact, I did," he said. "The bats were definitely there—"

"Were they still there?"

"No. But there were fifteen victims. All dead."

She was silent.

"Most of them looked like they'd been sleeping. They were badly lacerated and covered with guano."

"How fresh did the guano look?"

"Exactly like the stuff in the tunnel," Gentry said. "I'm waiting for lab results. Although there was one thing—my forensics guy said that one of the victims looked like she'd been attacked by a lion."

"Was he serious?"

"It wasn't a scientific judgment, if that's what you mean. Just an off-the-cuff observation. Nancy, can we talk about this face to face?"

"Why?"

"Because I want to brief you and I want to apologize for what happened down in the tunnel. I'm also sorry about the way it happened. I told you, it wasn't personal. It was just—the way it had to be."

"Had to be?"

"Yeah. It's a long story."

Joyce was silent again. Then she asked, "Can you come up to the museum?"

"I can."

"All right. When the professor and I are finished, we'll talk. We're on the fifth floor, Professor Lowery's lab. There's a private elevator—ask one of the security people."

"Thanks. I'll be there in twenty minutes."

Gentry hung up, then sped through the eight messages on his voicemail. He forwarded a few to Detectives Anthony and Malcolm, saved the rest, then hurried downstairs. Anyone who needed to reach him could get his pager number off the voicemail message. He stopped in Captain Sheehy's office and informed him that he'd like to spend time on the Grand Central killings. The precinct commander was surprised by Gentry's interest in a hardcore case but okayed the request, as long as the detective didn't step on the toes of the homicide team that was also investigating the deaths. Sheehy said he didn't want an IDPS—an intradepartmental political shitstorm. Gentry said he didn't anticipate the two investigations overlapping. Then he bummed a ride from a patrol car heading uptown.

While he was in the car, his pager beeped. He looked down, expecting it to be Chris Henry. It wasn't.

It was Ari Moreaux.

Fourteen

The Christopher Street subway station serves west Greenwich Village and New York University. To the south, it allows riders access to the World Trade Center, the Statue of Liberty and Ellis Island ferry, and a transfer-ride into Brooklyn. To the north, it's a short hop to Times Square, Lincoln Center, Columbia University, and Grant's Tomb.

The morning rush hour over, the crowd on the downtown platform built slowly. It consisted of a handful of tourists who were double-checking maps in guidebooks and a pair of slouching students wearing baggy clothes and blank expressions. A guitarist performed near the turnstiles, his instrument case open at his feet for donations. A businessman with a Walkman and a crisply folded *Wall Street Journal* stood alone at the end of the platform.

Save for the guitarist's unplugged sounds of Oingo Boingo, it was quiet on the platform. Then the first of the little brown bats flew in. It scratched a jagged course high over the tracks and snared the attention of one of the students.

"Hey, cool," he droned. His sullen eyes opened slightly as he raised a pale finger and pointed.

The girl had her back to the tracks. She turned and looked as the bat zigzagged toward them. It landed on the boy's black wool cap, and he suddenly came to life. He backed away, swinging his gangly arms at the creature as the talons pierced his scalp.

"Fuck, man!"

The girl stepped forward and swatted at the bat. The boy turned circles blindly as four more bats suddenly raced from the tunnel to the platform. Two of them descended on the girl from above and snatched at her long black-and-green hair while the other two dug at the back of a boy's neck. She screamed in pain as the bats pulled her head back.

The tourists finally looked over, and the guitarist stopped playing. Shouting for help, they all ran toward the kids. The businessman standing one hundred feet away saw and heard nothing. His eyes were on his newspaper and his ears were full of opera.

Sitting in her bulletproof booth and counting out five-dollar bills, subway clerk Meg Ricci heard the cries of the people on the platform. She looked up over her reading glasses and saw the tourists and students dancing and flailing. She saw the musician swinging his guitar around him. Then she saw the flapping wings and the dark little bats attacking their faces and hands. She snatched up the phone and called for police assistance.

As Meg told the dispatcher what was going on, something else happened. A well-dressed man at the end of the platform had removed his earphones and looked over. As he turned toward the others, a large shadow enveloped him. It came over the man from above, like poured paint, and then spilled quickly to the left. When the inky blackness was gone, so was the man.

Meg reported exactly what she saw before she realized how insane it must sound. The dispatcher matter-of-factly asked her to repeat it. Meg did. That was what had happened.

A few seconds later the bats suddenly stopped attacking the people on the platform. They fluttered around for a moment, circling just under the ceiling like leaves in an eddy. Then they darted back over the tracks and took off down the tunnel, following the inky shape.

While the dispatcher put out a call, Meg broke the rules. Pulling a first aid kit from under the counter, she left her booth and hopped the turnstile. She turned back long enough to tell new arrivals not to come in, then went to help the riders who had fallen.

Two patrolmen from the sixth precinct arrived moments later. While one of them called for an ambulance from St. Vincent's and kept other people from entering the station, the second officer went to help Meg.

She was extremely calm as she applied disinfectant and bandages to the students' scratches and told the officer about the bats and about the well-dressed man who must have fallen from the platform. What she saw, she decided, had been his jacket flying up. Or maybe it was the reflection of her own dark hair on the glass of the booth.

The officer went to the end of the platform to have a look. He hopped down onto the tracks. When he came back he was holding headphones from a Walkman. The foam ends were wet with blood.

He called for backup from the transit police and recommended that the station be closed.

Still calm, Meg went back to her booth and called her supervisor for instructions. He told her to lock the money drawer and the booth and to do whatever the police told her.

Transit police arrived. They took Meg's name, address, and phone number, and told her she could go.

She took the next bus back to Queens.

Fifteen

The American Museum of Natural History was built in 1874. Located along Central Park West between Seventy-seventh and Eighty-first streets, it is best known today for its unparalleled collection of prehistoric fossils and dinosaur skeletons. However, it was originally designed to be a showcase for contemporary nature and archaeological displays. The dioramas of modern-day animal life, from birds to bison to fish, remain among its most popular attractions.

But the galleries and spacious display halls are not the museum's only service. Research, exploration, and education are also important functions, and the fifth floor of the museum—closed to the public—has long been a haven for scientists and scholars. There, in hundred-year-old cabinets and drawers as well as in modern cryogenic chambers, the museum stores countless animal, vegetal, and fossil specimens for study.

Given what had happened in the tunnel, Gentry was in as good a mood as he could be. He was guardedly optimistic for a reconciliation. He liked Nancy Joyce, he admired her courage and determination, and he felt bad about what he'd done. He didn't feel repentant, for he'd do it again. Just bad. And all he wanted was the chance, at some point, to tell her everything—except the fact that he wouldn't have done anything differently.

Gentry got off the elevator at the fifth floor. A skinny young man was passing. The kid held a small plastic tray full of tiny bones, stringy sinew, and what looked like blood. The detective asked him for directions to Professor Lowery's laboratory. The young man pointed ahead and told him to hang a left and then a right.

Gentry thanked him then looked at the dish. "Mind if I ask what that is?" he asked.

"Lunch," the young man replied. "Chicken cacciatore."

The man continued down the corridor. Gentry followed him. There were framed portraits and photographs of various expeditions, going back to the Gobi expedition in the 1920s. The men and women portrayed reeked of scholarship and trailblazing. The detective made a point of not looking at them. He didn't want to start feeling inadequate between here and the laboratory.

Gentry had never been at ease in academic settings. He spent one semester at City College before bagging it for the NYPD. He liked finding things out for himself, not being lectured to. That was one of the many things he loved about his typesetter father. The man never talked at him. He talked to him and with him, as though it were always man-to-man. Even when it was man-to-seven-year-old.

Part of Gentry's discomfort also probably had to do with his mother having worked as a secretary for an intellectual snob of a college dean, Dr. Horst Acker. "Boss Tweed," he and his dad used to call him. His mother ended up leaving Gentry's father for him. The seven-year-old Gentry hated the red-cheeked, pipe-smoking creep with all the energy in his body, and after three months he ran away from his mother to live with his dad. His mother let him go, which was fine: Gentry wasn't crazy about her, either.

Before Gentry reached the laboratory, his beeper sounded again. He checked the number; this time it was Chris Henry. Give that dog a bone and there was no one who could chew it up faster. He kept walking.

At Lowery's laboratory, Gentry rapped on the frosted glass. His heart was thumping hard, harder than when he went into the hole in the service tunnel. He heard a Swiss-sounding voice and saw Joyce's shadow move toward the door. She hesitated a moment, then turned and opened it.

"Hi there," he said.

"Come in," she replied. There was a hint of distance in her voice, in the set of her mouth. But there was curiosity in her eyes, and Gentry latched onto it.

Gentry entered a room that was about three times the size of his office at the police station. Joyce walked the door shut so it wouldn't slam. Gentry glanced to the right. Along the wall was a wide black table. It was roughly half as wide and fully as long as a pool table, and it sat under a series of low, bright lights. A tall, elderly man in a white lab coat was bent over it, his back to Gentry. The man didn't turn when the detective entered.

"We've been working on the mold from the gouge in the deer bone," Joyce said. "We were waiting for a specimen to come up from storage. Now that it's here we're just finishing the scans."

"I see. I got paged on the way over. Is there a phone I can use?"

"Over here," she said, pointing to a desk.

The phone was nestled between a stuffed and mounted gerbil and chipmunk. Gentry called Ari first. The line was busy. Then he called the crime lab. Chris Henry came on and said he'd just finished measuring the trauma. He rattled off the dimensions and Gentry wrote them down. When Henry hung up, Gentry handed the page to Joyce.

"What's this?"

"The lab results I said I was waiting for. Fourteen of the bodies I found in the subway belonged to homeless people. They were pretty torn up. But not as badly as a fifteenth. That one belonged to a bicyclist who disappeared from way up on Riverside Drive early this morning."

"The one who had the strange bites."

"Right," Gentry said. "And two things I didn't tell you: She was gutted, just like the deer. And there were large, bloody hatch marks on the grate overhead."

Joyce's expression darkened.

Gentry pointed to the paper. "These are the dimensions of marks that were found on a rib belonging to the bicyclist."

Joyce read them. "They're the same as the deer," she said. "Professor?"

"I heard," he said. He still didn't turn. "Are you certain of their accuracy, Mr. Gentry?"

"It's Detective Gentry, and absolutely."

"Then input them, please, Nannie."

Joyce nodded and sat down at her computer. As she typed, Gentry walked over to the lab table. In the back of the room, to Gentry's left, was an industrial-size sink. Bookcases and shelves covered every other free foot of wall space. Books, magazines, papers, jars with floating things, and other taxidermied specimens were jammed into every available space. The room smelled faintly of mildew and formaldehyde.

Gentry stopped beside the professor. Kane Lowery had a long, priestly soft, white face, eyes the color of gunmetal, and thinning, slicked-back gray hair. There were three square aluminum pans lined up in front of him. The pan on the left contained what was obviously the cast of the wounds made from the deer bone. The second pan had a small dead bat about six inches from wingtip to wingtip. Lowery was holding a large, humming penlike instrument directly above the second pan; a cable ran from the back end to the computer, and he was moving a laser beam slowly from left to right.

The professor cleared his throat.

"Robert," Joyce said.

He looked back. She crooked a finger and motioned him over.

Gentry turned from Professor Lowery. He was annoyed by that little cough signal between them, and he was a little disappointed in

Nancy. For someone who just complained that she hadn't been treated like a professional, she'd been quick enough to help tug on Gentry's leash.

But he could live with that. He wasn't here to make friends with Professor Lowery. And unlike Nancy, he didn't have to work with the man.

Gentry stopped beside her. "What exactly is the professor doing?"

"He's using a laser to take very precise measurements of the bat's teeth." She pointed to the computer monitor. "The numbers in the left column are the dimensions of the wound in the deer bone. When the professor is finished, the column on the right will have the figures for the dentation of a little brown bat, like the ones that attacked at the field last night. If necessary, we'll also check the bat's claws and—"

"Explain it later, Nannie," the professor interrupted. "I'm just finishing the conic scan."

"I see," she said. "The data is coming up now," Joyce said. She read the new figures as they appeared. "The tangent angle at the bottom of the teeth is forty-two degrees."

"And it's forty-six on top," the professor said.

"That's correct. One point zero seven inches apart."

"Which gives us—?"

Nancy looked at the first column of figures. "The proportions are an exact match." Her eyes shifted to the figures Chris Henry had given to Gentry. "My God," she said.

"What?" Lowery said.

"They're all a match, all three sets of teeth."

The professor put down the laser. He turned and slipped his large hands into the pocket of his lab coat. "Incisors with a distinctive medial separation. The hint of a W-shaped impression from the molar cusps and ridges."

"It's unbelievable," Joyce said.

"But undeniable," Lowery responded.

"What is?" Gentry asked.

"The deer in Westchester was attacked and partly consumed by a giant predator," the professor said. "So, apparently, was your bicycle woman. And judging by the dentition, it appears in both cases to have been a bat. More precisely, a member of the family Vespertilionidae." The professor smiled for the first time. "This is amazing. And the simulated reconstruction we did earlier of the formation of the guano mound in the tunnel also supports the theory—well, it's more than a theory now, isn't it?—that there is a very large vespertilionid specimen in the tunnels under the city. Possibly the same creature, or a second one."

"I just can't believe it," Joyce said. "There's got to be another explanation."

"Such as?" Lowery asked. "A bear or mountain lion? That is more believable?"

"In a way," Joyce said.

"And did the lion also leave the guano? Did it shatter the tree limbs? Could it carry a grown woman seventy or eighty blocks, through city streets and subways, without being seen?"

Joyce just shook her head slowly. "I don't know, Professor. I don't know what to think."

"You're talking about a *giant* bat," Gentry said.

"It appears so, Mr. Gentry," Lowery said.

"This has to be some kind of sick joke. Where would it have come from?"

"I honestly don't know," Lowery said. "But for someone to execute a 'sick joke' with this kind of precision would take some doing. Why bother?"

"The same reason that people fake UFO abductions and Loch Ness monster sightings. Publicity."

"Are you so convinced that all of them are fake?" Lowery asked.

The three of them stood still. The only noise was the whirr of the computer hard drive backing up the data and the sound of the elevator opening and closing behind the laboratory. Joyce and Lowery were looking at each other, almost like predator and prey. The professor's arms were crossed, his brow hawklike. He seemed to be waiting for her to challenge the findings so he could slap her down with a fact.

Gentry decided he'd take the hit. "Assuming you're right about this, exactly how big is 'giant'?"

"That we don't know."

"Can't you just calculate up from—"

"No," Lowery interrupted impatiently. "That wouldn't work."

"Why not?"

Joyce explained, "The larger the bat's torso, head, and legs are, the greater the lift required from the animal's wings. But if you make the wings larger, then the muscles needed to control the wings must also be bigger and stronger. Increase the size of those muscles, and the wings must be larger still to lift that additional weight. Do you follow?"

"Some of it," Gentry said.

"If the bat is a vesper," Lowery said, thinking aloud, "then the musculature Nannie just described would make it a seriously deformed specimen. Almost like a flying bull."

"Why?" Gentry asked. "Aren't there are some pretty big nondeformed birds?"

"There are," Joyce agreed. "But birds have an entirely different anatomy from bats. A bird's feathers provide a great deal of lift, and they have just two opposing flight muscles. Bats have three pairs of pectoral muscles for the downstroke and a complex series of small back muscles for the upstroke. Bats don't so much flap as move through a rapid series of wing-beat cycles. So there would be a significant weight difference between, say, an albatross with a wingspan of twelve feet and a bat of the same size."

"All right," Gentry said. "I think I understand that. So how about this. Can't you figure out how big this hypothetical bat would have to be to lift a deer into a tree or fly carrying a dead body from somewhere around Riverside Drive to a subway tunnel under Forty-fifth Street?"

"Unfortunately," Joyce said, "that doesn't help us much either. As the professor said, we could be dealing with more than one big bat."

"I did not say they'd be flying in tandem," Lowery pointed

out. "The air currents from one would almost certainly upset the other."

"Well, you two can discuss all this later," Gentry said. "The question I need answered is if there is a big bat, do you think it'll want to stay here or is it just passing through?"

Joyce said she didn't know. Lowery didn't say anything. Gentry exhaled loudly.

"What puzzles me about all of this," Lowery said after a moment, "is if there is such a creature, how it came to be. And why the smaller bats seem to congregate around it. And how it's managed to remain hidden until now."

"Maybe it hasn't been hidden," Gentry said.

Lowery looked at him. "Explain, please."

"Earlier this morning I checked through New York state police reports of bat attacks over the last few days. In addition to the incident up in Westchester, there were two attacks by groups of small bats. They follow the Hudson River down from Albany. When I get back to the station house I can look back farther. There may be more."

"By all means do so," Lowery said.

Gentry definitely didn't like the man's manner. He turned toward Nancy. It was time to take a try-calling-Ari-again break.

"Can I use your phone again?" he asked Nancy.

She nodded.

Gentry walked to the desk and dialed. Captain Moreaux answered. "Ari, it's Gentry."

"Robert," Moreaux said, "I thought you'd want to know we've had another attack."

"Where?"

"The Christopher Street subway station, downtown," said Moreaux. "A man disappeared from the platform during an attack. With any luck, though, we may have some answers soon."

"Why?"

"Because an ESU team was just sent in to try and find him."

Sixteen

In addition to being extremely mobile, the NYPD Emergency Service Unit is fast.

Within fifteen minutes of being informed that man had been pulled from the downtown subway platform at Christopher Street, a Special Operations Division on the eight-to-four shift was down in the tunnel looking for him. They had arrived in two mobile Radio Emergency Patrol vehicles, 4x4 pickups stocked with rescue equipment, nonlethal weaponry, and body armor. The SOD was comprised of four men and one woman. Field Sergeant Laurie Rhodes was leading the team. They were dressed in heavy vests, blue construction helmets, and Kevlar boots and gloves to protect them from rat bites. They were armed with their service revolvers, two high-intensity hand lights, and a pair of tasers. Each weapon contained two cartridges that fired a pair of connected darts; when the barbs truck a target, they completed a circuit that generated a low-amperage fifty thousand volts. The jolt was sufficient to short-circuit nearby muscles for several seconds without stopping the heart. The subway clerk had said that the missing man had been pulled from the platform. Whoever did it could be an EDP, an emotionally disturbed person—"a Phantom of the Opera wannabe," Rhodes had said, based on the description of a cloak that had snared the man. The SOD officers wanted to be prepared.

They left the platform where the sixth precinct officer had found the headphones. For the duration of the operation, trains were not being permitted north of Houston Street or south of Fourteenth Street.

Officers Brophy, Hotchkiss, Lord, and Nicco and Sergeant Rhodes proceeded in side-by-side rows of two. The sergeant was in front. Rhodes held the radio in her left hand and kept the channel open, allowing her to stay in constant contact with the command truck. The large trailer was parked not far from the station along the southern side of Washington Square Park. Desk Lieutenant Francis Gary Kilar had been brought in from Manhattan South headquarters on Twenty-first Street to run the rescue operation.

Walking off to the left side of the tracks, the SOD team followed a trail of blood droplets along the track bed.

"If I didn't know differently," Rhodes said to Kilar, "I'd say the victim was hit by a train and carried along, bleeding. The drops of blood are lying in a long line down the center of the tracks."

"Have you ever come across anything like this, Sergeant?" Lord asked.

"Yeah," said Rhodes. "When my cat caught a mouse and ran across the living room carpet."

"Maybe the mice figure it's payback time," Lord said.

"Well," Kilar said, "the vic definitely wasn't hit by a train. As we speak I'm looking at the MTA log that was just E-mailed over. It confirms what the clerk said. There was no train on that track at that time."

"Then I've got no explanation for this," she said. "There's blood but no footprints. No Walkman. Nothing."

They were nearly two hundred yards in. Rhodes circled the light carefully and systematically along the walls, ceiling, and columns.

"Now that Lord mentioned it," Rhodes said, "I'm surprised we haven't seen any Jimmies down here." Jimmies were rats, named in honor of actor James "You-Dirty-Rat-You-Killed-My-Brother" Cagney. They usually moved along the rails searching for scraps that had been thrown on the tracks near the stations. And people moving through usually sent them running away.

"Sergeant Rhodes?" Kilar said suddenly.

"Yes?"

"Hold on."

Rhodes held up her left hand. Everyone stopped.

A moment later Kilar said, "Sergeant, you're being advised to turn back."

"Say again?"

"You're being advised to turn back. We have an incoming—shit," he said. "Just a minute. I've gotta figure this goddamn thing out."

Lord and Hotchkiss laughed nervously.

Rhodes acknowledged his last communication, then waited.

Lieutenant Kilar had given her an advisement, not an order. Though that could change at any moment, for now it was still her call as to what the team should do. She leaned her head to the right and peered ahead. She shined the light around some more. Up and down, left and right, diagonally in both directions, all very slowly. She didn't see anything.

She waited, chewing her cheek. She continued to look ahead. If she turned back to talk to the team, they'd look at her. That would leave zero eyes watching the track up ahead.

Lieutenant Kilar came back on the radio in less than a minute.

"Sergeant Rhodes, Sergeant Terry and I are going to attempt to patch through a call from a Dr. Nancy Joyce at the Museum of Natural History."

"Why?"

"The doctor will explain."

There was a short delay. Rhodes could just picture the lieutenant growing more and more frustrated as he and the technophobic Desk Sergeant Terry tried to work out the mechanics of switching the call. She also knew that Kilar wouldn't give up. He might pound the table and threaten to shove the radio up some part of Terry's anatomy, but he wouldn't give up.

Rhodes moved ahead several steps. She cast the light here and there, then came back to the group. The rear lip of the helmet was chafing her neck and the vest was hot. She was uncomfortable. But she wanted to do what the hell they came down here for.

A woman's voice crackled from the radio. "Hello? Are you there?"

"I'm here. This is Field Sergeant Laurie Rhodes. Are you Dr. Joyce?"

"Yes," the caller said urgently. "I've been talking to your sergeant. I don't believe that you're equipped to deal with what you may find in the tunnel."

"Why? What may we find?"

"A colony of bats," Joyce said.

"Bats?"

"Yes. Extremely vicious ones, probably belonging to the same colony that killed a group of homeless people under Grand Central Station this morning. There may also be a much bigger bat than the rest—we're not sure."

"Big enough to shoot?"

"If you were lucky enough to see it, and see it in time, maybe."

"Understood." She thought for a moment. "I just want to be clear about something. We're wearing heavy vests and helmets, as well as ratproof gloves and boots. Are you certain that these will *not* be sufficient to protect us?"

"Sergeant, it won't even *slow* the bats," Joyce said. "They'll crawl under whatever you've got on. They'll bring you down. And once you're down, you won't get up. Please—call off the search."

Rhodes glanced down the tracks. She moved the flashlight around even slower than before. "I don't see any bats," she said, "and we have an injured man somewhere down here."

"Bats don't store their food," Joyce said. "They eat on the run. The man is probably dead already."

"Dr. Joyce, are you saying they ate him?"

"Officer, I don't know. *Please come out.*"

Rhodes stood there a moment longer. Then she walked a few more yards into the tunnel. The blood on the ground had thinned. Then it stopped. She kept walking, her boots crunching on the black dirt beside the track. She shined the light ahead, then up. She still didn't see the victim, but he had to be near.

"Sergeant?" Joyce asked.

Rhodes hesitated. If it were just her life at risk, she'd stay and search for the missing man. But it wasn't. Reluctantly, the officer turned and walked back toward the team.

She never reached them. A pair of bats slammed into Rhodes's legs, directly behind the knees. It took only a second for them to bite through the trousers to her flesh.

"Son of a bitch!" she yelled.

She put the radio and the light on the ground and turned to smack at the animals. As she did, she was pelted by a dozen more bats. They hit in quick, stinging succession, like pellets from a BB gun. They pinched the back of her vest, arms, and legs.

The two officers closest to her, Brophy and Hotchkiss, ran over. The bats were too small, and Rhodes was squirming too much for them to use their tasers. This close, it would be easier and safer to attempt to pull them off. The officers began slapping and clawing at the bats, only to have the animals turn on them. More struck. Within seconds there were more than twenty of them.

"Are you coming out?" Joyce asked.

Rhodes didn't answer.

"Can you hear me?" Joyce yelled.

Rhodes picked up the radio. "Lieutenant!"

There was a click as Lieutenant Kilar cut Dr. Joyce off. "Rhodes, what's happening down there?"

She tried to answer, but she dropped the radio as she twitched and slapped at the bats.

"Sergeant, what's the nature of your problem?"

"She was right!" Rhodes screamed. "It's goddamn bats! They're all over the place!"

One of them crawled down her forearm and slipped into the flared bottom of her glove. The bat chewed at the heel of her palm.

"Fuck you, rodent!" Rhodes cried.

She slammed her hand onto the ground; the bat was crushed by the blow. The officer yanked off her glove and shook the creature out. The bloody bat plopped on the gravel. It was still alive, its wings broken, and it tried to crawl away. She drove her boot down in it.

"Heel!"

"*Rhodes!*" Kilar barked.

"Wait!" she cried.

Before Rhodes could pull her glove back on, two more bats flew from the darkness. They attached themselves to the sides of her hand. Their teeth pinched like staples. Their breath came fast and hot. Rhodes screamed and tried to shake them off. They held on, their wings folded tight. Pain flashed down her wrist and blood dribbled along her sleeve.

"God, these bastards don't give up!"

"I'm sending another unit down immediately," Kilar told her.

"Give them heavy armor!" Rhodes shouted. "I'm going to try to evacuate my own unit!"

Allowing the pain to fuel her anger, Rhodes tore into the bats and then tried to help the other two officers. Officer Brophy was on his knees; Officer Hotchkiss had thrown his back against a wall, mashing two bats under his heavy vest. Rhodes was forced to stop as four more bats swooped in low. They swung behind her, crawled under her helmet, and bit behind her ears.

Officers Lord and Nicco started forward.

"Don't!" Rhodes cried. "Get out! We'll follow."

The two officers stopped as Rhodes shrieked with pain. A bat had crawled into her boot and bit her ankle. She fell to one knee and pressed on the high Kevlar fabric with both hands. The bat dropped down to her heel to avoid being crushed. Her eyes wide, Rhodes wriggled her foot around as the bat bit it repeatedly. The others continued to pick at her arms, legs, and ears. Another attacked the nape of her neck. Her other knee hit the ground.

"I said go!" she yelled at the officers up ahead.

Just then Rhodes saw something move in the blackness. It was directly behind the two officers. As a bat crept under her neck and gnawed at her chin, the sergeant yelled for the officers to turn around.

Officers Lord and Nicco spun. Driving her chin into her chest to stop the pain, Rhodes grabbed her high-intensity light and swung it around. The bloody arm of a man had slipped from an overhead girder. She watched as the rest of his body followed slowly. The bloody corpse fell headfirst and landed heavily on the track bed, face down. Black dust clouded around the body and puffed up through a massive hole in the center.

With a growl, Rhodes snatched the tenacious bat from her raw chin. She wadded it like waste paper, squeezed hard, and threw it down just as something else appeared behind the officers.

Rhodes squinted ahead and stared. The apparition was just outside the glow of the light, and she tried to make it out. Drops of blood were spattered across it like stars. Its eyes were dull crimson, and its teeth were like red ice. There was the hint of what looked like a nose, two damp, oblong gashes sloping upward and outward from the mouth.

The shape was there for only a moment. Two objects, like great hooks, glistened and shot forward. They impaled Officers Lord and Nicco and lifted them off their feet. The two men hung several feet up for a moment, trembling, then were thrown down. The hooks and wings flashed up into the blackness, and then the teeth and eyes vanished.

Sergeant Rhodes managed to draw her service revolver. But the bats wouldn't let up, and the pain of countless bites had weakened her. She fell to one hand. Blood and perspiration blurred her vision. She tried to marshal her energies. But more bats came at her, attacking her wrists and forehead. The biting was constant now and much deeper behind her knees and elbows and neck. Each one felt like a staple fired nearly to the bone. Still kneeling, Rhodes dropped onto her chin.

And then she felt herself being hoisted up.

"Come on!" Officer Hotchkiss yelled. *"We're getting out!"*

Rhodes was startled, as though waking from a too-brief nap.

"Help me!" Hotchkiss said. "I can't do this myself!"

The policeman had slid his arm around the sergeant's waist. He pulled her halfway to her feet.

Rhodes collected her feet beneath her. "Brophy," she muttered. "What about Brophy?"

"He's coming!"

Rhodes turned weakly. She saw him running, then stumbling after them. Bats were clustered in the air around his head, like monstrous gnats.

"Help him," she said.

"He told me to help you. He was—*fuck* these things!" He slapped at a bat on his hip. "He was on his feet. You two can"—he pawed his leg—"fight this out"—he hammered the side of his thigh—"later! *Fuck!*"

They started running down the tracks. Hotchkiss was half-pulling, half-carrying Rhodes. As they ran past the fallen officers, Rhodes reached for her radio. She wanted to make sure emergency medical assistance came in with the backup. But the loop in her belt was empty. Then she remembered she'd dropped the radio.

Then she heard a scream behind her. She looked back, squinting through crimson sweat. She saw Brophy do a surreal forward somersault. Then the blackness filled in behind him, like ink, swallowing the faint lights along the tunnel wall.

"Oh my God," Rhodes said.

"Don't talk, run!" Hotchkiss screamed.

Rhodes looked ahead as she heard a scream. Then another and another. They degenerated into awful squeals of pain.

"Keep running," Hotchkiss said again. He was breathing hard and looking ahead hard. "Don't look back. Run."

Rhodes managed to find some strength and get her footing. After a moment she was able to carry more of her weight. The bats continued to nip at her, and a few of them flew at the other officer. They swarmed around his face and fought their way into her helmet. But the man ducked his head like a bull, shook them off, and kept going.

Soon the dimming light of the flashlight gave way to the distant glow of the station. The bats seemed to peel off the closer they came to the platform.

Hotchkiss screamed, "Help—anyone!"

He fell suddenly and Rhodes went with him. But they didn't lie there. Using everything she had to fight the few remaining bats as well as pain and exhaustion, Rhodes staggered back to her feet. Hotchkiss was struggling, wheezing. Rhodes helped him up and they continued running.

This time Rhodes called for help.

Moments later, three Sixth Precinct officers who had heard the screams met them coming the other way. They helped the injured officers out of the tunnel and laid them on benches along the platform wall. One of the officers called for an ambulance. Another of them said something about going in to help the other members of the ESU team.

He was startled when Rhodes grabbed his sleeve. She held tight with raw, bloody fingers.

"Don't go back!" she warned.

"What about—"

"*Don't!*" she snarled. "Not without infrared . . . armor . . . heavy weapons. Promise me."

The officer hesitated.

"Promise!"

He promised.

Sergeant Rhodes lay back on the bench. She shut her burning eyes. "It'll kill you," she muttered. "It'll kill you."

"What will?"

"It will," Rhodes said.

And then she passed out.

Seventeen

Detective Gentry and Dr. Joyce arrived by squad car at St. Vincent's Hospital on Seventh Avenue and Eleventh Street. That was where Field Sergeant Rhodes and Officer Hotchkiss had been taken.

Rhodes had been hurried from the emergency room to surgery. She'd suffered two badly broken ribs, a punctured lung—it had been penetrated from the outside, not by one of the ribs—and dozens of severe bite wounds up and down her body. The back of the top of her right thigh and one of her heels were practically gone. The bottoms of both ears had been chewed away. She had lost a great deal of blood.

Hotchkiss had suffered severe lacerations of the face, scalp, back, and legs. He was pale and bruised, and it hurt to move. But when Gentry and Joyce asked to see him, he agreed. His physician and a burly, balding ESU lieutenant were standing beside the bed when they arrived.

Gentry always felt honored to be with someone who had put it on the line like the ESU squad had. They'd known there was danger and they walked right the hell into it. Gentry felt miserable about the deaths but it was partially offset by the pride he felt in this man.

Gentry smiled as he walked toward the bed. The men moved aaway. "Officer, I'm Detective Gentry, Midtown South. I want you to know you've got a lot of people proud and pulling for you, Officer Hotchkiss."

"They cut us to pieces," young Hotchkiss replied thickly from between slashed lips.

"You went in knowing there was bad news down there," Gentry said. "That didn't stop you."

Lieutenant Kilar touched the officer's shoulder. "You also saved the life of Sergeant Rhodes. *That's* what happened down there."

Dr. Joyce walked toward the bed. The men moved away. "Officer, I'm Dr. Nancy Joyce. I'm with the Bronx Zoo. How are you?"

"Do I need . . . a vet?"

"No," she smiled.

She knelt beside him and touched his left cheek with the back of her fingers. It was the only part of his round face that appeared unhurt. The injured police officer smiled up at her with his eyes.

"I want to ask you a few questions. You okay with that?"

He nodded once.

She smiled back. "What can you tell me about the little bats?"

"Not much. It was dark."

"Do you know what size they were?"

He thought for a moment. "About mouse size. Mice with wings."

"Their color?"

"I don't know. I'm sorry."

"It's all right. You're doing fine. What did the bats do first?"

"They attacked Sergeant Rhodes."

"Where was she relative to you?"

"South of us, maybe two yards."

"Did the bats come at you in a wave?"

"There were several waves, I think. It was difficult to see."

"And they all flew at Sergeant Rhodes?"

He nodded. "Until we tried to help her."

"Then what happened?"

"Some of them peeled off," Hotchkiss said. "It felt like they were trying to push Brophy and me to the side while they also bit us."

"And when you were leaving the tunnel? Did they follow?"

"Some of them did for a while. Then they stopped. Very suddenly."

"One more question," Joyce said. "The other two officers who were down there with you—"

"Lord and Nicco."

"Lord and Nicco," Joyce repeated. "What happened to them?"

The remnants of Hotchkiss's smile vanished. The pain of the memory was evident in the slow downturn of his mouth, in his distant eyes. "The vic fell off a girder—"

"The who?"

Lieutenant Kilar explained, "The victim. The man they went in to find."

"He fell," Joyce repeated. "Then what happened? What did you see?"

Officer Hotchkiss continued slowly, "A shape. All I saw was a big, black, moving shape."

"Could that have been a bat too?"

"What?" Kilar said.

Hotchkiss's eyes grew red. "I don't know. It was like Lord and Nicco just rose off the ground and dropped. They didn't move after that. Brophy was fighting more of the bats than me, so he yelled that I should go get Sergeant Rhodes out of there. I did. Then we heard Brophy. He, uh . . . he wasn't having a real easy time, screaming . . ." Hotchkiss began to sob.

The doctor moved behind Joyce and said, "Let him rest."

Joyce nodded and rose. She looked down at Hotchkiss. "Thank you," she said.

Hotchkiss nodded once and tried to stop crying as she walked away. The lieutenant and Gentry joined Joyce by the door.

"Doctor, what kind of crap was that?"

"Lieutenant?"

"You can't be serious about what you were asking him," the lieutenant said. "A giant bat?"

"We're definitely looking into the possibility of a bat of unusual size and strength," Joyce replied.

Kilar sneered. "If this is a joke, I'm definitely not in the mood for it."

"Lieutenant, this is no joke," Gentry said.

Kilar looked at him. "How do you know?"

"A deer was found way up in a tree," Gentry went on. "People have been carried off and mauled. We've got impressions of teeth that match bat teeth, only much, much bigger."

"You've also got bats on the brain," the lieutenant said. "The two of you. This is ridiculous."

"What would you think?" Gentry asked.

"Exactly what we've told the media."

"That there's a wacko down in the tunnel—"

"That's right. An unbalanced individual who's swinging an ax or knife and scaring up the bats that live in the tunnel. Teeth and knives are sometimes difficult to tell apart in badly mauled corpses—"

"That's bullshit and you know it!" Gentry snapped.

"No, Detective," Kilar snapped back. "A giant bat or rat or alligator in the sewer—*that's* bullshit."

"Lieutenant," Joyce said, "I understand there's another team ready to go into the tunnel."

Kilar glanced over at Hotchkiss. He ushered the group into the hallway and shut the door.

"That's right, Doctor," the lieutenant said. "We've got three subway lines shut down. We've got the media way up our butts. The mayor has Gordy Weeks at the Office of Emergency Management ready to take this whole thing over if we don't clear it up by the evening rush hour. I don't want this slipping past the ESU, not on my watch. As soon as the mayor comes up to commend Officer Hotchkiss for his bravery, I'm going back to the command truck, and the team is going in. We're going to find and stop whoever or *whatever* is behind this."

"How will your people be protected?" Joyce asked.

"With exposure suits, which are thick and heavily insulated. They'll have self-contained breathing apparatus, goggles, and electrical gloves and boots tight at the wrists and ankles. They're to get in," he lowered his voice, "recover the bodies, and get out. Once they do that, we'll go in again, this time a little deeper."

Joyce said, "The problem is that if the bats—not the large one but the ordinary little ones—decide to attack, all of your protective clothing may not be enough."

"The team will also be armed."

"Bats are notoriously uncooperative targets."

"Look, Doctor," Kilar said. "I don't know enough to argue with what you're telling me. Do you know Al Doyle at pest control?"

Joyce shook her head.

"He's a good man. He's on his way to the site, and he's going to be running that side of things. He knows the weaponry, and he says we'll be all right. But if you'd like to come along and advise him—"

"Lieutenant," Joyce said, "these bats aren't pests. We've tested saliva we found in the wounds. They don't appear to be sick or rabid."

"Al's still in charge," Kilar said.

"That's not what I mean," she said through her teeth. "The way the attacks start and stop all seem to be tied to geography. That's not typical bat behavior—it's not typical *pest* behavior. This is a pattern no one's ever seen before. Not me, not a rat catcher, not anyone. What I'm saying is you have to approach this very, very carefully."

Kilar's radio came to life. The dispatcher informed him that the mayor's limousine was on the way. The lieutenant said he would inform the medical team, then come downstairs to meet him.

"As I said," Kilar told Joyce, "if you want to give us the benefit of your expertise, I'd love to have it."

"Thanks for the invitation, but I think I'll tackle this from another direction." She excused herself, then left.

Kilar glared at Gentry and stepped closer. "I lost some good people today. You oughta know when to back the fuck off."

"I'll back off when I'm sure more good people aren't going to be butchered—"

"Thanks for the advice. If you find out anything about this perp, something I can use, you'll let me know?"

Gentry nodded. Kilar returned to the hospital room.

Gentry ran after Joyce. He caught up to her, and the two walked quickly toward the elevator.

"Sorry about that," he said.

"Right."

"I am. You're not having a very good afternoon."

"You don't know the half of it."

"Tell me."

"I thought it was obvious back there. Another case of SDS."

"SDS?"

"Swinging dick syndrome. The idea that men do things better."

"Another? Is that what you thought I was doing in the tunnel?"

"Weren't you?"

"Oh, come on Nancy! I thought I explained—"

"You did. I never said I believed you."

"Well, it wasn't SDS," Gentry said. "And neither is this. The lieutenant may not have much of an imagination, and I can't say I blame him for not believing there's a giant bat on the loose. But he cares about the problem and he did want your help. He asked you to come to the command center."

"In support of his man."

"No. But it's like anyplace else. There's a pecking order—"

"A pecker order, you mean."

Gentry swung in front of her and stopped. So did she. "Look, I'm not saying that doesn't exist in the NYPD. But that's not what you got from the lieutenant and it's not what you got from me. You have to believe that."

"I'll try," she said, then moved around him.

He turned and walked with her. She reached the elevator and jabbed the button.

"Let them stick to their 'pecking' order," she went on. "Only if they do, there's going to be a lot less order and a lot more pecking. The kind you saw in the tunnel. This isn't a job for pseudoexperts."

The elevator arrived and they stepped into the empty car. Joyce leaned against a corner, her eyes downcast.

"Like I said before, Nancy, I'm sorry this hasn't worked out the way you wanted."

They were quiet for a moment. It was the silence of cooling off.

"I can't remember," Gentry said. "Did I ever thank you for coming?"

"I wanted to come."

"Well, thank you anyway. Whatever this thing is, we're going to figure it out and lick it."

She was silent again. Gentry didn't know what else to say, so he said nothing.

When the elevator door opened, they walked down a crowded corridor toward the Eleventh Street exit. Gentry had to hustle to keep up with the woman.

"What *are* you planning to do?" he asked.

"I was thinking about heading back to my office and getting online," she said. "I'm relatively up-to-date on all the current bat literature, but I could've missed some research somewhere. Occasionally the reports about bats show up under different headings."

"You mean like dead livestock or missing persons or things like that," Gentry said.

She nodded. "You may also be onto something with that Hudson route you mentioned before. I want to check it out."

"Y'know, I have access to a lot of reports that aren't a matter of public information."

"That could be useful."

"I was thinking that maybe we should pool our resources."

"Don't you have cases and crimes to work on?"

"Always. But this one's got me hooked. I've never seen anything like it." He smiled at her. "What about you?"

"My assistant Marc will cover the school lectures."

"Excellent. So how about it? We can work together."

She thought for a moment. "Sure. It makes sense."

"Then I have a suggestion. The subways are going to be screwed up for a while, and getting to the Bronx will be a pain. My apartment's a short walk away. Why don't we go there?"

"Nice one." She allowed the hint of a smile. "You inviting me up to see your guano?"

"Absolutely. It's a babe magnet."

Her smile flowered a little more.

"You can use my computer, and if you're hungry we can eat. Also, if they find anything in the subways, I'll hear about it and we can go right over."

Joyce nodded. Now Gentry smiled.

Fortunately, the mayor was arriving as they were leaving. The cluster of reporters gathered outside—Kathy Leung among them— failed to notice Nancy Joyce.

Gentry stopped at a pay phone and called NYPD ICCU, the Inter-city Correspondence Unit, also known as the Stat Unit. He wanted to get them working on the bat attacks as soon as possible. This small division, which is composed mainly of civilians, primarily involves itself with collecting information from and disseminating information to police departments in other cities. The wait time for information is typically a day or two. But Gentry got preferential treatment. That was because he made it a point to remember the birthdays of key personnel with flowers or Knicks tickets. It was a habit he'd started during his days as a narc, when he couldn't afford to wait more than a few hours for background checks on possible perps in Bridgeport or New Haven or White Plains.

Gentry asked Max Schneider to go back a year and check bat assaults in the northeast and up into Canada. Max promised to beep him as soon as he had something.

Ten minutes later, after paying for a sausage and onion pizza at a small shop on Hudson Street and Eleventh, Joyce and Gentry were on their way to the detective's apartment.

Eighteen

Nancy seemed a little more relaxed on the way to Washington Street. That allowed Gentry to stop thinking about her long enough to try and buy the idea that there could be a big bat under the streets of New York. Not a "giant" bat. That was too much. It was the stuff of fairy tales, like a dragon or a centaur or a flying horse. A "big" bat was like a python or a great white shark or a condor. Though it was a hell of a lot more than you wanted to meet in the woods or on a beach or on a hillside, it wasn't something that defied reason.

But even "big" bothered him, and his mind continually returned to logical explanations. A psychotic or sociopathic killer, as Lieutenant Kilar had said. Cultists. Prohunting radicals. An animal that had escaped from a zoo, like the big cat that ran free for several days down in Florida a year or so back. Or even like the ostrich that got its feathers up somewhere in South Africa and killed a woman by raking her to death with its claws. Gentry still wasn't entirely convinced that this wasn't the work of a mountain lion.

Yet Nancy and certainly her mentor believed in the big bat. Gentry could still hear Lowery responding, "Such as?" when Nancy said there had to be another explanation. He seemed so confident. Hell, maybe he was. Gentry didn't like the man, but he hadn't liked a lot of people, starting with the street scum he used to use as informants. Not liking them didn't make them wrong.

Thinking about dragons led Gentry to dinosaurs, and something suddenly occurred to him.

"Nancy," he said, "if there is a big bat, could it possibly be a throwback of some kind? I remember when I was a kid reading about a prehistoric fish that somebody found. It was about five or six feet long, ugly-looking thing. And it was still alive."

"That was different," Joyce said. "The fish was a coelacanth. It was discovered off South Africa in 1938."

"But it was prehistoric."

"Not exactly. It wasn't a product of genetic declension. It was an animal that was thought to be extinct but had simply gone unchanged since prehistoric times."

"Got it. Like cockroaches."

"Exactly like cockroaches. Science comes across those once in a while, like the Blewitt's owl that was thought extinct for over a century and was found a year ago in the woods of India, alive and well."

"That's too bad, about the fish. I thought I had something."

"Evolution doesn't work in reverse," Joyce said. "Elephants don't suddenly become woolly mammoths and cats don't become saber-toothed tigers. Once an attribute is discarded, it stays discarded."

"But didn't someone find woolly mammoths frozen somewhere in Siberia?" Gentry asked. "Weren't they perfectly preserved and didn't people even eat the meat?"

Joyce smiled slightly. It was a warmer smile than before. "Did you also read that when you were a kid?"

"As a matter of fact, I did. I read a lot back then. Books, comics, baseball card backs, cereal boxes. My mother left home, my dad worked, and we had shitty TV reception."

"You also said something like that back at Grand Central. About loving to learn things when you were a kid."

"I did love to learn. That's one reason I became a cop. To follow clues. Figure things out."

"Well, the thing about the mammoths is that they were dead. Even so, the fossil record doesn't show anything resembling a giant bat. Like cockroaches and the coelacanth, bats have been around for more than fifty million years in more or less the form that you see them now."

Gentry was silent again. This left him where he started, and his mind went looking for sensible explanations.

"Genetic drift is a possibility," Joyce said, thinking aloud.

"Which is?"

"New animals sometimes evolve when a species splits into two or more new forms. That sometimes happens due to geographical isolation. Genetic recombination is also a possibility."

"Is that the same as recombinant DNA?" Gentry said.

"Yes," Joyce said. "It's genetic engineering performed by nature. Sometimes chromosomes inherited from the parents swap segments because of physical breakage."

"Because of——?"

"Could be a number of things. Radiation. Chemicals. Internal mechanisms we don't understand. That can set up all new hereditary patterns."

"How long does genetic recombination usually take?"

"It can happen quickly or it can take years. Two parents under six feet tall can produce a child seven to eight feet tall. Or the height of humans can increase steadily over centuries. There are no rules."

They reached Gentry's apartment building. The front door was propped open with a wedge. One exterminator was spraying the hallway, another was in Mrs. Bundonis's apartment. The scent was like mildew. Gentry walked in holding the large pizza. Joyce was right behind him holding her nose.

"How's it look?" Gentry asked the woman spraying in the corridor.

"Like your usual *cucaracha* infestation," the middle-aged woman said as she continued spraying.

"Usual?"

"Hit-and-hide. They've got legs designed for running and antennae that tell them where to run. Toward food, away from danger. They pour into a place and then they seem to disappear. But they haven't. They're hiding in every damn place you can think of. In drains and behind cabinets and under refrigerators or stoves or toilets. They're also in some places you wouldn't think of, like Mr. Coffee filter pots and inside computer printers."

"Did you ever hear of a swarm this size?"

"I never see a swarm of any size. I usually get someplace after most of them are hiding."

"Right," Gentry said. "But have you *heard* of one? Why would they swarm in the thousands?"

"Roaches are funny. They find all kinds of reasons to move around. A change in temperature, a flood, a food shortage—"

"Predators?"

"Oh, yeah."

"Bats?"

The exterminator shrugged. "Why not? I found some kinda foul dung down in the basement. Could've been guano."

"Any idea how bats might have gotten in there?" Gentry asked.

"There's a drain in the floor down there," the exterminator told him. "Looks like it once emptied into the river, probably as part of an old sewage system. I found it when I saw cockroaches coming out from under an old desk and moved it. The metal drain cover was rusted. This close to the water, everything rusts. Your super'll have to get that taken care of. Maybe bats or even seagulls found a nest of roaches near the river and started feeding on them. One nest spills into another, that one into another—pretty soon you have a stampede."

Gentry thanked the woman. Then he and Joyce squeezed by her.

When they reached the apartment, Gentry handed Joyce the pizza and pulled his keys from his pocket. "This place was not exactly clean when I left."

Gentry stepped into the short hallway and switched on the light. The first impression wasn't as bad as he expected. Ahead, in the small living room, the blinds were up and the sunlight made things seem a little cleaner. And he'd thrown out the Thai food he'd been eating, so the cockroaches wouldn't get it. To the right, the bedroom door was shut. The detective took the pizza back, then held it high so Joyce could enter. She walked in and he kicked the door shut with his foot. He watched her slender form as she moved ahead, framed by the bright window.

"Very sunny," she said.

Joyce turned around in the living room and then faced him. He couldn't see her expression, but he could feel her eyes. His breath came a little faster, and he felt a kind of longing that he hadn't experienced in a very long time. He turned away—not to avoid the feeling but to freeze-frame it.

He walked into a small kitchenette to the left and put the pizza on a tiny drop-leaf table. "Where do you live?"

"Up in the Bronx."

"Is it pretty safe where you are?"

"Very. I carry a thirty-eight when I go to work. Licensed and loaded."

Gentry shot her an approving look. Not because she was a lady with a gun but because she was smart.

"You take it to a firing range, keep it in good shape?"

"Oh, yeah. I grew up with guns. The thirty-eight was a high school graduation present from my dad."

"We'll have to go shooting sometime."

"That might be fun."

Gentry went back to the pizza. He wasn't thinking about bats just then. A lot of longings were coming back.

He pulled a cookie sheet from under the sink and aluminum foil from a cabinet. "How long have you been at the zoo?"

"Going on three years."

"I bet there's a lot of competition for jobs like that. Curators and heads of departments, that sort of thing."

"It's pretty intense." Joyce's voice had dropped a little and she did not elaborate. She ambled toward the computer, then turned back. "Is there anything I can do?"

"Actually, yes," Gentry said. "Boot the computer. Just turn on the surge protector under the desk—everything else'll come on."

Joyce bent over the folding chair. The surge protector was lying on its side on the floor amid a cluster of dust bunnies. She switched it on. The computer and monitor snapped to life.

Joyce got onto the Internet and typed in two keywords: *bat* and *anomalies.* She sat back as Gentry put the pizza in the oven, then poured Cokes for them both.

The first list of ten articles and Web sites popped up after a few seconds. Joyce scanned the headings. The first article was about bats that had recently been lured from caves to farms in Colorado in the spring and so far ate nineteen million rootworms, saving a fortune in pesticides. There were also articles on the reproductive habits of the world's smallest bats, on bats that lived more than twenty-five years, and on tiger moths that emitted high-frequency clicks that disoriented attacking bats and forced them to break off their attacks.

"Anything?" Gentry asked as he brought the Cokes over.

"I've seen most of these," she said. "Nothing helpful unless you want the latest information on the bumblebee bat."

"Which is?"

"The world's tiniest mammal," she said. "From Thailand. Smaller than a penny."

"Why couldn't we have been infested with those bats?"

"Because then you're really be miserable," Joyce replied. "I had one fly in my ear while I was sleeping. You think a mosquito at night is bad? Bumblebee bats buzz and bite and leave very tiny, wet droppings that run into your ear canal and harden very, very fast. Not fun."

"But you love them," Gentry said.

"From behind a net, I love them very much."

Gentry went back to the kitchenette and slipped the pizza from the oven. He came over with two slices on a plate and a shirt pocket full of crumpled paper napkins. He pushed aside the stack of magazines and set the plate down next to the keyboard. Then he went and got his own plate and sat on the iron radiator beside the desk. He placed a napkin alongside Joyce's plate.

She asked the computer for a second list of articles. She sat back and took a bite of pizza. "What about you?"

"What about me?" Gentry asked.

"How long have you been in the West Village?"

"Five years."

She took a swallow of Coke and a second bite of pizza. "I had the impression—I don't know why—that police officers liked to get out of the city when their shift was finished."

"Some do," Gentry said. "Mostly the married ones. I've got a car in case I need to get away. But I was born and raised down here, on Perry Street. I did the suburbs thing when I got married. After the divorce, I came back. It's where I want to be."

The second list came up on the monitor, and Joyce began scrolling through the headings. Gentry leaned forward so that he was closer to the monitor. There were articles about fishing bats that can detect a minnow's fin sticking two millimeters above a pond's surface. Frog-eating bats that identify the edible from the poisonous by listening to the mating calls of the male frogs. Gentry kept his head facing forward, but his eyes shifted toward Joyce.

She clicked on the third list. "How long were you married, if you don't mind my asking?"

"I don't mind," he said. "Eight years. To Priscilla Nicole Francis. She was a bank teller I met on my beat. We bought a little house in Norwalk, Connecticut. She wanted a family, a real life. But after I went undercover I saw her maybe two or three nights a week. And I was kind of a drag to be with even then. Obsessed with the guy I was trying to bring down. I don't blame her for leaving."

"Do you still talk to her?"

He shook his head. "She remarried, to an up-and-coming

branch manager up there. They have a big house and a little daughter. I'm not really a part of any of that."

His voice had become wistful, though he wasn't aware of that until Joyce looked down at her lap.

"Sorry," she said. "I shouldn't be asking these things."

"It's okay," Gentry assured her. "I don't get to talk to people much, except to tell them to calm down or fill out a form or get me a report."

"Or get out of a tunnel."

"Or get out of a tunnel," he agreed.

"I've got the same problem," the young woman said with a little laugh. "I spend so much time looking after the bats at the zoo or telling school groups about them or keeping up on current literature and research that I actually forget how to talk to people sometimes."

Gentry's pager beeped while she was speaking. He looked down. "That's the Stat Unit."

"Do you need me to get off the Net?"

"No, I've got a second line." Gentry walked toward the kitchen and punched in the number. "By the way," he said. "You may not be around people much, but I've enjoyed the time we've spent together. Even the rough spots."

Even across the apartment Gentry could see her pale cheeks flush. She thanked him.

The conversation with the head of the Stat Unit was short, and Gentry didn't bother writing anything down. He hung up and walked back.

"Well?" Joyce asked.

"There isn't a lot to report. The only other bat attack they found that was like the others happened in New Paltz. That's about, what—thirty or forty miles west of the Hudson?"

"Something like that. What happened?"

"Three days ago a group of hikers in the Catskill Mountains got blitzed," he said. "They had to jump into a pond and stay underwater."

"Are they all right?"

"Except for cuts and never wanting to go back there, yes. They said the bats left them alone after about fifteen minutes."

"That was about how long the attack lasted at the Little League game," Joyce said. She drummed the desktop. "So we've got three attacks that lead toward New York. Aggressive bat behavior that is localized in time and place."

"No big bats," Gentry said. "Not in the three reports, anyway."

"Well," Joyce said, "like an old geometry teacher of mine used to say, a point is just a point. But two points make a line and three points make a plane and a plane is something you can stand on. After we finish going through these articles, we'll take a look at what we've got in the pattern of those bat attacks."

Joyce finished reading the third list of bat anomalies and clicked on the fourth and last collection. She took another bite of pizza while it downloaded.

As the headings appeared, Gentry bent closer and read along with Joyce. Once again, he forgot about the bats.

Priscilla used to joke, and then complain, that when he would come home he would always want sex. However tired he was, however unclean inside or out. What she never understood was that he needed her. He needed the sanity and beauty that she alone brought to his life. He needed to be reborn and reassured that those things did exist. Intimacy was the only way he knew to take that in perfectly. Soft words spoken close to the cheek, a soft touch, a soft breath. Sex was a transfusion of all that was good and wholesome and healthy in her to all that was worn out and spoiled and dead in him.

Maybe that was too much responsibility to put on any one person. But that was what he needed. And right now, for the first time in a very long time, he wanted that kind of closeness again. He was both relaxed and excited by the warmth of Nancy's bare neck and cheek. By the scent coming from her, not perfume but the slightly musky smell of dried sweat and fear that was almost like the smell of sex. By the smoothness of the flesh behind her ear. In a perfect world, where he could stop time and steal an indulgent moment without fear of rejection, he would touch that soft skin with his lips.

"Can you see okay?" she asked. She slid the chair to the left.

"Just fine," he replied.

The moment was gone, but it had been filed away with the others. He backed up a little.

"Now here's something I haven't seen," she said.

Gentry looked at the computer as she pointed to one of the items.

"A follow-up report from the town of Chelyabinsk in Siberia." Joyce clicked on the file and finished her pizza while she waited for it to download. The article appeared a minute later. It was a week-old posting from the *International Journal of Pediatrics*. "That's why I never saw it," Joyce said. "I usually just stick to the bat sites."

The paper was by radiation specialist Dr. Andrew Lipman. Lipman wrote in a preface that he'd returned to the Russian city on Lake Karachai where, just over eight years before, children had suffered from moderate radiation sickness at a newly opened camp near the lake. Accompanying a team of Russian scientists, he'd found leaking canisters of waste that had been buried years before by a secret munitions plant in nearby Kopeysk.

"'However,'" Joyce read, "'the illness suffered by the children was not due to the waste itself, which had been buried deep inside a cave two years before. It was due to radioactive bat guano that was found in the water. The guano was produced by bats that had been living in the cave and depositing droppings in a river that fed the lake.'"

"Radioactive waste," Gentry said. "That could've caused some seriously screwed-up chromosomes."

"Yes," Joyce said, "but around eight thousand miles away."

"You said bats migrate. Is there any way they could have flown here from Russia?"

"No."

"But radiation could cause serious mutations."

"Theoretically yes. If it didn't kill the bats. But it's still a huge, huge leap from finding radioactive guano in a lake in Russia eight years ago to what we're seeing here."

"That may be a huge leap in zoology," Gentry said. "In my line of work we call it a 'two-p'—poor prospect. But sometimes poor prospects pay off, even if it's only to send you in a direction you hadn't thought about. Maybe we should find this Dr. Lipman and ask him if there was anything unusual about the bats."

"I suppose it's worth a call."

"Does the article tell you anything about him?"

"There's usually a short biography at the end." Joyce scooted to the bottom of the posting. "It says he's a pediatrician who's done work around the world under the auspices of the United Nations Children's Fund. That was why he went to Siberia when they had the problem with the sick kids. It also says that he has a—" She stopped.

"What's wrong?" Gentry asked.

She pointed. Gentry looked at the rest of the bio. It said Dr. Lipman had a practice in New Paltz.

"That's got to be a coincidence," Joyce said.

"Maybe," Gentry said. "Or maybe he brought back samples."

"Jesus," Joyce said. "But even if he did, going from radioactive guano to completely aberrational bat behavior is a big step. And that was more than ten years ago."

"I meant that maybe Lipman brought back samples of the bats."

Joyce looked up at him. She didn't say anything.

"Let's call Dr. Lipman," Gentry said. "Just to find out. Just to make sure nothing strange went on."

Gentry called information, got the number of the office, and called. It would take just under two hours to drive to New Paltz. They made an appointment to see Dr. Lipman at six o'clock. Then they cabbed up to Gentry's garage on West Forty-sixth Street, picked up his car, and headed north.

Nineteen

Nancy Joyce felt herself winding down as she sat in Gentry's Cutlass. The running, the long hours, the thinking. Being stonewalled by the lieutenant and his rat catcher.

And the anger. Gentry and Lieutenant Kilar had both drilled in the same deep, rich oil field and gotten a gusher.

She was tired inside and out. But that was to be expected. What was unexpected was what came with the exhaustion. As Gentry picked his way through the moderately heavy afternoon traffic on the West Side Highway—he didn't grumble at the other cars the way she would have—Joyce found herself slipping into an unexpected contentment. The horrors of the day hadn't left her. But there was a welcome familiarity to at least one part of it: being back in the field. And this time it was not with a man she revered and feared, but someone who was more of an equal. A partner.

A companion?

Joyce opened her eyes wide to snap away the reverie and get off that track. She had known Gentry half a day. And it hadn't been love at first or second sight. But she couldn't shake the surprising awareness she felt of the man next to her. If there wasn't exactly a magnetic pull, there wasn't a desire to go anywhere either. And for her, Ms. Camp

Alone, Stay at Home, that was something truly different and a little unsettling.

"You can go ahead and shut your eyes if you want," Gentry said.

"Pardon?"

"I saw you start to doze a little."

"No," she said. "I'm fine."

He nodded. "If you want music there are a bunch of tapes in the glove compartment. I don't know if it's your taste, but you can look."

Joyce popped open the door and looked in at the tossed-in collection. "This reminds me of the way I used to store tapes of Professor Lowery's lectures. You have any preferences?"

"Anything's fine. It's all fifties and sixties rock."

"No seventies and eighties, huh?"

"Nope. Sorry."

"That was my era," Joyce said. "Queen. Prince. Michael Jackson."

"The King of Pop. All the royalty."

"You got it." Joyce began looking through the only occasionally labeled tapes.

"I used to like them too," Gentry said. "But when I was undercover, this guy we were trying to bring down always listened to contemporary rock in the car. His favorite was the Police, which I guess was kind of ironic. Now it's one of those association things. I can't listen to any of that music without thinking of the son of a bitch."

"Why did you give up undercover work?" Joyce asked.

"Because I was burned out. I was pretty close to quitting anyway."

"Anyway?"

"Yeah. Even if it weren't for what happened to Bernie Michaelson. My junior partner."

"What did he do to drive you out?"

"Exactly what I told him," Gentry said.

Joyce frowned. "You lost me."

"Never mind. It's a long story."

"That's what you said when you called before," she replied. "It's a long drive. I'm interested in hearing about it if you feel like talking."

Gentry looked at her. "I'll make a deal with you. I'll tell you mine if you tell me yours."

"Mine?"

"Whatever it was you said I had no idea about back at the hospital."

"I'm still not following—"

"What you said I didn't know the half of. When you told me about SDS."

"Sorry. No deal," she said emphatically. Then she added, slightly softer, "I can't, Robert. I'm not sure I could even articulate it all. I'm not sure I *understand* it."

Gentry turned his eyes back to the road. Joyce resumed going through the tapes, but her mind wasn't on them. She understood this much: men always *pushed*. Why? Because they wanted to help or because knowledge gave them some kind of control—

"Bernie Michaelson was my partner for seven years," Gentry said suddenly.

Joyce stopped shuffling the cassettes. She looked over. His hands were squirming slowly around the wheel.

"All he ever wanted to be was a cop. Son of cop, grandson of cop, that kind of thing. He started out as my ghost—someone who covers an undercover cop when he's making buys in the street. See, when you're undercover you can't wear a bulletproof vest. It's bulky, and if you get patted down you're screwed. The ghost stays until you're clear of the scene or makes the buy if you don't show. Mizuno, this guy we'd been after for years, spent the summers in Colombia and the winters in Bridgeport, Connecticut. He stayed at home every night during basketball season and watched the game. Every night, no exceptions. We finally had the goods on him—audiotapes, fingerprints, bank account numbers, paper trail—and arranged with the cops up there to pick a night for the pinch. On the night we picked, the Knicks were getting creamed so Mizuno decided to go out and see his girl in Fairfield. His two bodyguards got up to start the car and make sure the coast was clear. This is two minutes before the Bridgeport narc squad is due to move in. If the guys had left then, they would have seen the strike team taking up positions on the lawn and outside the doors. We have to keep everyone where they were, in front of the TV, for two more minutes.

"This Mizuno happened to like my sense of humor. So I told him he had to wait and listen to this joke I'd heard. I told the bodyguards I needed their help, it was a visual. I was going to make something up, some story. But Mizuno wasn't in the mood. He told the guys to go ahead, and then he started to get out of his chair. I was standing between him and the TV. The front door was a few steps to my left. Bernie was sitting in the chair next to Mizuno. We looked at each other. There was nothing to do but try to take the three of them down ourselves and have the narc guys back us up.

"I nodded toward Bernie and then toward Mizuno. I was going to go after the other two. Bernie nodded back. The problem was, we weren't allowed to wear guns around the boss. So I had to get one from the bodyguard who was coming toward me, and Bernie had to get Mizuno's. Bernie moved when I did. I succeeded. Bernie didn't. Mizuno shot him in the chest and leg. I nailed the bastard in the shoulder before I turned back to deal with the bodyguards. The narcs came in then and cleaned up. Bernie died en route to the hospital. I got out of the narc business a couple of weeks later. Commissioner Veltre shifted me over to Accident Investigations. Important, but a little less stressful."

Joyce had been sitting still. The glove compartment was still open. "Robert, I'm sorry."

He nodded.

"I can't even imagine what that was like."

"It was pretty bad for a while," he admitted. "Now it comes and goes, though I go through the drill almost every day—the should'ves and could'ves and why did I do this instead of that. I can't shake the idea that the narc squad might've been able to handle it without us. That maybe the best thing would have been for Bernie and me to do nothing."

"Maybe then it would have gone worse than it did."

"It's possible," Gentry admitted. "At least, that's what my new best friend Father Adams in the Chaplain Unit's been trying to tell me for six months now. He and I get together every other week for a spirited spiritual exchange. But this is pretty thick," he tapped his skull, "and what's inside is still telling me that I blew it. That's the reason you and I had out little to-do back in the tunnel. I love working with people. Always have. With my sources in the street way back when, with other detectives, with my forensics guys, even with our sorry goddamn softball team. I like working with you. But if something happens to anyone else I'm with, it's going to be an accident or an act of God. It's not going to be because I didn't look out for the people who were with me."

The car continued along the Hudson River. Sunlight and pleasure boats skipped across the waters. Joyce closed the glove compartment without selecting a tape. Her eyes drifted ahead to the George Washington Bridge.

"Everybody screws up," she said. "Sometimes it happens when you think you're doing the right thing. When you'd absolutely swear it. When you've thought about it, and gone back and forth about it, and had *weeks* to decide, not seconds. This field—the curatorships, the associate curatorships, the directorships, the assistant directorships—is every bit as competitive as you said it is. There are about fifty Ph.D.'s for every available position. If you manage to get one of those you can really vindicate yourself. Say 'fuck you' to all the people who thought you were crazy as a kid for liking what you did. For dreaming of being a circus aerialist or running cruises along the Amazon."

"Or devoting your life to bats."

"That too. But if you make a deal that gets you the vindication but costs you self-respect, it's worse than a wash. You never know if you could have done it without the deal. Or if failing on your own would have been better."

"Lowery," Gentry said.

Joyce nodded. She felt tears behind her eyes.

"I'm sorry I started this," Gentry said, "You don't have to—"

"I want to." She laughed and wept. "Hey, I'm crazy. Resentful one second, blubbering my heart out the next. But you did something not too many people do. You changed what you wanted to suit me. And then you trusted me with something very private. That gets to a girl faster than showing her your guano. Which, by the way, you never did."

Gentry smiled.

"Yeah," she sighed. "Professor Lowery. He was my mentor and he was my first lover."

Gentry's smile lost some of its glow.

"I fell for him big-time," she went on. "He was curator of the museum back then, curator emeritus now. Loves research. Controlled experiments. I thought, when we started our affair, that he was trying to help me reach my potential. And part of him was. Then I started to suspect he was trying to work some kind of "thing" through me. Like Eliza Doolittle. Take an unlikely student—a moody, introspective kid not from a rich or proper family and make her the top figure in her field. Give her the tools, the tutoring, the experiences no one else has. Take her around the world and make sure her papers are published in all the right journals, even if you don't agree with them." She snickered. "We had a big argument over the question of whether bats have rudimentary emotions. But he got behind my paper anyway."

"Because it wasn't about science," Gentry said. "None of this was."

"No. You're right. It was about ego. Make her a successful woman in a man's profession and it's your legacy. *Your* legacy, not hers. I went with the flow because I wanted to get where the river was going. And I was afraid to tell this towering figure, 'Wait a second.' But when you get there and look back, you realize that even though you know your stuff and may in fact be the best, you don't *feel* like it. So I'm a big shot in the bat world. A successful woman. *The* bat lady. But inside I'm Lowery's girl. And the worst part of it is, I still kowtow. Which I guess you saw."

"Yeah," Gentry said. "The 'Nannie' was kind of a giveaway. But it's not too late, you know."

"To tell him off?"

"Not in a rude way," Gentry said. "But you don't have to be so deferential either. I think that hurts you. It's also better than getting mad at everyone else you think might be trying to control you."

"I don't know if that'd solve things, Robert. Besides, part of the problem—the biggest part—is that I still care about Professor Lowery. I don't love him and I'm not sure I ever did. But I don't want to hurt him."

They were quiet for a moment. Then Gentry shrugged a shoulder. "Well, this was none of my business to begin with. And I do want to thank you."

"For what?"

"Trusting me," he said.

"You're welcome," she said. "Now I think we've had enough soul baring. How about some music?"

She selected a tape at random and slugged it into the cassette player.

Two hours later, with the sun setting along the Catskills, with their life stories having been told, with the Association and Simon and Garfunkel and Gary Puckett and the Union Gap having turned through the player, Gentry and Joyce arrived in New Paltz.

Twenty

Dr. Lipman's practice was located in a series of rooms in the back of his country home.

The three-story stone house was more than one hundred years old, situated near the Walkill River on seven thickly treed acres. The pediatrician had just begun examining his last patient when Joyce and Gentry pulled up the long, sloping gravel driveway. A young male receptionist invited them to sit in the waiting room, but they chose to go outside, behind the house. The quiet there was nearly absolute. The canopy of leaves was thick and the rolling grounds were dark. The river moved quietly around a bend, the surface rippling with the last glow of the dying sun. It was like a fairy tale forest, Joyce thought. And unlike the night before—she was happy to note—there were insects and unobtrusive bats.

"It's weird how the bats are behaving themselves," Gentry said. "Very."

"It reminds me of kids who used to get strung out. As long as they had their fix they were fine."

"I'd guess any addictive substance is like that," Joyce said. "Nicotine, alcohol."

Gentry picked up a stick and started peeling away the bark. "We could have a very serious problem on our hands, couldn't we?"

She nodded.

"How do you exterminate bats?"

"I've never had to do it," she said, "but I'd say poison or gas. The problem with the New York subways is that there are probably so many outlets, so many places the bats could sneak out. And it's not like rats where you can put out poison pellets. If these bats are all insectivorous, you'd have to poison the bugs first. I don't even know if that's possible. Then there's our giant bat. If it exists, it would probably be very fast and powerful."

"It's powerful, all right," Gentry said.

She gave him a look.

"Remember those hatch marks on the grate at Grand Central?" he said. "If there's a big bat, it may have left hanging upside down."

"Bats do that."

"Yeah, but like you said, holding up that much weight would take a lot of muscle."

"It would," Joyce agreed, "though it also could have been crawling along the roof using its feet and first fingers. Those are the ones located at the top of each wing. Which makes sense," she added. "The bat would have fed, crawled back into the tunnel, and left the guano mound after that. It's digestive system would have been stimulated after flying and eating."

When they heard a car pull away they walked back to the office. When they entered, Dr. Lipman was talking to his receptionist.

"Be with you two in a minute," he said pleasantly.

Andy Lipman looked as though he was in his early sixties. He was chunky and stood about five-foot-seven. He had a round face, a wide mouth, and lively eyes beneath thick brown eyebrows. His skin was dark from the sun, and he was bald save for a ring of short, light-brown hair. He had on a red bow tie, a white shirt, and jeans that were a little snug in the waist.

Lipman thanked the receptionist, told him to go home, then walked across the waiting room. He offered his hand.

"When you called," he said to Joyce, "I didn't realize you were Dr. Joyce of the Bronx Zoo. I took the liberty of having Warren look you up on the Net. You've published a great deal."

"Yes, sir."

"I always talk to my kids when they come in here," he said. "Ask them what they've been doing. A couple of them have come in talking about the tours they had with the 'bat lady.'"

"That's me," she said.

Lipman's eyes shifted to Gentry.

"Detective Robert Gentry," he said, "NYPD."

"Pleased to meet you. And also curious." He motioned toward a well-worn couch. "Sit down. Tell me what I can do for you."

Joyce sat. Gentry remained standing. Lipman slipped into an armchair at a right angle to the sofa.

"Doctor," said Joyce, "did you hear about the bat attack last night at the Little League game?"

"I did."

"There have been several incidents like that over the past few days," Joyce said. "The first was in New Paltz several days ago. The latest was this morning in New York—deadlier than all the others, I'm afraid."

"I'm very sorry to hear that."

"There was an indication at several of the sites that there may be an oversized specimen of vespertilionid bat. A mutation. After reading your paper, we wondered if there might be a connection between the bats you encountered in Russia and the bats we're seeing here."

"What we need to know, sir," Gentry said, "is whether you brought anything back from either trip to Siberia. Something that might have affected the bat population in some way?"

Lipman regarded Gentry. "Should I send for my attorney?"

"Doctor," Joyce said quickly, "this isn't an official inquiry. We're not interested in placing blame. We're simply trying to isolate a problem by tracing it to its source."

Lipman folded his hands in his lap. "The source of the problem is selfishness. Doing what is expedient. Russia, the Soviet Union, was very good at that. Did you ever hear of Dzerzhinsk?"

Joyce said she hadn't. Gentry shook his head.

"It's a city of three hundred thousand people, two hundred fifty miles east of Moscow. For forty years toxic gases were manufactured in factories there. Blister and mustard gas, rocket fuel, DDT—everything. When the Soviet Union shut down, do you know what was done with the poison that had not been distributed? It was buried. Rusted, bloated barrels were buried right there in the soil. I was called in when thousands of children became ill. And what do you suppose was causing the illnesses? Coal. Coal that was being burned in the homes. Coal that had absorbed lethal levels of dioxin while it was still in the ground." He snickered. "The Russian solution to the problem was not to try and clean up the city. No. It was, 'Don't burn coal from here,' or, 'Don't eat food grown here.' It was pathetic."

"You couldn't have been surprised," Joyce said. "The Soviets didn't admit there was a problem at Chernobyl until high radiation levels were detected in Sweden."

"I wasn't surprised," Lipman said. "Just sad for the people. Their solution to the radiation at the Chelyabinsk site was the same. Contain and downplay. So I would know how to treat the children, I tried to find out if there were anything else buried in that cave, any chemical barrels like the ones in Dzerzhinsk. But no one even *knew.* They simply didn't care."

"A toxicological soup," Joyce said.

"Nearly half a century old," Lipman remarked. "And who knows where else in the world there are similar 'soups'? China, Iraq, other sites in the former Soviet Union—maybe even the United States, God help us. The potential for ecological catastrophe is enormous. But getting back to Chelyabinsk, during my first visit there, the Russian military eradicated all the bats in the cave. There were thousands of them. Tens of thousands. I didn't see the colony myself, but I heard that they were not . . . normal."

"In what way?" Joyce asked.

"One of the soldiers who went into the cave said that some of them, in what looked like the nursery, had bodies the size of foxes."

"How were the bats destroyed?" Joyce asked.

"The troops used fire, flamethrowers. You could smell the death for more than a mile. The few bats that managed to escape were on fire, squealing. It was awful. The engineers dammed the river inside the cave, sealed the entrance with explosives, and then drained the section of lake near the camp. The water was trucked away, and the lake bed was filled with rocks and soil. The radiation count was negligible, and that was that. Except—" He stopped.

"Go on," Joyce said.

"I stayed on to help the United Nations team treat the children. Most of them were taken to a local clinic for observation. They were suffering from acute radiation syndrome—very, very mild cases that resulted in headaches, nausea and vomiting, malaise. All of them were ambulatory. I kept the children out in the daylight as much as possible. Sometimes, here, I treat my own patients out back. I've always believed in the therapeutic effects of the sun. I had my large medical case with me at all times. You never know what you'll need in a foreign country. Among the things I had in there were dried banana chips. They contain high levels of potassium, a very useful cleansing agent for bodily fluids, and children don't mind eating them—"

"One of the bats got in there," Joyce said.

Lipman steepled this thumbs and tapped them together. His expression was pinched, odd.

"Driven from its home. Hungry. Cold. It got in your case."

"I wasn't with the case at all times," Lipman admitted. "Sometimes I walked away with the children. I didn't think—didn't know."

"What happened?" Joyce passed.

Lipman looked down. "When I came home, the bag flew with

me in the cabin and was not inspected at customs. One of the perks of charity work. I put it in the backseat of the car, and because I got home very late, I left it there until the next morning. When I got it, I smelled something funny, so I opened the case. The banana chips were gone and there were feces in the bag. I moved my instruments aside and took out my journal. A bat was lying on its back beneath it."

"What did it look like?" Joyce asked.

"Like nothing I'd have wanted my kids to see." Lipman rubbed his mouth. "It was misshapen. The body was large, muscular, all shoulders, legs, and belly. The head was difficult to see because it was tucked low against the chest. But the mouth was extremely wide and the eyes were red and protruding—like the large marbles children used to play with. The ears were high, but I couldn't see them clearly. The wings were folded against its side, but I remember there was a very long hook on top of each wing.

"That's digit one," Joyce said. "The thumb."

"What happened to the bat?" Gentry asked.

"When I saw it, I was startled," Lipman said. "I jumped away and the bag spilled over. The bat crawled out."

"It didn't fly?" Joyce asked.

"No."

"Had the wings been hurt in the fire?"

"They didn't seem to be, but I never saw them spread. The bat crept along the carpet, right here," he said. "It was maybe nine or ten inches long and it moved slowly, arduously."

"But it never spread its wings?" Joyce asked.

"No. I wanted to help the poor thing. But when I walked toward it, it vaulted up to the window there"—he pointed to a double window above the couch—"tore through the screen, and jumped out. By the time I went outside, it was gone."

"Do you have any idea where?"

"I didn't then," he said. "I called the wildlife commissioner and told him there was something potentially dangerous out by the Walkill. I wasn't worried about it being radioactive, but just something alien in the wild. They searched for it up and down the river but found nothing. I didn't know what happened to it until about a month later."

"What did happen?" Gentry asked.

"Some hikers found it up the road a way. It was dead. They took a picture of it. I saw the photo in the wildlife section of the local newspaper, and it was unmistakably that bat. Same face, same general build, though it was somewhat desiccated from having been out in the sun. There was one difference, though."

"It was no longer as bloated as it had been," Joyce said.

Lipman looked at her. "That's right. How did you know?"

"Because," she said, "it was no longer pregnant."

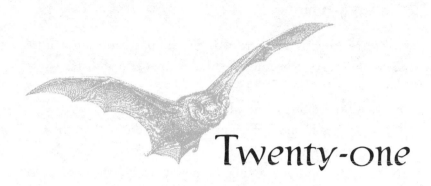

Twenty-one

I have a question," Gentry said.

The detective was driving slowly through the early evening dark. The sky was blue-black, and a very bright, clear star was already up in the northwest. Gentry's goal was a wooded area just off of Route 32 North. Located nearly a mile northeast of Dr. Lipman's home, that was where the newspaper article said the dead bat had been found. Gentry didn't know what Nancy expected to find there some eight years later, and she didn't say. But he agreed that since they were in the area it was probably worth a look.

The young woman was sitting with her knees up against the dashboard. She was holding a rough map the pediatrician had drawn for them on a sheet of prescription paper.

"It's Jupiter," Joyce said.

"Pardon?"

"The planet outside your window."

"What about it?"

"I saw you looking at it. I thought you were going to ask if I knew what it was."

"No, that wasn't my question. My dad had been in the navy—he used to point out all the planets and stars."

Joyce grew slightly embarrassed. She slumped forward a little, into her knees. "Sorry," she said. "I shouldn't have done that."

"Done what?"

"Assumed you didn't know what that was."

"Oh, come on. It's no different from what I did back in the subway, telling you about the third rail."

"Not many people go walking on subway tracks," she said. "A lot of people look up at the sky."

"I didn't," Gentry said. "That's why my dad made a point of telling me about it. About Jupiter and Venus and Orion and Polaris. I was a gutter kid. Bounced balls against the curb, swirled sticks in puddles, fished things out of grates. So ease up on yourself."

She seemed to, a little.

"If you really want to depress me," Gentry said, "you'll know off the top of your head how far it is from the sun."

She laughed. "About half a billion miles."

Gentry made a face.

"Hey, I used to be outside a lot at night," Joyce said. "I wondered about these things so I looked 'em up."

"You're amazing," Gentry said.

"Actually, Robert, what I am is a goddamn smarty-pants. All the kids used to say that."

"Hump 'em. They were jealous."

"No, they were kids. Two-legged pack animals. Anyway I don't want to talk about that. What was your question?"

"What I wanted to know was about radiation. Why is it that radioactivity sometimes causes mutations in living things but at other times it kills them?"

"It has to do with the levels of exposure different cells receive," Joyce said. "Back in grad school I took a course on the radiogenic effects of artificial and natural toxins on living tissue."

"Smarty-pants," he teased.

"I took it pass-fail," she grinned. "A lot of the physics and chemistry was over my head. But basically there are four ways radiation affects living things. Acute somatic or bodily effects, serious somatic effects, developmental effects, and genetic effects. They depend pretty much on the intensity of the irradiation and the ability of the irradiated tissue to replace damaged cells. For example, skin or the lining of the intestine recovers relatively quickly from low-level exposure, while the hair, eyes, and brain don't recover at all. Rapidly developing fetal tissue—in which the damaged cells can cause a cascade effect that creates damaged cells—are particularly susceptible to radioactivity."

"Okay, I think I've got that. So let's talk about our big bat. What's a bat's gestation period?"

"From three to six months."

"And how many babies do they have in a litter?"

"Normal bats don't have litters. They have one or two pups per birth. This particular vespertilionid, I don't know. Irradiated cells can divide in strange ways."

"So a high level of exposure could harm a mother and cause mutations in a fetus, but she still might live long enough to carry the pup to term. And the pup might survive."

"Yes."

"But then why wouldn't the pup be radioactive?"

"The radiation isn't passed along to the child," Joyce said. "Only the damage."

"So the mother acts like a filter."

"In a way. But the changes can be geometric. A mutated child can pass even greater changes on to its offspring."

Gentry glanced at her. "So a big bat like the Russian one could conceivably give birth to—"

"An even bigger bat," Joyce said.

"Shit," Gentry said.

"Yeah. Slow down," she said as they neared a dark stretch of road. "Up there."

The route narrowed and ended at a wooded region. Gentry's shoulders heaved and he sighed.

"Y'know, I can accept most of what you said. But I'm not sure I can make the leap of faith to the next part."

"Which part?"

"About one or more large predators living out here, in a small town, without being seen."

"Why not? How often do people see bears up here?"

"That's different."

"You're right," Joyce said. "A bat can fly. It feeds at night. It has a more diverse diet than a bear or a cougar or a deer. It apparently has a much wider range of predation, which would blunt its impact on the local fauna. And it has the Catskills to the west to prowl around in."

"Okay," he said. "It goes unnoticed. Flies too low even to be picked up on airport radar. Then answer one more question."

"I'll try."

"Can you fire a forty-four Magnum?"

She smiled. "Do bats fly?"

"Good. I've got two Ruger Super Blackhawks in the trunk," Gentry said, "and I'm not going mutant bat hunting without them."

They drove for another five minutes before reaching a clearing. There were no other vehicles in the area. Gentry parked and they got out. He removed the two handguns from the well where he stored the tire jack and grabbed a flashlight from the tool chest. When he closed the trunk, the slam of the door sounded disturbingly final.

It had gotten chilly since they left the doctor's house. An insistent breeze stirred the treetops, carrying an early hint of fall and a sense of isolation. Branches groaned softly. Gentry heard a train whistle far off. The detective had gone into crackhouses feeling less anxious than he did now. He knew that kind of enemy. The zoned-out junkie or the quick-on-the-trigger pusher. This was something—*primal* was the word that came to mind.

Stones and dirt crunched underfoot as they hiked up the sloping path. They proceeded slowly at Joyce's insistence. She didn't want to stumble into an "off-limits bat habitat," as she described it, the kind of area the Little Leaguer and his father had entered the evening before. If they did, the plan was that she'd back out immediately and Gentry would help her.

Twigs snapped as animals fled into the underbrush. Gentry kept his eyes ahead. He had the flashlight; Joyce had the lead. He liked the way she looked with the Magnum swinging comfortably alongside her thigh. He liked the way she looked period.

"Check the trees, not just the ground," Joyce said. "In case there are any animal remains up there."

"I am," Gentry said. "Have you seen any bats?"

"Not a one," she said. "Last night there were *only* bats in the woods. Tonight there's everything but."

"So we're wasting our time."

"To the contrary. What I'm saying is that there *should* be bats. I understand how massive bat predation like I found last night could eat up a lot of local animal life and force the remaining bugs or lizards to leave or hide. But I don't understand what could scare away *just* bats and leave everything else—"

She stopped. So did Gentry. She turned around.

"Holy shit."

"What?"

"Robert, what if the bats weren't *frightened* away?"

"I don't understand."

"Think about that path down the Hudson River you were talking about before."

"Yeah?"

"There are no bats here. There were relatively few bats by the time I went into the woods last night. There's a very high bat count in the city subways. What if they're all moving?"

"You mean migrating?"

"No. Moving. In a highly organized fashion."

"Is that possible?"

"Bats communicate," she said, thinking aloud. "We don't know how or to what extent, but we think they're a lot like dolphins in that sense. They send out short, pulselike sounds—'clicks'—that come so fast they sound like high-pitched duck quacks. Bats use those sounds mostly to hunt."

"Echolocation."

"Yes. But deeper in the throat, in the larynx, they generate a very high whistle that can change pitch very quickly. We think those sounds are used to communicate everything from the location of food sources to sexual interest to organizational commands."

"That's very nice," Gentry said. "But why would bats be moving to New York?"

"I don't know. Why do bats move anywhere? Shelter or food."

"Subways and cockroaches."

"There's also other wildlife," Joyce said. "Baby pigeons, mice, rats, fish—New York is a big, rich smorgasbord for bats."

"But so are the Catskills and Westchester and Connecticut. Right?"

Joyce started walking again. "For a normal colony, yes. But what if this one isn't normal?"

She stopped beside a sign that pointed out the various roads and scenic sites in the area. But she wasn't looking at the sign. She was looking at what was behind it. Gentry turned the flashlight in that direction.

There was a red and white iron bar waist-high across another dirt road. In the center was a sign with hours posted on it.

"Landfill," Joyce said.

Gentry shined his light beyond the pole.

"It's perfect," she said. "It's deserted at night. The remains of any animals would be bulldozed under, and the smell of the trash would cover the smell of guano."

"Are we going in there?"

Joyce ducked under the pole.

"I guess so," Gentry said as he followed her in.

They walked for roughly an eighth of a mile down the rutted dirt road. The full moon had risen above the mountains, casting the hills and thickly bunched trees in pale light. The only sounds were the crunch of their shoes on the stones, the leaves stirred by the night air, and now and then an animal fleeing through the underbrush. They moved slowly, Joyce reminding Gentry that the first time a bat came after either of them they were to back away immediately. Gentry understood and said he'd been less anxious raiding apartments when he was a narc. He knew and understood that kind of danger. Plus it was over in a few moments of intense activity. Now, he had no idea what to expect, or when.

When they reached the landfill, the vision was surreal. Crags of refuse, like blue-white lunar mountains, towered over the flat plains of dirt. The jagged peaks threw long, sharp shadows over their own lumpy foothills and across the occasional clumps of trash. Off to the right, near a shed, a bulldozer sat like a sleeping monster.

"Where do you want to look?" Gentry asked.

"I'm not sure." Joyce took the flashlight from him. "I'll just pick a spot."

She walked toward the hills that surrounded the landfill. The nearest slope was about three hundred yards away. When she reached it, she walked slowly along the base, shining the light up through the surrounding trees and then down along the ground.

Gentry stood alone at the entrance to the landfill. Despite the gun, he felt naked.

After several minutes, Joyce stopped in front of a steep section of hill. She looked up and then down. Then she got down on her hands and knees. "Robert?" Her voice seemed very far away.

"Yes?"

"I found something."

Gentry had had a feeling she would. She was like that, this lady. Had a sixth sense like a cop.

He walked quickly to where Joyce was standing. His pace wasn't dictated by fear but sickness; the smell down here was a curious mixture of pine and rot. The sooner he got past the trash, the happier he'd be. He reached the scientist's side and crouched beside her.

"What've you got?" he asked.

She pointed to a deep, damp rut cut by water. There was something dark lining the rut.

"Looks like diluted guano," she said, rubbing some of the muddy black substance between her fingers and smelling it. She shined the light up the hill. "And up there is where it could have come from."

Gentry looked.

Above them, maybe sixty feet, was a very large drain.

Twenty-two

Gentry insisted on leading the way up the hillside.

Joyce didn't argue. She wanted him to feel like he was contributing something other than the guns and the car. And she still felt bad about the Jupiter thing. She wasn't a show-off and she hated coming off like one. Especially to someone who was every bit as professional in his way as she was in hers. Even when he'd kept her from going into the sublevels of Grand Central Station, he hadn't insulted her intelligence or skill.

And Gentry *was* contributing to this, though he probably didn't realize it. He was making her feel like a member of a team, a partner in this search instead of an acolyte. Whenever she went on fieldtrips with Professor Lowery, he pushed her physically and intellectually. His prodding forced her to do things that established new high-water marks for where she could go and what she could accomplish. But they were always lonely experiences because he was looking down from his peak. He never pushed himself, made her feel like she was doing anything for him. That was why she'd allowed the professor to seduce her. It was an effort to bring him closer in a place and at a time of her life when she really needed it: her first year of grad school, her first time overseas. She did it to make him more accessible. Unfortunately, all it did was make her more "his."

Gentry did not seem like that kind of man at all. Even with a gun in his hand, even when he'd been ordering her out of the subway tunnel, there was something gentle about him.

"So let's work this forward from day one," Gentry said as they climbed.

"All right," she said.

"Mama bat gets away from Dr. Lipman. She makes her way to the river. She follows it and gives birth somewhere along the way."

"Not in the open," Joyce said.

"Why not?"

"Because hawks prowl the river. They'd have picked her pup off."

"So the mother finds a quiet, enclosed place to give birth," Gentry said.

"A place close to food and drink," Joyce said.

"What would she have done next?"

"The routine would have been for the mother to look after her pup, then go out to feed. Then one day during the month she didn't come back, probably succumbing to radiation poisoning. She's found relatively soon thereafter, or else scavengers would have picked at her remains."

"Could the baby bat have continued on its own after that?"

"Conceivably, as long as there was water and either insects or vegetation, depending on what kind of bat it was. Bats are pretty self-sufficient pretty early."

"Would it have continued to live alone?"

"Probably not. When male or female bats are in heat they can be very aggressive."

"How often does that happen?"

"In temperate regions that usually happens in the fall. That way they can give birth in the spring or summer when food is relatively populous. My guess is the bat would have tried to join an existing colony. If it was as big as we think, it could very well have taken over a colony."

Gentry reached the drain and stopped. It was difficult to stand there because of the slope, and he was forced to hold on to a tree. He shined the light around the opening.

The drain was about four feet in diameter, and the concrete was nearly green from the minerals in the water.

"This is an old one," Gentry said. "There's a faded WPA logo here."

"WPA?"

"Works Progress Administration. Government projects from the Depression. This was put in to give people work. They probably laid a whole lot of interconnected pipes through the town."

"I see," Joyce said. "So a bat that was born in one of the drains could get around quite a bit. It could listen at other openings, make sure that no one was near, then slip out unseen."

"I suppose so," Gentry said. "But would a bat be smart enough to do that?"

"Not an ordinary bat, no," Joyce said.

"This isn't an ordinary bat," Gentry said. "So in addition to being bigger and stronger than other bats, it might also be smarter."

"Very possibly," Joyce said. "But it wouldn't take intelligence to move around a system of pipes and listen until the coast was clear. That's instinct. Survival. In any case, that could be one reason the bat was never seen."

Cautiously, Gentry leaned across the mouth of the drain. He crinkled his nose. Even several feet below, Joyce could smell the odor coming from inside. It was definitely guano. The detective shined the light through the opening.

He screamed and jumped back.

"What's wrong?" Joyce shouted.

"Cuh-*rist!*" he said.

She clambered up, grabbed the flashlight, and looked inside.

There was a face staring out at them, the face of a sheep. It was just the face; the rest of the body was broken bone and bloody sinew scattered along the length of the drain.

"I'm sorry," Gentry said. "I wasn't expecting that."

"It's okay. I like a guy who's not afraid to scream." She leaned her head into the drain and raised the flashlight. There were long, deep gnaw marks on the sheep bone that resembled those on the deer carcass. She didn't move for several seconds.

"Anything wrong?" Gentry asked.

"It smells like there's guano," Joyce said. She crawled partway in. "There is. It's stuck to the back limbs. Jesus!"

"What?"

"There are two more sheep in there—"

"Bon fucking appetit!"

"—and—oh God!"

"What's wrong?"

"One of them is still alive."

Joyce slid back from the opening and motioned for Gentry to back away. Then she stepped back herself, raised the handgun, and fired into the drain. The clap echoed through the landfill. The sheep hopped back in a splash of red. Joyce lowered the gun.

"Robert," she said, "these animals were freshly killed. The blood is still pretty damp, and the guano is only about two hours old."

"Which means what? The big bat is back?"

"I don't think so," she said ominously. "I think it means the big bat is not alone."

Twenty-three

O*ne day,* thought Adrienne Hart, *the financial district is going to have a night life.*

The young investment banker hated the fact that after the stock market closed and the traders went to the bars and then home, the streets were empty. There were no movie theaters or museums or galleries, the apartments and most of the hotels were farther uptown, and every shop in and around Wall Street went into hibernation until morning. One day, when she had the money, she was going to open a comedy club that would draw people downtown. And she'd be the headliner. Give up the big bucks for the big yuks. After years in this male-dominated world, she had plenty of stories to tell.

Until then, the World Trade Center was a dead-lonely place after hours, and the smooth, swift elevator ride from the sixty-seventh floor was a quiet, eerie, cocoonlike experience.

She looked at her watch and immediately forgot what time it was. It didn't matter. By the time she got her car from the garage, drove back to her town house in New Jersey, and went to bed, it would be midnight. Then she'd be up at five-thirty and on-line to the markets in Tokyo and Hong Kong and London. Except for weekends, when the twenty-six-year-old went down to Philadelphia to see her fiancé, that was her life.

It happened so fast that she barely adjusted to one thing before the next thing hit.

The elevator shuddered violently, slapping her against the side wall. She slid into the corner, lost her briefcase, and put her arms out along the wall to keep from hitting the ground. The car stopped shaking.

Adrienne stood there, not moving, waiting to see what would happen.

A moment later the square door on the top of the car exploded in, shattering the lights, throwing the car into darkness, and *thunking* hard on the floor. The panel ricocheted into her left leg, gashing it just above the knee. The hot pain made Adrienne superalert. She swore and pushed away from the wall.

The car continued to descend as warm air spilled in through the opening. The young woman looked over at the lighted panel. She reached for the red emergency button.

She never got to it.

Something fell into the car. It was large and humid and it soaked up sound. Adrienne could no longer hear the whoosh of the air or the pings of the floor or anything but her own rapid breath. She also couldn't see the panel. Something had blacked it out. All she saw was creeping darkness, ripples of black, then dark brown, then black again.

Then there was red. Directly in front of her. Two fierce orbs that looked like warning lights but couldn't be, because what would they be doing right in front of her?

Adrienne turned to the right and reached out again, frantically trying to find the panel. She touched something that felt like satin. It was thin and soft and rippling. It was also moving closer. The woman wondered what the hell could have fallen through—

As the elevator eased to the bottom of the shaft, Adrienne suddenly felt a terrible pressure under each armpit. She stopped moving.

She *couldn't* move. It reminded her of when she was a kid on crutches—only the crutches were reversed. The pointy end was being driven up. She seemed to rise from her feet, but only for a moment. The pressure suddenly exploded into pain that obliterated the hurt in her leg. The nuclear fire raced up her shoulders to her neck, then down her arms to each fingertip. The awful heat ran its course in an instant, waking every nerve along the way. Then it blasted back up through her shoulders again, more intensely than before. She felt bone tear from sinew along her upper back and then something ripped through the flesh there. The pain was so severe that she would have given any-thing—including her life—to make it go away.

As Adrienne rose, her body quivered violently from her toes to the back of her head. Tides of heat and cold rushed over her in suc-cession, and her heart slapped erratically against her chest. Her mouth fell open in a silent scream. The pain turned her vision swirling red-black to white and her throat filled with saliva and blood.

And then, mercifully, she died.

Twenty-four

J oyce and Gentry stopped at the small New Paltz police station to
tell them about the dead sheep. Sergeant Katherine Mintz said she
appreciated the visit, and after asking what the two were doing at the
landfill—they told her they were trying to solve an old mystery about
Dr. Lipman's bat—Mintz informed them that a farmer, Brian Silverman, had called to report the sheep missing two hours before. Gentry
asked if Silverman had heard or seen anything. Mintz said he hadn't;
no bleating, no truck racing away, no sounds of a struggle. He simply
went outside to feed the animals and they were gone.

　　Gentry also used the phone to call the Emergency Service Unit
in Manhattan South. Joyce listened in on an extension. Lieutenant Kilar was still in the field, but Gentry learned from Sergeant Terry that
the second team had been able to retrieve the bodies of the unit members as well as the vic without incident. Power remained shut down on
the subway line when several small bats were spotted along the corridor. Al Doyle went in with a third ESU group and dealt with the bats
according to the book: hairspray and a tennis racket. The bats were
zapped with hair spray, which locked their fine-membraned wings.
Then they were swatted with tennis rackets. In all, thirty-seven bats
were destroyed. The MTA, the ESU, and Doyle then jointly decided

that the crime scene status would remain in effect on the Number 1 track while it was searched for any additional bats. But the adjacent Number 2 track could resume operation. According to Sergeant Terry, Lieutenant Kilar was still convinced that the vic had been murdered by a person and not by a bat. The sergeant said they'd know more after the medical examiner had completed his autopsy on the man. Joyce felt a little sorry for Kilar. After the autopsy, everything he thought he knew about the case would come under serious reevaluation. Especially when, as Gentry had suggested, they compared notes with Chris Henry about the autopsy on Barbara Mathis.

After picking up drive-through fast food, Joyce and Gentry got back on the road. Joyce wanted to go back to Manhattan instead of the Bronx. She was tired, but she wanted to be in the city if anything happened with the giant bat. If it was okay with Gentry, she said she didn't have a problem crashing on the floor; it couldn't be any less comfortable than some of the cold fields and rock ledges she'd camped on. Gentry said he had no problem with that.

They were silent for most of the ride back. Gentry had opened the windows and turned on the news, and they listened to reports about "the subway serial killer." Police Commissioner Veltre speculated that it was a homeless "tunnel person" who had massacred other tunnel people deep under Grand Central Station, attacked the man at Christopher Street, and was still on the loose. Extra buses were being put on for people who didn't want to ride the subways. Teams of police officers were being assigned to all the Manhattan subway stops for people who did. Gentry remarked that the police were making all the right moves for what they thought the problem was. Unfortunately, Joyce pointed out, if the bats behaved as they had elsewhere, those moves would be utterly ineffective.

They also listened to distressingly lighthearted reports about the "batfestation" in the West Village. Reporters had apparently bought the idea that they were stirred up by the serial killer who was prowling the subways.

Joyce wondered what they would say if she told them it was a giant bat. How many of them would believe her? Probably none. She still had trouble believing it herself. And as anxious as Joyce actually was to see the thing, to study a new breed of bat, the power of this creature—or creatures—terrified her. It wasn't just the physical strength she feared. The mere presence of a large bat would not have made the smaller bats go wild. Most bats were cowards; a large creature of any kind would have driven them away. What worried her was if a giant bat could communicate with the smaller bats, actually *instruct* them to attack people who strayed into their territory, then the situation could be catastrophic.

There were no other bat-related incidents in the news. Obviously, the vespers were resting. But she knew that wouldn't be the case for long. There was a reason the bat had come out of hiding after eight years. Perhaps it had finally grown too large for its roost or for the local food supply. If there were more than one bat, there might be another reason. One she didn't want to think about until she knew for certain the gender of the bats.

Joyce offered to drive part of the way and was glad when Gentry told her to relax. It was good to sit and semi-veg out. She shut her eyes and slumped in the seat. Her arms, shoulders, and legs were shot. The feeling of heaviness in her limbs reminded her how they used to feel years ago when she went off with Professor Lowery on his expeditions. When she climbed cliffs and bellied along the ground and scaled barn roofs to take pictures for his books about bats. Proving herself had always been hard work.

When they reached Manhattan, Gentry returned the car to the lot and they cabbed back to his apartment. They turned on the ten o'clock news. Doyle was on, congratulating himself and the NYPD on a successful pest-control operation. Gentry turned the TV off.

"You did good, Al," he said, "but it was only round one. Nancy, you ever play video games?"

"Just *Ms. Pac-Man* when I was a kid."

"This whole thing reminds me of *Space Invaders* or *Asteroids*. You clear one level and you feel pretty good about yourself. Then you get hit with the second level where everything's twice as fast and three times as nasty. And you're history in about two seconds."

"There's just one big difference," Joyce pointed out.

"I know," Gentry said. "The games have a reset button."

Twenty-five

Dori slowed as the traffic getting onto the George Washington Bridge began to thicken.

When she first started driving a bus six years before, thirty-nine-year-old Dori Dryfoos had the morning shift. The single mother thought she'd like shuttling businessmen between New York and northern New Jersey. They'd be neat, articulate, and reliable, everything her alcoholic, screwing-around, former jock of a husband wasn't. Maybe she'd even get to know some of the men, meet a single one, and get asked to coffee or dinner or a movie. It could happen. But it never did.

The reality was that at least half the businessmen were networking, lost in newspapers or cell-phone-using bores. The other half were busy hitting on the young, high-powered, up-and-coming women who rode the bus. Some of the men gave Dori a "good morning" with their tickets. But most didn't. And the women seemed condescending.

Dori hadn't asked for the night shift just to get away from the morning commuters. That was just a side benefit. She did it so that she'd be home during the day with her three-year-old son, Larry. Day care just hadn't worked out; poor Larry would sit in a corner and cry the entire time. Working the night shift, at least Dori could tuck the boy into bed while the baby-sitter looked on. Larry seemed much happier about that. And why not? No one liked to feel abandoned.

To Dori's surprise, she loved the night shift. It was relaxing and invigorating. One of the afternoon-to-evening drivers would park in the New Jersey terminal lot at eight o'clock, where the bus would get gas and a cleaning. Dori would collect it at nine. Her shift ended at five in the morning, right before the hellish rush-hour commute began over the George Washington Bridge. It was perfect.

The nighttime crowd was always delightfully eclectic and slightly wacky. There were aunts and uncles and grandparents who had spent the day with family. There were teenagers going to Manhattan for God knew what, workers heading in for late shifts as security guards or street cleaners or disc jockeys or whatever else people did at night, and even the occasional nun or lap dancer or hustler. Dori knew a few of the regulars by name. It was too bad: some of the male hustlers had better manners than the businessmen.

"Excuse me, miss."

Dori took a quick glance behind her. A thin, white-haired lady was standing in the aisle to her right.

"Yes ma'am?" Dori said.

"Is there something wrong with the lavatory?"

"Not that I'm aware of. Why?"

"I think it's locked."

"Maybe someone's in there."

"No. I'm sitting right in front of it. No one's gone in."

"Well, maybe it's stuck," Dori said. "This is a pretty old bus. Maybe one of the gentlemen back there will give it a tug for you."

"Thank you," the woman said. "I'll ask."

Slowed in the moderate late-evening traffic at the entrance to the bridge, Dori watched in the rearview mirror as the woman made her way back down the aisle. She held the backs of the seats as she walked, then stopped beside a young man. He was probably a college student. He had that look. Muscular, blond, clean-cut. The youth smiled up at the woman, listened to what she had to say, then went back to help her. The restroom was a small compartment on the left side of the bus. He pushed down hard on the handle.

The traffic started to move as she got on the bridge. Dori took her eyes from the mirror and looked ahead. You didn't see very many things like that in the morning, she thought. Simple courtesies. People who didn't mind getting off their butts and helping people.

Suddenly, a terrible cry tore through the bus. Dori touched the brake, and her eyes snapped back to the mirror.

The young man was stumbling backward. As Dori watched, he fell across the lap of a young woman who was sitting opposite the restroom. He was waving his hands wildly as things flew from the opened door. The old woman fell backward, landing hard on the rubber flooring. She didn't get up.

At first, in the subdued light of the bus, the things looked like campfire ash or fall leaves blown by a strong wind. They were swirling forward rapidly, an expanding spiral moving this way and that. Their approach caused most of the seventeen passengers to flail their arms, scream, and duck down. As the things continued toward her, Dori saw what they really were.

Bats.

Shrieks filled the bus as Dori crushed the brake. The vehicle stopped; the bats kept going. Four of the small, tawny creatures were on her a moment later. Their wings were dry and soft as they fluttered against her. She snarled at the bats as they tore at her face and scalp.

"Get off me!"

Dori leaned forward and tried to reach the level that opened the door. But she retreated an instant later, forced to cover her eyes. She shook her head violently, but the bats wouldn't leave. They clung to her bobbed black hair and ears, to her slender fingers and knuckles. Every move, every moment brought new pain. She felt like she'd run deep into a thorn bush and couldn't get out.

Screams bounced through the bus. Burying her eyes in the crook of her right elbow, Dori wrapped the arm tightly around her face.

Then she turned herself back toward the dashboard and felt blindly with her left hand for the lever. When she found it, she pulled hard.

The door folded open. The cool, brisk air rushed in off the Hudson River. The bats continued to attack.

Dori cried out in desperation. She half stood and threw herself against the window to her left. The bus began to roll forward. She hit the window again and again, banging her hands and forehead against the pane until bat blood mingled with her own blood and bat cries joined hers.

The bus angled toward the road divider, then rammed against it and stopped. Tires squealed as cars braked. A van smashed into the rear of the bus, jolting it forward. Horns blared angrily. Behind her, passengers screamed and shouted. But Dori wasn't aware of any of them. Her world was bounded by bats and defined by pain.

There were no longer any bats in the air. Two or three of them had latched onto each of the passengers. Most of the riders had folded themselves in the narrow space between their seats and the backs of seats in front of them. They were trying to duck in a face-down position. A few had fallen into the aisles and were pulling at stubborn bats or kicking the air in pain. No one was able to get free of the small, fast-flapping attackers. Not for more than a moment.

Suddenly, the cars went silent.

Then, as one, the bats stopped attacking the passengers and flew in a mad, cat's cradle pattern toward the door.

A motorist ran to the door to see what was wrong; the middle-aged woman ducked as the bats zigzagged past her. When they were gone, the woman hurried up the steps and knelt beside Dori. The driver was curled in a ball on the floor and crying softly.

"Are you all right?" the woman asked.

"It hurts," she said. Her face and the backs of her hands were a meshwork of fine, red stripes.

Several men arrived. They ran around the women and checked on the other passengers.

"I called nine-one-one," she said. "The police are on the way. You're going to be all right."

Dori attempted to get up. She was trembling. The woman gently pushed her back.

"Don't move."

"My passengers—"

"You stay still, Ms. Dryfoos," the woman said, reading her name tag. "They're being looked after."

"The bats?" Dori said.

"They're gone. They flew off."

Dori used the side of her hand to wipe blood from her eyes. Still shaking, she said, "Emergency brake," and pointed to a spot under the steering wheel. "Push it."

"Of course." As the woman went over to engage it, she looked out the windshield. She froze.

"Ms. Dryfoos, how do you close the door?" she asked urgently.

"The lever—there," Dori replied. "Why? What is it?"

The woman quickly pushed the bar. "Because the bats are coming back," she said. "A lot of them."

Twenty-six

Gentry was sitting back on the couch, enjoying the late summer breeze coming through the window and watching the end of some police show on TV. His eyes were half shut and his mood was one of dreamy satisfaction. He liked knowing that Nancy had fallen asleep in his bedroom, in his bed. Nancy Joyce was not a woman who needed looking after. But she did need sleep, badly, and it made him happy to know that she was comfortable enough to take it here.

His contentment evaporated when the show was interrupted by a news bulletin. Gentry was alert immediately.

"Good evening, I'm Patrick McDermot," said the local New York anchor. "There is a developing situation in upper Manhattan. For more information, we're going live to reporter Kathy Leung. Kathy?"

If Kathy was in New York, it had to be bats.

"Nancy!" Gentry shouted as Kathy came on. He grabbed the remote and punched up the volume. "Nancy, come here!"

He heard her stumble from the bed.

Kathy said, "Pat, just over an hour ago, a commuter bus starting across the George Washington Bridge from New Jersey was attacked by bats. According to passengers of the bus, the bats *poured* from the lavatory in the back and attacked every one of the seventeen people onboard, including the driver. Though there were no fatalities, that was only the start of what's shaping up to be a *major problem* for the city of New York."

Nancy shuffled into the living room. She was round shouldered and bleary-eyed. "What's wrong?"

"A bat attack on the George Washington Bridge," Gentry said.

Joyce was instantly alert. She remained standing as she watched.

"What you're looking at now," Kathy continued, "is a view of the skies over the Hudson River. Immediately after the attack on the bus, *thousands* of bats began gathering over the river. What's astonishing is that they've remained in the skies as their numbers swell."

"Kathy," the anchor asked, "where are these bats coming from?"

"Ernie, it seems like they're coming from *all* over," she said. "We've been talking to air traffic controllers at JFK and LaGuardia, at Newark, White Plains, and as far north as Newburgh. Their radar has been picking up movement that's *not* attributable to aircraft. They say it's being made by bats."

"Do you have binoculars?" Joyce asked.

"In the closet." He pointed to the hall.

Joyce hurried over.

"What are you going to do?" Gentry asked.

"I want to get to the river," she said. "See what's happening."

Gentry grabbed his pager, pulled on his shoes, and ran after her.

It was only a block to the West Side Highway. Traffic was thin and Joyce didn't wait for the light. She ran across, Gentry beside her. They jogged onto the pier at the end of Christopher Street. The wide, reconstructed deck extended several hundred feet into the Hudson, and during summer days it was jammed with sunbathers. Tonight there were about two dozen people. All of them were standing and looking north. They had probably been here already, enjoying the evening, when someone noticed what was happening.

Joyce reached the end of the pier and looked north through the binoculars. "Holy Mother of God."

Gentry peered up the river. Four police patrol boats had stopped around the lower Eighties. They were shining their spotlights up and toward the north. It looked like a scene out of an old war movie: the white lights crisscrossing against the black sky with waves of enemy aircraft moving overhead. Only instead of planes they were bats. More police boats would probably be taking up positions north and south of the bridge to keep sea traffic from the area.

"It looks like they're coming south," Gentry said.

"No, they're spreading," Joyce informed him.

"Spreading as in spreading out?"

"No. The group is growing. The bats are flying back and forth. Like a loom, knitting in and out."

"What are they doing?"

"I don't know. Waiting, maybe. It looks like a holding pattern. The bats that are already there wait for new bats to arrive. As more bats show up, they join the perimeter."

"Why?"

"I wonder—" she said thoughtfully.

Gentry's pager beeped. It was a Manhattan number he didn't recognize.

"What do you wonder?" Gentry asked.

"Do you have to check that out?"

"Yeah."

"I'll tell you when you get back. I want to think it through."

Gentry ran back toward the shore. There was a pay phone on the other side of the highway, and Gentry called the number.

It rang once before someone answered. "Yes?"

"Hi. This is detective Robert Gentry—"

"Detective," said the voice, a husky monotone, "this is Gordon Weeks, Office of Emergency Management."

So the guano has *hit the fan*, Gentry thought. Gordy Weeks was the big gun, "the lion tamer," the press had dubbed him. In a crisis situation, the former marine called all the plays. Even Mayor Taylor deferred to him, and Taylor—a longtime FBI man who'd run the bureau's New York field office—was not hesitant to take charge in most situations.

"I'm told you've been working with Dr. Nancy Joyce of the Bronx Zoo," Weeks said.

"That's right."

"We've been trying to find her."

"She's with me," Gentry said. "I'm at a pay phone. We're out on the Christopher Street pier watching the bats."

"Can you get her down to Seven World Trade Center?"

"Sure—"

"Robert!"

Joyce was running across the highway. A car had to jam on its brakes to keep from hitting her. She didn't seem to notice. He had never seen her this driven.

"Hold on," Gentry said into the phone. "Nancy's coming. I think something's up."

"Something is," Weeks said, "bats. They're stretched from the George Washington Bridge down to just below the Seventy-ninth Street Boat Basin. I need a think tank *fast* and ESU said she may have answers—"

"Wait a second, sir, *please!*" Gentry said. "She's pretty agitated. She may have something."

"Look, I've got the police commissioner on the other line," Weeks said. "Call me back as soon as possible."

Gentry said he would. The OEM director hung up.

Joyce arrived, breathless. She leaned against the phone. "Robert, I need to get above the bats."

"Above? You mean upriver?"

"No, I mean higher than. Can you get me a helicopter?"

"I suppose. Why?"

"Because I think I know what's happening, and I need to make certain."

"What's happening?"

Joyce said, "The courtiers are being assembled. The king is already here. And I believe the queen is on her way."

Twenty-seven

As they hurried back to Gentry's apartment, the detective told Joyce that if the Office of Emergency Management apparently had been put in charge of the crisis, Gordy Weeks would have to okay her plan to fly up into the bats.

"There may not be time to visit him and do a whole conference thing. Will he listen to me over the phone?"

"I think so," Gentry said.

"And will he listen to *me?*"

"He asked for you by name," Gentry said. "Look, I know Gordy Weeks only by reputation. He doesn't let bureaucracy, red tape, ego, or gender get in the way of fixing problems. He also doesn't have a lot of time to screw around here. They'll probably have to close the harbor, the Hudson air lane into LaGuardia—can't afford to have bats sucked into jet engines. He'll listen and you'll get a quick yea or nay."

"How much clout does he have?"

"In a crisis, Weeks reports directly to Taylor. And I don't think the mayor has ever gotten in the way of anything he wanted."

As they entered the apartment and Gentry punched in the phone number, Joyce quickly assembled her facts. Robert was right. A manager in the middle of an unprecedented crisis wouldn't have much time to listen—or to argue. She would have to make her point fast.

It was clear to her that the Russian female had had at least twin offspring, possibly more. The same bat could not have attacked the ESU team in New York and killed those sheep in New Paltz. And a male bat would not have come ahead, alone, to prepare a new home for another male bat. But a male bat would have come ahead for a female. He would have found a nest, settled in, and then relayed his signature cry from bat to bat—a distinctive series of bleats that would have told her exactly where he was.

He also would have gathered food for her arrival.

If a she-bat were on her way to New York, if she'd left New Paltz a few hours before, then she would be arriving very soon. Especially with an honor guard or a protective wall of drones already gathering. They, too, must have been summoned by the male.

If all that were true, it was important that Joyce be able to spot the female coming in. It was imperative that she watch where the female went so they could find the male. And she could do that most efficiently from the air.

When Weeks got on the phone, Joyce told him all of that. When she was finished, Weeks informed her that Al Doyle was in the command center with him helping to monitor and assess the situation. Doyle's contention was that the bats were here as part of a massive migration. Doyle said they would probably move on, since—like the subway bats—they were vespertilionids that didn't eat fruit and preferred flying insects to crawling insects.

"But," Weeks said, "Al can't explain what a night watchman just reported from the World Trade Center. The guard entered a bloody elevator carriage, shined his flashlight through the open hatchway, and saw a woman being hauled up the cable. He said that whatever was holding her was dark, about the size of a bull, and had wings."

The veteran watchman had never been drunk or stoned on the job. And the sighting corroborated what Lieutenant Kilar of the ESU had dutifully noted in his report on the subway killings: that bat expert Dr. Nancy Joyce of the Bronx Zoo believed there might be "an abnormally large specimen" of bat inhabiting the New York subway system.

"I'm having trouble signing onto this," Weeks said. "But people are dying and I've got to explore every possible lead. You can have your chopper."

Weeks told Joyce that he needed his helicopters for reconnaissance and transportation. His office would arrange with the police commissioner to have an ESU helicopter pick her up at the pier in fifteen minutes. The OEM director had only two requests: that she stay in constant radio communication with his assistant, Marius Pace, and that she not fuck up.

Joyce promised.

She kept the binoculars and grabbed her camera. Gentry went with her to the pier to wait. He had only one request: that she come back safely.

Joyce promised.

Ten minutes later, she and two ESU fliers were airborne in an Aviation Unit Bell-412.

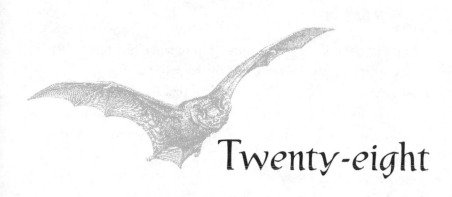

Twenty-eight

In all her years of bat hunting, Nancy Joyce had never had the opportunity to ride in a helicopter. Within five seconds of lifting off from the pier, she realized she'd have been happy to postpone the experience indefinitely.

The chopper ascended, which wasn't the same as taking off. Not to her. As it arced steeply from the pier, the sense of motion up and away and then forward was pronounced. It was like being in a bumper car that had suddenly added a third dimension of mobility.

But that wasn't all. The helicopter was incredibly loud. Even though Joyce was in the seat directly behind the pilot, she would have had to yell if she wanted to converse. Fortunately, as soon as they were airborne, the copilot handed back a headset. It fit entirely over her ears. That not only deadened the clapping-loud drone of the rotors, it enabled Joyce to communicate with the fliers and Mr. Pace without shouting.

The chopper was also fast. Joyce was accustomed to cabs picking and weaving their way through New York traffic. The helicopter was above the bats and just about ten blocks away before she even had a chance to adjust the mouthpiece of the headset and sit back.

All of that went through her mind in moments. She forced herself to concentrate on the horizon. On the bats.

The pilot said, "Dr. Joyce, all I was told is that you want to observe the bats. You're going to have to tell us from what height and where."

"I want to be able to watch the river facing north," she said. "How high are we now?"

"Seventeen hundred feet."

"How high would you say the bats are?"

"Maybe six hundred feet. Six fifty tops."

"Does your propeller cause any kind of downdraft?"

"It does," he said. "If we get on top of the bats and go much lower than above twelve hundred feet, we're gonna stir them up like a blender."

"Then make it twelve hundred feet," she said. "But the bats might ascend. If they do, we should be ready to get out of their way."

"Understood."

"Dr. Joyce?" said a voice with a gentle British accent. "This is Marius Pace."

"Hi," she said. "Sorry. I didn't mean to ignore you."

"You didn't," he assured her. "You were busy. Gordon advises me that what you're watching for is a very large bat."

"That's correct."

"How large is large?"

"I'm not sure," she said.

"Eagle? Condor?" he asked.

"More like a Cessna," she replied.

"You mean as in the private airplane?"

"Yes."

Pace said, "That's large, all right. And if and when you see this bat, is it your intention to pursue?"

"Only to watch where it's going," she replied. "If possible, I want to get close enough to see what it looks like, take some pictures."

"I understand," Pace said. "All right, then. From now on I'll just be listening in. If you need anything, ask."

She looked out as the helicopter reached the shifting carpet of bats. They were bottom-lit, twenty or thirty thousand of them swimming back and forth on a bright and luminous sea. It was majestic, mesmerizing, and inexplicable. Worse, she didn't know exactly where it was all going. If and when one of the big bats arrived, would these smaller bats go or stay? And if they stayed, would they stay peaceably?

Joyce hadn't really thought about the personal danger until now. If these bats became territorial like the others, things could get very bad. She also realized, suddenly and belatedly, that when she took off Gentry had really been worried about her. Joyce hadn't had anyone except her assistant feel that way for a long time. It felt nice.

Joyce wondered what Professor Lowery was making of all this. He would have a perfect view of the river from his apartment window. She also wondered what the bats were making of them. What they might be thinking, feeling. They'd be picking up the movement of every bat, every bird, every insect, the choppers, the people. The input had to be overwhelming.

"Can you hover?" Joyce asked the pilot.

He said he could.

The helicopter stopped moving forward.

As Joyce looked down on the thick mesh of bats, anticipation grew. Behind the helicopter, the dark cloud had spread southward almost down to Forty-second Street. To the west, the bats had reached nearly to the New Jersey shore. State police helicopters were already hovering over the New Jersey Palisades. Bats were still joining the group from all directions.

And then she saw something. Something large just beyond the bats.

She raised the binoculars, and the pilot nudged the nose of the chopper to the northwest to give her a better view. The George Washington Bridge was hidden save for an occasional glint of light.

"Go down!" she said suddenly.

"Where?" the pilot asked.

"Underneath the bats."

"You mean through them—"

"No. Go around—anywhere. I need to get under the bats. Something's out there, flying low. It's going to come in under the bats."

The chopper swung to the east, toward Manhattan. It moved so fast that if Joyce hadn't been wearing her seat belt she'd have been thrown against the door. The pilot dropped them lower as Joyce sat back up and watched through the binoculars.

"Where to now?" the pilot asked as they fell below the bat line.

"Stay about one hundred feet up. Go north slowly."

The pilot did. They passed through the Eighties. The Nineties. Joyce looked ahead. Something was there. It had ducked under the canopy of bats and was moving slowly. She unbuckled her seat belt for a better look.

"There it is!" she said excitedly. "Mr. Pace? Tell Mr. Weeks we found it! We found it and it's *huge*."

The bat was still beyond the range of the searchlights, but she knew it was there because she could make out its outline as it moved forward, blocking the shore light and headlights behind it.

And of course it was flying low. New Paltz was far, and there were no thermal currents from the sun to heat the air and help lift the bat. There was no reason for it to tire itself out by flying high.

As the bat neared, as it began to pick up the light, Joyce could see that it *was* enormous. There was nothing to compare it to but the other bats, and it dwarfed them. The wingspan looked to be about ten-to-twelve feet across—at this distance, in the dark, it was still difficult to tell. The body was thick, like a long barrel, with lumpy masses on the back. Joyce assumed they were muscle. The head was wide and pie round. She couldn't quite make out the ears, though they were nearly as high as the head was long, and they were extremely close together. There was a large bulge near the back of the bat, on the bottom. Joyce assumed they were the legs.

"Man oh man," the copilot said. "Are all these other bats here for—" He was interrupted when the helicopter shook.

The pilot and copilot both looked at their instruments.

"What was that?" the copilot said.

It happened again—a hard, spine-ringing thump from below.

"It feels like we're being hit from the bottom!" the pilot said.

There was a third strike, rougher than the others, this time from the pilot's side. Then something seemed to tug the helicopter toward the left. Joyce turned away from the distant giant and its entourage. She moved back to the pilot's side and looked out the window just as a monstrous face appeared beneath the portside landing skid. Joyce watched while it rose slowly, followed by two white hooks as thick and large as elephant ivory. The hooks were at least six feet apart.

"Get us out of here!" she screamed.

The copilot looked back. "Oh shit—"

A pair of large ruby eyes rolled toward Joyce just as a blast of vapor from the awesome mouth clouded the window. A moment later one of the hooks crashed against the pane. It didn't break though, but the tip raked downward, cutting a deep rut.

The pilot swung the chopper around and swept toward the southeast. Ahead, brightly lighted, the retired battleship *Intrepid* appeared through the window.

"What's wrong?" Pace demanded.

"It's one of them!" Joyce cried as the hook came again. It wasn't a hook, she knew, it was the bat's thumb. This time the tip of the finger came through the shatter-resistant window.

"One of *who?*" Pace said.

"One of the giant bats!" she screamed. "It's on the helicopter!"

"What do we need to do?" Pace asked, his voice calm.

The pilot rocked the helicopter from side to side as he flew down and toward the shore.

"Are you doing that or is he?" Joyce cried.

"I am," the pilot replied. "Trying to shake him—"

"Forget that!" she yelled. "Can you put us in the water?"

"I can't land on it—" the pilot said.

"I mean drag the runner through it! Bats hate submersion. It weighs them down."

"I can try," the pilot said tensely as he guided the chopper back to starboard and dropped toward the river.

The vapor had cleared from the window, and Joyce looked out again. The rotor was blasting the bat's fur, but the creature held on. The eyes were angry now, the crescent nostrils wide and trembling. Vibrating.

"He's calling the others," she muttered. "We've got to get him off—he's calling the other bats!"

Ther chopper was flying parallel to the water. They were seven feet up. Then five . . . four . . .

Joyce looked up. Bats were peeling off the edge of the colony. That was how he did it. The big bat called them, and they came. It was unbelievable.

She was rocked back hard as the skid shot across the water. Spray flew up on all sides, and the pilot immediately pulled up. The bat was still there, its head back, the mouth pulled taut, the eyes big and aflame.

The pilot dipped down again, this time dragging lower and for several seconds. He rose. The bat was dark and drenched, its hook still thrust through the window.

"Hold on!" the pilot said.

Joyce looked ahead. They were coming toward Yacht Harbor down by the World Financial Center.

Pace said, "N412, what's happening?"

"Just a second," the copilot said.

The chopper raced toward the nearest boat. The skid was level with the tower platform on the top of the flybridge.

"We're playing chicken," the copilot said into the mouthpiece. "Shit, man. Shit—"

The yacht was less than thirty feet away. The bat turned toward the boat. Suddenly, the creature snapped its thumb toward it. The pane flew out and the wind roared in, howling in Joyce's face. The bat turned toward her, glaring. Then it opened the claws of its feet, releasing its hold on the skids. It fell away, like a parachutist, its wings spreading and filling like a shroud.

The pilot swerved hard to starboard to avoid the tower. He missed it by less than two feet. Quickly righting the chopper, he steadied it and swung around the tip of Manhattan. He started to climb.

Joyce looked out the window. She withdrew her head quickly and cried, *"He's coming back!"*

The bat was about twenty feet behind the tail rotor on the portside. It was extremely muscular along its back and flapping vigorously. Definitely a male. Behind it was a stream of hundreds of small bats.

Joyce knew that it had to be difficult for the bat to keep up with them. Not only was the water weighing it down, but it was cooling fast and lowering the bat's body temperature. Bats did not fly well wet—or cold.

Pace said, "N412, come in."

"We managed to dislodge the bat," the copilot said, "but he's in pursuit. I clock him at about seventy-five miles an hour."

"He can't keep that up for long," Joyce said.

"Neither can we with that hole in our side," the copilot replied. "Got a lot of drag."

They passed the ferry buildings and sped up the east side of Manhattan.

The pilot said, "I'm going to land at the downtown heliport. I'll need support. The big bat and a shitload more are gonna be all over us."

"We'll never get out of the helicopter alive," Joyce said. "The bat will do anything to protect its sister."

"Its sister?" Pace said.

"Yes. The smaller bat coming from the north is a female. The male attacked because we were airborne, in her path. It sees us as a threat."

"Good for him," the pilot said. "What do we do?"

Joyce leaned between the pilot and copilot. She pointed ahead, toward the stone towers of the Brooklyn Bridge. "Head there," she said. "Take us between the cables and the span."

"Between them?" he said. "Doctor, there's a steel wire web truss in that area—"

"I know. But the bat doesn't. And it may not see them. It's dark, the bat has got to be tiring, and our rotors may mess up its echolocation. I've also got something it isn't expecting."

"Say no more," the pilot said.

He pushed the chopper ahead, maximum speed. The bridge was exactly a mile from their position. They'd reach it in less than a minute.

Joyce looked back. The big bat was well to the side of the chopper now and several feet closer. It was obviously trying to stay away from the tail rotor and get back alongside the helicopter. Now that she had her first good look at it, Joyce couldn't decide whether the bat was beautiful or hideous. The noseleaf construction was like an hourglass, with the crescent nostrils upright along the bottom half and a ridge of bone forming the top half. The bone formed a protective ridge around the eyes. The ears were large, a rose petal shape. They began, in front, just above the eye ridge. They twisted gracefully to the sides, just above the head, so that the upper third of each ear was turned nearly completely around. Unlike most bats, whose ears faced front, this creature could probably hear equally well in every direction. The mouth was a wide, deep slit very close to the chin, and the eyes were almost luminescent. Beautiful or hideous, the bat was astonishing.

Joyce picked up her camera. She faced backward and leaned toward the shattered window. The bat was gaining quickly. The strength and endurance of the thing were simply incredible.

She turned and looked toward the bridge. They sped past the Fulton Fish Market and the South Street Seaport. The bridge, nearly sixteen hundred feet long, loomed just ahead.

"I'm going to swing to the right and up," the pilot told Joyce. "In six . . . five . . . four . . ."

Joyce turned back. She leaned partway out the window. The creature was closing on them.

". . . three . . ."

She raised the camera. The face of the bat filled the lens.

". . . two . . ."

She took a flash picture.

"...one!"

The helicopter swerved to the starboard side and climbed. Joyce was tossed roughly toward the right side of the helicopter. She dropped the camera but put her foot against the starboard door to brace herself and looked back as the giant bat slammed into the mesh-work of steel strands. It hit at full speed, its head twisting to the side and almost completely back as the rest of its body struck. The wires sliced through the forearms, which connected the wings to the body, and continued cutting into the wing membrane. The body hovered straight out behind it for a moment, the legs kicking outward. Then the legs stopped moving and the body sagged and the bat hung crucified on the suspension wires just outside the Manhattan-side tower.

Below it, cars braked and horns screamed, and then nothing on the bridge moved. The copilot slapped his companion on the shoulder then updated Marius Pace. As the helicopter turned a gentle arc toward the East River helipad, Joyce slid into the seat behind the copilot. There was sweat on her back, and it was turning very cold. She looked out the window.

The thick stream of small bats had rushed past them. The animals fluttered close to the bridge but either peeled off or passed between the wires. After a few seconds they turned toward Manhattan, no longer as a group but hundreds of individuals. They vanished quickly in the darkness.

Joyce had no idea whether the bats were returning to the Hudson River group or leaving. There was no precedent for this kind of control by an individual bat over a supercolony.

As the helicopter touched down, Joyce knew only one thing. That wherever the female had gone, she would soon be aware of her brother's death.

Joyce had just seen what a guardian bat was capable of. She couldn't even begin to contemplate what a vengeful bat might do. . . .

Twenty-nine

The bat crept over the body.

She curled her lower legs beneath her and lowered her belly to the ground. Her short tail lay limp on the concrete, and she spread her wings wide. They were cold and tired, and the heat from the ground warmed them. She turned her red eyes to the torso of the dead woman.

She could not see the blood in the dark, but she smelled it. It had spilled in two long streams from under the arms of the body. The bat sniffed down the corpse to the belly. The body had been opened widthwise. The bat moved her mouth closer to the soft organs. Another smell was strong there. *His* smell.

She hesitated. She turned her nose to the air and searched for his scent. But it was very faint. He was gone.

He had driven away the things that were confusing her, that had been turning in circles. And then his voice was silent. He had not called out again, nor had he come to her.

She had never been without him. She felt need. She felt alone.

She turned back to her meal. After feeding on this soft tissue, she would call the colony of insect eaters. They would not be far. The bats would come to her out of fear, just as they had come to him whenever they were needed. For a bat knew only three voices: command, challenge, or acquiescence. Then the call would rise to the piercing heights that drove the insect eaters to a frenzy, and they would attack. And while they attacked, while the insect eaters kept the other predators away, the bat would leave her nest and follow his scent through these caves.

She would find him. And she would bring him back.

Her brother. Her mate.

Thirty

T he bats had begun to disperse from the skies over the Hudson.
    Though the vespertilionids remained in the city, Mayor
George Taylor did not call for a state of emergency. There were already
more people on the roads and trains than either could handle; turning
up the heat would only cause panic and draw police from where they
were needed: keeping people—especially journalists—from the subways and in the streets making sure bat-watch parties didn't get out of
hand. The air lanes over the Hudson River were reopened, people were
advised to remain inside, dog walks were discouraged because of fear
that their scent would draw bat attacks, and sanitation crews were put
on "snow alert" status to deal with possible guano cleanup. The sanitation commissioner and his deputies got together at one-thirty in the
morning to puzzle that one out, trying to decide whether hoses or
shovels would be their better weapons. Homeless "squeegee men"
were doing a steady business at stoplights and tunnel entrances. Because many people had already been in bed when the bats gathered,
windows had been left open and police lines were overloaded with
calls from people shrieking that there were bats in the bedrooms,
kitchens, and bathrooms. One man with eastern and western expo-
sures called 911 to report that while he was lying in his bed, literally

counting sheep, a line of bats had flown in one window and out the other.

Robert Gentry heard some of these stories as he was rushed by squad car from the Christopher Street pier to the downtown heliport to meet Nancy. When he arrived, ESU Emergency Medical Service paramedics were already treating her for lacerations she suffered during the attack. She looked a little shell-shocked but smiled broadly when she saw him. Gentry guessed that after the big bat even he looked good.

She told the paramedics that she didn't want to go to the hospital. She wanted to be present when the big bat was removed from the bridge. Gentry was proud of her as she got in the squad car, though he didn't have a chance to say anything then. The ESU pilot joined them as they drove out to the bridge, and he had a few dozen questions. Gentry wished the flier had been smart and gone home, like his copilot had done.

Al Doyle and Gordy Weeks were there when they arrived, standing at the windy edge of Dover Street, along with police from Manhattan and Brooklyn and literally dozens of reporters. Even though it was late at night, traffic was backing up in both directions.

Weeks wanted the bat off the bridge as quickly as possible so the cables could be checked for damage and the span could be ready for the morning rush hour. Because the bridge held landmark status, care would have to be taken when removing the bat. The initial idea, floated by Department of Transportation Acting Commissioner Marcy Chelmow, was that the Fire Department's marine division try to dislodge the creature using high-powered hoses from a fire boat. But Al Doyle said that an autopsy was vital, and he feared that the water pressure might further damage the bat. Inspector Steve Snider, ESU commander, suggested bringing another chopper in and having officers rappel to the bat, put a cable around it, and haul it off. But the pilot of the pursuit chopper, who had remained at the scene, was concerned that the downdraft could cause the animal to fall from the bridge before it could be secured. He was also worried about the weight of the personnel and the creature. The bat looked like it had a lot of muscle and meat on it.

The mayor arrived while the issue was still being debated. Conferring alone with Taylor, and then talking again to both Chelmow and Doyle, Weeks decided on a quick, conservative, low-risk approach; he didn't want to risk dropping the bat on anyone or anything, especially with TV cameras everywhere. He would have the bridges and tunnels division of the Department of Transportation send a quartet of "ironworkers" up the suspension cables. The engineers would attach a pair of slings around the bat's waist and lower it to the span. The remains would then be trucked away.

When Weeks had a second alone, Joyce went over and introduced herself. Gentry stayed several yards away. This was her moment.

The tall, silver-haired, African-American OEM chief seemed genuinely happy to meet the young woman. He said that her stock was "very high in the Weeks market" because she'd said the big bat was coming to town and it did.

"I like working with people who are right," he said.

Gentry was looking at the bridge, pretending not to eavesdrop. But he was proud of her all over again.

Joyce thanked the OEM director, then asked about the other bat.

"She turned northeast and went underground at Ninety-seventh Street," Weeks said. "She was obviously following the trail of the other bat that grabbed the woman at Riverside Drive this morning. Unfortunately, we had no way of following the bat inside the tunnels."

"What are you going to do next?"

"We'll have to talk about that," he said. "I want your input. For now, we've shut down all the west side subways and are deploying police teams at every subway entrance. They're carrying Ithaca shotguns—heavy duty—if the bat decides to do the town. I talked with the mayor and the police commissioner before coming out here. We're getting ready to send ESU teams into critical junctures of the tunnels. Once each of those junctures is secured, we can send in Remote Mobile Investigators—our six-wheeled robots with cameras—to check out tunnels ahead of them. With any luck, we can pin the creature down and let the Health Department take it from there."

Al Doyle wandered over. Weeks introduced Nancy. Chris Henry was right about him. Doyle was a short, round-shouldered man with an elongated nose, a sloping forehead, a small, recessed chin, and buck teeth. He looked like a mouse.

Joyce turned from Doyle back to Weeks. Even Gentry felt the chill rolling from her shoulders.

"What are you going to do about protecting your people from the small bats?" Joyce asked Weeks.

"The teams at the entrances are wearing their Viking dry suits—SCUBA gear. Al Doyle says that should afford the officers as much protection as they'll need. And when we do go in, they'll also have full face masks and air tanks so they're completely covered."

"That'll give them about fifteen to twenty seconds of protection," Joyce told him.

Doyle said, "Those suits have been tested in central South American freshwater against piranhas. They should hold against bats."

"They won't," Joyce said.

"Why not?" Weeks asked.

"Piranhas don't have claws. They can't make repeated attacks at the same part of the body."

Weeks arched a brow in Doyle's direction. Doyle kept his narrow eyes on Joyce. Neither man looked happy.

"There are also a few hundred thousand bats in the city now," Joyce said. "The male bat was able to summon them from miles around. I'm betting the female bat can do the same thing. If and when she moves in or out of the tunnel, she'll have an escort like the heavenly host. Their weight alone, piled on top of your suits, will make movement difficult. The heat of their bodies will cause the heat inside the suits to rise very quickly. And the sounds of a few hundred batting wings won't be pleasant."

"So what do we do?" Weeks asked.

"I agree with guarding the subway entrances in case the big bat shows up," Joyce said. "As for going inside, I'd wait. If we can find a way to jam her signal or lure her out, then we can capture her and kill her quickly. Then the other bats will either fly off or they can be disposed of through normal means." She looked at Doyle. "As pests."

"How do we lure her out?" Weeks asked.

Doyle said, "When the large bat flew down the Hudson, she was probably following the male's call. If we can duplicate that sound, we can take her anywhere we want."

"Is that possible?" Weeks asked Joyce.

"In theory, yes," Joyce said. "In practice, it could take months or years to replicate the male's call."

"Why?"

"For many reasons. First of all, bats generate sounds that range between twenty and one hundred kilohertz," Joyce said. "Humans can hear sounds only up to twenty kilohertz."

"So we can't hear what we're listening for," Weeks said.

"We can, but we'll need special equipment to do it. We can get the gear in a day or two. That's not the big problem. Where it gets complicated is that bat cries consist of both FM and CF elements. The frequency-modulated sounds cover a very wide range in a very short time—one hundred kilohertz down to fifty in about two milliseconds."

"So the sounds are fast," Weeks said.

"Incredibly so," Joyce replied. "On top of which you've got the CF, the constant frequency. That sound remains at a single frequency and lasts for about fifty milliseconds. Which means that each frequency has to be isolated and charted. Even if we can duplicate the sounds themselves, that won't give us the specific 'buzz' that called the female or summoned the small bats. That could be any combination of FM and CF sounds, in any range and duration. It could take months or even years to figure out."

"We obviously need a faster fix," Weeks said. "Any suggestions?"

"Yes. To start with, I suggest you try and get any videotape that may have been taken of the female's approach. There may be something that could help us. Her reaction to light, her control over the other bats, possible soft spots for your marksmen."

Weeks got on his radio and told Marius Pace to hit the TV stations for copies of their tapes.

"What else?" Weeks asked.

"Not much," Joyce admitted. "We may know more when we get a look at the dead bat. Cell structure, possible microbial weaknesses, circulation and respiration—to tell us how much sleep and food the big bats need.

"Dr. Joyce," Weeks said, "will you be available when we do the autopsy on the big bat?"

"Actually," Joyce said, "unless anyone has any objections, I was going to suggest that you let me handle it."

Weeks shoved his hands into the pockets of white windbreaker. He looked at Joyce. "Al?"

"We have a long-standing relationship with Dr. Berkowitz at the Central Park Zoo," Doyle said.

"Berkowitz is *not* a bat person," Joyce huffed.

Weeks said, "The long relationship aside, would you personally have any problem with Dr. Joyce conducting the autopsy?"

Doyle's thin lips and heavy eyebrows dipped in disapproval. "I'd have no problem with her *being* there—"

"Mr. Doyle," Joyce said, "I've done microdissections on more than seventy different species of bats. I know what to look for and how to get it without damaging the surrounding tissue."

"Al," Weeks said, "Dr. Joyce has been the point person on this situation from the get go. I'd like her to conduct the autopsy and write the report. Can we do that?"

Gentry was watching with interest. Weeks hadn't left Doyle much room to maneuver.

Doyle said, "Berkowitz probably won't let us use the zoo facility."

"That's not a problem," Joyce said quickly. "I'd be taking the bat to Professor Lowery's laboratory at the Museum of Natural History. I'd also want him to work with me on this."

"Professor Kane Lowery?" Doyle sniffed.

"That's right."

"He's very good."

"Right again."

"Then we're all okay?" Weeks said. "Let me know, because I've got to run."

Doyle nodded once. "We'll bring the bat to Professor Lowery's laboratory. But your report goes to me, Dr. Joyce, and I take it from there. And you don't talk to the press."

"I don't care about the press," she said.

Still standing off to the side, Gentry frowned.

"Excellent," Weeks said. "Thank you, Al. Thank you both."

Weeks went over to talk to the mayor, who was watching the ironworkers rig lifelines before walking up the cables. He was trailed by a small string of deputies who held reports about bat activity from around the city. From what Gentry could overhear, the worst problem at the moment was dogs going wild whenever bats flew past windows or went down chimneys. Weeks said he could live with that.

Doyle walked over to the DOT personnel at the bridge. Gentry came over to Joyce. She was looking across the river. The lights of the bridge were sparkling on its dark surface.

Gentry looked at Nancy. Her black hair was twisting away from her neck, riding the wind. There was a moment when her courage, her mind, her determination, her eyes, the smoothness of her skin, the delicate curve of her shoulders, her slender fingers, the way she stood with her feet pointing outward slightly—when everything came together and made his breath catch in his throat. It was a moment such as Gentry had never experienced.

"I can probably scare you up some coffee or a windbreaker if you want," he said.

"No thanks." She was frowning. "That bastard Doyle let me have the bat as soon as I put Lowery in the picture."

"At least you have it."

"Yeah, but it's still a boys' club."

"I'm still not sure I agree with that. Doyle jumped at your Lowery reference because it gave him a way out. Who could refuse letting a scientist of his stature examine the bat? He can sell that to Berkowitz and to the press. Anyway, like I said back at the apartment, Weeks is on your side."

"That's true, at least." She looked at Gentry. "You know what I'd really like?"

"What?"

"I'd like to sit down somewhere and close my eyes."

"I think we can arrange that," he said. "There are a couple of ESU REP trucks on the corner of Front Street. They're probably going to hang around in case they're needed for rescues or a bat attack. I'm sure no one would mind if you stretched out in one of them."

"Great," she said. "I just want to call President Lowery first and let him know I'll be coming in."

"With *your* trophy," Gentry said. "Make sure he knows that."

"He'll know."

She went to the closest truck. Gentry introduced her to the officers and she made her call from there. When she was finished, the ESU personnel were delighted to have her crash there. One of the younger officers, having heard of her exploits, declared his love for Joyce and asked if she would entertain a marriage proposal.

Gentry said, "Sorry, officer, but you'll have to take a number and wait in line."

Nancy didn't respond as she climbed into the backseat and lay down.

Gentry felt a little bad. After he said it, he realized he hadn't entirely been joking.

It took just over four hours to get the bat off the bridge. Once it was down and bundled in canvas—its wings carefully folded over—Doyle supervised its loading into an ESU Construction Accident Response Vehicle. Inside the wide CARV, the bat was laid out on a pair of four-person inflatable rafts. The rafts were arranged in two rows of two to cushion the creature. It was secured there with a 220-foot-long ⅝-inch lifeline.

Kathy Leung tried to get herself and her muscular camera operator T-Bone Harrold past the police barricade. She was turned back. Until the bat was down and the cables had been checked out, no one was going near the bridge. Then she tried to get Gentry's attention by shouting over. He pretended not to hear her. He didn't like ignoring anyone or helping to shut down the press. Four years ago, in one of those freak incidents that happens only in real life, *New York Times* crime reporter Sam Lawrence had scored an interview with Akira Mizuno up in Connecticut. Gentry was in the room when Lawrence arrived. The two of them used to bump into each other once or twice a week at the Lord Camelot diner on Forty-fifth Street and Eighth Avenue, just a few blocks from the *Times*. Lawrence would have had a hell of a story if he'd chosen to blow Gentry's cover. But he didn't. Things like that would give the press a good name if people ever heard about them.

Only when the bat was down, only when Doyle was finished with it, did Gentry go over and wake Nancy. He was a little light-headed from not having slept. But he'd wanted to make sure that Doyle didn't give the bat to Berkowitz while she slept. Doyle was the kind of clever bureaucrat who wouldn't hesitate to tell Weeks, *"Security came first. I couldn't find her so we took the bat to Berkowitz's lab."* When the big bat had come down, Gentry had gone over to the ESU drivers and personally made certain that they knew where to go.

Nancy hadn't moved from where she'd fallen across the seat of the REP truck. Gentry looked at her. Behind him, across the East River, the sun began to lighten the skies.

Gentry had no trouble seeing the girl in the woman. He hadn't always seen that in his wife or some of the other women he'd been with. But he saw it in Nancy. Despite the occasional bursts of indignation and anger, there was a sweetness that life hadn't squeezed from her.

He leaned into the truck, his hand on the back of the front seat. He reached down and lightly shook her arm.

She awoke with a jolt. "What's wrong?"

"Nothing," Gentry said quietly. "We've got the bat down. We're ready to head up to the museum."

"Right." She sat up and looked at her watch. "Almost six-thirty. That was pretty quick."

"You feel any better?"

"Yeah," she said. "Much."

Joyce swung her long legs from the seat. Gentry backed away from the truck and she slid out.

"Are we supposed to notify Professor Lowery?" Gentry asked.

"I will," Joyce told him. "He usually gets in at seven o'clock."

Gentry asked Joyce if she wanted something from the "chuck wagon," the coffee-and-muffin cart that the DOT had set up by the river for the crews. She said she wouldn't mind a bran something-or-other, so they got that and then headed over to CARV.

Gentry made sure that the paperwork from OEM had arrived, giving Joyce authority to take charge of the bat. It had, brought by one of Gordy Weeks's assistants who would be accompanying Dr. Joyce to the museum. The assistant, a twenty-something biologist named Heidi Daniels, would be taking notes and writing the report that was going to Al Doyle.

Joyce thanked Gentry for everything he'd done, then climbed into the back of the truck with Heidi and an ESU sergeant. They headed uptown.

Joyce was very intense and focused and she hadn't said anything about seeing Gentry later or getting together again. Maybe she didn't plan to. Or maybe she'd just assumed they would.

Gentry had. That was a swift, disturbing sock in the gut.

When she left, the slightly shell-shocked Gentry bummed a ride up to the station house. There would be paperwork and voice mail to attend to. He'd also try to stay on top of any other missing person or animal reports, information that might tell them something about the whereabouts of the female bat.

A reason to call Nancy.

And he'd get a little rest if possible. With all those bats roosting in town—including the big one—Gentry had a feeling that sundown was going to rock New York.

Thirty-one

Marc Ramirez joined the museum autopsy group in the late afternoon. He came to the fifth floor wearing a black leather jacket and carrying his bat helmet under his arm.

He noticed Heidi right off. He kept his eyes on her as he greeted Dr. Joyce and Professor Lowery. The young woman gave him only a passing look.

"How are things going?" Joyce asked.

"Outside?" He asked, shifting his eyes toward the scientist. "You've got a few quintillion reporters waiting at the delivery dock."

"I mean at the zoo," she said.

"Oh. No one is there. Zerobody. And even fewer people are coming to see the bats. There's a fall-of-Saigon rush to get out of town. Worse than the day before Thanksgiving."

Ramirez hung his jacket across the desk chair, then looked toward the black laboratory table. Joyce was in the center, Professor Lowery was on her left, and Heidi Daniels was on her right. All three were wearing lab coats and masks. The young man opened the locker beside the desk. He removed the last mask and lab coat and slipped them on.

"I thought it would be like when a singer dies and people put the

CDs back on the charts," Ramirez said as he walked over. "But uh-uh. After last night no one wants to know from bats."

"That's because most people are not curious by nature," Lowery said without turning.

"I think they're just scared shitless, Professor," Ramirez said. "And after the news footage I saw this morning, I don't blame them. Nobody wants anything to do with bats."

Lowery responded with silence. Even bent over the bat, Joyce was very much aware of his displeasure. That had always been his way: he passed on his wisdom, and you either accepted it or you didn't. If you didn't, he had no time for you. That could be hurtful to a career in a field as small as this one.

But Marc, bless his strange little self, didn't seem to care.

The grad student walked over and stood between Heidi and Dr. Joyce. The OEM deputy scooted over several steps so Ramirez could move in. He smiled at her through his mask. She looked at him again, nodded once, then went back to writing in her steno pad.

Then Ramirez saw the bat. *"Madre de Dios!"* he said.

The giant creature was lying on its belly on the canvas. Its wingtips were hanging over the sides of the table. Its head was turned sideways against the wall so the body could fit. An incision had been made along the shoulders and along the neck. There were dark, red muscles roped one over another, giving the bat fat mounds on the shoulders, down the back, and along the neck. Joyce was carefully re-moving layers of muscle with a scalpel while Lowery watched. A video camera set on a tripod behind Lowery was recording the dissection.

"Forget what you said last night about bats as territorial carni-vores," Ramirez told Joyce. *"This* is my doctoral thesis."

"Pretty amazing, isn't it?"

"Yeah. And you bagged it."

"Barely."

Ramirez glanced at her. "How're you doing?"

"I've had quieter nights," Joyce said.

Lowery exhaled impatiently.

Ramirez stopped talking. But only for a moment. "Is he a ves-pertilionid?"

"He is," Joyce said. *"Myotis mystacinus."*

"How much does he weigh?"

"Five hundred and sixty-six pounds, seven and one-half ounces," Joyce replied. "A lot of that's muscle, though not as much as you might think. There's an extremely high percentage of fat in the lower thorax, roughly forty-six percent of its body weight."

"That makes sense," Ramirez said. "He'd need to burn a lot of fuel when he flies."

"But he'd burn that up very fast," Joyce said, "which would ac-count for his enormous appetite and the need to shift, very quickly, from insects to other life-forms."

"And there's a female like it still out there."

"Right."

"She's probably, what? Seventy percent as large?"

"If the normal ratios hold, yes. I couldn't tell when I saw her. She was too far away. It's amazing, though, Marc. We were just looking in this one's chest. The lungs and heart are enlarged seven percent more than the bat's overall size increase, though all the other organs are pro-portionately smaller."

"Providing more oxygen and increased blood flow, less flying weight," Ramirez suggested.

"That would be my guess."

Ramirez slowly shook his head. "So what part of them did the radiation kick into overdrive?"

"I haven't gotten to the microscope yet," Joyce said, "but the database references a similar mutation among mice. In their case, probably this one as well, the mutation was centered in the muscle. Radiation affected the gene that encodes myostatin—"

"Right," Ramirez said. "So the growth-regulating protein shut down, growth continued unchecked outside the womb, and in just one generation you end up with Mothra."

"Exactly."

Ramirez thought for a moment. "How old is this bat?"

"About eight years."

"Long past the age when it could have sired pups."

"Right, and I know exactly where you're going with that. I've been thinking the same thing. Increased musculature usually leads to reduced fertility, just as it does with heavy-duty human weightlifters. So when an animal like this *does* become pregnant—"

"Its mate does everything it possibly can to ensure the safety of the offspring," Ramirez said. "It searches for a place where there's enough water, food, shelter, warmth, and privacy to suit the mother and child. It prepares a nest. Then it goes and gets her."

"Or given the infestation we saw last night, she or he summons an escort," Joyce said.

Lowery shook his head. "That kind of call-pattern communication among bats would be unprecedented, and I don't see how radiation would affect that."

"Not directly," Joyce said, "as in increased intelligence. But we have no way of knowing what effect a larger larynx and a lower vocal range would have on a colony."

"You haven't done the larynx yet?" Ramirez asked.

Joyce shook her head. "The pest control people wanted the mechanics of the bat itself first. What it's capable of, what its weaknesses might be in case they have to—"

There were pops in the distance. Joyce stopped cutting.

"What's the matter?" Lowery asked.

"That sounded like gunfire."

The others were silent. The sound came again; there were three muffled reports.

"That could be a car," Lowery said, "or one of those people who bang on plastic containers in the street—"

"I know guns," Joyce said. "That was a rifle."

The woman put down the scalpel, took off her mask, and walked to the door. Before she reached it there was a crash that rattled the building. The frosted glass wobbled in the door, and there was a deep creaking sound from the other side of the back wall.

"Maybe it's construction," Heidi said. "Aren't they building a new planetarium over on the north side of the building?"

Joyce opened the door and stuck her head out. The corridor was quiet. She listened. The creaking came again, from down the hall. There were shouts in the distance.

Joyce jumped when Lowery's phone beeped. Since she was closest to the desk she turned and answered it.

"Professor Low—"

"This is Rebecca Oliver at security!" a woman shouted on the other end. "They're all over!"

"What? Who is?"

"The *bats!* They're all over the lower level!" she shouted. "And another big one! It's trying to get—"

The line went dead. Joyce looked over at the others. Her eyes shifted to the big bat.

"Shit," she said.

"What's wrong?" Ramirez asked.

"The bats are here," Joyce said. "Little ones and a big one. And the phone just died."

Joyce stood staring down at the desk. Bats had a very highly developed sense of smell, which enabled them to identify bats of the same species. This was especially true during courtship and mating. It became even more intense in expectant bats, since it enables females who might have difficulty flying to follow males to rich food sources.

"She's here," Joyce droned. "The female bat. She followed the scent of her mate."

"But she went underground *miles* from here!" Lowery said as he tore off his mask.

"Right. And she tracked him."

"Yeah," Ramirez said, "but that's not the end of the love story, is it?"

Joyce looked at him. "What do you mean?"

"What if the lady doesn't know her big ugly's dead? She's not going to take that well at all."

Joyce agreed. She turned to the dead bat. It had taken six men to hoist it onto the table. There was no way they could move it down the hall, put it in the cryogenic freezer, and try to keep it from the female.

A loud series of groans and snaps echoed up through the floor. It sounded like a car wreck that kept on going. The building shuddered again and the lights snapped off.

"Passengers, I think we better get to the lifeboats," Ramirez said.

The room shook again as though it had been punched hard. Jars fell over and stuffed bats dropped from their perches. There was a muted crash right outside the wall on the other side of the laboratory, behind the sink.

"What's back there?" Ramirez asked.

"The elevator," Lowery said.

"The subway stops directly under the museum," Joyce thought aloud. "The bat goes from there to the elevator shaft to here." She wished she had the Magnum Gentry had given her back in New Paltz.

There was a sound like a whip on the other side of the wall.

Ramirez grabbed Joyce's forearm and tugged her toward the door. "I say we give the lovebirds some privacy."

Heidi and Professor Lowery had already walked past her. They opened the door and stopped.

"*God!*" Heidi screamed.

Hundreds of bats were coming down the corridor. Lowery reached past her and slammed the door. The bats crashed against the frosted glass, fluttering wildly on the other side.

Lowery went to the desk and snatched up the phone. It was dead. He threw it down. "Alright, think! What have we got in here to protect ourselves?"

Joyce's eyes drifted to the wings of the dead bat.

"Ultrasonic sound can disorient it, intense cold," Lowery thought aloud. "Come on, Nannie—think!"

She was thinking, but nothing was coming. She'd seen those two large claws in action.

The wall over the sink cracked. Plaster fell in thick chunks.

The door was rattling violently, and Joyce saw a tiny muzzle squeezing under the bottom.

She pulled off her lab coat and ran to jam it against the base of the door. While she did, Marc looked around. He disconnected the receiver from the phone and knelt next to Joyce. He smacked the creature on the head.

"It's for you!" he snarled.

The bat squealed and stopped moving. Marc used the phone to push it outside as Joyce plugged the remainder of the opening.

She stood. "That's not going to hold for long."

"I don't think it's gonna matter," Marc said as a hole appeared in the back wall. "Where's the goddamn cavalry?"

"They're probably fighting a few thousand vespers downstairs," Joyce said.

The laboratory was lit only by the bright light of an emergency lamp over the lab table. Heidi picked up a scalpel and began backing toward the desk. She stumbled into the chair and seemed startled by it. Moving it aside, she crouched under the desk, her back to the wall. The white surgical mask bore the damp outline of her open mouth.

"Wait," Lowery said. "Maybe this." He slipped a fire extinguisher from the wall beside the door. "Nancy, get the other one from behind the table and come here. We can spray it in the face, the ears."

The professor held out the hose and backed against the locker. It was the first time Joyce had ever seen him other than poised and collected.

A shower of plaster blasted into the room, leaving a hole nearly three feet across. The monster's hourglass-shaped nose filled the opening, then its right eye, and then one of its hooks slid through. It pulled on the top of the opening, breaking away more plaster.

Behind them, beneath the door, Joyce's lab coat began to move. The bats were shredding it and clawing through.

Heidi screamed. Ramirez tried to comfort her. Professor Lowery was facing the back wall, waiting.

And Joyce was looking around, praying for inspiration.

Thirty-two

Gentry spent the morning catching up on work. At noon he went to the chief's office to watch Mayor Taylor hold a televised press conference about the bats. The mayor said that he had some of the best "bat people" in the nation working on the problem, which was true, even though only Doyle and Berkowitz were with him at the press conference. The sixty-six-year-old second-term mayor said that a search was underway for the big bat and that the west side subways would not be reopened until it was found and "dealt with." He said that the small bats would probably not be "much more than an inconvenience" for most New Yorkers and chided Kathy Leung for suggesting that the bats could go wild here as they had in Westchester County.

Doyle elaborated. "We believe that they were being affected by the presence of the large male bat, which we have destroyed," Doyle said.

Gentry thought, *Nancy Joyce did that, you prick.*

"As we saw last night," Doyle continued, "the approach of the female had no effect on the bats over the Hudson."

When WABC's science reporter Bob Wallace asked exactly *how* the bats had been affected by the big male, Doyle replied, "We have someone working on that right now."

Nancy Joyce, you shit stain.

Mayor Taylor added that because the bat was apparently nesting downtown, Grand Central Station would remain open. He said that trains moving underground to and from Ninety-seventh Street would move through the tunnels slower than usual and that police would be standing watch along the way. He added that police vacation and days off were being canceled—which brought a very loud groan from the station house—so that the city's forty thousand officers would be available to help the city through this "unusual situation."

Though he said he would not be calling for a curfew, the mayor urged New Yorkers to remain inside after sundown. He said the number of bats in the city made accidental run-ins "inevitable," and he also discouraged rooftop "bat watch" parties. Police helicopters had spotted a number of these impromptu gatherings the night before.

Gentry spent the early afternoon catching up on sleep. His "power naps" used to amaze the hell out of Bernie Michaelson. Because Gentry never knew when it would be necessary to work undercover for several days and nights at a stretch, he had trained himself not only to sleep anywhere anytime but also to get into and out of it fast.

After resting, he pulled his radio from the desk drawer, turned it on low so he could hear what was going on with the bats, then went back to reading accident reports. There were dozens of them, some bat related, including fender benders due to a bat flying in a car window; a newsstand owner clocking a pedestrian while using a broom to shoo away a bat; window boxes dislodged by people trying to dislodge roosting bats. Gentry wondered how many people were going to be supremely unhappy when they discovered that these came under the "act of God" clauses in most insurance policies.

Several times during the day Gentry had to stop himself from calling Nancy. He knew she'd by busy with the big bat, and he hoped she'd let him know when she was finished or when she found something. It had been a long time since Gentry had been preoccupied with anything. The fact that it was a woman was surprising, exciting, and a little disturbing. He had become comfortable with the uncomplicated simplicity of his life.

He checked the central computer from time to time, and as of early evening the last missing persons report Gentry had heard about was the woman who vanished from the elevator at the World Trade Center. Investigators had followed the trail of blood up the elevator shaft but lost it around the fiftieth floor. A call to Marius Page confirmed that OEM was centering the search for the large bat in the downtown area between the financial district and the West Village. Despite the fact that there were more than five hundred police and transit officers taking part in the military-style maneuvers, progress was extremely slow. No one moved an inch without every section of tunnel being inspected.

And then came word that the giant bat and tens of thousands of small bats had ripped their way north along the B and D subway line. Gentry heard about it when a Times Square squad car called into division central, calls that were monitored by the station house. He turned up the volume.

"South Adam Patrol Sergeant!" said the caller. "We're on Broadway and Forty-second Street, and we have a major bat infestation here. They're attacking from the south. They're coming up Broadway and Seventh Avenue and converging in Times Square."

Gentry sat up and listened. He could hear the screams and car horns through his open office window. He went back to the radio.

The dispatcher said, "Sergeant, we've just been given a standard operating procedure notice. Have your officers get people inside. They'll stand a better chance in enclosed areas."

"Understood, but I need backup. People are running . . . being trampled. Looters are on the job."

"Sergeant, backup is being notified. I repeat: the priority is to get people inside."

The sergeant got off the radio for a moment. Though the box

was silent, Gentry could still hear the cries and shattering glass outside his window. He got his 9-mm pistol from the desk and slipped it in his shoulder holster. He rose and pulled on his jacket. He'd go out and help in a moment. First he wanted to hear where the giant bat was headed.

The patrol sergeant came back on. "Central, I've told my people to set up posts at three sites: the Palace Theater, the Virgin Megastore, and the Marriott Marquis Hotel. You got that?"

"Got it. Backup will be directed there."

"But it's a real madhouse here," the patrol sergeant said, "and it's getting worse by the second. All you can see are bats. They're shooting down like hawks—everyone outside is getting blitzed, including my people. If we can get inside, I'm hoping we can hold the interiors and get people to safety. I'm going out to try and—Jesus! *Jesus!*"

There was a short silence. Then Gentry heard and felt an explosion. He turned to the window as the distant blast lit the night.

"Get everyone away from there!" the sergeant yelled.

"What's happening?" demanded the dispatcher. "Sergeant, what's going on out there?"

"A cab just hit the liquid nitrogen air tanks on the—*back those other cars the hell away!*—on the west side of the office tower going up on Broadway and Forty-third—"

Silence.

"Shit—" the sergeant cried. "Oh, shit. God!"

"Sergeant?"

"Central, the construction platform's breaking—the crane's coming down! *It's coming down!*"

Gentry stood there feeling helpless. He heard the metal groan from ten blocks away. He heard the screams of the men and women in Times Square. He felt and then he heard the crash. The overhead lights danced. Books slipped from a shelf behind him, and pictures fell from the walls outside his office. People were shouting all over the station house.

The radio was silent.

There were eleven channels on Gentry's radio. His brain was numb, his body shaking as he tuned in to Midtown North. The bats had reached the west side of Central Park South, though they hadn't strayed past Columbus Circle. They were obviously sticking to the subway route.

Central was also receiving reports of events farther north, in the twentieth precinct. The dispatcher reported that so far three officers had been killed and seventy-eight wounded as the animals moved quickly along the subway line to the Eighty-first Street station. They stopped there.

At the American Museum of Natural History.

Immediately, Gentry was back. His mind kicked into drive as he stuck his radio in his jacket pocket and yelled for Detective Jason Anthony to come with him. They ran down the block to where the car was parked. Anthony turned on the siren and dashboard light and they sped off to the museum.

Thirty-three

The door of Professor Lowery's laboratory shuddered violently, and the room grew dark as more and more black shapes covered the frosted glass. The back wall of the lab was coming apart, and Nancy Joyce looked up while she screamed at God to give her a break. She continued to look up when she saw something. Then she took a quick look at the lab table and ran toward it.

"Yes," she said.

"Nannie, come back!" Lowery yelled.

"In a minute!"

"What are you going to do?" Ramirez yelled.

She snatched the burner from the lab table. "I'm going to set the coat on fire!"

"The coat?" Ramirez said.

"Don't!" Lowery said. "The smoke will—"

"Start the sprinklers on the ceiling," she interrupted. "The spray will put the fire out before we choke. The cold and the wet should also ground the little vespers if they get in."

"You totally rule," Ramirez said.

Joyce fired up the etna and crouched by the door. The rattling on the frosted glass pane and the mousy squealing of the bats were maddening, but at least they drowned out the sound of the crumbling plaster. She touched the flame to the lab coat.

It didn't burn.

"You fire-resistant son of a bitch!" she yelled.

Bats began to poke through and around the fabric. Muzzles, claws, wings. Joyce pulled over the swivel chair, stood under the sprinkler sensor, and held the flame to it.

"Come on!"

The first three bats made it under the door. They flew at Ramirez and he jumped under the desk, startling Heidi; he nearly impaled himself on her scalpel before she was able to pull it back. Snuggling toward her, Ramirez reached up around the front of the desk, slipped off the mouse pad, and held it almost like a Ping-Pong paddle. He used it to swat at the bats as they attacked. Heidi was bravely trying to slash at the bats as they darted in.

In the back of the lab the hole was big enough for the bat to fit her head through. She was using both claws now to hack at the wall. Bats began to fly through there just as the laboratory's two sprinklers came on. They sprayed the room with a cool, sturdy shower that caused the small bats to break off their attack and flutter around in confusion.

"Even better," Joyce muttered.

The water droplets were interfering with the bats' echolocation. Joyce stepped down from the chair and sidled up to Lowery. She kept the burner in case she needed it. The room was quite for a moment. In that moment of calm Joyce wished the professor would say something about what she'd just done. Nothing effusive. A "well done" would do it.

A moment later a door-sized section of the rear wall fell with a horrible crack. It sent dust billowing up into the water; it fell as pasty rain that covered the giant bat as she eased into the opening.

She came in with her folded left wing first, followed by her tawny body and then her right wing. She turned to face the room and spread her wings wide. As she did, Joyce moved into the room to get a better look at her lower belly.

It was extremely distended. The bat was pregnant.

The giant's head moved slowly toward the table, her nose wrinkling as she sniffed the air. After a moment she saw the male. Folding her wings, she crawled over to him. Joyce stepped toward the door to give her room. A chair and a stainless steel surgical table were knocked over as the bat approached. Lowery remained by the locker, trembling in the cold spray. Nearly a dozen small bats were hiding from the water and a few were flying above the spray. No more bats had entered the laboratory. In the distance a fire siren sounded.

The giant bat reached the table. She spread her wings and hopped up beside the other giant. She folded her wings again and dipped toward the face of the still, silent creature.

Joyce rubbed water from her eyes and watched the bat closely. There was no consensus among zoologists as to whether monogamous bats "felt" anything for their mates. They cared for their young but not for elderly bats; any sense of family, of community, seemed to revolve around the survival of the species. Professor Lowery had always been a student of the "survival-only" school. Joyce didn't share his sense of human superiority or bat inferiority, whichever it was.

She wished there were some way other than this to settle the debate.

Bats continued to slap against the outside of the frosted glass. Once in a while a bat in the laboratory would fly at one of the occupants, only to be driven away by the water. Now there were screams coming from other rooms. Joyce didn't want to think about what was happening there. The thick, thick swarms. The bloodletting. The death.

The head of the giant female was facing down. Her ears were turned toward the male. Joyce watched intently; she was strangely detached from the danger she was in.

How many days and nights had they been together? Joyce asked herself.

The dead bat was more than just the female's partner, her brother, and the father of her unborn pup. To the female, the sound of his heart and his breathing would be as familiar as her own. The closeness of his body would be the only warmth she'd ever known. He would have led her to food supplies and water and shelter and protected their nest from intruders. To the female, the dead bat might have been the greatest part of life itself.

The giant bat crept back a step and threw her wings out grandly. The right wing hit the wall behind the table, crushing the second fire extinguisher and shattering the emergency light above. Joyce turned up the burner. The long flame sizzled as water fell through it. In the hissing orange glow she saw the giant bat turn toward her. Spray from the sprinklers washed over the bat's face and wings and dark fur. The bat's gem red eyes fell on her and on Lowery. Then the animal's mouth pulled wide and turned upward and Joyce heard a sound she'd never heard from a bat or any other creature. It started low, like a moan, then grew louder and higher until Joyce had to put the burner down and cover her ears. Lowery dropped the fire extinguisher and it rolled away. Even with her palms pressed tightly against them, the shriek knifed through her ears, shattering the glass in the cabinets, until it finally passed from the audible to the inaudible.

The bat remained on the table, her mouth drawn open, the silent scream stirring the other bats from their hiding places.

The cry caused the frosted glass of the door to explode. The bats raced in, the crush causing some of them to become impaled on broken fragments that were still in the frame. They filled the room, flying in every direction, distracted by the water falling from above. A few, flying under the others and protected from the spray, started biting at Joyce. She dropped the burner, which rolled away and died in a puddle. A moment later she lost her footing on the wet tile floor and landed hard on her back. She managed to flop onto her belly to protect her face. Bats bit her back, neck, and legs.

"Nannie—"

She looked ahead.

Lowery was lying several feet away at the foot of the locker. The scientist was curled on his left side in a fetal position, his arms wrapped around his head. Bats covered his side and hands.

"*Nannie!*"

He was reaching blindly for something.

The fire extinguisher. It had fallen over and rolled several feel away.

The woman scrambled across the slippery floor. As she did, bats gathered on her, biting and scratching. She'd been nipped by bats before, though not by as many or so often. She did what she'd learned long ago to do on cold nights: relax. It didn't lessen the prickling pain, but it kept her from jerking this way and that each time a bat nipped or clawed.

As Joyce neared the fire extinguisher, the giant bat suddenly leaped down. The floor wobbled as she landed. In almost the same movement she slammed her right hook into Lowery's back, dragging him across the wet floor as she turned toward Joyce. The ivory white claw penetrated the professor's right shoulder amid a fountain of blood; he writhed and pulled at it but the she bat didn't seem to notice. After a moment he went limp.

The bat raised her other hook.

There wasn't time to think. Joyce was moments from being impaled. Rolling toward the bat, she grabbed the fire extinguisher. The enormous bat hopped toward her as Joyce lay on her back and turned the nozzle up and sprayed the contents into the bat's face.

The giant staggered back, still holding Professor Lowery. Joyce fired again, this time into her mouth. The other bats instantly broke off their attack, flying back to shelter out of the rain.

Joyce looked at Lowery. Blood was pouring from his body. His arms and legs were limp.

"Marc!" she cried.

"Yeah!"

"Get out *now!*"

The young man slid from under the desk, pulling the reluctant Heidi with him. He continued to hold her hand as he helped her to her feet. He pushed her ahead of him and looked back at Joyce.

"*Go!* I'll hold her back!"

"I'll get help!" he said.

He ran out, and Joyce turned back to the giant bat. The bat had pulled her claw from Professor Lowery and was shaking her head violently. The water was washing the foam away. Joyce hit her again.

The bat stumbled back against the sink, her great wings stiffening, her body deflating as she exhaled.

Joyce knew that wasn't going to hold the bat much longer. She also didn't want to run. The thing would chase her through the museum where other people might be injured. Firing one more blast of foam, Joyce slung her arm behind her and threw the fire extinguisher at the bat. It hit the creature in the left forearm. Then, turning to her left, Joyce reached for the handle of the locker door. She yanked it open, stood, and squeezed in sideways. She took a wire hanger from a hook, slipped it through one of the vents in the door, and pulled it shut.

It was dry in here, though water dripped from her hair into her ears and mouth. She began to tremble from the cold and ended up crying with fear and the horror of what had happened to Professor Lowery.

Joyce listened. As she did, her mind beat up on her.

Lowery is dead.

She breathed rapidly and the locker warmed.

I should have done what he told me.

The dark made everything seem louder, closer. She heard the flap of the bat's wings, like someone shaking out a rug. She couldn't tell whether or not it was coming closer.

No. That wouldn't have made any difference. Two fire extinguishers wouldn't have helped.

She heard shouts from downstairs.

You did the right thing.

Then there was silence, but only for a moment. Suddenly the world turned sideways as the locker was wrenched away from the wall and dragged loudly across the laboratory floor. A moment later the top and bottom of the metal cabinet slammed hard against something. There was a brief respite, the locker tilted farther, and then it was slammed again—

The hole in the wall. The locker was being pulled against it.

Joyce's breath came faster as panic gripped her. She thought of the deer in the tree, the bicyclist carried into the tunnel, the man swept from the train platform at Christopher Street.

The bat was trying to take her away.

Thirty-four

Detective Anthony raced along Eighth Avenue to Columbus Circle. En route, Gentry used the car phone to try to raise Professor Lowery's office.

The phones were not working in the laboratory. The detective also wasn't able to reach museum security and was furious with himself for not having accompanied Nancy.

The car rounded Columbus Circle. Anthony cut through the traffic coming the other way and sped alongside the park. As they headed north, Gentry was overwhelmed by the panic he saw. Anthony had to swerve, stop, and start as people ran and stumbled into the street, trying to get away from the bats. It reminded him of the cockroaches that had been flushed from the walls of his apartment building. People didn't seem to be running *to* anything, just away. And there weren't many people helping other people. They were looking after themselves. Not out of selfishness but out of necessity. The bats turned each person, each part of the body, into a battle zone.

And the people were losing.

"Isn't there anything we can do to help?" Anthony asked.

"If we get out, the bats will bring us down," he said. "And if we stop to let anyone into the car, we may be overrun."

Overrun by bats and by people. Overrun by panic and fear.

The detective looked up as they drove past the rows of stately and exclusive apartment buildings that lined the broad street. Small fires were burning in the windows of several apartments. They could have been caused by struggles around candlelit dinners, by bats that had flown too close to gas burners, by people who tried to chase away the creatures using makeshift torches. Gentry could also hear the high-pitched whine of the smoke detectors, which seemed to make the bats even more agitated.

Midtown South and Midtown North used the same radio frequency and Gentry called in the locations of the 10-59s to be relayed to the engine and ladder company on West Eighty-third Street. He didn't know how the firefighters would deal with the bats—hoses, perhaps—but they'd have to try. That was all the city needed now, to burn.

The car pulled up across the street from the museum. The old gothic towers were alive with bats. Gentry told Anthony to wait; he didn't want an officer who was inexperienced with the bats either getting hurt or getting in his way. Pulling his coat over his head, Gentry ran across the wide street and raced up the stairs into the rotunda.

He was not surprised to find bats everywhere. In the bright glare of the emergency lights he could see them circling in the high ceiling, knitting in and out of the skeleton of the giant, rearing barosaurus, flying through the dark halls beyond. What did surprise him was that they weren't attacking, though it was obvious they had been: wounded museum personnel and visitors were everywhere. People were just beginning to stir after the assault.

Gentry took his coat from around his head. The subdued state of the bats meant that the giant had left or had been killed. As he sped toward the stairway, he prayed it was the latter.

Gentry reached the fourth floor, the last of the public floors. There, he had to ask a wounded guard how to get to the fifth floor. Bleeding on the cheeks and hands, the man told him. Out of breath, Gentry ran to the door and put three bullets through the security scanner. The door clicked open. He took the stairs two at a time and hurried to Professor Lowery's laboratory. He heard awful banging coming from that direction.

The spotlit halls were deserted save for several confused, slip-stream flows of bats and two people who were limping toward him. As they neared, Gentry recognized Heidi Daniels. The detective stopped her.

"Heidi, where's Nancy?"

"She's still in the lab!" Marc Ramirez said urgently.

"What happened?"

"The female bat broke through—"

Gentry didn't hear the rest. He ran on, damning himself with every other step. He should have been here. He *should* have.

Though the main lights were down, the emergency lights had come on in the hallway. The laboratory was just ahead. Gentry approached boldly; it didn't pay to tiptoe, not with bats.

When he reached the lab, he saw bats drinking from a puddle just outside the doorway. He heard the gentle spray of water inside under the steady beat of *wham* . . . silence . . . *wham.* The bats didn't bother him, even though he was just a few feet away.

He saw the shattered glass lying just inside the door. His heart punching hard, he raised his gun and held his breath and swung through the wooden frame.

Years of entering drug dens and hideouts had taught Gentry to see everything as a snapshot when he went into a room: front vision, peripheral vision, top and bottom, it was all processed at once. The emergency lights in the hall barely lit the laboratory, but it was enough. Virtually every inch of the walls, cabinets, and ceiling was covered with a rippling black carpet of bats. Everything except for the dead giant, which was lying on the table to the left. A fine spray was raining down in the midst of the bats, and Professor Lowery lay soaked with water and blood near the desk. He wasn't moving. Behind the spray was what the narcotics squad used to call "the big story," the head of the gang.

The giant bat.

The creature was mostly in shadow, its giant off-white hooks trying to pull the laboratory clothes locker through an opening in the wall. The animal was hidden inside the opening. The banging came from the monster's awkward attempts to maneuver the tall locker through the wide hole.

The creature stopped moving. Gentry stood with his right arm extended, his left hand supporting his wrist, his index finger on the trigger. The locker was resting in the creature's hooks, lying diagonally across its body. Gentry couldn't see the bat's head, wings, or legs.

Suddenly, the creature wailed. The echoing cry reminded Gentry of a street musician he used to hear on his beat, a man who dragged a violin bow across the mouth of glass bottles. It was a high, sustained, hollow sound, almost like weeping. The other bats didn't move. Obviously, that wasn't the sound that sent them into their frenzy.

Gentry raised the gun slightly and fired twice, once to the left and once to the right. The giant bat's wail became a shriek of pain. The locker clattered loudly to the floor.

The twin reports of the 9-mm stirred the small bats from their perches. Hundreds of them dashed through the spray, weaving up and down and from side to side. The droplets seemed to confuse them. Gentry lowered his weapon and walked into the spray. Behind the thick swarm he could see the locker lying on its side. The giant hooks were gone.

Gentry walked ahead. He stopped short of the crisscrossing bats and peered into the dark. With awful, kick-in-the-groin suddenness, the detective wished he had thought about what he'd seen in the subway. A moment later he saw the monster's gaping mouth and serrated teeth inside the dark opening. He saw the ruby eyes beneath them.

The head was inverted.

The goddamn thing had been hanging upside down. Gentry had probably shot the bat in its fucking tail.

The detective raised his gun to fire again, but by then the giant bat had vanished. He holstered his weapon and ran into the laboratory. He had to duck bats as they wove to an fro.

"Nancy!" he yelled. "Nancy, are you all right?"

There was no answer. He half skidded, half splashed to a stop and knelt by the locker. The door was facing him. It fell open.

Joyce was bundled inside. She looked up at him, trembling, and he slipped his arms around her.

"It's okay," he said, hugging her. "It's okay."

"That's easy for you to say," she said, shivering. "Did you get her?"

"No," he said, "but she's gone."

"Probably got tired. She's very pregnant."

"We can talk about this later," Gentry said softly as he helped her out. "Let's get you out of here."

He had to work her from the tight spot in pieces—head, right shoulder, left shoulder, lower right leg, lower left leg, torso, hips. He held her close to him, warming her as they stood.

Gentry pulled Ramirez's leather coat from the locker. It was soaked and he threw it aside. There was nothing to wrap her in.

Joyce turned toward the opening in the wall. "I thought I heard a shot and a cry," she said.

"You did," Gentry told her, "but I fucked up. She was hanging from something inside there. I only hit her foot or her tail."

Joyce turned and touched his wet, unshaven cheek. "You didn't fuck up. You saved my life." Then she looked past him at Lowery. Her expression had told Gentry that she knew exactly what she'd see.

Gentry slid between them. "Let the medical people take care of the professor. I want to get you out of—"

A bat dove at him. Then another.

"What the hell?" he said.

"It's the female," Joyce said as she swatted at the bats. "She stopped wailing, but that doesn't mean she's quiet. She's probably making her way back toward the subway."

"Come on!" Gentry said as he hustled her toward the door.

As more and more bats resumed their attack, the detective was not optimistic about making it back down the stairs. Just getting into the hallway with Nancy was a nightmare of slipping on water and swatting at bats. He was trying to shield the woman. But the bats that had been streaming above when he arrived were attacking now. They had scattered before when he fired his gun, and he tried to frighten them again.

This time they weren't buying.

Gentry had his left arm over Nancy. He pulled her close and used his body and coat to shield her as best as he could. She had her arms wrapped tightly around his waist, her damp head bent against his chest. He could feel her heart drumming. His own was getting up there too: they'd gone only a few yards down the corridor when Gentry realized they weren't going to get much farther. The bats were really starting to pile on. He couldn't see or hear, wasn't even sure in which direction they were headed. And he felt like he was being hit from ankle to scalp with snapping rubber bands. Each bite made some part of him jump.

Finally, Gentry stopped, took off his coat, and started to wrap it around Nancy's head.

"You go!" he yelled. "Make a run for it!"

Joyce refused and pushed blindly at his coat to make him take it back; she stopped suddenly and desperately patted the coat. The top, on the left.

"What's in here?" she asked.

"My radio—"

Joyce tore frantically at the coat to get it out. She fell to her knees, pulling at the coat with one hand while swatting at the bats with the other. Gentry dropped and helped her get it out.

He handed it to her then pulled the coat over them both.

"Turn it on!" she yelled.

"It's on."

"*Louder!* I want static, as much as you can get!"

Gentry took the slender radio. He held it close to his face, curling his arm around them both for protection, and turned it to talk. Then he pushed up the volume in order to generate feedback. After a moment he got a thunderous, seashore-breaker drone.

He gave the radio back to Nancy. "Now what?"

"We jam them!" she shouted as she took the radio and held it outside the garment.

The bats broke off their attack at once. They fluttered around aimlessly. When Nancy was sure the retreat would hold, she removed the coat.

"Okay," she said. "Let's get up and walk out of here."

Gentry rose and helped her up. They started toward the stairs. It was astonishing. The bats would approach and then fly off, as though they were bouncing into a force field.

"It's like you said about the tiger moth, isn't it?" Gentry said. "High-frequency sounds interrupting the normal flow of information."

"Not exactly," Joyce said. "This isn't blocking whatever the she-bat's sending. It's hiding it—confusing them."

They hobbled ahead, bleeding from numerous puncture wounds. Gentry's mind leaped from being proud of Nancy yet again, to thinking about the rabies shots they'd certainly have to undergo after being attacked, to focusing on the larger problem: how to stop the giant bat. If they didn't do that soon, New York City would be destroyed in a matter of days.

The bats in the rotunda had gone back on the offensive, flying, clinging, and ripping at everyone who moved. The radio afforded Gentry and Joyce protection as they made their way to the exit; she left it behind with a museum official who was trying to get workers into a windowless office. She and Gentry ducked back under his coat.

Detective Anthony was still waiting across from the museum, his windows shut as bats poured from Central Park. Dogs were howling everywhere, and many were running free in the streets, no doubt driven wild by the ultrasonic cry of the she-bat. There were screams coming from people lying on the sidewalks, from windows of the apartments that lined Central Park West, from cars and buses. They had stopped or plowed into one another, into trees or hydrants, or had rolled up onto sidewalks. Bats had come in through open windows. Passengers were struggling to get them off.

There were loud cries to the right. As Joyce and Gentry crossed the street, the detective pulled the coat off his head and looked back. The skies high and low were full of bats. They were like layers of clouds, moving at different speeds, in different directions. Just north of Seventy-sixth Street, where the loud screams had come from, a cloud of bats had descended on a rooftop bat party. "Guano shelter" tents were ripped, and ghostly shapes flitted through the night as bats became tangled in the torn fabric.

Gentry opened the car door and helped Nancy in. A bat flew at him, and he whipped his coat around, smacking it to the ground. He stepped on the coat, then pulled it under his arm. The bat was crushed on the asphalt. Gentry took another look back.

The air was full of bats. It was like watching thousands of dark Ping-Pong balls blowing in a huge lotto tank. The creatures were moving everywhere and every way. The detective watched as some rooftop partygoers stumbled against the low brick wall. There was a horrified shriek as one man went over. He managed to grab a cement planter that ran along the edge of the roof; he dangled there while other guests attempted to pull him up. But the growing swarm of bats drove the rescuers back, and the man fell eleven stories to the sidewalk. He didn't scream, but he hit the concrete with an audible crack.

Gentry slid into the back, behind the passenger's seat. He slammed the door, catching an incoming bat as he did. The detective opened the door, let the bat drop out, and reshut it firmly.

"What in God's name is going on?" Anthony cried.

"We've been demoted to insects," Gentry said.

"I don't understand."

"Never mind," Gentry replied. He told Detective Anthony to head downtown to OEM headquarters at 7 World Trade Center. The detective hoped the place was still operational.

Anthony activated the flasher and siren, turned the car around, and sped back down Central Park West. He wove around a zigzag of fire engines that had responded to their call. The firefighters were backed against their trucks using the water to beat back bats. Obviously, the giant female was still close enough for her cries to affect these vespers.

"I'm going to keep off the highway," Anthony said. "The radio says it's jammed with abandoned cars and wrecks and people who are still trying to get out of town."

"Fine," Gentry replied. "Just don't stop. It'll give these bastards a chance to swarm."

"Understood."

The driver cut west at Sixty-fourth Street, then turned onto Columbus Avenue at Lincoln Center. The bat attack was not limited to the Central Park region. Well-dressed patrons who had come to hear the 125th anniversary production of *Die Fledermaus*—a perverse coincidence—at the Metropolitan Opera were running through the lobby or hiding under tables in the vast courtyard. Several bodies were bobbing under a sea of bats in the large, lighted circular fountain.

Gentry turned to Joyce. She was staring ahead, her expression flat. He took her hand and squeezed it. She turned toward him, and as they passed a streetlight he could see the sadness in her eyes.

The driver slowed to avoid a body that had crawled onto the street. A moment later, Anthony screamed, jammed hard on the brakes, and started slapping at his lap. Gentry looked over the seat.

A bat was chewing on the inside of the driver's thigh, and two more were crawling into the car from under the dashboard.

"Get the hell *off!*" Anthony cried.

He grabbed the bat and tried to pull it away as the other two flew at his hands. Two more bats came in behind them.

"Where's your radio?" Gentry demanded.

"In the passenger door!"

Gentry reached over to get it as four more bats squirmed in from under the dashboard. The animals flew for his face, and Gentry dropped back into his seat.

A bat flew at Joyce's chin; she snatched it from the air with her right hand and slammed it against the window to her left. There was a mushy *splat* and a short squeal.

As the dead bat slid from the window, Joyce leaned over the seat toward the dashboard. She turned the air conditioner on and cranked it to *high.*

"Turn the vents on the bats!" she said to Anthony as she turned to help get the bats off Gentry.

With bloody fingers, Anthony adjusted the vents so they blew on his lap and face. The bats immediately slowed down, and the young officer was able to pull them away. They flew at him again, this time less vigorously. He snatched them off and crushed them like tissues and discarded them on the floor. No other bats entered the car.

When Gentry's bats had been crushed, he looked at Nancy. "They hate cold," he said.

"That's right."

"You never fail to amaze me. Neither do the bats."

"I can't decide whether they're trying to get away from the female's cry or whether they're controlled by it," she said. "But whatever it is, if there's a way into a place, they'll find it."

Gentry turned to the officer. "Can you drive?"

"Yes," he said. "And thank you, ma'am."

"It was my pleasure," she said.

They had stopped at Fifty-sixth Street, near the Symphony House. He flipped on a loudspeaker and turned back onto the road.

"Turn on your air conditioners!" he shouted as he went around other stopped cars.

Gentry reached over and got the radio. There were different channels broken into divisions, with three precincts in each division. Anthony's radio was still set to Midtown South. On the other end, dispatcher Caroline Andoscia was trying to listen to several people at once. Each of them was shouting, probably because they were under attack. Gentry turned down the volume and put the radio on the seat. They heard a dispatcher call for backup at Grace Church on Broadway and Tenth Street. The 10-66 "unusual incident" call reported that the building was jammed with people and under attack. Bats had come up through the pipe organ. When people tried to escape, the bats swarmed in through the doors.

"Should we go there?" Detective Anthony asked. "We don't know how many units are operational."

"There isn't time," Gentry said. "We've got to get Dr. Joyce downtown."

"Say your prayers," she said quietly to the radio.

Gentry looked out the window. It was like a scene from an old science-fiction movie where a monster or alien invaders had gone through a city reducing lively streets to acres of bodies, idling vehicles, smashed windows, and windblown litter. And all of it in just under an hour. People who had ignored the mayor's suggestion to stay inside had dropped where they were walking or jogging or waiting to cross the street. In the road and on the sidewalk, bicycle delivery men were lying where they fell. Dogs that hadn't been brought down in attacks were fighting each other or jumping into the air trying to bite the bats. The car had to swerve even more than before to avoid hitting injured people. Dead pigeons were everywhere. Occasionally, Gentry saw a bird streak through the air, pursued by bats. At least the furry bastards weren't playing favorites.

The handful of people who were still mobile were attempting to ignore the bats clustered around their heads and arms and were trying to crawl to the nearest doorway. Those who had managed to get to shelter—small bodegas or newsstands that could be closed up in a hurry—were looking through windows or shouting for help. But help was nowhere near.

"What would happen if we pumped the radio feedback through the loudspeaker?" Gentry asked Joyce. "Would that drive the bats away?"

Joyce shook her head once. "The interference was the equivalent of a weak magnetic force. Beyond a very local perimeter it wouldn't affect the stronger cry of the female."

Gentry started as bats slammed at his window in succession and bounced away. The bats were thicker downtown, flying in every direction like black confetti caught in a fan. Just below Forty-second Street, the Port Authority Bus Terminal was a disaster, with evening commuters and police looking as if they'd been cut down by poison gas. They were lying side by side or one atop the other under the wide overhang.

To the east, the top floors of the Empire State Building were dark—not because the lights were off, but because the top of the building was crawling with bats. There must be trapped prey on the observation deck and inside the spire. Occasionally, light would poke through the shroud of bats as they shifted or as a window broke and a body fell through.

Car sirens and bank alarms screamed on all sides. Occasionally, police cars and ambulances sped by. Gentry couldn't imagine how they were deciding who got help. Probably doctors or surgeons or city officials, he guessed. People who would be needed to fight the bats. Gentry had never seen a system crash so fast or so completely.

He turned back to Nancy. "Assuming the OEM is still functioning, Weeks is definitely going to want to talk to you. Al Doyle spent the last of his credibility coin at the mayor's press conference this morning. He told everyone there was nothing to worry about, it was the male bat that was controlling the others. Will you be up for meeting with Weeks?"

She nodded. "That she-bat is still out there. And it's a lot more dangerous than these people realize. She's definitely pregnant; I could see that when she was in the lab. She's probably within a week or so of giving birth, which is why she's come to New York. Her offspring will be very vocal within a few days, and they'll probably have the same effect on bats that she has. If there are two or three giants running loose in the subways, protected by other bats, it'll be damn near impossible to get near them." Her voice snagged and she looked away. "The one time I could really use his help and he's not here."

Gentry took her hand. "I'm very, very sorry about Professor Lowery."

"Me too." Joyce looked back at Gentry. "But I'm responsible for this, you know."

"For what?"

"For all this. The destruction, the death."

"How?"

"By killing the male."

"Oh, bullshit."

"No," Joyce said, "it's true. I should have expected it. I always believed bats were capable of feeling emotion, and I should have taken that into consideration before I started cutting the male apart. I certainly shouldn't have left the body where the female could find it."

"You couldn't have known she'd do that, or that she'd find you. She was in a subway miles away."

"You're thinking like a human, not like a bat—"

"Yeah, well, that's always been one of my problems."

Joyce looked at him for a moment more. Then she pressed her lips together and looked down.

"Look, Nancy," Gentry said, "I'm just trying to help you put this in perspective. Everyone's been under incredible pressure. We all did what we thought was right, up and down the line. And as far as I'm concerned, you've done more things faster, better, and righter than anyone could have in your position."

She continued to look down. She looked like she wanted to cry. Gentry wished she would, just let it all out. He had, a couple of hours after Bernie Michaelson had been shot. It was like a good rain, cleaning away all kinds of grime. Some of it about Bernie, some of it about losing his wife, some of it about things even Father Adams in the Chaplain Unit was still trying to figure out. But he'd obviously needed it.

As they were approaching Twenty-third Street, something came through Detective Anthony's radio that caught Gentry's ear. He grabbed it and turned up the volume.

". . . at the Prolly House on Twenty-third and Seventh. Repeat: the giant bat is attacking the Prolly House at Twenty-third and Seventh. Request immediate assistance."

Anthony didn't have to be told. He turned left and raced toward the shelter for battered women.

Thirty-five

They were too late.

Several police cars and fire trucks were pulled up in front of the three-story center for abused women. The cars were parked on the sidewalk so police and firefighters could get inside without being exposed to the bats outside for very long. A hose hooked to a fire hydrant had been used to douse the bats inside while the women and children were evacuated into ESU recovery vans. Once the bats were down, police officers with heavy-duty vests and helmets kept them down permanently using shovels. Deeper inside the building, police were using pressurized water extinguishers to knock the creatures from the air. When word came through that all the visitors and staff had been evacuated and accounted for, the officers had begun using scatterguns on the doused bats.

The giant bat had left shortly before the first police car had arrived. Around that time, the police reported, all the bats in the area had ceased their aggressive behavior, including bats that had gotten inside the shelter. They appeared frantic and disoriented but were non-violent. Reports from other precincts indicated that the bats had calmed down all across Manhattan and were being exterminated by any and every means possible.

While Gentry headed in to assist the other officers, Joyce hurried toward the vans to talk to the evacuees.

Up and down Twenty-third Street, New Yorkers were literally trying to get back on their feet. Those who could walk were helping those who could not. Many people were just sitting where they'd fallen, staring. Joyce imagined that the same scene was being repeated everywhere from Eighty-first Street to wherever the bat was nesting.

That, and the quiet. There were occasional shouts for help and moans of pain. But the fact that they could be heard only emphasized the silence that had settled on the city. There were no cars or growling buses, no air traffic, no bicyclists shouting for people to make way. There were no car radios or boom boxes, no loud conversations or kids shouting to other kids or the rattling coin cups of the homeless. There was no construction, no one selling hot watches from a briefcase or bundles of socks from a cardboard box. Save for the countless sirens and alarms, the stillness was abnormal, like during a blizzard.

New York sounded like Nancy felt. Numb. She still couldn't believe what had happened back at the museum, that Professor Lowery was dead. She was glad she had these interviews to do, the problem of finding and destroying the bat to wrestle with.

According to the only adult eyewitness, a woman who had been in the playroom with several children, the creature had come through a skylight on the top floor and went right to that room. The woman said that while she crouched with the kids in a corner, trying to protect them but fully expecting to die, the bat ignored them all. She said that after looking around the room for several moments, the bat spread its wings, knocking over furniture and shelves. Then it wailed loudly, returned to the hallway, and flew back through the skylight. It was in the shelter for less than a minute.

One of the children, a young boy named Chaka, got up from one of the benches inside the van. He walked over to Joyce and said that the bat looked mean but wasn't mean.

"That's a pretty silly way to be, isn't it?" Joyce asked. She took his hand.

"You're cold," he said.

"Very cold. I got sprinkled on."

"How?"

"Water was putting out a fire. And I forgot my umbrella."

Chaka smiled.

"Can you tell me a little more about the bat?" Joyce asked.

"It's big."

"It is. But it didn't hurt anyone?"

Chaka shook his head.

A little girl from one of the benches said, "It reminded me of Oscar the Grouch."

Joyce looked at the petite blonde. "Let's see. That's one of the Muppets from *Sesame Street*, isn't it?"

She nodded.

Chaka said, "It looked mean, but it didn't do anything bad to anyone. It just looked sad."

Joyce thanked him, thanked everyone, then left the van. She chewed on the problem as she walked toward the townhouse.

The bat hadn't come to feed. She hadn't come to give birth. But she had left the subway searching for *something* and wailed or wept when she didn't get it.

What?

Joyce hoped the answer was in the playroom.

She walked inside. Dead, hurt, or unconscious bats were being swept aside with brooms. She made her way carefully down the wet corridor to the stairs in the back. On the third floor, she found herself standing under the shattered skylight. The playroom was directly ahead. She walked in.

The room smelled of wet fur. There were crushed toys and snacks, an upended TV, tattered sleeping bags, and overturned racks of videotapes and video games. Joyce stood with her hands on her hips, looking around.

Gentry walked in a minute later. "I think we got most of the bats," he announced. "The cops're shoveling them into Hefty bags. How were the people you talked to?"

"Pretty shaken up. Are you sure everyone is safe? No one's missing?"

"Not a one," Gentry said. "I talked to the police downstairs. The two ESU officers at the Twenty-third Street stop got knocked silly when she burned through the station and flew up the stairs, but she didn't attack them."

Joyce shook her head. "Then I just don't understand."

"Maybe she was conserving her strength. Maybe I hurt her when I fired those rounds back at the museum, and she came up to rest, get some fresh air."

"She would have rested in the subway tunnel," Joyce said. "Besides, there's no blood."

Gentry looked around. "So I didn't even hit her freakin' tail!"

"No," Joyce said. "You didn't. You only scared the bat off and saved my life. What was it you said to me back in the car? About asking too much of yourself?"

"I said *you* shouldn't. I can, though."

"Right." Joyce knew he was joking but not. She let it go for now. She continued pacing in a circle as she looked around the room. The sleeping bags were ripped where the bat had walked across them. A few videocassettes had been crushed, and the TV was blank.

"So what do you think?" Gentry asked.

"I don't know. I just don't know."

"How do I start thinking like a bat?"

"You ask yourself what sensory input could have brought you here," she said. "All right. Let's go back. The bat left the museum and entered the subway. She got down here fast, which meant she had to be flying. Flying and echolocating because the subway tunnels are a snug fit and she'd have to watch out for girders and posts. She probably intended to stay underground until she reached her nest."

"Maybe she came out to eat."

"Unlikely."

"What makes you so sure?"

"Because she *didn't* eat. She didn't attack the police at the station stop or the people here. Besides, if she were hungry she would have waited until she was closer to home. Less distance to carry her meal. No. As she neared here she either heard or smelled something that made her leave the subway. She flew straight to the roof and came down through the skylight. Then she entered the playroom. She attacked no one but encountered something here that made her cry again."

"Wait. Again?"

Joyce nodded. "The bat also cried when she realized that her mate was dead."

"You mean she cried like a human being?"

"I believe that's exactly what it was, yes. Of course, that grew into rage back at the museum and caused the other bats to go berserk. But not here. She left without hurting anyone. Why?"

"What were the kids doing?" Gentry asked.

Joyce was still walking around the room. "Coloring, reading, resting, snacking." She looked down at a half-eaten peanut butter sandwich, an overturned container of milk, a banana. The bat hadn't touched any of the food.

Was it a scent? Someone who smelled like Joyce? The bat could have detected that from the subway, but she didn't come here to kill. She was looking for something.

"Maybe some of the kids were watching TV," Gentry suggested.

"Possibly." Joyce walked toward the overturned set.

"Maybe the bat heard her mate's voice on the news."

"A lot of people would have been watching TV along her route," Joyce said. "Why would she stop here? Anyway, even if a tape of the male bat was on the news, she'd hear the sounds differently from the way we do. They would register as a series of strobing pulses, not as a continuous sound. It would be like you mistaking a black-and-white newspaper photograph for reality." She stopped at the TV and looked down. "On the other hand—"

"What?" Gentry asked.

"She could have heard something that we recognize as one thing but that she heard as something else."

"Such as?"

Joyce righted the stand and the TV. She reconnected a loose cable in back. The static vanished and a solid blue screen appeared. Joyce looked at the VCR that was on a bookcase behind the TV. The unit was off. "They weren't watching a videotape," she said.

Gentry moved one of the sleeping bags. There was a small plastic console beneath it. The red "on" light was glowing. "No," he said. "They were playing video games."

Joyce stepped over and crouched beside it. The game cartridge had popped partway out. She pushed it back in and then looked at the TV. The title screen of the game came on. "Feather Jackson," she read. She pushed "start." The legend scrolled down the screen, recounting the history of the girl who could fly. As it did, the theme music came on.

Gentry said, "Maybe we ought to ask one of the kids what part they were up to."

Joyce nodded absently. She was listening to the game.

Gentry turned to go.

"Wait!" Joyce said suddenly.

Gentry came over and squatted beside her. "What've you got?"

She punched up the volume on the TV. "Do you hear that?"

"The music?"

"No." She raised the volume. "The drum underneath it."

Gentry listened again then nodded with the beat. "Drums of doom," he said, then read from the screen. "'The approaching armies of the Pillow People want to conquer Featherland and turn its inhabitants into—'"

"Robert, don't you get it?"

He shook his head. She turned the volume higher. The music it-self became a broken, crackling noise, but she could still hear the drum.

"This is just a hint of how the bat heard it. Loud and thumping."

"Okay. But there had to be thousands of radios on along the way, a lot of beats. Why would she respond to this particular drum?"

"The drumbeats in music change, don't they?"

"Most do, I suppose."

"This doesn't. It's constant."

He listened.

"*Ba-dum. Ba-dum.* Hear it?" Joyce asked.

"Yeah."

The legend finished, and the game began. The drums continued.

"The beat keeps going when the introduction ends," she said with growing excitement. "The sound probably continues through the entire game. Don't you *see?*"

"No."

"Robert, that sound is in the audible range. When would the bat have been exposed to a regular drumbeat like it?"

"I have no idea."

Joyce rose. She shut off the video game and started toward the door. "In the womb, Robert. The bat came here looking for her mother."

Thirty-six

Gentry and Joyce went back to the car and continued downtown. Joyce was revved up again. Gentry was not. He had some major problems with what Joyce had come up with.

"You really believe that a bat flying through a subway tunnel heard a video game that sounded like her mother—

"Her mother's heart."

"Like her mother's heart," he said. "She heard that and she flew over to check it out?"

"Yes. It's very possible."

"One sound in a city of millions upon millions of sounds."

"That's right. Again, think like a bat. Its hearing is extraordinarily sensitive and multidirectional. A bat can pick up and follow a distinctive sound the same way a shark sniffs blood in the water."

"But even if that's true, her mother died eight years ago," Gentry said. "How could the bat remember that?"

"It's not in the conscious mind, but it's *there*," Joyce said. "The sound triggered some kind of memory. Think about it. She left at peace, without hurting anyone, without stirring up the small bats again. She was obviously calmed by whatever happened here."

"All right. Assuming that's true, why didn't she get angry when she saw that her mother wasn't here? She was in a rage when she left the museum."

"You just said why."

"I did?"

"All the giant bat knows is that her mother wasn't in the play-room," Joyce said. "As far as the bat knows, she might still be alive somewhere. But when the bat came to the museum laboratory, she *saw* that her mate was dead. She didn't see or smell anything to suggest death here in the shelter. Maybe one of the kids accidentally pulled out the cable when the bat came in. Maybe the bat did. So the video sound stopped suddenly, and the bat—"

"—thinks that mommy may still be alive?" Gentry said.

"We've got a name for that at the zoo," she said. "It's called the Dumbo effect. We use smells and sounds to wean animals from their parents."

"Nancy, I just don't know."

"Robert, it's *possible.* As far as our bat knows, this is the same thing that happened once before, a month or so after she was born."

"Abandonment." Gentry rose. "How did our lady bat find the dead male bat?"

"She probably traced it by smell."

"By smell. So wouldn't the big bat also have smelled that her mother *wasn't* here?"

"Olfactory memory doesn't work that way. Bats, people, most animals recognize a smell if they encounter it again. But they can't summon it up like they can sounds or images. If she heard something that sounded like her mother, she would believe it was her mother, smell or no smell."

"And you're saying this is the *only* sound that ever reminded her of her mother's heartbeat?"

"Why not? Until yesterday this bat lived her entire life in the wild. And she was with her sibling. They were brother and sister, mother and father to each other, mates."

"Death, incest, and Oedipus," Gentry said. "This is a goddamn Greek tragedy."

"That's the way some mammals are. And now, for the first time, the bat's alone. When better to listen for her mother?"

Gentry still had problems with it, problems with all of it. Big mutant bats. Little bats driven mad by echolocation. But it didn't change the fact that New York was under siege, and that the bats had to be dealt with.

"So how does this help us?" Gentry asked.

"I'm not sure," Joyce said.

Once they crossed West Houston Street, the city was deserted except for police officers patrolling in cars and riot gear—and bats. They were hanging from streetlamps and awnings, from walk signs and traffic lights.

A tired-looking Marius Pace met Joyce and Gentry in the lobby of the new Office of Emergency Management headquarters. Pace took the pair directly to the elevator; on the way to the eighteenth floor, he reported where things stood as of one hour before. That was when Gordy Weeks had come out from his meeting and briefed his deputies during a short recess.

"The impact assessment is obviously pretty grim." Pace consulted a legal notepad that was spotted with round coffee mug stains. "The subway patrols obviously weren't able to deal with the bat, so all of New York's roadways, rails, and bridges have been shut down. Nothing leaves or enters the borough. All businesses here and in Queens, Brooklyn, Staten Island, and the Bronx are closed except for food-service and health-care providers, but the roads are still open. The area airports have also been closed from Westchester down to New Jersey, and all incoming traffic is being diverted to Hartford, Philadelphia, and Buffalo. Only emergency aircraft can come or go locally."

"Have there been any incidents?" Joyce asked.

"Yes. Not attacks per se, but two aircraft had to be evacuated just before takeoff, after they sucked groups of bats into the engines. The towers at all the fields are reporting radar problems due to the bats. If we haven't cleared this up by tomorrow night, the National Guard will be mobilized to get food and medical supplies into the city. An immediate curfew will be in effect from six-thirty P.M. until six-thirty A.M. We've got a good group of people working with the media to keep the public informed, and each of the officials you'll meet upstairs has teams dealing with problems involving health, fire, looting, sanitation, and other issues. As it happens, your timing is very good. When I E-mailed Director Weeks to tell him you were here, he informed me that they'd just started discussing what kind of offensive the city is going to mount."

"Who's in charge of going after the big bat?" Joyce asked.

"That information," said Pace, "I do not have."

They emerged in a brightly lit hallway decorated with framed newspapers of disasters going back to the blizzard of 1888. It was almost as unsettling here as it was in the streets. People were moving quickly in all directions, shouting into phones and passing papers, folders, and diskettes like batons in a relay race. The conference room was in a corner on the southwest side of the building, overlooking the Hudson River and Upper New York Bay. After they entered, Pace closed the door and left. The room was refreshingly quiet. There was artwork on the walls here, very loud and busy expressionistic prints of New York landmarks.

"To bring you up to speed, I have declared a state of emergency," Mayor Taylor said as Joyce and Gentry took empty seats at the far end of the long table. Everyone chuckled.

The mayor was seated at the head of the table, his back to the door. He was the only one in shirtsleeves and the only one without a laptop or cellular phone in front of him.

Gordy Weeks was seated to his left. Al Doyle was on his right. Weeks introduced the others who were present: Police Commissioner Veltre, Fire Chief Pat Rosati, Department of Health director Kim

Whalen, Emergency Medical Services head Barry Lipsey, and the mayor's press secretary Caroline Hardaway.

The newcomers sat beside Department of Environmental Protection director Carlos Irizzary and Child Welfare commissioner Valari Barocas. Everyone looked a little emotionally threadbare—eyes tired, hair wandering, jaws locked. But Gentry got the impression from the very tight expressions worn by Carlos and Valari that this was the outcast section of the conference room. The people who got in the way of action with finger-wagging "what-ifs." Of everyone present, only Commissioner Veltre seemed happy—proud?—to see Gentry. When the patrol car had radioed OEM that they were coming in, Weeks had asked that Gentry be brought up with Dr. Joyce. Veltre was pleased that "one of his own" had been in the thick of this from the start.

Doyle did not appear pleased to see either of them.

"Thank you for coming," the mayor said.

Mayor George Taylor was a tall, robust man. He had a resonant voice that started from somewhere around his knees and picked up power in his broad chest.

"I know it's been a long, hard day for the two of you, and we all very much appreciate everything you've both done." He turned his steel gray eyes on Nancy. "I understand, Dr. Joyce, that you have specific knowledge of the oversized bat."

"I do, sir."

"If you would, bring us up to speed."

There was strength and confidence in Nancy's voice and in her eyes, even in her straight posture. After everything that had happened, Gentry couldn't imagine where it was coming from.

From knowing what you're talking about, he decided.

"Mr. Mayor, this bat is a mutation, the offspring of an irradiated vespertilionid bat from Russia."

"Vespertilionid is the name of the species," Doyle said, leaning toward the mayor.

"Actually, that's the family," Joyce said to the mayor. "Vespertilionidae. Forty-two separate genera, three hundred and fifty-five species. They live almost everywhere in the world—very hardy. This particular bat and her mate came to the city from New Paltz to have pups. I believe, sir, that the birth is imminent."

Doyle gave her a look.

"Excuse me," Weeks said, "but how many 'pups' do bats have at one time?"

"One or two," Doyle said.

Joyce glared a look at the pest control chief. Gentry could see the steel in her eyes go molten. After a moment Joyce looked down, took a shallow breath, and continued.

"The small bats—also vespertilionids—apparently came to the city in response to a signal emitted by the male. We don't know whether the female has the same ability to control the bats. But we do know that whenever she echolocates or generates any sound in the ultrasonic, the bats go wild."

"Meaning," Weeks said, "if we stop her, we stop the others."

"Yes. And I think I have a way to stop her."

Save for the sound of forced air coming from the vents in the ceiling and Doyle turning a paper clip over and over against the table, the room was silent.

"The bat came to a women's shelter on Twenty-third Street, I believe, because—and I know this may be a little difficult to accept—she heard a television video game that she thought was her mother's heartbeat."

Doyle tossed the paper clip on the table and sat back. The room was somehow much quieter. Even Gentry had to admit that, hearing it spoken here, the notion sounded absurd.

"Why do you believe that?" Weeks asked. There was nothing judgmental in his tone.

"Because there was nothing else in that building that would have attracted the bat. She ate nothing at the shelter. She was there only a minute or two. And she attacked no one, which suggests a mollifying factor, a mollifying *presence*. God knows she wasn't calm when she left the museum. The children at the shelter were playing the game when the bat came. It apparently became unplugged after that, but when we put it back on it had a sound very much like a heartbeat."

"You put it back on?" Doyle said.

"Yes."

"Then why didn't your bat return?"

"Because she would have been out of range by then."

Weeks asked, "Assuming this is true, about the heartbeat, what do you propose?"

"I suggest we set a trap for her," Joyce said. "The bat is nesting somewhere downtown. We'll probably know her exact location very soon. She's very close to giving birth, and I suspect she's stockpiling food for the event even as we speak."

"Human victims?" Commissioner Veltre asked.

"Possibly. No, probably. She'll want enough food to tide her over for several days."

"Gordy," Veltre said, "I want to pull my people out of the subway stations. I'll put them on the street where they stand less chance of being caught like that man at Christopher Street."

"Do it," said Weeks.

Veltre turned from the table and called on his cell phone.

"How large will this offspring be?" Weeks asked.

"Maybe twenty or thirty pounds," Joyce said. "A wingspan of possibly two feet, maybe a little more. But its size won't be the big problem. Nor will its mobility, which will be limited for a few days. The problem is if it starts making the same high-frequency sounds as its mother. The bats in the area will probably respond just as they did to the giant male and female."

"By gathering around it," Weeks said.

Joyce nodded.

The mayor said, "Gordy, if Dr. Joyce is correct and we find out exactly where she is, why don't we just throw everything we've got at her?"

"Because, Mr. Mayor," said Joyce, "you'll still have the little bats to deal with."

"You mean her offspring?"

"No. The million other vespers in the city. When she came to the shelter, the small bats were nonagressive because the giant bat was calm. We have to keep her that way. If you try to sneak up on her, she'll hear. If she hears, she'll call for backup, as it were."

Weeks turned back to Joyce. "So what's your plan?"

"I'm sort of improvising," she said, "but I propose we lure the she bat out of her nest using the video game sound. Bring her to where *we* want her, whether that's somewhere in the subway tunnels or out in the open. Once we have her there, we kill her in a way that doesn't involve anyone trying to close in on her."

"Kill a pregnant female animal," said Press Secretary Hardaway. "The animal rights activists will excoriate us for that."

"Sane humans will applaud us," the mayor said dismissively.

"The question is, how do we kill the bat without getting close to her?" Weeks asked. "Could we put snipers on surrounding rooftops?"

"No," Joyce said. "The smaller bats would muck things up for a telescopic sight."

Commissioner Veltre looked at her. "You're sure of that?"

"I do a lot of shooting," Joyce said. "The little bats would crisscross the line of fire at different depths of field, making it extremely difficult for a marksman to focus on the target."

"What about poison gas?" the mayor asked. "We were talking about this before you arrived, Dr. Joyce. The Pied Piper aspect could be perfect. If we have the ability to bring the bat to a specific section of tunnel, then all we have to do is keep everyone away from that area until we're finished."

"And I still say that's much too dangerous," Department of Health director Whalen and Environmental Protection head Irizzary both said almost at once and with the same exasperation.

"As if a few hundred thousand bats, a mad giant, and tons of bat shit *aren't* dangerous," contributed Doyle.

"They are," Whalen agreed, "only we don't even know how large a dose it will take to kill the bat."

"Plus leaks can and will happen," added Irizzary. "Especially if we have to keep pouring it on."

"And then there's the cleanup afterward," Whalen said. "It could leak into the water, kill fish, birds—"

"We can always use a shitload of hair spray and a really big tennis racket," Veltre suggested, only half in jest.

"There is one thing to keep in mind," Joyce said. "I have no idea how long the bat will sit still when she realizes that the heartbeat isn't a heartbeat. We may have only a few seconds to destroy her. And I don't think we'll be able to draw her out a second time. This creature's smart."

Doyle said, "Assuming we can even get the bat where we want her using this dubious Pac-Man gambit, we can always use ethyl chloride."

"Yes," Weeks said. "Yes, I like that."

"What's ethyl chloride?" the mayor asked.

"It's a congealant," Weeks said. "A liquid that vaporizes at room temperature and freezes whatever it comes in contact with."

"We use it as a local to numb kids' skin before we give them stitches," said Emergency Medical Services chief Lipsey. "Fast-freeze—turns everything white. A large enough dose will induce hypothermia."

"We've got a lot of it on hand from the rat sweep we just finished. All we'd have to do is barge it down from the boat basin on West Seventy-ninth," Doyle said.

"What are the risks?" the mayor asked.

"Frankly, not many," Weeks said.

"Do you agree?" Taylor asked Whalen and Irizzary.

They both nodded.

The mayor looked at Joyce. "So we have the agent. But do we have the subject? Doctor, I'm more than a little worried about betting everything on—what did you call it, Al?"

"The Pac-Man gambit."

"It's the Dumbo effect," Gentry muttered.

"The what?"

"The Dumbo effect," Gentry repeated. "Using a mother image to lure out a child. But you knew that, didn't you?"

Doyle said nothing. Joyce smiled slightly.

Weeks asked Joyce, "If what you're saying is true, why not use a recording of a real bat heartbeat?"

"Because the video game *worked*. The bat's mother had been exposed to nuclear waste and God knows what else in Russia, then came to a totally new environment in New Paltz. I have no idea what effect the radiation and the change in climate and diet had on her metabolism—whether her heartbeat was normal or irregular, whether it was stronger or weaker than that of a normal bat. Whatever the special sound or rhythm was in that video game, it 'spoke' to the giant vesper. I suggest we stick with it." .

Everyone was silent.

The mayor nodded thoughtfully. "Gordy?".

Weeks sighed. "Dr. Joyce is the expert on bats." He looked over at her. "I say we bet on her game plan."

The mayor slapped the table. "Then let's make it happen. Otherwise we'll all be living in Jersey."

The mayor thanked everyone, rose, and left the room. The press secretary was sitting to Joyce's left and thanked her for her efforts. Commissioner Veltre came over to congratulate Gentry on the fine work he'd done since the crisis began.

"The fine work you've done *again*," was how Veltre put it.

Doyle slipped away without a glance.

As everyone else left, Weeks came over, thanked them both, and asked them to continue as members of the team.

"There's a lot of work we're going to have to do over the next few hours," the OEM director said. "We'll have to get the ethyl chloride down here and figure out exactly where to draw the bat to, and also how loud the video game has to be relative to where the bat is."

"You don't want to make it so loud that the sound is distorted,"

Joyce said. "Then it may not sound like what she heard. And the time factor is very important. Bats usually stop flying twelve to twenty-four hours before giving birth."

"We're going to move this along as fast as possible," Weeks assured her. "What I think is that you and Detective Gentry should get some food and rest. We've got a cafeteria downstairs and rooms you can use. When we need you, we'll come and get you." He smiled. "I'll also scare up a pair of jumpsuits. Looks like you two've been living in those clothes for quite a while."

Joyce and Gentry both smiled, after which Marius Pace led them to the small, busy cafeteria. After picking up a few sandwiches and sodas, they were taken to the "crash pads" on the tenth floor—small, quiet, prison-size cubicles each with a cot, a shower, and a toilet.

Gentry made sure that Joyce was comfortable before heading to his own cubicle next door. After showering, eating, and pulling on the baggy blue jumpsuit Weeks had sent to the room, Gentry felt three things. One was pain from all the cuts and gashes the bats had inflicted. They were superficial enough that they could be washed out and seemed to disappear. But each of those little cussers stung. He also felt totally exhausted. Now that he'd stopped running, all his muscles wanted to do was nothing. They didn't want to lift, adjust, or move in any way. They let him know that by complaining each time he shifted his shoulders, his arms, his legs, and even his fingers.

As he lay there, he forced himself to enjoy the respite, the sense of accomplishment—of survival—and he imagined he could hear Nancy's heartbeat from the other side of the wall.

Thirty-seven

Gentry woke at three-thirty A.M. He wasn't accustomed to the quiet, and it finally got to him. He left his room, warmed with the expectation of seeing Joyce's door shut. When he saw that it was open, he tracked her down to the conference room. There were blueprints spread on the table; Joyce, Marius, and a team of OEM tacticians were collected around them and talking animatedly.

Marius spotted Gentry and motioned him in. Joyce looked up and smiled.

"I think we've got something, Robert," she said enthusiastically and went back to work.

There was a coffee maker in the corner of the room, and as Gentry poured himself a cup he glanced at Nancy. She looked great in the jumpsuit, but he was more concerned that she looked exhausted.

He went and stood next to her.

"Marius, do you want to—"

"No," Pace said. "You explain it. I'm going to check in with Gordy." He went to the phone.

Joyce leaned on the table with one arm. With another, she pointed to diagrams of the Brooklyn Battery Tunnel and Upper New York Bay.

"Okay," she said. "Here's the deal. About two blocks from the entrance to the subway station is the Manhattan entrance to the Brooklyn Battery Tunnel. We're going to use the video game to bring the bat into the tunnel—about here." She pointed to a spot where it intersected Governors Island just over a half mile from the tip of Manhattan, a mile east of Liberty Island and Ellis Island. "The Brooklyn side of the tunnel is being sealed off with sandbags. Once the bat goes inside, plastic sheets will be rolled down from the portal on the Manhattan side and secured with sandbags on the bottom. If the bat tries to get out, the plastic will slow her down long enough for marksmen to take her out."

"Assuming the little vespers don't attack them," Gentry said.

"The officers will be inside armored cars," she said.

"A pair of Emergency Rescue Vehicles," Pace added as he hung up the phone. "M75 armored personnel carriers."

Gentry nodded. The police kept the tanklike ERVs in case it became necessary to extricate casualties under fire.

"And since the big bat will be stuck in one place behind the plastic," Joyce said, "the marksmen should be able to sight her and get their shots off without the other vespers interfering. Once the big bat dies, the little bats will quiet down. Now, if the bat doesn't try to escape, we'll be waiting for her with ethyl chloride. It'll be pumped through the fans in the tunnel. The drums containing the compound are already inside the vent house on Governors Island."

Gentry knew the building. It was a five-story-tall hexagonal fortress on the 160-acre island.

"If we can hit her quick," Joyce said, "her metabolism will drop and she'll be dead in minutes."

Gentry asked, "Where will you be while all this is going on?"

She jabbed a finger at the map of Governors Island. "Here. Monitoring that end on security cameras."

He nodded again. This time he wasn't going to blow his chance. "Mind if I come along?"

"No," she smiled again. "I was kind of hoping you would."

Pace triumphantly closed his cellular phone. "Gordy has given this his final thumbs-up. He's calling the mayor's office now, and we should have our go-ahead within fifteen minutes." He looked at Joyce. "Then it's all up to your little video game heroine."

Pace and his aides left the room. Joyce sagged in her chair. Gentry asked if she wanted coffee. She shook her head.

"You didn't even try to sleep, did you?" Gentry asked.

She shook her head. "I've never been much of a rester."

"Waste of time?"

"Pretty much."

"Afraid you might miss something?"

"Yeah, there's a job to do here, but that isn't the only thing. When I lie down I always think about stuff I don't want to think about. People I miss. People I don't miss. Right now I don't want to think about Professor Lowery."

"I understand."

"No, it isn't what you think. I'm not real happy about the thoughts I'm having. How I'm going to miss his knowledge, his guidance, but not him."

They looked at each other in comfortable silence. But it was silent for only a moment as Pace suddenly swung around the jamb.

"It's showtime, folks," he said.

Joyce and Gentry followed him out.

An OEM car drove them the short distance to Pier A where an NYPD harbor boat from Harbor Charlie in Brooklyn would take them to Governors Island. Pace went with them to the riverside. En route, he gave Joyce a radio and said that both he and Weeks would be listening for her reports. When they arrived, Pace wished Joyce and Gentry good luck. He stayed until they were on board and the tuglike vessel was headed into the bay.

The two officers who were on board went inside the cabin. Joyce and Gentry remained on deck. The detective had been on the Staten Island Ferry at night, and it was always a thrill to see the New York skyline. Millions of windows lit in the patchwork way of a big city, planes and helicopters moving overhead, headlights on the surrounding highways. It was deeply unsettling to see the city dark and seemingly dead.

The small, compact vessel plowed loudly through the salty early morning air. The engine droned and water slapped the hull. The boat felt every swell and dip of the powerful river current, and Gentry held the wood railing tightly. He hadn't spent much time on the sea—he once went motorboating on the Long Island Sound with Priscilla—and he couldn't get used to the ground heaving sharply up and then down while his feet remained unassailably flat.

He looked out at Governors Island. Since 1966, when it was abandoned by the Army, the island had been a Coast Guard base of operations for search and rescue missions and the interception of seagoing contraband. But the cost of housing four thousand sailors and support personnel and their families was more than thirty million dollars annually, so—save for a skeleton crew—the Coast Guard had all but shut down operations in 1997.

The ventilation tower was built on a small section of landfill just off the island proper. It was surrounded by a walkway some twenty feet wide, and there was a narrow boardwalk that led to the main island. The lights were on there as Coast Guard personnel and officers from the Triborough Bridge and Tunnel Authority worked with city engineers, harbor police, and fire department marine units to set up "the icebox," as they were calling it.

The barge that brought the ethyl chloride had docked on the north side of the islet, so the harbor boat swung around to the south side to deposit the passengers. It was good to walk on stable land again, though Gentry continued to sway for a short while. Despite the fact that helicopters had been grounded, boats from various networks and news services were docked at the island, covering the preparations. Kathy Leung was there, of course. They were kept behind a police barricade, though Gentry shouted to Kathy that he'd talk to her when he was finished inside. That didn't seem to satisfy her, but it was the best he could do.

Neither the mayor nor Weeks had forbidden anyone to speak with the press. No one was afraid the bats would overhear. But despite pleas from the reporters, there wasn't time to stop and talk now. Gentry and Joyce entered the gray stone building.

Gentry's first impression was that the tower was a huge jet engine. The floor was honeycombed with a dozen trapdoors that covered ladders and access to the fans and ducts. The doors were open and surrounded by twenty-four of the ethyl chloride canisters. Technicians were in the process of feeding coils of hard rubber tubing into the ducts. One end of each tube was attached to a canister. Gentry had no idea how far into the shafts the other ends went.

Above the fan ducts were four levels of grated metal floors that were accessible by stairs on the north side of the tower and by an elevator on the south side. The floors were eerily reminiscent of the ones in the catacombs under the subway at Grand Central Station. Gentry wondered if the rooms where he found the homeless people had originally been designed to ventilate the subways. It made sense, he thought.

This part of the operation was under the direction of the Triborough Bridge and Tunnel Authority head Charlie Schrank. Schrank was a slender, easygoing, shirtsleeves man with thinning brown hair and a chronically bemused expression. He seemed genuinely pleased as he shook Joyce's hand.

"Gordy Weeks told me you're a pro," Schrank said, "and he doesn't say that about a lot of people."

"Thank you," Joyce said.

She introduced Gentry, after which Schrank walked them up to the command center, a curved bank of panels, computers, and monitors along the east wall of the second floor of the cavernous tower.

"The audio portion of the operation is being controlled from the Emergency Broadcast Center at the OEM," Schrank said. "As soon as we're set here we'll call the EBC. Their involvement will last until the bat enters the tunnel and the Manhattan entrance is closed off. Then we take over."

"How will you know when the bat's in position?" Joyce asked.

"We have security cameras in the tunnel." Schrank pointed to the black-and-white images on the monitors.

Gentry stepped closer. There was also a feed from the video camera the police had left at the South Ferry subway station. Despite the intimate views of the surveillance cameras, Gentry felt curiously detached from the proceedings. He was accustomed to being in the middle of the action, not watching it from the outside. He looked down at the crew. Many of them had never worked with one another, but they were all pulling together. When Gentry thought of all the people and materiel that had been brought together in just a few hours, he was impressed. The machine had worked fast and it had worked well.

"I only wish we had time to test the delivery system," Schrank said.

Joyce pointed out, "A lot of things are going to have to work right the first time."

She was fidgeting with the zipper on the front of her jumpsuit. Gentry couldn't imagine what was going through her mind and heart. So much had happened since this began and, more than ever, so much was sitting squarely on her shoulders.

"What exactly is going to happen?" Gentry asked. He was interested, but he also wanted to give Joyce something else to think about.

"The fans are twenty-seven feet down each shaft," Schrank said. "They change six million cubic feet of air every minute and a half. You see the ladders?"

Gentry nodded.

"Ordinarily, they facilitate repair and cleaning. Now we're using them as braces. One technician inside each shaft is fastening the tube to the ladder."

"You had enough qualified technicians for that?" Gentry asked.

"Just enough," Schrank laughed, "with a supervisor left over. What we didn't have were enough plastic straps to attach the pipes to the ladders. We needed something with a little 'give' for when the fans start rattling."

"What did you use?" Joyce asked.

Schrank pointed to his waist. "Trouser belts. Punched new holes in the sides, just the right size. It's a little *Apollo 13*—and, like I said, I wish we had time to test it. Once the pipes are secured and we see that the bat is in the tunnel, the ethyl chloride will be released and the fans will be turned on. The liquid will vaporize and, within seconds, the gaseous agent will be circulating through the tunnel, which is sixty feet below us."

Schrank's radio beeped. "That's my supervisor," he said as he slipped the unit from his back pocket. "Yes?"

Gentry watched as people climbed quickly from the shafts. He saw the supervisor standing directly below, beside the elevator door.

"We're ready down here," the supervisor said.

"Thanks," Schrank said. "Tell everyone 'good job.'" He put the radio back in his pocket and picked up a black phone under the bank of monitors. He punched in a number.

"Gordy?" he said. "We're all set here."

Gentry could see Joyce draw a sharp breath. He reached over and took her fingers in his.

She squeezed his hand.

A few seconds later the drumbeat came softly through a speaker on the console.

Thirty-eight

The great bat was lying in her nest. Her large wings were unfurled
and her ears were relaxed. Despite the pains in her tail, arm, and
belly, she was trying to sleep.

Suddenly, in the midst of the quiet, she heard the sound again.
Muscle after muscle inside her ears contracted within milliseconds of
one another, refining and sharpening and pinpointing the sound. Fatty
tissue in the base of the ear dampened everything outside the focus of
the external ear, absorbing all sounds but the one she wanted to hear.

It was more comforting than the sound of her mate had ever
been. Yet it was so much less familiar. In her mind she couldn't see
what made it. Yet when she heard it she couldn't think of anything but
the sound.

Slowly, she raised her head and pulled her wings toward her. It
was strange to be on the ground like this and not suspended in the air.
But it had not been an ordinary night. She had seen death, his death.
She had sought to destroy the one who had taken him from her. And
then she had felt the call of new life. She had returned here to await
its arrival.

Now the sound had returned. The sound that had stopped her

enraged flight from death and filled her with peace and with an unfamiliar yearning. A need so old yet so near . . .

It was coming from outside her cave. Despite her discomfort, the bat had to go to it. She had to find the source. She had to smell, see, and touch it. She had to understand it.

She had to have it again.

The giant threw back her head and wailed. Throughout the tunnel, her voice stirred her minions. When she heard them moving, she drew her powerful legs beneath her and stretched her hooks before her. She looked back at her nest, then began crawling through the blackness. As the sound grew closer, louder, her need for it became greater.

Then, when she was free of the cave, the sound suddenly disappeared—just as it had before.

The bat stopped. She listened. She heard countless smaller sounds ahead and above and to the sides. But she knew what those were: food. There were also lesser bats flying around her in all directions. She stopped wailing as she felt the loss again. Along the top of her wings, her fingers moved as though searching for something.

Where had it gone?

And then, as the lesser bats settled onto posts and ledges and wires, as the fluttering of their wings stopped, she heard it again. The sound, distant but distinct. She turned to the side.

There was another cave, larger than her own. That was where the sound was coming from. And the sound was making an echo. This cave had a back. Whatever was making the sound would not be able to leave.

Bunching her wings beside her and turning, the bat flung herself forward and soared into the air.

Thirty-nine

S he's in!"

Charlie Schrank's shout punched through the silence in the ventilation tower. No one cheered, though. Getting the bat in the tunnel was only the first step. Now everything was up to this crew.

Joyce watched the tired, wounded creature crawl, leap, or occasionally fly past the succession of wide-angle video cameras. Because the optics for the black-and-white security cameras were designed to show stopped vehicles in low light, not to capture motion, the moving bat was a blur whenever she passed. It was difficult to see details, though only one seemed to matter: the bat had entered the tunnel. Joyce experienced a soaring sense of vindication. Not only had the bat gone in, she'd entered the tunnel alone and she wasn't wailing. She'd bought the fact that the video game was her mother.

It also felt very good having Gentry hold her hand. He'd been with her almost every step of this, and she knew that he shared the satisfaction she was feeling right now.

Schrank had told them that the twelve vents in this tower covered the center section of the tunnel. That was the section farthest from populated areas. Three other ventilation buildings—two in lower Manhattan, one across Buttermilk Channel in Brooklyn—were responsible for the ends of the tunnel. If for any reason the fans overshot their sections, the chance of spreading ethyl chloride into Manhattan or Brooklyn was remote.

The center of the tunnel was slightly northwest of Governors Island, closer to Manhattan. Once the bat had passed that point, the four fans of Group One would begin blowing. That would make it impossible for her to go back. Then the four fans of Group Three would be engaged. Those were closer to the Brooklyn side and would trap her in the middle. Then Group Two, the four center fans, would be turned on. Joyce wondered if she'd still feel vindicated while she watched the pregnant bat freeze to death.

"On Group One," Schrank said calmly as the bat moved past the video camera there.

The supervisor had come upstairs. He shouted down for the Group One canisters to be opened. When there were four hands in the air, signaling that the flow was underway, he pressed the buttons that started the fans. The blades began to spin below them. They caused a deep, pleasant hum and a gentle vibration that could be felt throughout the building.

"On Group Three," Schrank said.

The next batch of canisters and fans was activated. The noise and vibration increased proportionately.

"She's trapped," Gentry said as he looked at the monitors. "Son of a bitch, we got her!"

Suddenly, the bat stopped. Her wings held wide, she turned toward the northern side wall of the tunnel. She was just shy of the center vents.

"That's strange," Joyce said. "She must be tired."

"Or maybe she's already feeling the cold," Schrank said.

"It's possible," Joyce said, "though she's not doing anything about it."

"Like what?" Gentry asked.

"Folding her wings around her. Going back the way she came. Trying to get to the top of the tunnel where it'd be warmer."

"Charlie, can we still zap her there?" Gentry asked.

"Yeah," Schrank said. "It'll just take longer. Let's wait a minute and see if she starts up again."

The view was from nearly directly overhead. Joyce watched as the bat moved her head around in slow, wide circles.

"That's weird," Joyce said. "She's not listening anymore—" And then it hit her. "Shit! *Shit!*"

"What?" Gentry asked.

She smacked her forehead. "I'm a fucking *idiot!* The sound of the fans is drowning out the video game." Still watching the monitor she said to Schrank, "Tell OEM to turn up the sound of—"

She didn't finish. She watched as the bat unexpectedly cocked her first digits back, well past her head, and slammed them forward. Joyce couldn't see what she was hitting, but she heard and felt the assault.

Schrank looked straight down. "Oh crap. The elevator."

"Don't tell me," Gentry said. "The shaft—"

"—leads right from the tunnel to here," Schrank finished. "The bat's trying to get out."

"Turn on Group Two *fast!*" Joyce yelled.

Schrank ordered the last group of fans turned on. The video screens went white as the freezing gas rolled in.

"Man, did I fuck up big-time," Joyce said.

"No," Gentry said. "It's going to be okay."

"I don't mean that," Joyce said. "This isn't about the bat hearing the video game anymore. She isn't trying to get *out*. She's trying to get *in*—here."

"Why?" Gentry asked.

Joyce glanced at the monitor as the bat reared back and slammed her hooks forward again. The elevator door rattled, the sound echoing through the tower. They saw the bat retreat, then bend, then put her muscled shoulders against the doorway. Joyce felt completely and utterly inept.

"You saw what she was doing before?" Joyce asked. "Moving her head around?"

"Yeah."

"She was smelling."

"Smelling what?" Gentry asked.

"*Me*, Robert. When the fans came on, my scent was one of the things they drew into the tunnel!"

The phone beeped and Schrank snapped it up. Pace was calling to report that the vespers along the tunnel entrance on the Manhattan side had turned violent. Obviously, the bat had started wailing again. Schrank informed Pace what had happened on the tower end; Pace told him to hold on. Schrank was perspiring along the temples, neck, and forehead.

They heard metal tear. Everyone downstairs was looking up.

"There's nothing else your people can do here," Joyce said. "You better start getting them out, just in case."

Schrank nodded. He sent the supervisor downstairs to evacuate the team; he said he wanted everyone to go to the old air raid shelters in the hospital ward. The crew didn't have to be told a second time.

"You really think she's going to get out of the tunnel before she freezes?" Gentry asked.

"Very probably," Joyce said.

The building shook. There was a series of metallic slaps.

"That has to be the elevator car," Schrank said. "The shaft is made of concrete."

"She's coming through," Gentry muttered. He turned to Joyce. "I say we make a stand."

"Sure, fine. *How?*"

"We call the police in from downstairs," Gentry said. "When the bat comes out we tag her."

"Uh, that might be a good idea ordinarily," Schrank said, "but not with all those ethyl chloride canisters down there and the building shaking. If they fall over, you're iced."

"All right," Gentry said, "then can we *use* the canisters somehow? Spray her with them, or dump them into the elevator shaft?"

"We haven't got any nozzles," Schrank said, "and if we open the canisters and pour them down the shaft, the liquid will only vaporize and rise."

Gentry swore.

Weeks came on the line and Schrank briefed him. When he was finished, the OEM director said that they'd made a good try but he was preparing to send over a launch with two six-person SWAT teams. He had no intention of letting the giant bat get back into New York.

Schrank hung up. He told the others what Weeks had said as the tower rumbled again. This time the lights went out and the fans shut down.

"I was afraid of that," Schrank said.

"What?" Gentry asked.

"The electric cables. They run up through the shaft."

Emergency spotlights had snapped on up and down the stairways. The fan blades continued to turn for several seconds and then they died. The quiet was unnerving, though it didn't last long. After a few moments there were shouts from outside.

"The other vespers," Joyce said. "Goddamn this all. Goddamn it to hell." It was maddening that something so small, so preventable as her own smell getting into the tunnel had brought them to this point.

Directly below them, under the concrete floor of the tower, metal broke in thunderous volleys.

"Charlie, you'd better get out of here," Gentry said. "Join your people in the shelters."

He nodded. "What about you?"

"I don't know," Joyce said.

"The bat's going to go wherever Nancy is," Gentry said. "We'll think of something else."

"No!" Joyce snapped. "*You're* getting out of here."

"Sorry, but that's not an option."

"Robert, *go!*"

Gentry had let go of Joyce's hand when Schrank was on the telephone with Weeks. He took it again and held it hard. She looked at him for a long moment. He looked back. They said nothing more.

Outside, the cries of the reporters were joined by the sound of boat engines being fired up.

Schrank started jogging toward the steps. "I think you're both crazy, but I wish you luck. If you change your mind, the hospital is—"

"Wait!" Gentry shouted suddenly.

Schrank stopped.

"No, not you," Gentry said.

Schrank waved and disappeared down the steps.

Gentry regarded Joyce. "How spry did the bat look to you?"

"You saw. It's tough to say."

The floor shuddered. Still holding Joyce's hand, Gentry turned and followed Schrank toward the steps.

"Where are we going?"

"How far do you think our girl can fly?"

"God, Robert, I don't know. Why? What are you going to do?"

They started down the rattling steps. "I'm going to find out how bad Kathy Leung wants an exclusive."

Forty

Leaving the ventilation tower and running across the boardwalk, Gentry found Kathy Leung and her brawny camera operator T-Bone Harrold where he knew they'd be: right where he'd left them. Waiting for a story.

The small bats were beginning to swarm around the ventilation tower, and police were asking the reporters to withdraw to the nearby Coast Guard buildings. Several of the print journalists were cooperating but not Kathy, T-Bone, and their small mobile crew. Gentry knew that she wouldn't be going anywhere without a video of the bat. In fact, he had been counting on that.

As they'd run from the tower, Joyce and Gentry had agreed that they couldn't go back to Manhattan. With the tunnel fans shut down, the giant bat would be able to backtrack through the tunnel and fight her way back to her nest. Or if she got free of the elevator shaft, she would be able to follow Nancy by air. Either way, it would be bad for the city.

When the bat's attack became audible on the island itself, Gentry surprised Kathy by asking for a ride.

"Sorry, but I'm not going back!" she informed him. T-Bone had the video camera on his shoulder. Kathy motioned for him to snap on his lights.

"I'm not asking you to go back," Gentry said.

She seemed startled.

"I'm asking for a ride to Liberty Island."

Kathy regarded him suspiciously. "Why?"

"Because the big bat made Nancy."

"The bat what?"

"It knows she's the one who killed her mate!" Gentry said.

"The bat's breaking through the tunnel to *get* to me," Joyce said. "When we leave she'll probably follow us. What we want to do is lead her and the other vespers *away* from the city."

"And you want us to take you."

"Right, Kath," Gentry said.

"What a story," Kathy said. "Thank you, God."

Gentry said, "I've gotta warn you, though. Things will get hairy if the bat reaches the island."

"If?"

Joyce said, "She's tired and extremely pregnant, and we're hoping she belly flops into the sea."

"T-Bone."

"I'll keep my camera pointed in her direction."

As they started toward the boat, Gentry reiterated that the bat was obviously very determined. Kathy said she understood the risks. T-Bone shrugged his big shoulders and said that he was with the lady.

As large chunks of stone fell from the south side of the ventilation tower, the reporter dismissed her mobile unit. She said that she and T-Bone would go directly to the studio when they had their footage. In time for the morning news show, she promised.

Meanwhile, Gentry and Joyce helped T-Bone load his equipment behind the two pedestal seats of his producer's twenty-one-foot fishing boat. Gentry knew there was no way he'd be leaving that behind, so he didn't even attempt to persuade him. The three of them had to stop every few seconds to swat at vesper advance guards. More than the crashes echoing from the tower, the vespers were an indication of how close the female was.

Kathy started the engine and took the helm. Gentry slid into the seat beside her. Joyce and T-Bone crouched in the cramped stern, looking back at the tower. T-Bone pulled a bottle of seltzer from his equipment vest and offered some to Joyce. She declined. When everyone was secure, Kathy pushed the 225-horsepower engine to its maximum speed and tore from the dock.

As the island receded, Gentry ducked low behind the windscreen. He turned and asked Joyce for her radio. Holding it close to protect it from the wild sea spray, Gentry called Weeks.

"Where are you?" Weeks demanded.

"We're in one of the news boats heading west!" Gentry shouted into the mouthpiece

"Where west?"

"I'll explain in a second. What's the status of your SWAT teams?"

"Their launch is pinned down," Weeks informed him. "The bats are in an uproar again. What the hell is going on out there?"

Gentry said, "The big bat was nearly through the floor of the ventilation tower."

"Jesus! What's that fucking animal *made* of?"

"Muscle, mostly," Gentry replied. "And she's after Nancy. Instead of coming back into the city we decided to head to Liberty Island. Nancy feels that even if the bat can make the trip, a mile-long flight in strong air currents will exhaust her. What kind of personnel are on the island?"

"Hold on. I'll—"

"*Robert!*" Joyce cried.

"*Comin' atcha!*" added T-Bone, who had hoisted his camera onto his shoulder.

The detective spun around. T-Bone hadn't turned on the floodlight so Gentry squinted into the dark.

There was an emergency lamp over the front entrance to the

tower. In the small, sharp cone of light Gentry saw the giant bat literally push down the door. A cloud of ethyl chloride followed the animal out, dusting its back with a frigid coat. The bat took two hops
toward the sea and vaulted skyward. She flew close to the water, followed by a train of small bats. Occasionally, the bat would rise, glide
for a moment, then drop and resume flapping.

"She's got to be within minutes of giving birth," Joyce said.
"She's having trouble staying aloft."

"Not trouble enough! She's closing the gap," Gentry said. He
turned and looked at the control panel. "Fifty-three miles an hour. Is
that the best we can do, Kath?"

"That's top speed!" Kathy shouted apologetically.

Gentry ducked back down behind the windscreen. "Gordon? Are
you still there?"

"Here!"

"The bat's out and she's following us."

"Do you have a weapon?"

"Yeah. An empty one. Listen, we'll be at the Statue of Liberty
dock in less than a minute. What've you got for me?"

"Wait," Weeks said. "Marius is talking to the park police."

Gentry waited. He glanced ahead. The statue was brightly lit, an
ethereal, washed-out green against the starless sky. They were less than
a half mile from the low wall that surrounded the island.

Hope, he thought as he looked out at the statue. Wasn't that what
Lady Liberty was all about?"

Weeks came back on. "Okay, here it is. Sergeant Julie Gilheany is
opening the main door, back of the monument. She and another officer will lay down cover fire for as long as they can. Listen. I'm assuming the bats are going to follow you out there. When they do, we're
going to get our SWAT teams onto the water. If they can get close
enough to pick off the giant—"

"I understand," Gentry said. "We'll lay low."

Weeks wished him luck. Gentry thanked him, then put the radio
in his jacket pocket. Holding on to the windscreen, he stood, half

turned, and told the others the game plan. As he did he could see the giant bat illuminated by the reflected glow of the statue. The thing was roughly a quarter of a mile away and coming after them slowly but doggedly. Her dark army was spread behind her, their numbers growing.

"This is unfuckingreal," T-Bone said as he videotaped the swarm. "I feel like I'm in *The Outer Limits.*"

Nancy was also watching the bats. She was hunched over and seemed beaten. Gentry leaned toward her and lightly squeezed her left shoulder. Without turning, she reached across and touched his hand. Her fingers were cold. He wished he could think of something hopeful to say that wasn't naive or a lie.

He looked back toward the island.

Roughly two hundred feet separated the dock from the entrance to Fort Wood, the star-shaped structure that serves as the foundation for the statue. Kathy swung around to the east side of the island and came to a hard, jolting stop alongside the dock.

Kathy jumped out and Gentry followed. He told her to run ahead while he helped Nancy out. Instead, she stayed to give T-Bone a hand with his camera and equipment case. Together, the foursome ran along the asphalt walk toward the large doors. Gentry stayed close to Joyce. She was tired and not moving as fast as the others. They swung around the left side of the statue. The tall double bronze doors were open. Inside the statue's lobby entranceway stood two United States Park police officers. One held a 9-mm pistol, the other a pump-action shotgun.

The park police sergeant had stepped outside with her shotgun. She aimed skyward.

"You'd better move!" she shouted to the group without taking her eyes from the bat.

They were about thirty feet from the doors. Gentry glanced behind him. The giant bat had just crossed the shoreline and was bearing down. The advance guard of vespers had slipped around the female and were slicing toward them.

Nancy screamed as two of the bats bit her shin. She stumbled, but Gentry wouldn't let her fall. He caught her around the waist and pulled her up even as a flurry of bats dug into the back of his neck and chewed on his left leg.

Gentry heard Kathy shriek as bats descended. The reporter kept running. She dropped the lights she was holding and pushed both hands through her hair, trying to dislodge the bats. Her cries were followed by the distinctive *pup-pup-pup* of the 9-mm as the second officer raced from the fort.

"Berk, get back!" the sergeant cried.

"I'll be okay!" the young man said. Still firing, he ran past Gentry.

"*No!*" Gentry barked. But he was tired from the run and his voice was a raw wheeze. He wished he could turn and pull the officer back, but he didn't want to let go of Nancy.

Suddenly, Gentry felt a sharp shooting pain run up his left leg from his ankle. Several bats were attacking his shin and one of them had taken a bite from his Achilles tendon. But the detective refused to go down. The bats were growing more numerous every second. If Gentry dropped he wouldn't be getting back up. He swallowed a cry and dragged the leg behind him.

Kathy reached the entrance, followed by T-Bone. She was still struggling with bats. T-Bone pulled two from his own head, crushed them in his giant hands, then did the same with the vespers that were in Kathy's hair.

"*Berk!*" the sergeant cried again.

Gentry heard a scream. He turned and saw bats attacking the officer's hands. A moment later hundreds of small bats slammed into his torso. The force of the impact lifted him several inches off the stone walkway and dropped him on his back. Then the giant bat crashed down on his chest. The officer's arms flew out and he vomited a plume of blood.

"Berk! *God*—" The sergeant wailed and raised her shotgun.

The giant bat's eyes and ears were not on her victim. They were on Joyce. Shaking her head angrily and closing her wings, the creature crawled from the body and lumbered through a cloud of thousands of small bats. Her eyes were narrow, her mouth fierce. Bent low and moving slowly, she clawed across the twenty yards to the door.

Gentry and Joyce ran past the sergeant. A fist of bats flew in with them, knocking the sergeant down before she could fire. T-Bone rushed over and pulled the second door shut. It closed with a heavy slam just as the giant bat hopped toward it. There were six smaller doors behind the ornamental front doors.

Gentry wrestled the bats from his neck, then helped Nancy with the vespers that were viciously biting her hands and forearms. When she was finally free of bats, Joyce ran to help T-Bone and Kathy, who had gone to assist the sergeant. Apart from being vocally angry at herself for having lost the camera lights, Gentry was pleased to see that Kathy had it pretty well together.

The enormous bat hit the outer door hard. The lobby resounded with a thick, echoing *thud.*

While the others were still struggling, Gentry tied a handkerchief around his ankle to try and stanch the bleeding. Then he rose. The pain had abated somewhat and he put his weight on the foot. It wobbled as if it were asleep and his ankle flared hotly. Favoring his right leg, Gentry looked around for the shotgun. He spotted it lying near the display of the statue's original torch, which had been replaced during the centenary restoration. The bat continued to hit the door. Gentry limped toward it, stopping several feet away, off to the side. He slipped his arm securely through the strap. He cradled the heavy rifle in his left hand and raised it to his shoulder.

"Come on, you misery," he said through his teeth. "Come on."

Behind Gentry, obviously frustrated with the tenacity of the remaining vespers, T-Bone had reached into his vest and retrieved the seltzer bottle. After shaking it vigorously, he shouted for the women to back away from the sergeant. Placing his thumb over the mouth of the bottle he turned the spray on the bats, concentrating on the ones clustered around Sergeant Gilheany's head. The vespers hopped off;

when they did, he stomped them as though they were spiders. Then, with the help of Kathy and Joyce, the sergeant was able to crush the rest of the bats.

Suddenly, the pounding at the front door stopped. After standing frozen for several seconds, Gentry lowered the shotgun.

T-Bone absently wiped his wet thumb on his trousers. "What coulda happened to her?"

"I don't know," Joyce said.

Kathy helped Sergeant Gilheany to her feet. "As soon as I can I want to go out and get Officer Berk's remains."

With the pounding stopped, they could hear the clawing of all the other bats. They were scratching on the stone walls, on the door, on the roof. It was claustrophobic and unnerving.

Gentry jumped when he heard a voice in his pocket. The radio. He slipped it out. "Gentry here."

"Are you all okay?" It was Weeks.

"We lost one of the park officers," Gentry said. "The rest of us are inside the fort. Can you see what's happening?"

"We're watching the statue from our window," Weeks said. "And it looks like you've got two problems. The first is that every bat in New York seems to be nesting on the statue."

"We know. What's the second problem?"

Weeks said, "It looks like the giant bat found a way inside."

Forty-one

When the Statue of Liberty was dedicated in October of 1886 it was the tallest structure built since the Pyramids of ancient Egypt.

A gift from France celebrating the hundredth anniversary of American independence, the 152-foot-tall statue was designed by Frédéric Auguste Bartholdi. It portrays a woman stepping from broken chains and raising a torch of freedom. In her arm is a tablet representing law; on her head is a crown whose seven spikes represent the seven continents and seven seas over which it was hoped the light of liberty would shine. She looks toward one of those seas, the Atlantic, from atop a 152-foot-high pedestal.

Three hundred thousand rivets hold the statue's beaten-copper skin to a metal framework designed by Gustave Eiffel. These supports function like springs, designed to give in winds reaching up to 125 miles an hour. This crisscrossing skeleton is attached to a central metal core that runs up the center of the statue. The core also supports a 168-step spiral staircase that enables visitors to walk from the foot to crown. Only the upraised arm that holds the torch is off-limits to tourists. When the statue was first constructed, a design miscalculation caused the spikes of the crown to pierce the arm. The framework of the arm had to be reconfigured on the spot, weakening it.

The statue's stone pedestal rests in the center of the star-shaped Fort Wood that once guarded the entrance to New York Harbor. More than a century after being decommissioned, the fort was once again guarding the lives of those inside.

According to Gordy Weeks, the giant bat was using her hooks to make her way up and around the statue's pedestal, and she appeared to be holding a human body in her claws. Weeks told Gentry he'd update him in a moment.

Sergeant Gilheany moaned when she heard about Officer Berk. She started for the door.

"Where are you going?" Gentry asked.

"No way am I letting that thing take him."

T-Bone got in front of her. "You can't do anything about it now."

"Like hell. I can kill that monster."

"No," T-Bone said, "you can't. You can get your own ass seriously killed though, and I ain't gonna let you."

"Sergeant, the man's right," Joyce said. "If you step outside, those little bats will be all over you."

The sergeant looked from T-Bone to Joyce. Then she looked ahead as she wiped blood from a gash across her nose.

"You dumb rookie," she said to the door. "I ordered you to come back. Why the hell didn't you listen?"

"Because he knew what every cop knows," Gentry said. "If we don't block the shot, the bad guys score."

"Save the pep talk for the cadets, Detective. If the four of you hadn't come in like a bunch of—"

"What? Scared people who just got our butts kicked?"

"Yeah, something like that. . . ."

The sergeant stopped speaking as a new sound came from above. It was high, muffled, and continuous. It sounded like a dumpster lid slowly being opened and shut.

"What the hell?" T-Bone said.

Weeks came back on. "Detective, it looks like the bat's gone into the pedestal."

"We're hearing that," Gentry said.

Just then the creaking stopped. A moment later so did the scratching outside the lobby.

"Now what?" Kathy asked.

"Maybe it's naptime," T-Bone said.

"No," Joyce said. She turned quickly to Gentry. "It's birth time. The statue's right on the water. It's cold down here, warmer up there. By how much, Sergeant?"

"About thirty degrees."

"Which would make it well over eighty inside," Joyce said. "That's perfect for a new nest."

"Detective, is that Dr. Joyce?" Weeks asked.

"It is." Gentry held the radio closer to her.

"Tell her the small bats are starting to leave the statue. Some are heading back, some to Jersey, some to the other islands. Ask her if she has any idea why."

"I do," Joyce said. "The big bat's dropped out of the ultrasonic range. She'll be making vocal sounds while she gives birth, which means we've got to take her out *now*. Otherwise we'll have to deal with her *and* her wailing brood."

"I hear you," Weeks said. "I'm sending the SWAT teams right away."

"They won't get here in time," Joyce told him. "If the bat's like a normal vesper, we have about ten minutes to get to her."

Gentry turned to Gilheany. "How do I get up there?"

"You don't." She came forward, her fingers wriggling for the shotgun. "This is my beat. I'm going up."

Joyce fell in beside her. "I'm going with you."

"I take it you're a scientist?" Gilheany asked.

"Yes."

"Good," the sergeant said. "Then you can tell her 'fuck you' in bat talk before I blow her away."

Gentry looked from Joyce to Gilheany. "All right," he said as he handed the officer the shotgun. "But I'm going with you."

"No you're not. You're limping."

"I'll be fine."

"You'll slow us down. And you don't have a weapon," Gilheany pointed out. "I can't watch your back and hers." She pulled her radio from a loop in her gunbelt. "Besides, I may need you down here. There are security cameras in the communications center. It's located in the administration building about two hundred yards directly behind the fort. Code 6453359 will get you in. Go there. We'll stay in touch."

Gentry hesitated. He looked at Nancy.

"Robert, we haven't got a lot of time," the scientist said.

Nancy was right. What rubbed Gentry raw was not that she was going. It was that she was going with an officer who was on the warpath. And he was afraid that saying something about calming down or being careful would only piss Gilheany off more.

So Gentry just nodded. Then he and Gilheany set their radios on the same channel.

The women turned and jogged toward the short staircase that led to the pedestal as Gentry brought Weeks up to date. Then he switched the radio back to Gilheany's frequency.

Kathy and T-Bone wished them good luck as they passed. T-Bone had picked up his camera and was videotaping their departure.

Before they disappeared through the gate at the top of the stairs, Gentry thought *Fuck it* and called after them. "She's going to smell you coming, Nancy. Don't forget that!"

"I won't!" she called back. "I'm counting on it."

Forty-two

Joyce hadn't been to the Statue of Liberty since her first-grade field trip. All she remembered from that visit was the very long, very winding, very hot climb to the top. It was still long, winding, and hot.

The women took the stairs toward the top of the pedestal. The staircase wound around a wide, open shaft for the elevator that went to the observation deck at the top of the pedestal. They made their way cautiously in case the bat had decided to come down instead of up. She hadn't. As they neared the balcony level that led to the statue itself, Gentry radioed. They stopped while Gilheany took the call.

"We're in the communications center," Gentry said, "and the security cameras are all dark."

"Impossible," Gilheany said. "Each of them has an internal power system."

"Then maybe it's the statue that's dark," Gentry replied.

"I don't see how," Gilheany said. "The transformers are in the base of the monument. I'm looking at them now."

"What about the cables that service the lights?"

"They run up the statue's central column," she said. "They're encased in inch-thick steel pipe."

Joyce said, "I haven't met a metal yet that could stop that bat. Maybe she slashed it on her way up."

"On purpose?" Gilheany asked.

"No," Joyce said. "But the inside of the statue would be a very tight space for her to maneuver. She could have used the column as a hookhold or punctured it by accident."

"Nancy, this is not looking good," Gentry said.

"And we're wasting time," Sergeant Gilheany said. She slipped a flashlight from her gunbelt. She switched the shotgun to her left hand. "I'm still going up. Are you coming?"

"I am," Joyce said. "But I'll take the light."

Gilheany handed it to her along with the radio. Gentry said nothing.

They moved from the pedestal into the sculpture itself. The stairs had ascended along the sides of the pedestal. Now they fed into the ceiling and up the very steep spiral staircase that led to the crown. Gilheany was in the lead. As they proceeded, Joyce circled the flashlight slowly from the steps to the copper skin of the statue to the stairs overhead.

The steps ascended in a tight, dizzying spiral up the central steel core. Almost at once they saw that the central column had been breached. There was a gouge in the side, and it appeared as if the rent metal had sliced the cables. Sparks sizzled from the frayed ends and Joyce wondered if the statue had ever seen a lonelier fireworks display.

Gilheany was stepping quietly and Joyce was wearing running shoes. The scientist listened carefully for sounds from above; the mother wailing, the pups mewling, the noise of nursing or movement—anything. But there was nothing save the distant howl of the wind as it slipped around the statue. At least there was no scratching from outside. Whatever bats were left were inactive.

All around them were the monument's zig-zagging stainless-steel support struts. Joyce knew that the bat could be hanging from any one of them. Or from the steps. Or from the central column itself.

Or the dark folds of the statue's skin.

The light from the flashlight threw ever-changing shadows on the copper plates that comprised the statue's robe. The shifting light and dark made the skin appear to crawl, made it seem more liquid than solid. And though her mind told her the bat was nestled some-where above them, Joyce couldn't rid herself of the feelings she'd had as a child, that the night, the darkness, held more than she could ever know. That any of those fluid changes to the side or above them could have been the bat moving its wings, preparing to jump—

Joyce started when Gilheany spoke. As if her heart weren't thumping fast enough from the climb.

"How soon before she knows we're here?" the sergeant asked quietly.

"She already knows," Joyce assured her. "The bat heard us as soon as we entered the pedestal."

"So there's no reason to whisper."

"None. And she'll smell us soon, if she hasn't already."

"You said downstairs that you were hoping she would. Why?"

"Because if the bat gives birth quickly, and if she feels strong enough, she may try and intercept us. We'll hear her."

"If she's already given birth, how dangerous will the babies be?"

"I don't know," Joyce admitted. "Vesper pups tend to be about twenty-five percent as large as the parent. Their wings aren't developed enough for flight, and many of them are born with their eyes shut. But the way this bat was mutated it's impossible to say."

They passed the statue's midriff. The tablet in the figure's left arm loomed above. Joyce turned her light there and made sure the bat wasn't inside. In the dull light that bounced back she could see Sergeant Gilheany's expression. A great deal of her gung-ho had been sucked into the shadows. If time hadn't been so short, Joyce might have insisted that Gilheany stay behind with Gentry and let her have the shotgun. She probably had more wildlife experience than either of them.

But Joyce was glad it hadn't worked out that way because she might not have been able to get off a steady shot. Her thigh muscles were aflame and trembling from the running she'd done and now from the climbing. She'd had to put the radio in her back pocket, hold on to the handrail, and pull herself along. The higher they went the hotter it also became. Her jumpsuit was thick with perspiration, and the fresh bites she'd suffered stung continuously as sweat dripped into them. Her hand was clammy around the flashlight's rubber handle.

The climb did provide one unexpected compensation for Joyce. She liked knowing that Gentry was on the other end of the radio, listening silently, worrying about her. Not being alone was a new and different kind of feeling for her.

Just above them were the statue's massive shoulders; straight above them was the neck and the ascent to the crown. Between the shoulders, to the right, was a small rest area with a relatively wide landing beyond it. Past that, Joyce saw dark, narrow steps that rose into the statue's raised arm to the torch. The ladder that rose through the statue's raised arm to the torch was there. Joyce heard the wind rushing around the arm, swift and ghostly. And while she heard only that, she knew that wherever the bat was it could hear everything. She wished there were something she could do to neutralize that advantage. Feedback from the radio wouldn't distract the bat because there was no signal to disrupt. The flashlight might blind her momentarily, but she'd still be able to hear. They could fire a shotgun blast and deafen her, but they'd also deafen themselves. And there was still the bat's olfactory sense.

Joyce shined the flashlight toward the upraised arm. She ducked under a low strut and walked slowly toward it. She looked up inside.

The wind blew hard in the crown above, almost as though the statue were drawing a breath.

"I don't think she can fit in the arm," Gilheany said, without looking over. She was peering up. "The neck would give her a little more room."

"You're probably right, but I want to check anyway," Joyce said. "How thick are the copper plates?"

"Three-thirty-seconds of an inch. About the thickness of a dime."

"The bat could bend them out, make herself fit. Squeezing into places is something bats are very good at. They also like to hang upside down and there's a ladder in the arm."

Gilheany was walking close behind Joyce. She was breathing heavily. "When we do see the bat, where should I aim?"

"For her head," Joyce said. "She's got sheets of muscles around her torso. It may be difficult to inflict a fatal wound below the neck."

The wind stopped blowing for a moment, and Joyce stopped. They heard a scraping sound behind them. She and Gilheany both spun around. The officer raised the shotgun to her shoulder.

There was nothing there. But the scraping came again, definitely from above the neck.

"She's in the crown," Gilheany said softly.

Joyce slipped the radio from her pocket. Then she walked around the sergeant toward the statue's neck.

The staircase here was like a large loop with the right side higher than the left. The upward steps curved up along the back of the statue's neck and followed the contour of the statue's right cheek, past her right eye into the crown. The downward steps were different. They didn't follow the curve on the left side. At the end of the observation area they turned sharply toward the right, dropping and passing under the ascending stairs.

Joyce stood on the bottom step and shined the light up. The beam glinted off the curving rails of the staircase. They were bent away from the deck, as though something had pushed them outward. She saw the rolling copper curves of the statue's hair and heard more scratching. Slowly, she went up another step. The flashlight roamed higher to the upright support beams that ran up the crown and along the top of the head. Joyce saw that they bulged outward, slightly distorting the shape of the head.

She put the radio to her mouth. "Robert?"

"I'm here."

"The bat was definitely in the crown. She may still be up there."

"I know. I heard Sergeant Gilheany. Nancy, the SWAT team will be here soon. Why don't you leave this—"

"*Shit!*" Gilheany screamed.

Joyce had heard it too. The loud creak of metal. She ran down the stairs to the landing. Gilheany was facing the statue's arm. She raised the shotgun as Joyce shined the flashlight in that direction.

"I don't get up here a lot. I didn't even notice that before."

"What?" Joyce asked. Gilheany pointed the light to an area left of the arm, at the very edge of the ledge. A gate that had been erected to keep tourists out lay wadded and crushed off to the side. The light climbed higher.

Officer Berk's body fell to the landing an instant before the giant bat dropped from the arm. The copper sides rattled as she landed. There was blood on the creature's mouth and nose; she was no longer pregnant and looked thin and bedraggled. The birth had obviously been an ordeal for her.

Gentry shouted something, but his voice was swallowed by Gilheany's oath as she fired. The blast was deafening, and Joyce screamed from the pain. The shot punched a bloody wound in the side of the bat's neck, but it didn't stop her. The giant screamed audibly as she jumped forward, her wings folded against her sides so that she could move through the confines of the statue. Gilheany raised her sights and fired a second shot. But the bat lowered her head and charged like a bull, and the bullet flew past her, blowing a hole in the copper.

Joyce ran to the left and Gilheany dove to the right. The sergeant landed hard on her shoulder. She rolled to the edge of the landing, losing the shotgun. The bat cannonballed past, toward the spiral staircase. A moment later the severity of the wound finally seemed to hit the creature as she staggered forward and struck the side of the spiral staircase with her shoulder.

Gilheany scrambled toward the shotgun. Joyce had had the same idea, but the sergeant got in her way. Joyce kept running toward the arm, hugging the radio and flashlight to her chest to keep from losing them.

The bat turned quickly and looked back. Blood trickled down her front and back. Her expression fierce, she leaned forward and snapped her wings ahead of her. The thick muscles of her shoulders bunched and rolled as she pulled her wings back and sailed across the landing.

Sergeant Gilheany reached the gun and dropped onto her back. She swung it around as the bat bore down, but the creature landed on Gilheany before she could fire. The impact caused the gun to spin free and drop from the landing. Joyce heard it clatter down through the struts. The claws of the bat's feet dug deeply into the officer's hips, and the sergeant cried out. She screamed again as the bat drove her hooks into Gilheany's chest.

Joyce fell against the steps that led up the statue's arm. She heard the sergeant's cries but didn't look back; she knew what was happening. Physically and emotionally exhausted, she sobbed as she scrambled up the rickety, steep steps toward the next small landing. The staircase was slippery with blood and guano from when the bat had roosted here, and Joyce stumbled as she ascended. She dropped the flashlight but kept going until she reached the landing. Her eyes were blurry with tears and sweat, and there was nothing to see here anyway except the narrowing confines of the arm and the dead end of the torch.

"Nancy!"

She was startled to find herself still holding the radio. She brought it to her lips. "Robert!"

"Where are you?"

"I'm in the arm. The sergeant's dead. The bat's wounded and it's chasing me—"

Just then the creature slammed against the stairs at the base of the arm. The entire structure rattled; the support struts creaked around her. Joyce looked down. The flashlight beam spilled across the floor, silhouetting the bat in its glow. Joyce was just ten feet above the animal.

She turned to the ladder and started climbing. The ladder twisted as she reached the elbow. It was awkward to negotiate as the copper literally rubbed against her hips and shoulders. Still holding the radio, she tucked it in her belt, followed the trapezoidal turn, then retrieved the radio.

"Robert, I blew it and I'm sorry," she said. "I'm so sorry—"

"Nancy, this is Kathy Leung! Robert and T-Bone are coming up. Do you hear me?"

Joyce was about to acknowledge this when the bat pulled her wings to her body and forced herself into the opening. The arm shook more violently than before, and the scientist lost the radio as she was forced to hold on with both hands. . . .

Forty-three

Gentry and T-Bone had left the communications center with no plan other than to reach the statue's arm and attempt to get Nancy out. T-Bone was holding a crowbar he'd found in a broom closet; that was their only weapon.

Gentry was carrying a flashlight he'd taken from a tool rack and wearing a bandage he'd found in a first aid kit. The pain of his wounded Achilles tendon was a hobbling constant, but it was tolerable.

He was also carrying a lot of anger.

"I never should have let her go up there," he'd said as he handed the radio to Kathy. "Never."

"You didn't 'let' her do anything," Kathy had pointed out. "Bats are her livelihood."

Bats, yes—not monsters.

As they reentered the fort he couldn't have been more disgusted with himself. There was an unpleasant groaning high above them, like a tree listing in the wind. Gentry also thought he heard scratching outside the statue.

"Uh-oh," T-Bone said. "The little peckers are back."

"I hear."

The men started up through the pedestal, Gentry in front. He was struggling to keep the weight off his foot.

"You gonna be okay?" T-Bone asked.

"Yeah," Gentry said. He was using the pain to stay alert. He was aware of every damn step.

As they entered the statue, Gentry felt the way he used to when he chased scum through the tunnels under Grand Central. His senses were high-intensity, as they were as he listened for quarry, watched for trains, stayed wide of the third rail.

Gentry stopped suddenly. T-Bone ran into him.

"Hey," the camera operator complained, panting.

Gentry turned the flashlight back toward the pedestal. "The third rail," he muttered.

"What?"

"The third rail," he repeated, as he moved the light down the stairs. "You step on it and you're fried."

"Man, what the *hell* are you talkin' about?"

"T-Bone," Gentry said urgently, "didn't Gilheany say there was a transformer down here?"

"She did, but we ain't got time to fix the lights—"

"Not the lights," Gentry said. "She said they passed them at the bottom of the statue. And that the transformer was intact."

"Yeah, she said that," T-Bone said impatiently. *"And?"*

Gentry hurried down the steps. He kept his left palm pressed against the left side of the stairwell to keep as much weight as possible off his leg. He felt like he was on a caffeine high, his heart racing and nerves crawling. He could see and hear the faint crackling of the broken wire above. He kept the light directed at the core of the statue.

"De-*tec*-tive," T-Bone said.

"There!" Gentry said. He shined the light on a series of large metal boxes that lined the stone walls.

"Okay," T-Bone said. "The juice. And the fuse boxes. So?"

"Situated less then fifteen feet from a shaft that goes all the way up the statue," Gentry said. "A shaft made of steel."

T-Bone said, "Fuck, man. Yeah. *Yeah!*"

The big man elbowed around Gentry. He looked at the locked boxes then put the crowbar to the faceplate of one of them.

"You worked with transformers when you were a lineman, didn't you?" Gentry asked.

"Every friggin' day," he said as he drew back the crowbar.

"How much power would it take to kill that bat?"

"Five amperes of current at two thousand volts should do it."

The panel snapped open. Gentry took the crowbar and handed him the flashlight.

"They sure have solid-stated a lot of this shit," T-Bone said.

"Can you work with it?"

"I'm lookin'."

The scratching outside became louder. The bat was echolocating again. He hoped that meant Nancy was still on the run.

"This is a major transformer," he said. "I bet they're runnin' Ellis Island from here too."

"Can you *do* it?" Gentry pressed.

"I don't know——!" He looked at the bundles of wires tucked above and behind the transformer. Pulling a pocket knife from his vest, he carefully stripped away some of the casing.

Gentry was growing impatient. But he stood there quietly and waited.

T-Bone shined the flashlight on the wires and bent close. "High temperature wire. Looks like adequate ampacity . . . galvanized steel armor." He backed away and slipped a screwdriver and pliers from his tool vest. "I can run some of this to the steel core, close the circuit, and turn the juice back on—yeah. I think it's doable. But I seem to recall it's all metal up there. Anyplace you stand you're gonna get zapped."

Gentry started limping up the staircase. "You rig it and wait for me to come back with Nancy."

"Man, you sure? The two of us stand a better chance up there—"

"I'm sure," he said. "Just be ready to turn the transformer on when I give you the word."

"It'll take me about five minutes," T-Bone called after him. "Just don't bring that motherfucking bat with you!"

"I'll try not to," he called back.

It was dark inside the statue but not black; the earliest rays of dawn were beginning to filter down from the statue's eyes and from the windows in the crown. He heard the sound of grinding metal and he saw several vespers flitting above. He also saw the body of Sergeant Gilheany crumpled on one of the rest platforms off the staircase.

There was a slight breeze coming from above. The statue had obviously been breached somewhere, which was how the bats were getting in. But there was no way he was going to let the vespers stop him. As his heart and legs pumped ferociously, as he prepared to take the pain of the vesper attack to do whatever it took to draw the big bat away, Gentry had just one concern.

That he wasn't too late to help Nancy.

Forty-four

When there was nowhere left for her to go and nothing else she could do, Nancy Joyce had become surprisingly calm. It wasn't peace but a combination of things that gave the semblance of that state: being drained, frightened, numb, and resigned.

She had climbed to the top of the arm and was standing on a small platform beside the highest rung of the ladder. There were two handrails, and there was room for only one person. Above her was the solid base of the torch. Behind her was a steel door. The door obviously led to the small balcony that surrounded the torch, but it was double-locked. And even if she went out there, what would she do? Jump?

Perhaps. She'd rather leap than die under the hooks and teeth of the bat. And if she jumped she would live an extra—how long would it take to fall? A second or two?

Why not? Right now that seemed like a lot. She might also black out as she fell and die painlessly. That was a comforting thought, given the alternative.

So was this, a non sequitur which came to her in a flow of thoughts. She hadn't had time to contemplate death up at the mu-

seum. She'd been too busy surviving. Now that she did she was surprised to find herself not bitter but grateful. She was happy to have
had the time she had, the life she did, the experiences.

The entire arm shuddered, and she squeezed the handrails. For
some reason the thought of death wasn't as scary as the thought of being vulnerable like this. She wished this part would pass.

It was dark below, the entrance to the forearm stuffed with the
giant bat. The creature was no longer trying to get up here. Rather, it
would enter, hack, back down to the second landing, then twist
around and enter again. Each time it did, it tore at the support structure, trying to rip the steel beams, steps, and ladder out of its way.
Every now and then the hint of sunlight entering through the crown
gave her a glimpse of the giant's face. Motherhood had not softened
the creature's disposition. If there could be such a thing as hate in an
animal's expression, it was there. Joyce could also hear the giant even
after it stopped wailing aloud and began panting in long, chilling,
hisses. She knew that each suspiration was comprised of hundreds of
high blats, the barely audible aspect of her echolocation.

Steel support struts buckled. Rivets strained and the copper
plates that comprised the skin of the statue popped on one or two
sides. After a short time the smaller vespers began returning to the
statue; Joyce could see them outside through the broken seams in
the arm.

That was it, she thought. Gentry was on his way from the communications center, and the giant bat must have heard him coming.
That was why it was echolocating. The scientist in Joyce found it an
amazing synergy. So simple, yet so effective that nothing—no living
thing other than a bat—could get near the creature. Not even an insect.

She prayed that Gentry would have the good sense to turn
around. If the bats came back in force he'd never make it.

The young woman felt the arm sag and rotate slightly. The platform she was on angled backward so that she was leaning more than
slightly against the door. She heard it squeak.

Then she heard something else.

Her name.

And all the calm, all the pensive resignation, was gone in a finger-snap instant as she gripped the handrails and screamed, *"Robert—go back!"*

Forty-five

About midway up the twelve-story statue, vespers had begun swirling around Gentry, scratching and biting. The detective ducked his head into his arms and continued running up. He didn't have to see where he was going in order to get there. All he needed to do was keep his right side pressed to the railing and follow it up. The pain in his ankle had become a constant ache, which was preferable to the sharp jabs he'd been suffering before.

Every once in a while he shouted Nancy's name, hoping that she might hear him and respond. Hoping that she might find a way to buy herself another second or two until he could get to her.

It wasn't until he was near the statue's shoulders that he heard a response. He also heard something else: the continuous grind of metal against metal. He felt gusts of fresh air. Still holding the crowbar, he crouched when he was just below the landing. With his arm slung across his face to protect it from the vespers, he raised his eyes above the crook of his elbow. He peered through the crisscrossing support beams.

He saw the bat on the staircase of the upraised arm. She was tucked up in the folds of the bunched sleeve. All around her, copper plates had been torn away while others were swinging on single rivets.

Though none of the support beams were broken, several were bent, and the arm was tilting slightly toward the front of the monument. He could tell because the stairs had torn away from the landing and were leaning seaward.

The belligerent vespers forced him to move before he'd had more than a moment to reconnoiter. He clambered up to the landing, leaning as much as possible on his right leg. God help him if the bats hobbled that one too. His immediate goal was to try and get the big bat away from the statue's arm so Joyce could get out.

As the detective began to move forward, the creature dropped from the stairs, landed heavily, then turned slowly. The animal was bowed very low, its chin nearly on the platform. It was bleeding from its neck. Swatting vespers away from his face, Gentry watched as the wounded giant crept slowly across the broken body of Officer Berk. The bat inadvertently dragged the corpse several feet as it crawled toward him. Berk's shredded belt came off. Blood-soaked shreds of his uniform stuck to the landing.

Gentry backed away as more and more vespers picked at his arms, his shoulders, his legs. He held the crowbar in one hand and clawed desperately at vespers with the other. Between close-up glimpses of tiny white teeth and velvety wings he thought he saw movement behind the giant—

The giant bat heard it and turned, still low to the ground. As she did, her head snapped to the side as Joyce smashed it with Officer Berk's nightstick.

The creature reared up, shrieking, its huge body centered on the tripod of its powerful legs and thick tail. Its head and shoulders pushed against the top of the statue's sleeve. The copper bulged and broke as the creature rose into the dawn sky.

"Nancy!" Gentry cried. He motioned her toward him.

"No, go back!"

"Not without you! Come *on!*"

The young woman hesitated a moment longer. Then she tossed

the stick aside, scrambled around the bat, and ran toward Gentry. An instant later the creature came down hard, causing the metal landing to bend in the center. The floor tilted and seemed to suck Joyce back; she grabbed the handrail of the spiral staircase to keep from sliding toward the creature. The monster swept at her with its hook, but Gentry had dropped the crowbar and pulled Joyce up and over the railing just as the claw sliced by. Roaring with rage, the wounded creature hunched its head deep in its huge shoulders and charged forward.

Holding Joyce close to him, Gentry started running down the stairs. He was glad he'd tied the ankle bandage tight. It was all that kept his foot from crumbling beneath his weight. The giant bat crushed the railing and crawled after them, facedown, vespers spiraling ahead of it.

"What are you *doing?*" Joyce screamed.

Gentry couldn't answer. He was out of breath and concentrating on staying ahead of the main body of vespers. He was also watching his feet, paying attention to what was below them.

Waiting.

The steps shook as the creature descended. It was difficult to tell how far behind she was, but it wasn't far enough: Gentry could not only hear but feel each *chung* as the bat's hooks came down ahead of her.

It was a dizzying descent, and when they were nearly at the bottom Joyce stumbled and fell. Gentry stopped, turned to help her up, and saw the bat just yards above. The lowest of the vespers attacked them as Gentry grabbed Joyce under the arms, held her against his chest, and pulled her down. Just a few more steps.

"Get ready, T-Bone!" he shouted.

Gentry reached the rubber-topped landing in the pedestal. He threw himself on top of Nancy.

"*Now*, T-Bone!"

"Almost there!" T-Bone shouted back.

Gentry looked anxiously around the base of the column in the center of the room. There was a cable attached to it; at the other end, T-Bone was lying on his back, working beneath the transformer box.

Gentry looked up. The bat was winding its way down the last turn of the spiral staircase. Gentry saw its bloody mouth and flaming eyes and more of the small bats swirling down.

"We're out of time, man!" Gentry cried.

"No shit!" T-Bone said. He slid out and quickly knee-walked to a smaller box beside the transformer.

The bat crawled down the last few steps. The detective and Nancy moved to the other side of the column. The creature looked at them over the railing and spread its wings.

"Say cheese," T-Bone said as he punched the circuit breaker on.

There was a click, then a hum as electricity shot through the cable to the steel core. The giant bat stiffened. Its wings trembled at its side and its mouth spread silently in every direction. There was a sizzle from the column as wisps of smoke curled from the torso and right wing where the bat was still touching it. The white bone around its hourglass nose quickly grew black, and the bat's head rolled down. Its eyes and claws went wide and stayed that way. The huge muscles of its chest and shoulders grew taut and the fur seemed to dissolve, then the skin darkened and smoked. From behind came a flood of death as bat after bat brushed the column and exploded into small, living torches. Some of the vespers dropped quickly, others circled widely for a moment before falling, a few tried to fly away. Many of them squealed, but most of them died silently.

As he looked back at the fiery cascade, Gentry covered Nancy with his arms and chest to protect her from the burning bats. He didn't want to move from the rubber ledge and risk touching the handrail. Not while the power was still on. Her head was tucked against his armpit, her breath coming fast and hot, and she hugged him tightly. Her fingers were in constant motion, running over any part of him she could find. Gentry didn't take it personally. He suspected that Nancy was happy to be feeling anything at all.

After several long, long seconds, the giant bat finally moved. It looked down, though Gentry wondered it if was even aware of them. Slowly, it rose on violently trembling legs and opened its wings as though it wanted to fly. It lifted its head and looked up—at its nest, Gentry wondered?

Its wings opened wider, to their fullest extent. The left wing rose and touched the copper skin of the statue's foot. Sparks and a sound like crumbling paper rolled up the side, in and out of the folds of her robe, lighting the statue as it rose. The electrical wave ran into the statue's arm and up the torch and ignited the cluster of thousand-watt bulbs behind the yellow and red glass of the flame. It burned, bright and brief, as the rising sun lit the millions of windows in the countless buildings across the breadth of Manhattan.

And then the electrical fire died. The bat relaxed. Its burned wings descended like shrouds, and its eyes shut and its legs crumpled. Smoke rising from its flesh, the bat did a slow pirouette as it dropped into the narrow space between the staircase and the pedestal wall. It fell for just a moment, landing hard on a cross-section of metal struts, and then everything was quiet. The light of the sun quickly diluted the strong orange glow of the bats that burned on the steps around them. The surviving vespers flew off quickly to the top of the statue.

Only now did Gentry become aware of the fact that Nancy was crying. He continued to crouch where he was and hold the young woman.

"Gentry! Hey, Detective, you guys okay?"

"We're fine, T-Bone," he said. "Good work. Thanks."

"You're very welcome," the big man said as he walked around the column. He was smiling broadly.

Kathy Leung came running up the stairs. She was carrying the camera on her shoulder, videotaping her ascent. When she arrived, she shut the camera off and handed it to T-Bone. Then she knelt on the step below Gentry. She smiled at the detective and winked. "Thanks for the exclusive, Robert."

"I did it all for you, Kath."

"Were you able to get some of those fireworks?" T-Bone asked.

"Oh yeah." Kathy looked up at Joyce.

"Cool," T-Bone said. "There's your transfer and my raise."

Kathy regarded Joyce. "Doctor, is there anything I can get you?"

Gentry lifted his arm. Joyce slipped from under it. "No thanks."

"You sure?"

She looked at Gentry and smiled faintly. "I'm sure."

T-Bone looked over the side. "Kath, you may want to shoot this too, before the SWAT guys get here and seal it all off."

"We will," she told him.

"Hey, and thanks for listening to me, Detective," T-Bone went on.

"What do you mean?"

"Didn't I *tell* you not to bring that motherfucking bat down here? Man, that is some nasty smelling fried animal."

"Sorry," Gentry said. He looked at Joyce. "The air *is* a little foul in here. You up to walking outside for some of the fresh stuff? Assuming I can get my legs to work."

"Not just yet," Joyce said. She rose unsteadily. "There's something we have to do."

Forty-six

The walk back to the statue's crown was slow and painful. It also hurt because Joyce knew what she and Gentry were going to find when they got there.

Joyce wasn't sure she would have been able to kill the spawn of the giant bats. But when Gentry told her about the charge that had flowed up the statue, she knew that that probably wouldn't be necessary.

They were breathing heavily, their nostrils stinging from the tart electric smell that hung inside the statue, as they dragged themselves up the final leg of the climb—the stairs that led along the right side of the crown. As they ascended toward the landing, they saw a sky turning blue through the twenty-five small windows and sunlight skimming across the bay. The sun warmed the crown, though Joyce felt cold as they stepped onto the studded steel floor. It was singed black in spots where the electricity had shot through it.

When they finally entered the small chamber, neither Gentry nor Joyce was looking at the floor or even at the new day. They were looking at what was on the opposite side.

"Aw, jeez." Gentry stopped walking and turned away.

Two enormous baby bats were lying spoonlike on their sides.

They were nearly three feet long and facing the back of the crown. Their eyes were shut and their heads were resting near the newcomers. Their fur was off-white and their wings—relatively small for their size— were translucent and folded around them. Neither of them was moving. Their faces were turned out slightly as though they were watching for someone . . . waiting.

Joyce continued toward the bats.

"Are you sure they're dead?" Gentry asked.

"Pretty sure," she said.

"Nancy—"

"It's okay. If they were breathing rapidly, normally, the windows would be steamed up." She reached the bats and knelt by the one in back. She reached around it, put her hand gently on its chest, and felt for a heartbeat. After a moment she leaned over it and felt the chest of the bat in front. "They're dead," she said quietly.

Joyce let her fingers linger on the pup's fine fur before rising. It was like touching the surface of a bubble bath, the fur was that soft. And it was that innocent. These creatures had done nothing wrong except to be born where and when and how they were.

She felt miserable.

"So history won't quite be repeating itself," Gentry said.

"No," Joyce said sadly. "It won't."

Gentry limped up behind Joyce and put his hands on her shoulders. "I'm sorry. I can't even imagine everything you're feeling right now."

She reached across her chest and rubbed the back of his hand. "You'd be surprised what I'm feeling right now. Come on," she said. "We're finished here."

They went back downstairs where they were met by the incoming SWAT team. The heavily armored police officers ushered them outside quickly, as though they were in danger. Joyce and Gentry were taken to the administration building first aid center. Kathy and T-Bone were already there, sitting in plastic chairs as a pair of paramedics examined them. T-Bone had his camera on the floor and Kathy had the tape in her hand. She refused to put it down.

After receiving emergency medical treatment for cuts and burns, the four were bundled onto a harbor boat. Kathy and T-Bone stood in the front of the boat; Joyce and Gentry sat on an equipment locker in the stern. They watched as the last remaining vespers scattered through the bright daylight, headed for shelter.

As soon as they were underway, senior police officer John Esty brought a radio to Gentry. It was Weeks. Gentry held the radio between them where Nancy could hear.

"That was a very nice fireworks display," Weeks said.

"You should have seen it from the inside," Gentry replied.

"I'm sure. You both okay?"

"We're a little banged up, and we'll have to do the rabies shot thing, but we're alive," Gentry said. "A lot of good people aren't."

"I hear you," Weeks said. "There are going to be a lot of questions when you get back, about the museum attack, the tunnel operation, and what happened at the statue. But I've spoken with the mayor and the police commissioner and we're going to put you two in the hospital for observation. While you're there we'll minimize the bullshit as much as we can. You did a helluva job, both of you, and we're all very grateful."

"Thanks," Gentry said.

Joyce asked what was going to be done with the remains of the bats. Weeks informed her that their disposition would be decided in a day or two and that Al Doyle was on his way over to collect them. She said that she wanted to be part of any team that was put together to examine the remains.

"Of course," Weeks said. "Absolutely."

Weeks said he'd see them in a few minutes. He and the mayor had a few matters to attend to, like making sure traffic could start coming into the city again, that any remaining vespers were cleared from the subway, and that Albany and Washington sent people and money to help clean up guano, fix the tunnel, and make sure that Lady Liberty didn't lose her arm.

Gentry turned the radio off.

Joyce looked at him. "How's your ankle?"

"A little surgery, a little rest, no more bats, and it should be as good as new."

"I think we've pretty much guaranteed the no-bats part," she smiled.

"I hope so," Gentry said. "So. Can I buy you coffee when we get back?"

"No thanks."

He seemed wounded.

Her smile broadened. "Hasn't it occurred to you, Robert, that I just don't like the stuff?"

"Actually, no. I thought you were turning *me* down."

"Uh-uh. It's coffee I don't like. Not the server."

He smiled back and put his arm around her.

She hadn't felt cold, but now she felt wonderfully warm.

Forty-seven

Al Doyle spent the day supervising his pest control personnel as they removed the giant bats from the statue. He left the cleanup of the remaining vespers to the National Park Service police and the Hazardous Materials unit of the Coast Guard. He would return later in the day when officials from the United States Agriculture Department were scheduled to arrive from Washington.

The three giant bats were packed in crates lined with plastic and loaded with ice. The crates were sealed, placed on a barge, and floated up the Hudson River to the Seventy-ninth Street Boat Basin. There, they were met by ESU personnel who loaded them into vans and brought them to the Central Park Zoo's veterinary department.

Zoo chief Berkowitz had suggested that the remains of the bats could be put on display to help raise money for the zoo and for future pest control efforts. Doyle was all for that. But several things Dr. Joyce had said about the creatures intrigued him. Not just about the bats themselves but about the circumstances that had caused them to mutate.

Whatever accident had created these monsters offered many opportunities to science—and to the scientists who were clever enough to decipher the chemical and biological processes involved. Decipher them, understand them, and one thing more. The most important thing of all.

Replicate them.